AMONG THE C

ISBN 978-0-9821023-3-6
0-9821023-3-X

P orzia Amard has left her French-Italian roots and her beloved wine making family behind in Tuscany to pursue her journalistic studies in the USA, eventually settling in Florida; Pensacola, to be exact, where hurricanes abound. And it is on the forceful tail end of one such hurricane that her life suddenly takes a mystical turn and the story begins.

Porzia is a fairy tale archetype disguised as a pragmatic food writer leading a satisfying professional life as an epicurean globetrotter. Never mind the fact that her pathetic love life amounted to nothing more than a devastating relationship with an alcoholic pastry chef.

Stubborn and beautiful, yet often playful, her colorful and sometimes blunt comments make her irresistible in the eyes of one special man.

When she unexpectedly inherits the legacy of unusual powers at her beloved grandmother's deathbed, her usual self-assurance is shaken, yet she stays true to her promise to accept the challenge before her. Tormented by doubts, Porzia has no time to fully absorb the enormity of her life-changing decision before she finds herself in the middle of events she cannot comprehend.

Under the caring guidance of her spiritual mentor Evalena, Porzia abandons the straightforward path after a past life regression introduces a distant soul mate, revealing a love so intense it has resisted the tarnishing of time.

On her way to Australia to write about a new Shiraz being released, she meets famed off-road racer Gabe Miller. Their attraction is immediate and impossible to resist. As they experience a love only few of us can imagine, let alone have ever savored, she finds herself believing Gabe to be her lost soul mate reincarnated. But Gabe's past holds secrets and a destiny to fulfill which keep Porzia constantly questioning herself and her choices as their romantic encounter leads to intense passion, mystery, and a journey of self-discovery.

With mystical powers in full swing, a Tarot card reading triggers conflict and a profound transformation, and for Porzia, once the key has been inserted into the magic portal, the inherent powers— held dormant for so long— sweep her off her feet and there is no turning back.

AMONG THE Cloud Dwellers

GIULIANA SICA

GEMELLI PRESS

Published by Gemelli Press LLC
9600 Stone Avenue North
Seattle, Washington 98103

Copyright 2012 Giuliana Sica
All rights reserved.
No Part of this book may be reproduced or transmitted in any form or by any means, electronic or mechanical, including photocopying, recording or by any information storage and retrieval system, with out permission in writing of the copyright owner.

Cover design and typesetting by Enterline Design Services LLC

ISBN: 978-0-9821023-3-6
Library of Congress Control Number: 2011940511

This book is dedicated to the Fallen...it was too soon.

Ringraziamenti/Acknowledgements

Porzia believes that a gourmet meal without wine is like a song that has great music but lacks intelligent lyrics. I believe that a life without magic is like a song with intelligent lyrics but it lacks the quintessential ingredient necessary for us to truly live and not merely survive.

Magic manifests itself in a smile, an extended hand, a spark of recognition in the eyes of someone who, having just read a written-under-the-influence manuscript, sniffs the intoxicating aromas of the truffle in the dirt and believes in it.

My magic has names, many names. To me it came in vibrant shapes and forms. Occasionally it shyly awaited, lingering in midair by my windows for my terrestrial eyes to acknowledge it, but more often than not, it barged in and brutally ruffled my feathers; mostly, my enormous Leonine-ego feathers, as in the case of Brad Hopkins of Russell Dean and Company, author of the most atrocious ruffling, which began to pick at the earth-caked nugget, wondering how in the world a Tuscan truffle ended up in the Pacific Northwest. Brad, your advice to "write to the extreme, there is always time for the editors to reel you in" is still my motto today.

To Justin for eating scrambled eggs for an entire week and brainstorming Gabe's name in front of beer, not wine. To Cheri, Marta, and Yvonne, the three fairy godmothers who cradled the manuscript and, reverently brushing off some dirt, told me it was timeless. To Ilene for wanting to live in it. To Johnny for forcing me to face the Wizard of Oz.

To the gang at Gemelli Press – Jason for tapping into my vision; Kari and Sally who rather than fluff my feathers, decided to fluff Porzia's instead. I am eternally in debt to you both, but the Brunello I am drinking alone.

To Aurora, Andrea, and Marcellina – more than Magic, you are angels. To Melissa for her encouragement and friendship and for holding my hand when most needed while birthing this baby.

To my beloved Artur for steering away from car manuals and reading the whole thing. You are my King and my Merlin.

And to my father who gave me markers and walls at the tender age of 4 … and my mother who, three months later, finally gave me paper so I would stop doodling on those walls.

~ Grazie

LA PERSEVERANZA

Love found me all disarmed and found the way
was clear to reach my heart down through the eyes
which have become the halls and doors of tears.
—Francesco Petrarca, *Rhymes in Life & Death of Madonna Laura*

PROLOGUE

Firenze, Italia. Galleria degli Uffizi.

The echo of the security guard's footsteps slowly faded toward the distant museum exit.
Silence.

Silence echoed along the austere arcades on the first floor. Sunset filtered through the ancient windows, the sunrays interrupted in their paths by massive walls. Golden light ricocheted and dispersed off myriads of confused dust motes. At the end of the high-windowed galleria, the heartbeat began to pound within the chilled white marble of Michelangelo's Davide. Life's essence stirred through his perfectly chiseled body until strength and heat gave him power to move. He slipped from his pedestal and headed toward Venere in Botticelli's room.

From the darkening sky, a full moon replaced eternity and cast an inquisitive look down. Davide's shadow glided undisturbed amongst dozing masterpieces. On the upper level, beneath gilded ceilings, silence reigned.

Venere stepped out of her golden frame, and leaving her seashell behind, she entered reality. The angels' gazes followed her progress while her *ancella* gently smiled and wiped a lonesome tear.

Still wet from the scented sea mist, Venere's long auburn hair trailed, barely covering her glowing body. Desire stirred deep within her soul, conjuring rhythmic waves within her.

She met Davide on a sunset-lit windowsill. Doubts dissipated, washed away by the high tide of her will. The lovers allowed the salt-scented mist to subdue them, slowly, to unfold erotic dreams.

Please let reality be what fantasy was.

As the sun's light faded away she drew him in, savoring primitive rituals, riding the moist rhythm of the waves to slowly drown their thirst. With the moon silently smiling, they reached for the sky and left agony behind.

That was the night my parents gave me life.

This life.

If I were a color, I would be gold. Born under the blessing of the full moon, protected by ageless winged guardians, I played hopscotch with Giotto on checkered floors and hide-and-seek with masterpieces along marble staircases, among their golden frames and moth-dappled velvet drapes. My tiny hands pressed against rain-streaked windows while outside the river Arno swelled and found its way to the sea.

I grew up by the shadow of the leaning tower of Pisa. And although the colors of Tuscany in August blush my skin, it is the Manouche mystery that pounds through my veins. I know the woods where Dante lost his way like the palm of my hand. I could escort you to the inferno door blindfolded, for I have knocked on it often myself. I crossed the Mississippi River and heard Jesse James ask Huckleberry Finn if he was real.

I swam with dolphins in the Gulf of Mexico and danced with the Queen of New Orleans on a wet, humid winter night. I got drunk with Ezili in Savannah and cursed life, screaming at the moon in rage. I wandered in meadows restlessly and watched the winds with a longing I could not understand.

Absolutely still in a Veronica, I held a crimson cape of fears, enticed a crippled wolf to charge, and defied time.

I challenged the Goddess, belied my powers, and regretted it all. I soared with a majestic eagle toward a sinking sun and caught up to it by Ayers Rock where, anguished, I bowed. Subjugated at last, I embraced magic.

Too wild, too strong to be mortal, I wove a dream with love in my heart, passion in my soul, and the breath of my life.

I have summoned the elements, conjured my yearning into a spell to be taken away across the endless sky. I have swallowed my pride and begged the gods to give me proof that life is worth the fight. Now I walk through sorrow barefoot, careful not to step on the sharp, shattered pieces of my broken dream.

Now I lie still, numb and spent, waiting.

CHAPTER 1

In the *anno domini* 1300, midway upon the journey of his life, Dante found himself within a forest dark, for the *straightforward* pathway had been lost . . .

Precisely 699 years later, I wandered as well. And *found* myself.

Only it wasn't the inferno I entered.

And God had nothing to do with it. This was more likely the Goddess, subtle and beckoning.

As someone who—up to that point in her life—had never gambled, I claim full responsibility for abandoning the straightforward pathway.

I rolled the dice, and I have no regrets.

Exactly on the eve of one of Florida's most prolific hurricane seasons, while everyone boarded shut their windows against the wrath of Hurricane Erin, I left mine wide open. And magic stormed in.

Metaphorically speaking, the timing was impeccable.

I had no time to bother with trivialities such as shutting windows. Across the Atlantic, a family emergency demanded me. Although back then I still had not learned how to face Death, I rushed to France and my grandmother's side.

Beyond the expanse of the Atlantic Ocean, over the somber peaks of the Pyrénées, down into the dampness of the Camargue, across fields of fragrant lavender, in a room where someone *had* remembered to shut the windows against the scorching July sun, my *grand-mère* Joséphine was dying.

Her delirious eyes swept the darkness in the far corner. "*Zut! Attend toi!*" she spat. "*Je ne suis encore prête.*"

Chills ran down my spine. "Who are you talking to Joséphine?"

"*La Mort.*" Her voice echoed hollowness.

Resigned looks spread across the faces of my family. My father bowed his dark (despite the age), luscious crown of hair and covered his eyes. My mother's aquamarine eyes welled up with tears, like the sea on high tide, and my younger brother Alex, a born skeptic as myself, turned to see if he could actually catch a glimpse of Death.

I did too.

In the far corner, ghastly folds of shadow quivered.

Alex's eyes met mine and he shrugged.

Joséphine's gnarled hand gripped my arm and pulled me closer. My knees met the side of her bed, and yet she kept on drawing me to her. Choking in sorrow, I bent down to give her my undivided attention.

"*Ma petite miette—*," she sighed, short of breath.

"Joséphine—" My shoulders shook with grief.

"I kept you in the dark. I thought I would protect you. But how do we love that which we don't know?" She unclasped her beloved amber pendant from her fragile, birdlike neck and pressed it into my hand. It pulsed warm with her heat. "I renounced The Craft and now it's too late! A lifetime with no magic wasn't worth it." With extraordinary strength for someone in such weak condition she shook her head. "But you must rekindle the power!" Her eyes bulged. "*Promets-moi!*"

In one inhuman last effort, her shoulders pushed off the pillows. "*Promets-moi! Ma petite miette!* You must return to magic!"

Tears spilled from my eyes, her face liquefied, and I nodded frantically—against all my principles. I gripped her cold hands in mine. Pain flared as the amber pendant cut into the tender flesh of my palm. "*D'accord,* Joséphine. I promise."

Her shoulders collapsed back on the pillows. "*Merci.*"

*

The very first time my grandfather set eyes on Joséphine he thought, "*Le premier soufflé du Divin était la Femme. Et voilà, elle vient.*" The Divine first breath was Woman. And here She comes.

And I think: *The Divine must have been lonely. We are born alone. We die alone.*

Despite my grandfather's romantic heart, I remain guarded. Why waste time believing in soul mates?

It is perhaps because the Divine created us in her image? And if the Divine is Love, therefore are we, as well, Love? Moreover, in our desire to express our true nature, then aren't we doomed to Love?

Grief does not heal prettily. Especially when morbidly and persistently poked, it scabs. Then, if we are lucky, it finally scars.

After the burial, this sort of thinking flew with me back to the Florida Panhandle where Hurricane Erin had made landfall only days earlier.

Pensacola was still on its knees. Surprisingly, my place had sustained no damage.

*

A month later, I kept my promise and took my first wayward step.

CHAPTER 2

A yellow light blinked furiously as I sped through the intersection and landed on the Gulf Breeze Bridge with the car's shock absorbers cringing. The speedometer read eighty-five miles per hour. *Oddio!* Adrenaline jolted through me like a strong buzz. I shot a glance at the rearview mirrors almost expecting the flashing lights of a police car. I caught sight of my own makeup-free eyes instead. I frowned, puzzled by their unusual aqua clarity; so much like my mother's.

Some people are here for answers while others only have questions, tesoro mio. Her voice echoed in my head, her eyes spiraled back into mine, and I smiled wryly.

My heart and mind struggled in disagreement. I felt like the rope in a tug o' war game. This time I *wanted* to change my mind, but I feared my heart.

My brow creased as I raced across the deserted bridge. I eased my foot off the gas pedal in a futile attempt to delay my appointment. A pang of disappointment shot through my gut. Second-guessing my promises is not something I do. Usually, once I make a choice, I stick with it—often despite vociferous warning signs.

To make matters worse, the Category 3 hurricane had re-tailored the Florida Panhandle's hems and destroyed many homes on Navarre Beach, my friend Evalena's included. She and Rex now dwelled in Gulf Breeze, in a house lent them by a friend—my destination only a few miles ahead, according to the crumpled napkin I had scribbled with hasty directions. I hate not knowing where I am headed. I hate changes in my habitual routine, and I can't believe I do what I do for a living with such irrational fears as faithful companions.

After a last glance I tossed the napkin back on the passenger seat where it landed in my overstuffed bag and soaked the sweat off a chilled bottle of San Pellegrino. I cranked the air conditioner and wondered grumpily about this new place Evalena now called home. Energetically speaking, I questioned whether the atypical environment, with its unfamiliar vibes, might possibly affect my past life regression.

I wondered whether it would be a good idea to postpone the session until Evalena's house was restored. *Yeah. Right.* With all the destruction the hurricane had left in its path, the Panhandle faced at least a year of intense reconstruction.

I could never wait that long.

I still churned about the whole deal and idiotically questioned Evalena's metaphysical powers. The absurdity of my own doubts shook my head. I needed answers now.

I braked the car to a halt in front of a low bungalow painted in an extremely unsuited-for-the-circumstances jolly yellow. I pushed my cheap plastic sunglasses up my head and heard a cracking noise. Under the mass of my unruly hair, the sunglasses snapped and broke in two. Fine. Cringing with pain, I raked the ruined pieces off my head along with some hair, tossed them on the backseat, and finally killed the engine, leaving my feet on the pedals. I leaned to rest my chin on my white-knuckled hands, still clenching the sweaty steering wheel. Through the bug-speckled windshield, I silently observed the house.

My heaving chest echoed the engine's struggle to cool down. I resented the jovial yellow.

Nobody in sight, I could still bail . . .

But didn't. I had a promise to keep.

The weak end of daylight dimly lit the living room where tottering, knee-high stacks of books edged an erratic path to a rolltop desk. A brass incense burner towered over several carelessly scattered bills. Tendrils of the ever-lingering moldy odor of all that is wet in Florida swirled, almost visible in the milky light.

Evalena was her usual self: part matter-of-fact, part esoteric. Gray streaked her bright auburn hair like reality creeping into fantasy. The pink chenille sofa she motioned me to lie on had seen better days, but once I sank in, the faded cushions felt familiar and comfortable. Somewhat reassured, I made an effort to relax and inhaled deeply. My nostrils flared with the pungent smell of eucalyptus. Evalena eased me into her warm energies and began to slowly rub Tiger Balm on my third eye. She followed with a soothing foot massage while her calm but firm voice walked me through the necessary steps to fade back in time.

I closed my eyes and trusted her voice. "Imagine a sphere of golden, warm light at the bottom of your feet and a second, identical one above your head," she guided me soothingly. "Now, move them simultaneously, about one foot away from the extremities of your body. Focus. Take deep breaths, and when you exhale, push both spheres one more foot away."

The concentration came slowly. I struggled to split my focus between both my extremities at once, finding it incredibly difficult. Evalena sensed my hesitation and began to massage my shoulders. Lowering her voice, she instructed me to push the bright energies away, again and again and again, until one rested about six feet above my head and the other the same distance beneath my feet.

It felt like quite an accomplishment to be able to control the luminescent spheres that floated weightlessly in midair. I felt the pride of a magician but with no tricks, just my will.

So it had always been within reach . . .

Under Evalena's instruction, I began to count backwards from one hundred to one.

*

Stairs appeared and I descended the narrow spiral staircase, surrounded by damp stone walls. As I slowly made my way down, my left hand helped me balance. The darkness in front of me dissipated with every step, yet remained impenetrable and dense at arm's length. I could sense it closing silently behind me.

An old clock tick-tocked in the background. Fading time? *Or perhaps my only conscious link to the present?*

I felt no fear. My clear mind focused on counting the numbers backwards, leaving little room to dwell in either apprehension or expectation. The temperature dropped, cooling with each descending step I took. A cold chill uncoiled at the base of my spine, crawled upward, and wrapped itself at the back of my neck. Finally, I set foot on one last step and counted: *One.*

I stood in front of a closed door. I felt as though I had reached a long-forgotten cellar, abandoned since the beginning of time.

"Describe the door."

I heard my voice answer from a distant present, "It's a dark wooden door, old and beaten, with a brass handle on the left. I'm going to have to move back to be able to open it. It will swing inwards, toward me. I don't see a keyhole, either." *But I don't need a key,* my mind whispered.

"Porzia, open the door," she commanded.

With a sudden impulse of confidence, my hand wrapped around the cold, tarnished handle and turned. The door gave silently.

*

A clear blue sky fills my vision while the strength of a warm breeze supports me above distant, deep-blue waters; not a cloud in sight, just warm sunshine.

"*Mamma mia!* Evalena, I'm flying!"

"Have you got a broom?" she asked, amused.

"No, I'm using my body," I replied, my arms outstretched like an airplane. It feels a tad ridiculous.

"Where are you?"

"Somewhere warm and bright, above water."

"Are you alive?"

Hmm, good question. How would I know? "I think I'm in between lives."

"Do you see anybody?"

"No."

"Porzia, do you need to stay there?" Evalena asked.

"No, I don't think so." I sensed this to be an introduction to what I was about to see and learn about myself. *No need to linger here.*

"Ok, then go back up in the sky, and as you fly away, time comes with you."

I drift ever upward into a darkening sky until I am surrounded by blackness.

Soundlessly, I land in a dimly lit room, like an intruder on a theater stage while a scene is unfolding. I hear soft voices and listen for a few seconds to two men discussing my future. I know one to be my father, a distinguished older Japanese aristocrat, and the other, my future consort. I see the woman I was in this particular life hide behind an inlaid wooden screen. I shift to be closer to her, like a silent shadow in a play I have acted in as a young Japanese woman with shiny black hair, wrapped in an elegant red kimono. A hint of sweet jasmine flutters in the air. The vividness of the scent amazes me.

I know every thought she has.

She's listening, trying to catch a glimpse of her future husband. Outlined in a foreign blue and gold uniform, his shoulders are solid. He's handsome, even if not Asian, very exotic, and surrounded by a powerful, beckoning aura.

The scene is so captivating that I barely hear Evalena's voice ask me to move ahead in time, just a few weeks.

"I have been given to him." Surprise and panic tangle my vocal cords. Something isn't right. "He's hurting me, Evalena—" I stir in my discomfort. "He's forcing himself on me." I shift on the couch to get away. "He's raping me." *Bastard*, I think, *he doesn't care about my pain.* "He's got blue eyes," I whisper to myself while staring through my own tears straight into his icy glare. The pain he's inflicting on me quickly builds his lust; it shatters his ice, melts away his liquid coldness, until my pain becomes unbearable and his eyes blaze.

"Ok, Porzia, you must leave." When it finally reached me, Evalena's command was choking with concern.

I tore myself from painful tentacles and traveled into darkness again.

"Are you safe?"

"Yes, I'm safe. I'm in a garden surrounded by massive stone walls. I see mountains in the distance. There are flowers blooming around and shoji doors facing east. I can breathe the crisp morning air. It must be springtime because the mountains are snowcapped but I'm surrounded by flowers." *I like this garden, and I don't want to leave.*

Sadness sweeps over me in a longing sensation I will have to examine again ... maybe in this lifetime, but in any case, sooner than expected.

Gently, Evalena asks me to drift away, toward a happy time.

All of a sudden, I feel lulling water. I balance on bare feet on the gently rolling floor of a wooden boat. A sunset spreads in front of me while I tenderly rock a chubby baby in my arms. The boat is my home.

Evalena does not ask me anything. Sensing my peace, she lets me bask in the warm memory.

The baby stirs in my arms. He's a boy, Asian, not quite one year old. He's happy to play with my hair and touch my cheeks with his pudgy hand. I am loved unconditionally.

There is no father. *Am I the woman of the previous life?*

I feel the weight of war in my near past. The agony of slow death is a wet, blood-painted memory; the stench of piled bodies left to rot in filthy ditches is stagnant in my nostrils. Along a country road an endless line of slow-walking figures, shrouded in rags, chokes in oppressive smoke. With her feet wrapped in bloody bandages, a young girl in front of me struggles along, holding her mother's torn arm like a precious rag doll; it is all she has left.

It's an exodus. A Moviola-paced run from hell to purgatory. There is no heaven. Nobody around me believes in it anymore. Chinese soldiers have raped, brutalized, and tortured us out of pure hatred, stripping us of hope, dignity, and our future. Nobody believes it will ever be over.

But I survive. The tragic memories will seal into scars when I finally reach Hong Kong. I will sail for peace on my wooden boat.

Shifting my gaze away from the sinking sun, I focus on a thousand boats like mine, all content like me to merely roll on the breathing water.

"Porzia."

"Hmm...?"

"Porzia, move closer—closer to see your quest in this lifetime."

I embrace darkness again, knowing with profound certainty that my child in that life is somebody dear to me today.

Now, that's a thought.

Suddenly, I see an older man wearing a powdered, poufy wig. His enraged gray eyes are screaming in my face along with the venom in his voice. I am a disgrace to the family. He's furious; I cringe when his spit hits my powdered cheeks.

My firstborn is a girl I have named Marie Claire, after my mother. My husband is about to explode. I have not given him a male heir.

Uh, is that a fake mole on his upper lip?

Disgusted, I jerk my face away.

"Where are you?" Evalena asks, concerned.

"France," I answer, "in a baroque bedroom. My husband is outraged! I have failed his expectations . . ." Speed blurs time, and images fast-forward through my mind. "He has locked me up . . . I am alone most of the time . . . He only comes in to try to conceive a boy child. I am not allowed to see my daughter, but I hear her cry with the nursemaid."

Pitiful. What a disaster. *Who the hell is this woman?*

Although I don't like myself, I'm fascinated by the platinum-blond ringlets piled high up on my head and the angelic blue eyes, made even brighter by all the tears.

This time I see it all clearly, as if in a silent movie. The scenes run through my memory like rolling subtitles. My closed eyelids tremble as I fill in blank pages with events as they unfold: My husband's indifference when Pierre-Jacques, my son, is finally born appalls me; his cruel, twisted sexual abuse toward the maids and me turns my stomach. I can't cope with it any longer. I vow revenge, and a plot to escape evolves in my mind.

I see myself running through a dark forest wearing a black, hooded cape. A strand of blond hair sparks bright against the velvet night. Behind me the ostentatious castle disappears against the thickening wall of fragrant trees. I finally reach a small wooden cabin with a lonely window glowing in soft candlelight.

Xavier is opening the door.

The hard impact of his bare golden chest scorches my frozen hands, like holy water on sin. His coal eyes, feverish with desire, are all I yearn for. Impatient hands unfasten my cape; the hood falls, unleashing a golden cascade of curls down the swell of my backside, and I am naked in his arms. His hands cup my face and his mouth hungrily captures mine.

I love this man. I have loved him forever. I'm swept away. The feelings of that distant night drown me.

Our tangled bodies embrace. They fall urgently on a heap of hay. The dry scent spills into the present, raising hair at the nape of my neck. His strong hands caress, stroke, and knead my aching body, releasing warm liquid melodies. His raven hair is coarse silk through my fingers. His dusky voice whispers sin against my navel as his tongue darts along a sensitive path between my thighs, lured by the pearly dew moistening my swollen bud. My feet wrap around his waist, my back arches, reacting to his intimate suckling and . . . I choke on a scream strangling up my throat.

On the couch my body responded to the passionate stimulation, and I found myself physically aroused. Hot and sweaty, I stirred and struggled with the wetness that drenched my trapped hair and my back, only to find myself wet in more private places. I'm a prisoner of my own past.

I yank his head upward and plunge my tongue into his mouth, sucking my own wetness off his lips, and spread my legs, ready to receive him. Cupping my backside, he lifts me up to meet him, hard, swollen, thick. I can barely breathe as I feel moist tissue stretch to accommodate such virile invasion. In a rush of French, with passionate words, I call his name. I beg for more, plead for satisfaction. *Oh! Mon Dieu!* I hope this never ends. Please, this is absolute ecstasy. This is how it's supposed to be between man and woman.

Our lovemaking is a perfect unison of drumming heartbeats, of entwined limbs taut with blind, aching yearning for sexual fulfillment. Our souls merge, effortlessly soaring beyond earthly boundaries to fly an endless flight along the trail of a shooting star.

Time shifts, blurring memories into later, more tragic events.

In the castle courtyard, a crowd had gathered to gawk at Xavier's perfect body slumped at my feet, lifeless. His beautiful, loving heart is torn open, reduced to a caked pulp. In front of a disapproving mob, my husband looks at his bloody sword and slowly wipes it against the candid lace cupping my heaving breasts. His satisfied glare at having once again mortified me is something I will never forget.

Unbearable pain flares through time, through my veins. It lights my blood on fire and explodes, shattering my heart. I clench my fists and jerk as if struck by lightning on the couch. I can barely speak. "Xavier's dead," I seethe.

"Honey, are you OK?" Evalena's voice elbowed its way through thick curtains of folded pain and stirred me. "Do you want out?"

"No—," I panicked. *This is not over yet.* "I need to know what happens next."

"Ok, then slowly move away a few days ahead, and tell me what you see."

"I believe I'm about to shoot somebody." Through clenched teeth, I didn't recognize my own voice. My big blue eyes are strong and hard. My hand is steady on the ivory butt. My right thumb on the shiny hammer slowly clicks it backward. I am using both hands. *Making sure I do this right.*

The rage spilled over into *this* present.

"Who?" Evalena asked.

"I can't see who." I cringe. "I can only see myself aiming a pistol."

"Well then, move forward a few days and tell me where you are."

"I'm in a carriage pulled by horses. I'm with my children. We're leaving the castle behind. I've killed him. It's evening time—dusk, I believe."

I'm exhausted.

*

Evalena's voice guided me upward, away from the vivid past into a weak present. From the bottom of an inscrutable darkness, I struggled upward toward a feeble glimmer of beckoning light.

Through the sheer gauze of billowing drapes, a marine breeze brushed my cheeks, and the memories swirled to finally settle, like leaves on freshly upturned soil.

I blinked and looked at Evalena. She smiled softly, and I thought of *liquid women*. Grateful, I accepted her offer of a lavender-scented wipe and ran it over my soaking neck and face.

"I would like you to meditate on today's events. Take your time. No hurry. It will dawn on you. Then come back and share it with me, if you will.

"By doing a past life regression, you summon Transformation. You commit to respect your path and you embark on a soul-searching quest. *Your* soul, Porzia."

Here she paused, sighed, and cast me a piercing look. "Be aware. This is not a straightforward path, Porzia."

I smirked at her choice of words and raised my usual wary eyebrow.

"I explained the seriousness of this commitment before you accepted. Today I guided you in front of the tabernacle of your soul in such a manner that fears were your last concern. Stripped of obstacles, you faced your own truth. Be aware of this, Porzia." Evalena stared at me, entranced. "The immensity of your soul is quite capable of embracing knowledge. You must use what you have seen today wisely." Her arm arched and spread in a rainbow. "Discover your soul . . . for how do we love that which we don't know?"

Evalena is a world-renowned herbalist I interviewed a few years back for one of my culinary articles; we've been friends and collaborators ever since. Aside from being such a skilled herbalist, Evalena is a natural-born clairvoyant. Still, despite her accuracy, my entire being exuded cynicism.

"That's exactly what Joséphine told me before dying." I shot her a penetrating look. "Excuse me if, after an eclipsed lifetime in dark exile, my soul remains skeptical about paganism and its powers to help me." *No, that wasn't entirely true.*

She tapped into my uneasiness and nodded soothingly. "It's not your soul that is the skeptic, Porzia. And you know it." Her certainty arrowed my cynicism and incinerated it.

"So, do you seriously believe Xavier is my soul mate?" My instinct had already answered.

"Porzia, it's been a year since you broke up your last relationship. Can you honestly tell me that you're healed, that you're whole? At your grandmother's passing, through the promise you made her, a timeless power has reawakened. You are a special creature with a powerful magic lineage coursing through your veins. I believe it is time to consecrate your divine awareness; embrace your spirituality. Transformation rests in your hands, Porzia. You begin this quest rich in unharnessed powers. You must find your magic and rise to access such richness. As in every archetypal fable, only the gods know what might pass along the journey. Moreover, it will be a long journey, perhaps involving an emotional death, anger, and grief.

"Liberation from boundaries is always a loss, Porzia. You must grow strong enough to ask for what you want, for it will be the glowing awareness of having been touched by magic that ultimately will attract your soul mate. And what you felt with Xavier is strong. So strong it spilled into the present and crawled over my skin, for as you were re-living it, I felt it. In my entire life, only one other time have I experienced such emotional strength."

My left eyebrow shot up, questioning.

"When I put Rex under and saw us together centuries ago," she said very matter-of-factly.

I knew she was married to her soul mate, but to actually think that it could happen to me was an extremely abstract concept. Perhaps I ought to raise the ceiling of the room where my ambitions are stored away collecting dust.

Oddio! It had been such a long time since my last date.

I shook my head. "I don't know what to do now. Do I go around asking everybody I suspect to be Xavier if they suffer from nightmares of being killed in France by a nutcase wearing a powdered wig?" I had to smile at that.

Humor sparkled in Evalena's eyes as well, but her voice remained serious. "How did you feel when you were with him? Unless terrestrial matters will obfuscate your senses, you'll know him when you meet again, just as you recognize your own face in the mirror every morning. Consider also that there is an enormous chance he won't know about all this and will be puzzled by the fact that he'll be extremely attracted to you." She smiled. "If he's anything like Rex, he'll think it's just strong sexual chemistry. I suspected it, but he didn't know about our bond through the centuries until he finally consented to regress. And we had been dating a while by then."

"On a more material note," I hesitated, anticipating the answer in fear, "how come, despite having left the windows open, my place was spared by the hurricane?"

Evalena winked, "Nothing *material* about it—why are you surprised?"

CHAPTER 3

Engulfed in a daze, I barely held the steering wheel. My car just about drove itself back home.

A lump plunged up and down my throat like an oversized buoy, making it impossible to swallow. From the safety of my car, I swept the sky in a glance, hoping to find familiar surroundings, only to crash against the surprising remains of a sunset-stricken, darkening sky across the bridge. It had taken a little over an hour for the regression. *It's going to take a lot longer to sort it out and digest it,* I thought.

I didn't have such luxury. I had to be on a plane to South Australia the following afternoon for one of my gourmet assignments.

I faced *un accidenti di viaggio*—a bitch of a journey—when the only thing I wanted was to lock the bright Florida sunshine out of my front door and use the shaded coolness inside to help me think. I needed days. Weeks. Another hurricane would have helped; weren't they in season?

What the hell possessed me to initiate my quest with a past life regression anyway? Truth be told, it was Evalena and her disarming ability to reach within me and caress my soul.

Upon my return from Joséphine's funeral I had called her, disregarding the fact she doesn't particularly care for lengthy phone conversations. Reaching out to her with all my might, I asked for guidance. Her response encouraged me to think in ways I'd never even dreamed about.

"Every journey of self-discovery begins with unburying our past and coming to terms with our humanity, as fragile as we might discover it to be. I believe a past life regression may be the ideal first step in your sensitive case. It may reveal why your grandmother asked you to embrace her legacy. At present, it's as if your lost soul, wandering through darkened night skies, has landed on the roof of a fast-speeding train about to be swallowed by an even darker tunnel. You're holding on for dear life to a thin metal ledge and, being so utterly devoted to this enormous task, you ignore the rest of the train, which has so much to show you: the lengthy past behind you and the undisclosed future ahead. But more importantly, why are these the most auspicious times for such events to unfold?"

When put to me in these terms, my curiosity was certainly piqued. I absolutely can't refuse a challenge, and so I bit.

*

Joséphine and Evalena pulling the tug o' war rope . . . I smiled and lifted one arm to observe the thin bluish veins marbling my wrist—a powerful magic lineage.

There are women and then there are *liquid* women.

Liquid women are ageless, mystical, Atlantis-worthy creatures with skin like impalpable water. Their diluted features shift as light dances on mermaid profiles to re-adjust quietly after a smile. Their skin is smooth, like a lake surface after a pebble sinks.

When they cry, their eyelids flutter and tremble in wonderment, speckled by shy lashes; their moist rims well with a salty tear. Breaths quiver in anticipation when such a gem finally surrenders down the silkiness of a pearly cheek. Their bodies sway following ancient rhythms of silent waves, birthing endless surging and receding tides.

Grand-mère was one of such women. I suspected Evalena to be another, and without a doubt, my mother is a liquid woman. I never thought I would see the day I'd fall in her footprints. For a child walking behind her on the Tuscan seashore, it was an impossible game. Frothy waves kept beating me to it.

When life becomes mere survival, one begins to question matters, ask more of relationships, and, ultimately, find elusive fulfillment.

*

I parked beneath my balcony and noticed Peridot's face peeking through the sheer blue curtains. I climbed upstairs, almost tripped on my own hurry, managed to balance myself before miserably falling, and opened the door slowly, holding back my curious cat. Once inside, I threw my keys on the dining table, and for the second time in a day, I slumped, exhausted, on a sofa. I just needed to think for a few minutes.

Peridot climbed on the cushions and rubbed his soft chin on my feet. He blinked his light green eyes, inviting rougher play, wanting to bite my toes. "Come here, *micio*," I called. He meowed and settled on my lap.

So I had a couple of cruel husbands. A war. But I know I can fly now. I thought of this and smiled, resigned. What to do with these newly discovered powers? Pretend I never cracked the door open? Slam it back shut and move on? Appealing. Hmm . . . extremely appealing.

I had been Japanese. No wonder I appreciated their cuisine, customs, and culture so much. Still, I don't look Asian today. My hair is layered, past shoulder length, the color of chestnuts. I wear it curly if I let it dry naturally or straight if I take the time to blow it dry. My eyes are aqua green, bright and catlike, not almond and angled. I have a curvy figure so I'm no willowy Asian beauty anymore, nor a delicate, pale French flower. I'm more like a Mediterranean sunset, as somebody once described me.

Xavier. What a name, I thought.

I repeated it quietly. "Xavier."

"Xavier."

"Xavier." The harsh impact of the X ignited sparks at the back of my throat, the rest quickly released in a whispered rush of breath.

I recalled the strength of his hands cupping my face. The smoothness of his chest came alive in my vivid memory, and I found myself swept backwards, pressing my cheek against his heartbeat. And his eyes . . . such rich eyes, eyes of dark chocolate speckled with gold; eyes warm and profound, with flames lingering behind long black lashes. I remembered how that single candle magically lit the entire cabin, how the dark brown of his pupils had turned into pools of dark blood. I remembered . . .

Xavier.

My pulse quickened with the vivid memory of his chiseled profile and high cheekbones, the smoothness of his skin and fullness of his mouth parting when I pulled his thick, dark hair to kiss his throat.

Xavier. *Where are you now?* I thought of his strong hands and how safe I felt in his embrace. After Steve, I'd promised myself to never again place my life in any man's hands, but Xavier's hands felt damn right. Those private places ached as I thought of him.

The realization that I had once loved so unconditionally hit me suddenly. A rush of tangled emotions surged through me.

Do I believe in it again? Do I wait for it to happen? What does he look like in this life? How lonely have I been in all my wrong choices? How can I even believe it could happen again? I have no guarantees. How can I even begin to believe in it?

I felt stupid and gullible, manipulated—and then, with appalling clarity, I realized that these were not emotions but fears, fears hindering my wayward path.

Xavier.

How does one divest of fears? I asked. But his name kept on beating in my head, like steady drums echoing in my heart. It lulled me gently until no more doubts swirled inside me; just Xavier and my longing.

A few tired tears ran down my cheeks. My eyes closed heavy with sleep, and I drifted into Morpheus's embrace.

*

After a restless night on the sofa, I woke up late to a gloomy, rainy morning, still groggy from yesterday's events. Wishing I could sleep longer, I stumbled into the bedroom and began to fumble with luggage. I still had to pack, check my travel itinerary, and assemble my phone contacts. If only I could freeze time and think; instead, I barely had time to hurry through a quick shower and jump on a plane.

August in Florida meant winter in Australia. I should be used to packing by now, with all the traveling behind me. But each location is different. Each occasion is unique, requiring different casual outfits or formal ensembles.

I threw in my old faithful jeans, my periwinkle cashmere sweater and the chocolate suede trousers, along with two pairs of boots, one black and dressier than my other choice of the brown aged-leather boots I usually wear with jeans. And then? I looked around . . . Ah! Of course, I could not forget my favorite gypsy blouse. I always travel with it. I absolutely love the way the sleeves bloom at my elbows and how the lacey black flowers graze my navel. What else? I scanned my closet for the ankle-length, claret velvet dress I planned to wear to the presentation with the black boots and smiled when my hands brushed the luxurious fabric. I always feel like a goddess when I wear it. A pair of black thigh-highs went in next, the length of my dress compensating for the low, feminine stockings beneath. What more? I thought about the Australian climate and added a couple more sweaters to wear with the jeans. I picked out more lingerie, socks, and an insulated goose down jacket that I dropped on the oversized peach chair by the window, until I saw Peridot jump on the jacket in purring nap mode, ready to settle and knead with his huge clawed paws. I moved the jacket.

I prepared a couple of panini and some extra things to munch on and took a quick shower. Once dressed and ready to go, I filled my beauty case with toiletries, makeup, and my amber-scented oils.

The doorbell rang as I shut the suitcase. I hoped it would be Benedetta, my best friend, occasional pet and house sitter, and ad hoc chauffeur. I walked to the front door thinking I'd have to remind her to water the herbs in the windowsills, especially the oregano. It makes the difference between a mediocre marinara sauce and a want-to-wipe-the-plate-clean, tangy success!

*

I was grateful for the ride until we were on the highway, and I panicked in her car thinking we'd never make it to the airport alive. During a mere thirty-minute drive, I swallowed my heart several times. She was driving like a maniac while simultaneously pressing me with questions. Skilled chick, I had to give her that. I, on the other hand, am incapable of multitasking, even when I'm cooking.

"So, when will you get back?" Benedetta asked, keeping her eyes on the road.

"Next Saturday, if all goes well and I have no delays."

"Ok, ring me if anything changes or e-mail me the new flight details. I'll pick you up as planned if I don't hear from you." She barreled around a van, passing on the right, and zipped back into the fast lane.

Somebody honked at us.

"Benedetta! You cut him off!"

"*Eh?*" She jerked her head to look at me, taking her bright blue eyes off the road as we approached the airport exit.

We missed it.

"Hard to see the signs when it's raining." She blamed the weather.

We drove up to the next exit and turned around. She laughed about missing the exit all the way to the check-in. I ended up grinning as well. I couldn't help it.

"I'll see you in a week," I said, hugging her.

"Be good, Porzia. Watch out for dingoes, bugs, and whatever else they eat down there." She winked. "Bring me back a rugby player."

"Take care of yourself. And don't let Peridot drink out of the toilet. He thinks he's a dog."

"What's wrong with drinking out of the toilet?" she asked, a portrait of innocence.

"Please go away."

Struggling to keep a straight face, the airline clerk took my suitcase. I finished the check-in formalities and went looking for coffee. I found it, along with a key chain dangling two shiny dice that I bought on a whim.

Pensacola–Houston–Los Angeles–Melbourne–Adelaide; I hoped for all my connections to be on time and not full.

Just shoot me now, I thought as we boarded. If I could have flown as I had in my past life regression, then I'd probably be halfway over there already. Not only can I not multitask, I also have no patience. Resignedly, I settled into my seat and flipped through my notes, silently thanking Helen, my magazine liaison at *A' la Carte,* for being exquisitely efficient once again and for booking my flights in business class.

Frank and Beverly Jourdain, the owners of Umeracha Winery, had requested me especially to cover an intimate release of their new Shiraz. They had made headlines in the past with their Cabernet, and I felt confident they would do so again with the sophisticated Shiraz. Frank made wine with his heart. Good things come from passion such as his. Bless Beverly to be the business brains behind the enterprise, or Frank probably would not have survived in the trade long enough to produce such exquisite corking.

Their winery was located some miles outside of Adelaide, on the outskirts of a small town called Gumeracha; from the Aboriginal word *Umeracha*, meaning "good water hole." Frank used the word to name the winery in 1961 out of respect for the Aboriginal people of Kaurna, the first inhabitants of the region. He's that sort of man. They have been successful ever since.

I can't wait to get there! I thought as I crept from airplane to airplane and finally plunged into my next-to-last seat in LA I suppressed a pang of frustration sprouting in my stomach. The thought of facing another twelve hours straight on this leg of the flight made me queasy. I closed my eyes and gently rubbed the bridge of my nose between thumb and forefinger for a few seconds, wondering what movie selection they would offer.

A soft jingle of keys interrupted my short-lived meditation. Feeling a tad better, I opened my eyes, glanced over at the passenger by the window, and almost broke my neck with whiplash.

His fingers casually toyed with a feather on a key chain. But that wasn't what caught my breath.

It was his hair. A sudden need to run my hands through it rushed through me. I knew it would feel like golden silk. Cut short on the side, the dark blond hair exposed his right ear and a thin strip of sun-kissed, golden skin. I followed the skin path down to where the hair faded into pale sunshine, shaved at the nape of a tanned neck.

I crossed my legs. I shifted my eyes higher to the top of his head where lighter and darker strands gelled into soft spikes, daring me to reach over and . . . pull.

Holding my breath, I waited for him to turn so I could see his face. He seemed lost in thought, gazing out the window while his fingers still jingled the keys.

I exhaled and looked away. *Does everybody react like this to a perfect stranger?* Naw! *Full moon in a few days,* I heard Evalena's voice say.

That must be why I felt so sensitive. I glanced over at him again only to be interrupted by a flight attendant's light tap on my shoulder and an offer of a small airline bag.

"Thanks, mate." Stretching a perfect arm only inches above my head, the perfect stranger reached over to grab his goodie bag.

Australian. Great voice, incredible hair . . . *OK, Porzia, turn and see if the rest is just as breathtaking.*

Veins ran along the perfect arm now raised to hide his face from my view. Carelessly, his right hand combed the thick, golden hair back, just as I'd thought of doing moments earlier. A black, short sleeve T-shirt stretched tightly where his bicep flexed with the raking movement of his hand.

Back and forth . . . back and forth . . . hypnotic. A light spiced scent reached me and I swallowed and shook my head, dislodging chunks of a quickset concrete stupor that rattled between my ears.

The plane was backed free of the gate and rolled out on the taxiway where it paused after a turn.

"Would you mind holding my hand?"

I looked at him, astonished.

"I hate takeoffs." He crooked a smile apologetically, extending his right hand.

The plane surged forward, gaining speed and thunder. The roaring engines buzzed loudly in my ears as I stared at the darkest, bluest eyes I had ever seen.

My hand reached out to his.

Loads of humor spilled from behind his dark lashes, and he engulfed my hand in a firm handshake.

"Gabe Miller," he said, stretching his grin. "Pleasure to meet you."

"Porzia." That's all I could manage.

My hand disappeared inside his firm hold. *This man is not afraid of his strength—or takeoffs,* I thought in the flash of time it takes to blink. My awareness struggled upwards from deep down a bottomless pit full of . . . leashed sexual frustrations? Where was my voice?

"Porzia Amard," I croaked. "Nice to meet you too. You had me there for a moment." I smiled and slowly pulled my hand back, ignoring the agonizing supplications of my entire body.

"Yeah, that was the idea." He grinned back.

Great mouth, I thought, noticing the chipped corner of his right upper incisor. It added something lethal to his smile.

He shifted back in his seat and stretched his legs in front of him. "Might as well make the best of being trapped up here."

What the hell was wrong with me? I didn't know what kind of 'best' *he* had in mind, but mine was not going to be G-rated. I gripped the seat arms and sank my nails in.

Shocked with myself, I seriously questioned my sanity. For heaven's sake! I never react to strangers like this. *Merda!* Absolutely ludicrous behavior! I *never* talk to strangers . . . unless I need to. That's part of why I write about food for a living. I am either alone writing or my mouth is full.

I have only a small circle of what I consider good friends. A couple of them live overseas and that suits me just fine. Benedetta is my only local close friend. Although born and raised in Mobile, and her knowledge of Italian limited to a few curses, her family is originally from Castiglione della Pescaia, about two hours south from where I grew up in Toscana. She spent every summer of her childhood there until age eight, when her parents split up. Her mother stayed in Italy; her father left for the United States. He raised Benedetta with his new wife, American-style. Still, we have in common the same childhood summer memories of juicy figs and *salame,* sun-ripened blackberry-stained mouths, and the occasional jellyfish encounter while snorkeling in the Mar Tirreno. We met in college, stunned at our similar pasts, spent months sharing stories, and slowly bonded like two goldfish in piranha-infested waters.

Bene doesn't cook, gets tipsy after a single glass of Chianti, and has the most contagious laugh I've ever heard. I've often suggested to her that she ought to go work for a hospital to help patients recover. She's perfectly happy to just 'spread the noise,' as she describes teaching music. I love her to death but I still remember it took me a while to warm up to her.

The seatbelt sign went off with a piercing *Bing!* That brought me back to the present and to Gabe Miller, who was observing me silently.

"I just witnessed several days of weather forecast unfold with your expressions," he said quietly, wonderment in his voice. "Clouds gathering quickly over a perfect blue sky. Darkness and rain pouring down while a couple of distant thunderclaps rumbled. Finally the smell of wet earth as the sun breaks through, warming everything up. I'm now waiting for a rainbow . . ."

I smiled slowly, granting his wish. "What do you do? Write greeting cards for a living?"

"No, I own an off-road specialty shop for cars, trucks, and four-wheel drives. My father writes the cards."

"No, he doesn't." I frowned, half-believing him. Nobody reads me like that.

"Where did you learn to make rainbows like that?"

"Boot camp," I blurted, dead serious.

Surprise caught his features and brightened his eyes, as if he didn't expect me to make him laugh. And when he did laugh, it was a rich, velvet sound. His happiness reached out to me like a glittering aura. Shiny bits of joy sprinkled over me. I liked that. I liked how the lines at the corners of his eyes deepened, how his lips stretched with his smile, how his five o'clock shadow made a man out of him, not a boy. But most of all, I liked how I felt about it: glad I had made him laugh. I don't know why it struck me as so important but it was.

"Where are you from?" he asked, laughter fading in his voice. "I hear an American accent, but there is something else mixed with it."

"Europe. My mother is Italian and my father French. And you?"

"Australian. Sixth generation, both parents from Adelaide."

"Is that where you live?" A hint of hope sparkled in darkness, like the twinkle of the first evening star. *Ouch, ouch, here we go.*

"Yes, just outside, on the hills."

"That's where I'm going." My heart quickened awaiting his reaction.

"You're flying into Adelaide?" He arched an eyebrow, but his tone remained enigmatic.

"Yes, I'm visiting a winery called Umeracha."

"Work or leisure?"

"Both." I smiled. "I'm fortunate enough to have a job that is also a passion. I absolutely adore food, and I freelance gourmet articles for magazines. So I get to cook, eat, travel, and make a living."

A soft-spoken flight attendant interrupted the conversation to offer a snack and drinks.

Gabe Miller asked for Scotch, water on the side. I ordered a glass of Merlot and they promptly brought a bottle.

"This ought to be interesting," he said. "It's going to be a long flight, and usually I end up being stuck next to boring executives fidgeting with their laptops the entire time." He leaned close to top the wine glass the flight attendant had adequately mid-filled already. "You're definitely not boring." He lightly toasted my glass with his.

Golden speckles dappled the cobalt of his pupils. These were no ordinary eyes; they were predatory eyes. I wondered if he would mind if I spent the entire flight counting those golden sparks.

I shook my head and leaned back in my seat. "So, you travel a lot?" I sipped the strong wine and pushed my black case under the seat in front of me with the tip of my shoe. *Mmmh . . . good wine.* I held the glass up to check the color and swirled. *Good legs as well.*

"Twice a year to California to check out new top-of-the-line accessories at an international off-road show in Anaheim, then Osaka in the fall, and Montreal in the spring. I don't think I travel as often as you do but it's enough for me." He shot me a tired look. "I hate flying. If I didn't have to,

I wouldn't. I like Australia and exploring by car. I've seen a lot, but there is still plenty left."

"So you were in California this time?"

"Roight. How about you? First time in Oz?"

I absolutely loved how he said "roight."

"No, I have been once before to Barossa, never to Adelaide." The velvety wine bouquet warmed my stomach, liquefying my usual reserve and skepticism.

"Oh, you'll like it. It's a great place. You can still see the styles of the first settlers reflected in the buildings, but there are plenty of parks and nature around to respect the environment." His sensuous mouth broke into a quick grin.

I took another sip.

"I've never heard of the winery you mentioned, but I don't really know much about wine. It's becoming a successful business in South Australia," he observed, "although, I must admit I don't know much about the subject." He paused and trapped my gaze with his spellbinding eyes. They crinkled at the corners as his lips curved. "Got plenty of time if you'd care to enlighten me."

Lethal.

I cleared my throat, searching for my business voice. I could do this. My father had been making wine since before he could walk. Back in France, his family has been making wine since the crusades. He brought his craft to Tuscany when he married my mother and applied it to the local grape varieties. Grapes are my compass. I can forecast the weather by observing the stalks, the leaves, the soil. Following family tradition, I learned how to walk stomping my stubborn legs in a vat filled with sun-ripened grapes. My brother eagerly imitated my every move, both of us turning purple, giggling ecstatically, blessing the *mosto* with our joy. Yes, this was familiar territory for me. Simply put: my own back yard.

"Well, you seem to have all the ingredients for producing high-quality wines: perfect climate, excellent soil, fewer competitors than California or even South America, where production is focused more on large scale than quality."

"Do you believe then that quality is more important than quantity?" he asked. Amusement warmed his voice.

"Absolutely," I replied with conviction, although a speckle of suspicion that he might not be talking about wine anymore tickled my warning sensors.

I ignored it. "Think about it like this: which is more satisfying, a delicious meal with a single, well-matched bottle of wine or that same meal with several low-quality bottles? And honestly, price is irrelevant more often than not. I would prefer the perfectly paired meal."

"Do you apply this parameter only to food, or does it happen to spill into other areas of your life?" His voice had dropped dangerously low.

I looked at him squarely. "That depends..."

He raised an eyebrow, folded his arms across his chest, and invited me to elaborate. I glanced at the wine bottle label, trying to find a way out of this spiraling trap. He unfolded his arms and swiftly stirred his Scotch. I watched his strong hand, the tumbler, and a single stubborn ice cube slowly drowning in ambered malt.

Add patience to his already long list of good qualities, I thought, still stalling.

"You're blushing, Porzia," he breathed.

Flames blazed across my cheeks. I raised my head and locked eyes with him. "Say my name like that one more time and I'll catch fire," I blurted.

"Porzia," his voice issued, low and time-stilling, like an inquisitive caress beneath my skirt.

Accidenti. Who did he think he was dealing with? I nearly burst out of my seams but held my own and managed to give him back a taste of his own medicine. Thinking of dark, rich chocolate mousse rolling over my tongue, I whispered his name, "*Gabe*—mortals often wrongfully believe monogamy to be a sign of absence of libido. That is not necessarily the case."

I sipped my wine.

It was his turn to catch his breath. His eyes swirled into a darker shade of troubled skies. "*Touché!*" He raised his right hand and touched his heart.

"You speak French?" My heart just about leaped into the wine glass I had just managed to drain.

"A little," he said. "Is it important?"

Panic bled my cheeks white. Had I been thinking of *Xavier*? It would explain my overreacting.

"I believe that in order to do well in business you need to give back. So every time I travel back to Canada or Japan, I try to learn more of the language. I've found it helps in your travels to be able to speak the local language."

"Yes, it does."

"What else besides English do you speak? Italian? French?" he inquired.

"That's it. A little Japanese, but I don't get over there often enough to be fluent, although I'd love to." I remembered the red kimono.

The acrylic smell of airline meals and heated plastic trays wafted through the pressurized cabin. Static on the movie screens launched the featured programs. I was surprised to see we had been flying for over an hour already. A few passengers had fallen asleep. The pilot's voice came over the intercom giving out flight details and wishing us "bon appétit."

CHAPTER 4

I politely declined dinner. I reached for my carry-on and found my snacks, realizing that besides coffee at the airport, I hadn't eaten in ages. I was famished. The wine had stirred a light buzz and food sounded delicious, especially the two focaccia sandwiches with prosciutto, mozzarella, and pesto I had packed. I set them on the tray along with a clutch of grapes, Belgian endive and cucumber sticks from ziplock bags, and a handful of Baci chocolates Benedetta had added at the last minute. To *bless* her would be redundant.

I eyed Gabe and debated whether I liked him enough to share my treasure. He was poking suspiciously at his food with a fork. I offered him a sandwich. "Here. This is going to beat anything they might try to pass for food around here." I nudged it toward him.

He reached over and lifted it to his tray. "Thanks," he said, unwrapping his sandwich. "It smells great, what is it?"

"Panino. Italian for sandwich." I handed him some grapes and vegetables. I had not yet decided if I liked him enough to share the chocolates.

Gabe reached for the Merlot and poured me another glass, then took his remaining Scotch and toasted my wine. "Cheers."

"*Salute!*" I added, raising my glass to meet his.

We ate in comfortable silence, enjoying the food until a flight attendant appeared balancing two enormous brownie sundaes. He grinned and almost dumped one on my lap. I stared at the heap of ice cream, steaming brownie, and melting fudge syrup. I sighed, "I'm sorry, but I'm afraid this is just too much for me."

"How about you take one back, mate? And leave us two spoons?" Gabe offered.

"Yes, sir, no worries." The flight attendant bounced away with the other dessert and Gabe's untouched airline meal.

My spoon, precariously hanging on the edge of the tray, didn't make it and fell, tumbling backwards under my seat until, even with my head between my knees, I couldn't see it anymore. I raised my head, bumped the tray, managed to save the wine bottle, and felt grateful Gabe had grabbed my full glass before it spilled. I settled back somewhat, took my wine glass back without touching his fingers, swallowed disappointment, and was about to ring to have a new spoon brought to me, when Gabe reached for his and smiled wickedly. He scooped some ice cream, brought the spoon up to my mouth, and waited, tempting me.

This man has initiative. I lowered my eyelids to stare at the perfect bite: a little chunk of brownie covered in vanilla ice cream laced with thick fudge and a melting dollop of whipped cream. Not a single nut in sight. I bit. I closed my eyes for a minute and savored the richness. It tasted heavenly in my mouth. Gabe chuckled and took a bite himself. Several blissful minutes of perfect bites followed, from my mouth to the frosty glass to his mouth.

The mood coated us with intimacy. Silence lingered around us, a willing accomplice. We exchanged not a single word.

Attraction and wonder glimmered in his eyes.

I thought of calm lights reflecting gold before sunset. Holding his gaze, I exhaled and let my guard fall. I hadn't realized until that moment how much I had been shielding. He sensed the change and looked at me with such intensity I thought about warding myself again. I handed the empty sundae glass to the flight attendant, who had magically appeared at my elbow, and wondered how or what the hell I knew about warding and shields.

Good that the ice cream was gone. It would have melted in such intense heat.

Clearing his throat, Gabe reached for his bag. "Do you like music?" he asked. I watched him mess around with a portable CD player.

"Yes, I do." I held my breath. As if on cue, the cabin lights dimmed slowly.

He reached over and placed small earphones on my head. He hit the play button and I recognized the first notes of one of my favorite Depeche Mode songs. He unfolded his right leg, leaned forward, and gently brushed a lock of hair off my face. His fingertips lingered just enough for me to shiver.

I didn't resist when his arms lifted me over his knee and pulled me until my back met his chest. I tilted my head, brushing the curve of his chin with my hair, and nestled in. Purrs tickled my throat.

His left hand brushed my hair away from my neck, exposing the earphone. He traced my ear with his hot fingertips, drawing a line from my earlobe down the base of my neck, and I shivered. In a caress, his fingers trailed down my shoulder, along my arm, and finally entwined with mine. His right hand slid under my right elbow and found my waist.

I closed my eyes against the intensity. I was on fire.

The music washed over me, and I relaxed my back against his strong chest. I exhaled, and his chocolate-scented breath mingled with mine. When I squeezed his hand, his grip tightened in response.

I listened to the lyrics, realizing Gabe had chosen that specific song on purpose.

Seized by fear, I couldn't turn to look into his eyes.

What kind of *world* did he want me to see?

I shoved doubts out of my head with a firm push, and since my heart had already settled, I surrendered, relaxing against his chest completely. Several songs unraveled—all from different musicians, some just instrumental versions of classics.

Gabe never said a word. He just held me against his chest, comfortable in the darkness around us at over thirty-eight thousand feet altitude. I covered his right hand with mine and he began to caress my fingers. Quick electric shocks climbed up my arm, like flames flickering over my skin. It was as if he could hear the music spilling from the earphones, and he moved his fingers along my hand to the rhythm. My own heartbeat echoed that same pulse, matching the rhythm. I felt his head move backwards to rest against the seat and his hand slowed down and finally stilled as he drifted to sleep.

I absolutely refused to think. I used the music as a shield to keep me from stirring my rational brain from its ice cream-induced hibernation.

Yeah! Let's blame the ice cream. Fight one weakness with another.

But was this weakness? Is it weak to allow yourself to be real and do as you feel instead of hiding behind pretense when your entire being screams otherwise? How many times do we make scalding-hot eye contact with a stranger and fail to act upon it? We hide behind worn-out panels of decorum. The excuse of fear, the terror of being hurt restrains us from life.

Joséphine used to say that to feel pain is better than not to feel at all. I find myself agreeing with her more often than not.

I lifted my feet to the side, kicked my sneakers off, and readjusted my legs to rest on Gabe's. He must have felt extremely comfortable to fall asleep with me in his arms. Or maybe he was just exhausted.

I felt sleep crawl over me like a familiar blanket, but I didn't give in.

Like thunder chasing lightning, expectation follows the high tide of emotions that a brand-new attraction raises. It's a mistake, an enormous mistake. Would I start making plans for us to see each other in Adelaide? I might not ever see him again after the flight.

I had so many questions. Benedetta calls this "jerking off mentally." Why was I even bothering?

Because I'm human, a tiny voice whispered inside me.

Why can't I just be grateful I had the chance to feel this, if only fleetingly? Why can't I stop doubting and just ride the high tide?

Because I know the low one will follow. I wondered if magic was at work already, steering me in the right direction. I shook my head. Too much had happened in my life for me to believe in fairy tales with happy endings. After Steve, I started thinking that Gretel and the witch should hook up after killing, peeling, boiling, and eating Hansel. It would make a great sequel.

The music stopped with a soft click. I rubbed my eyes, lifted the earphones off my head, and slid my feet into the complimentary slippers. Gabe didn't wake as I moved out of his arms. I stood and walked to the lavatory.

Funny how we use the word 'lavatory' only on airplanes because any other time it would be considered an odd word, perplexing. *Maybe they use it in Australia,* I thought. I'm often prone to random mind-wandering, especially during uncomfortable or stressful situations. But was I really nervous?

I splashed cold water on my face. I looked in the mirror and realized that none of my previous names had come up in the regression. I was Porzia, with my face, my personality, my flaws, and my baggage of timeless memories. To try to be any of those women would mean to *regress* literally, in *this* life and perhaps acquire more baggage. To try to find Xavier would mean limiting my choices in partners to somebody that fit his profile.

Wrong.

It meant I had embarked on a quest of self-discovery, to learn to love myself—including my magic powers—and ultimately merge again with my true love. That's what Evalena meant.

Good luck, I silently mouthed to myself in the mirror. But the awareness of sharing a time-defying bond with someone flared through a secret part of my soul I had no idea I owned and filled it up for the first time in ages. Warmth radiated from my navel outward like a spreading aura, heating my body from the inside out.

I bowed my head in acceptance and secretly smiled as I chose to take my second wayward step and walked back to my seat self-consciously, musing that I might actually glow in the dark. I wished I had a volume knob to turn it down.

The movie screen flickered azure lights against the seat.

Gabe was still asleep. I adjusted myself sideways against his chest, kicked the slippers off, and closed my eyes. I snuggled my face against his chest, brushing the softness of his T-shirt with my cheek, and inhaled musk and spice. His heart, beating strong and steady beneath my ear, comforted me.

*

I woke up to his hand smoothing my hair. I usually don't fall asleep on airplanes.

We had crossed the Pacific and were following the Australian coast toward Melbourne, now less than a couple of hours ahead according to the video screen.

Gabe got up, gently readjusted me on the seat, and covered me with the blue blanket.

With a hand, he wiped sleep off his face and quickly combed his hair back. "I'll be roight back," he whispered.

I watched him walk away. I wanted to sleep more, but they were turning the lights on and I could smell coffee.

Ahhh . . . coffee.

Gabe came back as I struggled with the blanket; it insisted on wrapping itself around me. I must have looked a mess. He didn't seem to notice, just balanced two cups of coffee in one hand and peeled me out of the blanket, making it look like the easiest thing in the world. Then handed me coffee—sweet, creamy coffee.

How did he know?

"I never sleep like that." His eyes held a spark of involuntary admission. "You're an unexpected, precious gift, Porzia. I know it's hard to believe, but I think you understand."

Gift? I kind of liked that. I nodded.

"I'll ask the flight attendant to seat us together on the next flight home," he invited. "So you can hold my hand again."

I laughed.

Once we landed in Melbourne he waited for me to clear Customs, and we walked to catch the other plane hand in hand. So I ended up next to him all the way to Adelaide.

As we settled back in our seats he took my hand in his again and held it until the end of the flight.

Maybe he really is afraid of flying, I mused.

"Clark is picking me up at the airport. Have you got a lift to the winery? I could drive you up there if you need me to, I'm sure he won't mind," he offered.

"Clark?"

"Clark's my father. I've taken to calling him by his first name. He told me it makes him feel way too old to have a son my age." He winked mischievously.

"How old are you?" I asked suspiciously.

"Thirty-six. And you?"

"Thirty," I smiled. "I'd love to meet Clark, but I've got a ride to the winery. Thank you for offering."

"How long will you be up there? Have you got a number I can ring you?" He reached for his wallet and handed me a business card. "That's my work number roight there." He took the card back. "Here—let me write my home number on the back." He scribbled numbers on the back of the card and handed it back to me.

I rummaged in my bag and found a small brochure from Umeracha Winery. "I'm planning on being there about five days. I'll be busy for the first few with the wine presentations, but I'm sure if you'd like to come along, they'd be glad to have you there."

"Get settled and give me a ring when you have a moment." He brought my hand to his lips and gently kissed it. "Until then, I want you to know I'll be thinking of you."

I found myself responding naturally to the unequivocal message in his eyes. Mesmerized, I leaned forward. Shrouded by fear my true feelings skimmed behind my half-parted eyelids.

"Your eyes are getting greener—Porzia."

Dangerous warning but I couldn't care less so close to his delicious grin. I found myself responding in a rush of arousal—irrefutably *sexual* arousal. "Well then, you'll need something to fuel all that thinking," I whispered, bringing the hand he had just kissed to his heart. My fingers found the smooth swell of his chest. In a daze, I fist-filled his shirt and tugged, pulling him closer to me. I tilted my head, parted my lips, and closed my eyes.

I kissed him.

My lips met his. I let them dance slowly—tease, like a butterfly on velvet petals. I tasted coffee, coffee much more bitter than mine, on the tip of his tongue as I dared explore deeper. I felt his hands cup my face, pulling me even closer, and the kiss flared. Heat, lust, and passion twisted and braided in a struggle to possess us.

He became the aggressor and I the consenting victim. I moaned against his mouth, overwhelmed with burning emotions. My insides melted into hot lava, running scalding, liquid paths. His heated scent enveloped me, seduced my senses, and teased my animal instinct until a primal beat began to pulse between my legs. His hands left my face to follow the curve of my shoulders down my arms where they gripped and pulled me against him.

My hands became an obstacle trapped between us. I slowly moved them up, my lips never leaving his mouth, until my heartbeat pressed madly against his. His hand reached the nape of my neck and yanked a fistful of hair.

"That's supposed to help me think?"

My lips throbbed against his words.

His mouth moved to brush my throat. Slowly I opened my eyes and saw his incredible hair tease my chin. I plunged both hands into those thick strands of golden silk, pulling his head back up. I hungered to taste his mouth again.

Suddenly I felt my brain bounce around in my head as the plane tilted and slowed down, dipping toward the ocean below.

"I think we're landing," Gabe said, his voice thick against my mouth once again.

"Where are we?" I blinked, totally lost.

He laughed and pulled back just enough to look at me. His eyes shifted to clear aquamarine, his hair remained an untamed mess. He looked sexier than ever.

"If this is what it's like to be bewitched—"

"I'm not a witch, Gabe, why do you think—"

"Yeah? What was in that panino you gave me?"

"Nothing! If you feel like you've been bewitched, maybe it's because you want to." I was only half joking.

"It's OK, plenty of antidotes in my outback supplies stash . . ."

"I've never heard that one before," I laughed.

"I've never been kissed like that before." His serious eyes caressed my mouth.

"Yes, you have," I told him. "Perhaps you just don't remember."

He raised a questioning eyebrow. "What would make me forget?"

"Death."

Seats in upright position; we were landing.

CHAPTER 5

I had instructions to keep my eyes open for a sign with my name on it, but Gabe saw Clark before I could even begin to look around for Dom, my driver. My eyes followed his and stumbled upon a sun-parched version of the man holding my hand.

Clark stood tall and solid, wearing a timeless smile matched by a faded denim shirt that looked just as old. Where Gabe's eyes still reflected honesty, Clark's wore an astute smart-ass look, framed by myriad laugh lines that appeared to deepen as we got closer to him. He looked at me as he would at something exotic on his plate, wondering if I were good to eat or if he should just ask for the check, go home, and fix a Vegemite sandwich.

I held his gaze.

Gabe briefly let go of my hand to shake his father's.

"Hey, son! How was the flight?" Clark asked.

"Not bad, thanks. I slept most of the way."

Clark's eyebrows went up. Way up. "I'll be stuffed! You *slept*?" He looked at me.

I grinned.

"Yes. I did. Clark, this is Porzia Amard. Porzia, this is my father, Clark Miller."

Clark re-orchestrated his eyebrows, smiled, and extended his hand. "It's indeed a pleasure to meet you, Miss Amard."

"The pleasure is mine, Mr. Miller. Please, call me Porzia." I returned the firm handshake.

"Well then, splendid! I'm Clark." He turned to look at Gabe, still holding my hand. "Is she the reason you slept?"

"Yes, she is," Gabe mused. "She gave me a panino."

"Ah! That explains it," Clark conceded, bringing my hand to his lips, amusement in his voice. "I have no clue what he's talking about," he said, kissing my hand, "but if it cures his high-altitude insomnia then I'm all for it. Welcome to Oz, Porzia."

Charming old devil, I thought, taking my hand back. "Thank you." I would leave him wondering about the panino mystery a while longer.

"What brings you all the way Down Under?" Clark asked as we walked to collect our luggage.

"Wine."

"Excellent!" He took my left arm under his right and patted my hand. "We have heaps of beer as well."

"Do you now?" I smiled, as I caught sight of a flustered man waving a sign with my name on it. I waved back at him. Gabe followed my gaze to a very relieved Dom.

"Miss Amard? I'm terribly sorry. Please forgive me. Traffic was horrible on the way over," he panted, pumping my hand.

"Please, no reason to apologize. I'm glad you've made it here safe."

"Yes, yes. Thank you. I'm parked right outside—will I be driving everybody back to the vineyard?"

"Oh no, we have our own car, thanks," Clark answered. He let go of my arm to follow Gabe to the carousel as it started to move.

A freezing winter wind hit us outside. I wrapped myself inside my jacket and shoved my hands deep inside my pockets where my fingers closed around a few more Baci chocolates. Benedetta must have slipped extra ones in there. I was about to say good-bye and follow Dom when Gabe took my arm and pulled me aside. Clark winked at me. Feigning nonchalance, he loaded bags into a top-of-the-line SUV parked a few car spaces behind Dom's Jeep.

Gabe sieved his hands through my hair and held my head while he kissed me, keeping his eyes open. I know because I didn't close mine either. I just looked at him. I kissed him back.

"I'm going to remember every moment spent with you until I see you again."

He kissed the tip of my nose. "Ring when you have a chance. If I don't hear from you in about two hours, I'm calling *you*." He smiled.

"OK." I pulled my hands out of my pockets and gave him a chocolate. "Eat it on your way home," I said and hugged him. The hell with freezing. I kissed him one more time, forgetting the cold, warming up under his touch. I closed my eyes and melted against his heat.

It took a lot of control for both of us to come out of it; his hair was all messed up again. *Did I do that? With my fingers?*

Dom and Clark shook hands. It was time to go.

Clark dangled car keys in front of Gabe. "Would you like me to drive, son?" he asked with a smirk. He waved at me. "It's London to a brick I'll be seeing you again—"

I blew him a kiss, walked to the Jeep, and climbed into . . . the driver's seat. A puzzled Dom held the opposite door open for me. Of course. They drive on the other side of the road. How silly of me to forget.

I was silent on the drive back to the winery. Having slept incredibly well in Gabe's arms, I didn't feel too tired even after such a long journey. But I needed a few moments to assess what had happened to me. To us. *Was* there even an 'us'? A somber palette of winter monochromatic colors shrouded Adelaide. The trees were mostly bare, and above us pregnant clouds shifted slowly against a low ceiling, reminding me of drowsy elephants.

Dom quietly hummed along with the radio.

I thought of Gabe. I closed my eyes. I thought of Xavier. I opened my eyes. Maybe I should stop thinking of both . . . *but what would I do with my eyes then?*

We left Adelaide behind to climb up the hills. The road was wet; it must have rained minutes earlier. Homes became sparse and the landscape waxed foreign to my Florida-accustomed eyes. I felt ages away from home. Winter crawled under my skin, frosting whatever trace of Florida sunshine I carried within. The clouds dropped much lower and loomed so closely over me I struggled with the urge to reach out and touch them.

I tried to remember what the weather had been like the day Xavier died. I frowned in effort to focus on the background instead of his lifeless body slumped at my feet. I recalled the castle courtyard paved in damp gray cobblestones. No rain that day but wetness still lingered around. It must have been the end of winter, still cold enough to make one long for spring as a distant mirage. Xavier would never enjoy warmth again.

I wondered what had happened before that day. What brought us to love each other so? I could make up so many ways. I had opened a theater door in the middle of a movie playing, taken a peek at the screen, and shut the door again. There seemed no beginning, no end. Just a few strategically placed images scattered on a black velvet background.

A majestic eagle split a seam amid the grayness of the low clouds. It made me think of Gabe. Now *he* felt real. His deep voice, thick with his Australian accent when he said my name, rippled along my skin raising my hair from head to toe. How easy it had been to just let him hold me. Sometimes it takes months to fall into such a safe trust zone. Sometimes it never happens. With Gabe it had been instantaneous.

Endless rows of knotty, bare vines announced our approach to Umeracha Winery. A solid two-story mansion with a wrap-around porch stood at the end of a long, curved, gravel-paved driveway. A couple of caramel-coated dogs barked and chased around the Jeep as it slowed.

"Welcome to Umeracha, Miss Amard," Dom announced, bringing the car to a stop in front of the main entrance.

Beverly Jourdain's freckles spilled abundantly across her perky nose as she greeted me at the door and fussed around me like a busy bee on a ripe blossom.

We had met over a year earlier in Barossa when I came to write an extensive article about the Australian wine scene for *In Vino Veritas*. They had been there to receive a prize for their Cabernet. I remembered Frank, her husband, as a somber bear of a man, not nearly as gregarious as his wife. Beverly and Frank had three sons: Luke and Ronnald took after Frank, but Nicolas, the youngest one, had Beverly's sparkle twinkling from his eyes beneath an untamed mane of auburn hair.

The main house smelled of lemon-scented wood polish. Votive candles napped on a rustic sideboard. Resigned sepia family photographs dozed on the dark wood walls.

I walked with feet of felt to my room on the second floor. Down below, a naked garden slept through winter. I found it hard to make out what kind of tree those stark branches belonged to, even harder to imagine eventual buds on such knobby limbs. Impossible to imagine magic blooming in my barren life as well, I grimaced. Least of all true love.

I reached inside my pockets where I found a lonesome Baci chocolate and the dice key chain I had bought at the Pensacola airport. I unclasped the dice off the key chain and rolled. Two. How sad. Irrationally I had hoped for an immediate answer to all my problems. I unwrapped the chocolate and read the quote as I chewed the delicious morsel: "This being is free from servile bonds of hope to rise or fear to fall; Lord of himself, though no lands, and having nothing, yet hath all". *Interesting.*

A spacious bathroom hid behind an alcove screen. A large tub and plush towels beckoned me to run a bath. It was too early to go straight to bed, and I wanted to call Gabe. *After the bath,* I thought . . . *and then, sleep.*

I sat on the edge of the tub and turned the water on. In a small basket a scrumptious selection of herbal bath gels captured my attention, and I poured an entire lavender bottle into the steaming waters. I quickly undressed and sank into the bubbly, scented water and closed my eyes. Too tired to even think, my mind drifted and my limbs relaxed, absorbing the heat until the water finally cooled down.

I felt much better afterwards. I was wrapping my hair in a towel when the phone rang.

"Porzia, I have a . . . uh . . . Gabe? . . . on the line. Shall I put him through?" Beverly's voice asked politely.

"Yes, thank you." Excited, I sat on the tall bed and noticed my naked feet could not reach the rug. My toes had shriveled in the bath down to the look of semi-comatose raisins. How attractive.

"Porzia."

My heart skipped a beat. "Hello."

"Hey, you got there alroight?"

"Yes, it's beautiful up here. I even saw an eagle on the way up."

"You did?" he asked, surprised.

"Yes."

He switched the subject. "Hey, you didn't tell me the chocolate had a quote hidden in its wrap."

"What did it say?"

"'Leap and the net will open. The key to change is to let go of fear.'"

"I believe that may be meant for me." I smiled and repeated the one I had found.

"If that's about me it's not accurate," he commented inscrutably and switched the subject again. "Do they have you drunk yet?"

"Why yes, of course. Dom had me going as soon as we left the airport."

I heard him chuckle. "You must be exhausted. I just wanted to wish you goodnight."

I tried not to yawn but wasn't able to hide it. Yes, I was tired. "You must be tired yourself." I let myself fall back on the bed.

"Well, yeah, but I'll be fine by tomorrow," he said. "I'll let you go."

"Ok, I'll call you tomorrow." My eyelids won the fight and shut. "Goodnight."

"Goodnight."

Summoning my last reserve of will, I rang Beverly downstairs and told her not to worry about supper for me, that I would see them for breakfast. She offered to have a tray brought up, but as I was almost asleep, I told her it wasn't necessary.

With my wet hair wrapped in a towel, I fell asleep on top of the covers. I woke up sometime during the night to slip under the blankets and pull the damp towel off my head.

CHAPTER 6

I slept like a baby for the rest of the night and woke up at the sound of heavy rain tapping against the window. The room hummed, warm and cozy. My eyes lazily followed rivulets of rain weaving erratic patterns along the glass pane. I didn't want to get up. I could have spent the rest of my morning under the blankets, snoozing off and on. I wondered about breakfast in bed but decided against it. After a quick search through my luggage for clothes, I wrapped my still-damp hair in a low bun and went looking for coffee. I followed the sound of laughter and the scent of strong coffee to the dining hall, where I found the gathered family enjoying a buffet worthy of Pantagruel. The rustic table almost bent under such abundance. Three baskets of wheat, rye, and sunflower seed country breads exchanged hands over a soundtrack of chatter, laughter, and silverware clatter.

Nicolas noticed me first. With a flamboyant "G'day," he stood, bowed, and offered the chair next to his.

"Thank you and good morning," I greeted everybody, accepting the seat.

Frank sat at the head of the table opposite Beverly and nodded at me. Ronnald and Luke smiled as they simultaneously handed me serving platters of fluffy scrambled eggs laced with chives and wild mushrooms, grilled lamb chops with mint sauce, roasted new potatoes with rosemary and sage, and the breadbaskets.

Nicolas poured me a cup of steaming coffee, pushed away the Vegemite jar, and almost miraculously handed me cream and sugar.

Beverly quietly nurtured a steaming tea mug, her arms propped on her chair armrests, her rust-colored cashmere sweater only a shade darker than her cheerful freckles. "I trust you slept well, my dear?" she asked, smiling.

"Yes, I slept great, thank you," I replied, helping myself to some of the eggs and spearing a lamb chop with the serving fork.

"How was your trip?" Frank asked, waving an empty mug under Nicolas's nose. Biting into an oversized, generously buttered slice of rye bread, the cheerful kid promptly refilled it for his father with both hands.

"Long, but I was able to sleep for quite a while. Thank you for asking."

"Well, we have a long day ahead of us. If you'll excuse us, Porzia—I reckon if you need anything, Beverly will be able to assist you. Also, you're welcome to join us down in the cellar for a private sampling later on, if you'd like." He stood as I nodded, taking his mug with him. The boys followed, saying goodbye. Nicolas winked and grabbed one last lamb chop on his way out.

Beverly watched them leave in pensive silence.

I tasted the food. The eggs were excellent. It might not seem like such a difficulty but to make good scrambled eggs actually takes a measure of skill. It took me ages to finally manage a decent outcome and Benedetta still makes better ones, although that's all she can cook. One can't hurry the cooking or over-beat the eggs. I know several chefs who actually separate the yolks from the egg whites. They then beat the whites into soft peaks and fold in the yolks after slightly whisking them with some whole milk, salt, and freshly ground white pepper. The result is a heavenly explosion of lightness in the mouth.

The sunflower seed bread tasted great with the fantastic eggs. It stood on its own with no need for butter. I had just about wiped my plate clean before I even reached for my mug to sip some coffee. Yes! Strong and sweet.

Beverly poured herself more tea, added milk, and stirred in some sugar. "It's indeed a pleasure to see you again, Porzia," she said, raising her cup to her lips where it steamed up her galaxy of freckles. "You've been making quite a name for yourself in the gourmet world and international wine circles. I have been following your articles, and I know it was quite a challenge to book you for this event, but I wouldn't want anybody else to have the exclusive coverage of the presentation. We're delighted to have Desmond Tanier as the photographer. You probably remember him from Barossa. He'll be arriving later tonight. *Driving* from Melbourne, he is." Beverly chuckled at her own last remark.

Desmond Tanier looks like the ear Van Gogh cut off.

He established his own recognition during the Vietnam War, risking his life taking pictures of things nobody back home wanted to know about. His work earned him several prizes. He took to drinking, though and shifted his skills to make a living taking pictures of his favorite subject: alcohol. He's a legend, if not just because people can't seem to figure out if he's dead or still alive. I had worked with him on several previous occasions, and I do believe he is alive; seldom sober, but alive.

"How did you manage to book him?" Helen had graciously warned me of his potential presence. I knew how irreverent and outrageous he could be.

"He gave Frank his business card back in Barossa, told him anybody who wins a prize for excellent wine has earned a special place in his heart. So I called him up and told him about the Shiraz and that you'd be writing the article. He seemed quite fond of you." Beverly's bright green eyes sparkled just short of twinkling.

I looked at her and caught the light beaming from the window rearranging the freckles on her nose.

"He's fond of me because I owe him a bottle of Scotch," I clarified, laying my linen napkin on the table.

Beverly's eyebrows shot up, questioning.

"I lost a bet. I owe him a bottle but haven't seen him since. He just wants me to pay my debt." I smoothed out the napkin creases with my fingers.

"Indeed. And how's that charming young man who accompanied you at Barossa? What was his name? Steve, I believe?"

"Last I heard he was on his way to California for a sous-chef internship somewhere in Napa. We're no longer together," I shared, with a lot less pain than I had expected to feel. How surprising. What relief.

"Oh dear, I didn't mean to pry or bring up painful memories for you, sweetie," she said, concerned. Her hand reached out to mine over the napkin.

"No need to apologize," I told her. "It's been long enough, and I'm over it." I tried to smile but failed.

"Has it been that long already since we met at Barossa?"

"Over a year." I thought of all the water that had passed under my daily bridges, carrying the debris of memories and events out to sea.

*

I had met Steve at Seville Quarter, a local hangout in downtown Pensacola, during a spring break from my journalism program up in New York.

I wasn't looking for love. I wasn't looking for anything but some time off for life and relaxation. I guess that is always when love finds you: when you're not looking. When all your energies, or what is left of them, are focused on just going your merry way.

I remember it had rained earlier and the New Orleans-style courtyard was still damp, smelling sweetly of night jasmine. Citronella lanterns kept the mosquitoes at bay. I could hear my hair begging for mercy, struggling as the humid air turned my curls into a frizzy mop. Perseus would have chopped my head off instead of Medusa's had he seen me that night.

Steve had just moved from England on an exchange program to train as a pastry chef at Chez Jacques in New Orleans. Chez Jacques is the only French pastry school worth attending in this country, according to *Monsieur Jacques* himself, *naturellement*! He was visiting some friends in Florida when I met him, using them as guinea pigs for his culinary experiments. They were gaining weight by the minute.

I loved his British aplomb. I loved how that night he never commented on my messy hair, how it took him forever to ask me to dance, how candidly he told me he was trying to find things to say because he didn't want the evening to come to an end. It all attracted me.

I fell in love with Steve *and* the Florida Emerald Coast.

After culinary and sommelier schools, and my first serious assignment to the Chianti region for *Bacchus Grapeyard* magazine, I moved down to Pensacola. Steve and I became inseparable, sometimes driving the three hours between us just to have an evening together.

He brought me Peridot one stormy evening. That night we shared *choux* filled with Chantilly cream covered in chocolate ganache. We made love outside under a starry velvet blanket, and I toyed with the idea of marriage.

That was eons ago and things changed.

He never asked me to marry him. My assignments took me all over the world, and he started resenting my success. He dove headfirst into his job, trying to prove he was just as good at what he did as I was. In the process, he won several national prizes for Chez Jacques, but his successes were never enough and by then he was addicted to the challenge of working harder and harder. Pretty soon the uniform shrank a couple of sizes too small, the jealousy mounted, and he hit the wall. He quit. He had never hinted at his dissatisfaction, but when he moved in with me, things took a turn for the worse.

I still loved him at that point. Hell, I loved him for months after we broke up. But he didn't want my help. He slumped into depression and blamed it on everything but himself.

It was right after we got back from Barossa. That trip is the last good memory I have of us together.

He couldn't stop drinking —I even caught him throwing empty bottles of whiskey into the neighbor's trash one evening—and he blamed me. His envy of my blossoming career and my hard work left such a bitter aftertaste, I could not help him. My words fell like deaf stones into the waters of his drunken stupor. He chose to keep on drinking; no matter how much pain he caused us. But there was nothing I had done to bring this on. He was battling his own private demons.

My help rejected, my love useless, I slipped into co-dependency. I hated myself. I loved him. I hated myself for loving him.

And then it happened. I caught him cheating and told him to leave. We had been together for over five years. He never forgave me.

I was heartbroken.

Ask Evalena. She was there and caught the tail end of the comet.

CHAPTER 7

I spent the day exploring the winery, escorted by an extremely informative and most courteous Dom. I shrugged off some of the painful memories and plunged my thoughts into musty-scented cellars full of aging wooden barrels and decanters ready to be sampled.

It was mid-afternoon when I remembered Frank's invitation to an informal tasting.

I hurried to the cellar's entrance in the main kitchen where the scent of the tarragon beef stew we had enjoyed for lunch still lingered. By the pantry I found the door I was looking for, opened it, and took the stairs down. The temperature dropped by at least fifteen degrees as I stepped onto the bare brick floor. Naked light bulbs hung from the raw-stoned ceiling, casting shadows in alcoves where dusty wine bottles rested; each alcove was numbered, named, and dated with plaques. I glanced at some Grand Reserve bottles dating back to the 1960s.

Frank and the boys had gathered around an ancient rustic table where opened bottles of Shiraz stood at attention like obedient soldiers. Frank had a couple of half-filled decanters in front of him and was pouring thick purple wine into Riedel glasses.

Greeting me, they shifted around the table to make room. I mumbled an apology for being late and bumped into Nicolas on my left. He winked at me. I cracked a grin and then turned serious as Frank cast a sidelong glance at us.

The wines that benefit from decanting are usually the robust reds, such as the most mature red Bordeaux, Italian Barolos, and, occasionally, Australian and California reds. Shiraz (known in France as Syrah) also responds well to decanting. Decanting, in addition to filtering out sediment, aerates the wine, allowing it to breathe or, as they say, 'open up,' which enhances the flavor.

The Shiraz grape appears to be named after a city in Persia (Shiraz) where the grape variety probably originated. It was brought into Southern France by a returning crusader, Guy De' Sterimberg. He became a hermit and developed a vineyard on a steep hill where he lived in the Rhone River Valley. It became known as Hermitage. This is the sort of story I fell asleep to as a child. The occasional princess tale intruded once in a while but my mother always had an uncanny ability to lace true history with fantasy at our bedside and *those* stories I truly enjoyed. As I pursued my sommelier studies, all grown up, I mused every time I discovered and validated real tidbits of history she'd so skillfully woven between her vivid imagination and immeasurable knowledge. Only later was I able to figure out and distinguish that she was the creative part while my father and Joséphine had provided the historical facts.

The Shiraz grape produces a tannic, purple wine with a peppery flavor that was originally used to bring strength to Grenache wines in the Southern Rhone and with Bordeaux and Burgundy, until it was legally excluded from this last role by "*appellation contrôlée*" rules. It has become extremely important in Australia, producing rich, spicy, intense reds, but it also does well in blends with Cabernet Sauvignon.

We followed a simple wine-tasting ritual. Frank handed each of us a glass filled to one third of its capacity and, with a general "*à votre santé*," raised his glass to toast ours.

Color, smell, and then taste are the essentials to look for when sampling a new wine for the first time. Held against the light, Frank's Shiraz revealed a deep purple, almost inky color.

We sipped in silence.

The nose evoked intense, rich blackberry aromas. The flavor on the palate showed mouth-filling fruit, massive structure, and a long, sweet finish. It coated my throat like a velvet caress, glazed my stomach with warmth, and shot straight up to my head.

Have I mentioned that I'm a sensible drinker?

A plate of paper-thin sliced *salame* and hearty bread appeared as if by magic on the table. Nicolas passed it around while Frank refilled us, a satisfied smile lingering on his face.

I looked at Frank and cleared my throat. "I believe there is no need for me to mention how excellent a product you have here. I know by experience that the producer is his own biggest critic, and if I'm not mistaken, you're having a hard time hiding that grin of yours." I must have been getting drunk at the speed of light to use such a tone with him. Faintly appalled at my gaffe, I begged, "Pardon my *hauteur*."

A loud racket coming from the stairs made us all turn at once.

"Bloody hell! You've been as busy as cats burying shit! I can't believe you've hit the turps without me!" Desmond Tanier's voice boomed like a cannonball, ricocheting against the dark stone walls. Beverly followed at a safe distance, her flustered freckles blanching with chagrin.

Tanier spotted me. "Porzia! Dear lass! How long have you been going at it? You seem a bit flushed." He hugged me, then abruptly pushed me to arm's distance and eyed me critically. "Have you gained weight since last I saw you? Having romantic troubles as usual?" Desmond Tanier would never win awards for manners; we all knew that by now.

"Desmond! *Mon petit fleur*, did you just get in?" I asked, smiling sweetly. I threw French at him in a futile attempt to trigger Vietnam flashbacks in his mind. It didn't seem to shackle him at all.

"Yes, indeed! Just drove up the coast from Melbourne. I reckon I beat my own previous record, but I'm as dry as a nun's wrinkle." He snatched the glass Frank was handing him.

Beverly got hold of a bottle and looked like she had all intentions of drinking straight from it. Who could blame her? Heaven knows what had happened upstairs before they actually made it down to the cellar.

Desmond quickly sniffed his glass. With a sharp motion of his wrist he swirled the dark wine once around the smooth crystal, grunted satisfaction, and gulped the contents. Briefly, he closed his eyes. Wiping his mouth on his sleeve, he declared, "Excellent!" He raised the empty glass up to Beverly who promptly refilled it from her precious bottle. Frank and the boys shared an idiotic, amused look that reminded me they were definitely related.

Dom appeared, legs first, and announced dinner to be served in less than an hour.

As I followed everybody upstairs, I realized the thought of Gabe had been humming in the back of my mind the entire day. I couldn't wait to talk to him again. I climbed the steps two at a time.

The sun had set and dusk spread twinkling stars one by one on a violet velvet stretch of sky. A gentle winter breeze fluttered softly along . . . or maybe it was just my head buzzing. I made it to my room and dialed Gabe's home number from the back of his business card and sat on the edge of the bed. The anticipation of speaking to him again rose with every ring. I tried to imagine him on the other end, wondered what he was wearing, who he had thought could be calling him . . .

He answered, catching me by surprise, and just hearing his simple hello made my heart jump.

"Hello, Mr. Miller, my name is Porzia Amard. You don't know me, but I heard all about your extensive antidote collection, and I was wondering if you had anything that would cure acute light-drinker syndrome?" I used my most scholarly tone. I should have pinched my nose. Oh well, too late.

"Hey, I've been thinking about you."

"Have you now?" I warmed from the inside out. I kicked my boots off and sat on the bed, folding my legs crosswise. With my free hand I pulled my hair out of the constricting bun and combed it out as if he could see me. I thought of Japanese people who bow on the phone as if the person they're talking to could actually see them.

"Of course I have. How's everything going up there?" he asked.

"Great. I've slept, I've been fed, and I've tried the new wine. It's excellent."

"That's why you need the antidote?" His laughter spilled out of the receiver.

"Yes," I laughed. "I also wanted to know if you and Clark would be interested in coming up tomorrow around six for the presentation."

"I don't know about tearing Clark away from his card-writing business, but if you tell me there's forage involved, I'm sure he won't mind."

"Great. It's not formal, so no tuxedo or anything. I'm sure whatever you both wear will make you the most handsome men of the evening."

"Oh . . . adulation," he said, suspiciously. "Do you need something?"

Wow! If he wasn't quick. "Well, as a matter of fact, I do."

"And—?"

"A bottle of Scotch," I blurted, retracting my head turtle-style between my shoulders.

"Porzia, what in the world? Is this in case the wine sucks?" he asked in disbelief.

My head snapped back up in surprise. "You know, for an Australian, you speak pretty good American slang," I remarked.

"Don't try to change the subject."

"OK, I need the Scotch to pay a bet I lost with the photographer."

"If I get you the Scotch, will you tell me what sort of bet you're talking about here?"

"I guess it would be only fair," I agreed. "Ok, you have a deal."

"What do I get if I bring the antidote to your acute light-drinker syndrome?"

"Oh, I don't know. What would you like?" I held my breath.

"How about you spend the next evening with me?" A pause; *was he holding his breath?* "If you're free, that is," he added.

"Well, that's easy. I'd love to spend time with you, antidote or not." I smiled.

"Great. I've just wasted a perfect chance to take advantage of you."

"Perhaps the gods will be generous and will grant you plenty more," I laughed.

"It's great to hear you laugh, Porzia," he whispered. "I believe I'm the one who needs an antidote here," he said. "I can't stop thinking about you. About how close you are to me, and yet I have to wait until tomorrow to see you again."

"Thank you." I stretched my legs, leaned against the pillows, and wiggled my toes inside the warm socks.

"Well then, I will pass on your invitation to Clark, and I'll see you tomorrow evening."

"Sounds wonderful. Thank you, Gabe."

"No worries. I wish you goodnight, Porzia."

"Same to you. Bye—"

"Goodnight."

I sat on the bed for a few precious moments, savoring his voice and the pleasant feeling stirring in my heart. I smiled, absently combing through my nearly dry hair. I wanted to change for dinner but realized I was running late already. I pulled my boots back up and walked to the bathroom where I freshened up with cold water. I made a face or two at myself in the mirror. All things considered, and no makeup time, I was holding up quite well. Finally, I rushed downstairs taking the steps two at a time again and collided with Desmond at the foot of the stairs. He took my right arm and escorted me to the dining room where the family had gathered to start supper.

The table took center stage, elegantly covered in linen dignified by Limoges plates and polished silverware. Crystal wine and water goblets reflected candlelight discreetly around the room. The table centerpiece, an exquisite Limoges tureen, carried an earthy bouillabaisse. I inhaled; my nose sorted out saffron, cayenne, and bay leaf, among other ingredients. My mouth watered.

Madame Framboise Jourdain, Frank's mother, sat regally at the head of the table. Frank sat to her right, quietly speaking to her. Totally captivated by her son, she seemed unaware of the others. I took time and observed her. Until now, I had only heard of her legendary reputation in the wine circles. I had to admit I was apprehensive at the thought of finally meeting her. She seldom left her quarters, especially in winter when the harsh weather affected her fragile health the most. Her bright black eyes shone like polished opals. Although her patrician face reflected her age, her aristocratic profile was still sharp, her chin firm as she turned it to study me intently.

"*Bonsoir, Mademoiselle Amard.* It's a pleasure to have you here with us." She tilted her head and extended her right hand to greet me. Her English was unblemished, barely laced with a subtle Provençal accent.

"*Bonsoir, Madame Jourdain.* Please call me Porzia." I walked up to her to shake her hand.

"Thank you, my dear." Once again she graciously tilted her head toward Beverly, who was busy serving the bouillabaisse. "Beverly, *cheri*, I would never think of distressing your dinner placements but I would love to have Porzia sit next to me this evening," she kindly requested.

"Of course, Maman," Beverly nodded, smiling at both of us.

I sat down on her left. Frank nodded and everybody else took their seats. Nicolas jumped to sit next to me, cutting Desmond off in his path.

"François, would you mind saying grace this evening?" Madame Framboise asked her son. "Unless *Monsieur Tanier* would rather do the honor himself." A hint of mischief danced in her eyes.

Desmond Tanier, busy tucking his linen napkin into his shirt collar, almost burst into flames in a spontaneous combustion of discomfort. "Oh no, Madam! I wouldn't dream of robbing the lord of the manor of such an honor!" he thundered, waving his open palms like windshield wipers.

Frank and Dom struggled to keep straight faces. Nicolas didn't even try. The sound of Beverly's soft giggle stopped my smile in midair while Luke and Ronnald struggled to catch up with the rest of us.

Frank cleared his throat. "Dear Lord, thank you for another bountiful season. We give thanks for our health and for the joy of sharing your blessed gifts among friends and family. Amen." A choir of "amens" and a dysfunctional "no worries" from Desmond sealed the deal.

The bouillabaisse was thick with a rich fish and white wine stock. Juicy butterflied prawns, baby oysters, cubed cod filets, and shredded crabmeat gave texture to the soup along with chopped celery, onions, and tiny tomato bits. The saffron, mixed with cayenne, chopped parsley, and bay leaf, enriched the seafood flavors, conjuring up images of blazing red Provençal sunsets, salt-scorched fishermen mending nets, and children running along the seashore chasing crabs. Beverly had drizzled raw extra virgin olive oil into the Limoges tureen right before serving to tie the ingredients together. It was delicious.

Frank had brought up several chilled bottles of Sauvignon Blanc, a pleasant surprise, for I thought Umeracha specialized in red grapes. Dark grilled country bread accompanied the soup, and a light spring greens salad dressed in raspberry-walnut vinaigrette followed. Cheeses and juicy Anjou pears completed the meal.

On some more recent occasions, the host has tended to be a bit overly concerned with me as a guest at their table. In the Jourdains' case I was treated with respect and warmth. Through each course of supper, fine food combined with entertaining conversation flowed smoothly along the wine riverbed. I slipped into my rusty, rudimentary French occasionally as Madame Framboise asked me questions and intrigued the rest of the table with her charm and humor. Frank surprised me as his reserve melted, revealing an extremely intelligent dry wit that had Desmond booming with laughter, bringing him to the verge of tears a couple of times.

After promising Madame Framboise to visit her the following afternoon for tea, I found my way upstairs, thinking about Gabe and what tomorrow would bring. A gentle tapping against my window told me it was raining outside. I quickly undressed and was soon under the covers, sound asleep.

*

I had no ground beneath my feet.

As I fell through pitch darkness, a voice commanded me to stop fighting, and I woke up suddenly, soaked in chills from a terrible nightmare. Sweat pearled my forehead, drenching the back of my hand when I wiped my soaked hair off my face. Darkness surrounded me. Fear seized me, gripping me breathless. Bitter panic curdled at the back of my throat, paralyzing me. I didn't dare blink, swallow, or move. My heartbeat pounded like a thief caught in the blasted, trapping rubble of a bank vault, a prisoner of its own mistakes.

Scared to death, I panicked.

I had no idea what drove the fear. The images vanished on awakening, unavailable to my conscious mind. I couldn't remember what had happened in my sleep to frighten me so, and honestly, I didn't really try hard to recollect.

It was ages before I finally summoned the courage to reach out and turn the nightstand lamp on. I rubbed my eyes and took a sip of water. I glanced at a wooden clock faithfully ticking away and saw I had been asleep only a few hours.

Evalena had once told me that nightmares alert us to face issues that need tending. Recurring nightmares happen when we ignore such warnings. How was I supposed to face my issues if I couldn't remember my nightmares in the first place? I don't have bad dreams often, and I'm usually not insanely affected by them, but I had a feeling this one was going to linger like a nagging runny nose, probably until something in my living reality triggered the memory of it.

Until then I'm going to try and catch some seriously soothing sleep, I thought, hiding my head under the pillow. I left the light on. Apparently this wayward path sometimes held no ground.

Afraid? Chi, io?

CHAPTER 8

I woke up late—extremely late. I had missed breakfast. I grabbed some coffee and spent the rest of the morning in the kitchen with Beverly going over recipes for that evening's menu. Desmond was out with Frank and Dom taking advantage of a break in the overcast sky to shoot outdoor photographs. I doubted we would see them until later in the evening. A flower delivery van took Beverly's attention away from me, and I decided to start jotting down ideas for my article as I warmed up beside a scorching fire that roared in the kitchen fireplace.

Lori, a charming pixie lady who turned out to be Dom's wife, kept me company. She answered my culinary questions in her thick Australian accent, repeating her words slowly at every puzzled look of my face.

I always marvel at a chef's skill to match, pair, and marry flavors. I grew up with simple earthy flavors straight from the family garden, and now I know I was truly blessed since I can't grow anything but herbs, and those merely due to Evalena's guidance.

I went into this line of work mostly because of my familiarity with wine and quickly discovered I needed to learn at least the basics of gourmet cuisine to make a decent living. Desmond is the only human I know capable of making a living strictly on spirits.

I could manage wine pairing but in order to decide what to cook, I have to begin with the wine and then retrace my steps from there. I could never be offered gourmet choices and then match them to their ideal wines. So, I shop for wines and then I buy my ingredients and groceries based on that decision. My choices are often simple and limited to what I know best or, better yet, like to eat. I am quite aware of the fact that this is not an orthodox way of looking at it, but it works for me, and isn't that what we do? Work with the skills we've got? And leave the rest to professionals I can always write about . . .

I shared all this to Lori while a symphony of intense flavors and subtle, enticing spices unraveled in the kitchen. Nutmeg and thick cream bubbled happily with butter, white wine, and black peppercorns in a deep copper skillet. The pungent scent of lamb mingled with tangy rosemary and chanterelle mushrooms seeped from the oven. Several loaves of hot country bread slowly cooled on a wire rack.

By lunchtime I was famished and extremely grateful when Beverly, Lori, and I shared *jambon* sandwiches, a delicious cherry tomato salad, and a pitcher of freshly squeezed lemonade.

I finished my notes while Beverly prepared a tea tray for Madame Framboise and then eagerly followed her upstairs.

Madam's room smelled pleasantly of chamomile and lavender. A lively fire burned in a massive stone fireplace, warming up the entire room. A pastel-yellow angora shawl fastened with a garnet brooch hugged her shoulders while a single lacquered chopstick held her upswept, silvering hair. Her bright eyes greeted us, and her hand motioned me to sit across from her in a comfy-looking sage chenille chair with a beautiful antique three-legged table set between us. She waited for Beverly to leave before she finally spoke, pouring tea. "I trust you're enjoying yourself with us, my dear?" she inquired. Her steady hand offered me a dainty china cup filled with steaming amber liquid.

"Yes, thank you, Madame Jourdain." I took the cup and helped myself to sugar.

"It must be difficult to shift from different weather and time zones." Her gypsy eyes watched me attentively.

"It takes some adjustment, but I seem to manage after a few hours." I could barely hold her gaze.

"Are you sleeping well, my dear?" She leaned forward and took my right hand in hers. She never broke eye contact with me. Her warm hands poured heat into mine like some sort of tension-relieving drug that spread its effects from my fingertips to my hand, coiled around my wrist, and slowly worked its way to my elbow, up my shoulder, and around my nerve-stiff neck. There it diluted my tension until I dropped my shoulders. I found myself relaxing and eager to confess anything, as if it were most natural to spill my secrets to an almost perfect stranger.

"I had a nightmare last night," I told her, squeezing her hand back. Suddenly, her familiarity hit me like a distant flavor from a long-forgotten childhood memory. She was no stranger. Framboise was the living example of what Joséphine would have been if she hadn't renounced her power.

"And you don't remember it."

Astounded that she had gone right to it, I could only agree. "No, I don't. But I'm still a bit shaken." I recalled the fear that had paralyzed me in the darkness. I swallowed hard against the bitter tide surging up in my stomach.

She let go of my hand and sipped her tea. She added sugar. I settled back in my chair, my tea untouched. The lingering chamomile scent soothed me. I felt myself slipping into a gentle trance; any apprehension I had ever felt about meeting this woman had been evaporated by the familiar magic of her divine magnetism.

"I get the impression that you're wading through some shifting waters," she ventured.

I nodded once, silently waiting for her to continue, still unsure of where this was leading.

"You strike me as a very realistic, rational creature . . . you believe in ingredients assembled . . . *et voilà*, there is a dish." Her hand fluttered swiftly. "If the ingredients were a poor selection, the outcome would reflect it. But when the right combination is achieved, then the result is superb."

I nodded again in agreement.

"All of a sudden abstract concepts are introduced into this schematic world of yours. Things are no longer either black or white. Unexplainable events, emotional tides, the past is revealing itself to you." There went her hand again, up in the air like a flutter of wings. "But of course, *ma chère*—life is so much more profound than mere reality as it appears to our mortal eyes . . . alas, once magic stirs in your life, my dear child, you can only accept it, learn to expect it. Perhaps you can even learn to use it to your advantage—never to harm, of course." She blinked. "Perhaps your background? Your family? *Oui?* You are part French?"

"*Oui, la famille de mon père,*" I explained.

"*Bien sûr, alors ta grand-mère?*"

"*Oui, Joséphine Amard.*" I whispered my dearest grandmother's name. "*Mais elle n'est pas vraiment Française, sa famille vient de l'Hongrie. Ils sont d'origines Manouche.*"

Enlightenment brightened Madam's eyes at the mention of the gypsy Manouche tribe my paternal grandmother belonged to. She reached behind her and took a carved wooden box from the windowsill. "*Et ton nom?*"

I smiled. "*Porzia Joséphine Amard.*" I had been named after my grandmothers.

"Would you make some room on the table, dear?" she asked. She pulled a worn tarot deck out of the box.

I hadn't seen the cards in ages; ever since I got caught snooping in Joséphine's secret *coffre au trésor* and got such a whipping that just thinking about it still makes me cringe.

Reluctantly, I cleared the table, leaving only our teacups and saucers. Maybe it wasn't chamomile scenting the room. Maybe it was opium.

Her hands expertly shuffled the cards. "Porzia, when is your birthday?"

"July 30th."

She pulled the Queen of Wands out of the deck and laid it out in the center of the table, face up. At her direction, I cut the deck with my left hand. The left hand is connected to the heart, my mother once told me. That's why you wear your wedding band on it.

Madam laid the cards in what looked like a random order to my inexperienced eyes. Two cards covered the Queen, forming a cross. I sat up, moved closer to the table, and looked down at the vibrantly colored images trying to understand the various figures upside-down. Meanwhile, what I had mistaken for a fluffy white pillow thrown nonchalantly on the massive bed caught the corner of my eye as it stretched, yawned, and unfolded itself into a huge Persian cat. Its deep emerald eyes looked at me, decided I wasn't worthy of further attention, and commenced grooming places I will not mention.

Madame Jourdain pointed at the Queen of Wands. "This card is the significator: it represents you in the reading. Wands are backed up by the fire element, just as your zodiac sign Leo is. That is my reason for its selection." She paused and looked at the spread. "*Ah! Le Pape!*" She indicated the first card across the Queen of Wands.

"You have had a recent revelation. Your astral connection with an ancient soul mate has been revealed to you. To be blessed with such knowledge carries responsibility for the manner in which you will use this information. You have much to learn. Free will lies in your soul-searching path, and you have the power to use this knowledge either foolishly or wisely."

The second card completing the cross was the Magician.

"*Le Bateleur.* He represents brewing forces. Not necessarily negative, just out of the ordinary realm. Will and trust are his strengths. He is a fierce one, extremely powerful. He holds the strings and offers protection from danger. Remember, Porzia, danger is sometimes healthy, shaking us up from torpor."

Who the hell could that be? I tried to identify the role among the people I knew but was distracted by the beauty of the next card. A naked woman stood in a golden circle framed by a yellow-eyed snake biting its own tail.

"*Le Monde.* The World. How odd." Madame Framboise frowned. "My intuition is incapable of reading this one at the moment." She paused to sip her tea and scrutinized the space around me. "Someone does not want us to interfere."

I felt like getting the hell out of there but sank my nails into the chair's armrests instead. I cast my own intuition out there and felt my blood rush, my lineage reclaiming its power. But it was too new, too weak to breach through the mystical barrier surrounding *Le Monde.*

"You've met someone recently." She caught my attention, pointing at the Two of Cups. "But perhaps influences from a recent past are still at work. The card's advice is to be open. Keep honesty and an open heart up front, if you will. Fears and hesitation regarding new decisive steps are only lingering aftershocks of past failures. Be as childlike as possible, for only such a magic-infused demeanor will allow the ensuing cards to manifest the outcome."

Gabe came to mind with such intensity I thought he would materialize right in front of us. Instead, what did materialize—with a loud meow—was the fluffy white cat. That he chose such an inopportune moment to jump on the table put an end to my reading. He landed on the spread, scattering Queen, Pope, Two of Cups, and the World into disarray. Then he straightened his tail, bounced off the remaining deck, and leaped to Madame Framboise's lap, where he curled up and began to purr.

I bent to pick up fallen cards off the Persian rug. *Don't fight . . . allow free will. Don't resist free falling.* The echo of my nightmare ricocheted through my brain and dissolved, to be echoed by the Baci chocolate message Gabe had read to me over the phone. I looked at the cards in my hands with the momentarily delusional thought that I could figure out what they meant.

"Madame Jourdain, it seems like I wasn't meant to find out about my future after all."

"I guess not, *ma chère*. This is most baffling. Neige knows better than to jump on the table in such an awful manner." She frowned at the remorseless bundle on her lap.

I handed her the remaining cards and glanced at my watch.

"I need to get going to be ready for tonight's event." I looked at her. "Will you be there, Madame Jourdain?"

"Why, of course, my dear child. I would love to meet the Two of Cups." She smiled, sending a chill down my spine.

How on earth?

CHAPTER 9

I usually don't spend much time getting ready. Benedetta teases, tells me I get ready like a man. She says I shop like a man too. I walk into a store as if equipped with radar, go directly to what I need, and get out. Same deal when I get ready. I am intimidated at the thought of applying much makeup. Foundation always ends up streaking and staining my clothes, and lipstick is a rarity with my lifestyle of tasting and constant eating, so I usually never need more than ten minutes. Not tonight. Gabe was going to be there, and I was going to take my time; the final result should be well worth the extra labor.

First sign of falling for someone: taking extra time to get ready. I washed and styled my hair until it shone in a thick, luscious cascade over the dark claret velvet of my dress.

For makeup, I dusted a faint blush onto my cheeks and applied a subtle eyeliner under my eyes before brushing on a couple of coats of mascara. Why do we feminine creatures part our lips in a perfect O, worthy of Giotto's free hand, while applying mascara? I closed my mouth, too impatient to wait around for the universe to answer the mystery, and slicked on a finishing touch of a light, nude lip gloss. I took a step back and eyed my reflection in the full-length mirror, frowning. Then I broke into a rainbow. Queen of Wands or not, it was time to tango.

Although the presentation guest list was limited to family, some close friends, Desmond, and of course *la sottoscritta*, Beverly had kindly accommodated my request to include Gabe and his father for the evening, assuring me it would be a delight.

As I glided downstairs, I heard soft notes of music rise like dainty butterflies in the darkness surrounding me.

I realized I was early. Countless candles and strategically placed oil lamps trembled in the elegant but silent dining hall I thought empty at first glance—but poised regally on a deep pillow in front of the glowing fireplace, Neige watched me curiously. The blazing orange fire danced in his eyes. I felt awe as I approached him, exposed under his unfaltering stare. Purring, he stretched his front paws, arched his back, and met my hand with his nose so that I could pet him. He closed his eyes and tilted his head. I scratched behind his ears. The fire had warmed his coat. I sat on a low stool next to him, thinking about how different his fur was from Peridot's back home. I ran my fingers through his long, fluffy coat, hypnotized by his loud purring. Telepathically I asked him why he had jumped on the cards.

He kept on purring, totally ignoring my silent question.

Joséphine Amard, my paternal grandmother, had been a rebel to family traditions, breaking with a long chain of wanderers, nomadic travelers, and gypsy freedom believers. At the age of sixteen, during one of many family pilgrimages, she fell in love with a Christian farmer and winemaker and settled in Provence. She continued to use herbs from her garden to cure naturally and cook with but left all that she considered pagan charlatanism behind, including tarot cards, dream interpretation, and most importantly, her divination powers.

Until the day she died.

Apparently, along with her pragmatism, I had inherited her last-minute reclaimed clairvoyance as well. Wondering if just inheriting it made it tangible, I cast a futile attempt at connecting with Gabe but failed miserably. Although I imagined a feeble flutter of wings, I met only inscrutable darkness. I shook my head.

I didn't believe.

Neige had flipped on his back, exposing his tummy to my nails. I smiled and kept on scratching. Forget telepathic communication; cats will be cats no matter where in the world you connect with one.

Nicolas found me like that when he entered the room juggling several bottles of wine in his arms. He looked older than his seventeen years, all dressed up for the evening. Even his unruly hair was combed back and smartly styled with some gel. He smiled at me, fumbled the wine onto the table, and began to inspect several decanters one by one against the candlelight. "That's interesting," he said, throwing his chin in Neige's direction. "He's not a friendly cat. He usually doesn't let anybody but *Grand-mère* pet him."

"It seems our young friend has a special touch, Nicolas," responded Madame Framboise as she entered the room aided by a walking stick. She looked regal in vintage black silk. Her bright smile matched the purity of the single strand of pearls gracing her neck. The rest of the family followed, headed by Frank in a black dinner jacket livened by a burgundy bowtie. Beverly beamed in forest-green lace, and the boys looked stiffly uncomfortable in starched white shirts.

I stood as the doorbell announced the arrival of the first guests. My heart jumped in my throat. Neige rubbed himself against my ankles, and Desmond boomed in with a camera dangling from his neck like a jolly monkey on a jungle vine. A bouquet of feminine laughter spilled from the foyer. It told my pounding heart that my wait wasn't over yet. Then my brain took over and curtly stopped the intense emotional nonsense, enabling me to greet the Dassaevs, the Jourdain's friends and fellow winemakers, without making a fool of myself. I turned professional, grabbed two glasses of apéritifs, and went in search of Lori, following a trail of mouthwatering aromas back toward the kitchen.

Beverly had hired catering help for the evening, and the kitchen resembled a very organized war camp. Lori accepted her glass gracefully and showed me around the scrumptious array.

I believe that a gourmet meal without wine is like a song with great music but lacking intelligent lyrics. What lay in front of my eyes confirmed that the Jourdains shared my belief in the concept.

Where to begin looking?

My mind surged into overdrive, striving with enormous effort to master the entire menu concept at once. I began the tedious task of taking notes, the least appealing side of my job. The breads could hold court per se. I counted honey rolls, poppy seed muffins, whole wheat *bâtards*, crusty thin baguettes, and one of my favorites, Tuscan focaccia drizzled in an embrace of extra virgin olive oil that could make you forget about your hottest lover, unless you were lucky enough to be sleeping with the baker. I nodded to a smiling young fellow about to wheel several trays of *crostini* out of the kitchen: grilled country bread topped with a variety of mushrooms, cheeses, tomatoes, tapenade, and *pâté*.

The first course consisted of a red chicory risotto presently bubbling on the stove.

"The risotto looks happy," I observed.

"Could you blame it?" Lori laughed. "What a life, even if short. Hot in a copper pan snuggled with butter, sweet onions, radicchio, and Arborio rice, drowned in rich vegetable and saffron stock."

Lori moved on to Beverly's choice of entrée: a slow oven-roasted rack of lamb and side dish of rosemary potatoes. She commented on the ideal pairing with the new wine.

I groaned to hide my stomach's rumble and walked to the salad to pick a cherry tomato from the bed, saw the baby green beans glistening with olive oil, and struggled to control myself. "Lori? What about dessert?" If I had to suffer, I might as well inflict my own coup de grâce.

Fruit compote followed en suite by rich French coffee.

Engrossed in jotting down material for my article, I didn't realize I was being observed; my sixth sense kicked in. I turned and saw a flustered Nicolas watching me with something close to . . . renewed respect. How long had he been standing there? "Porzia, G—*Gabe Miller* is out there with his father, asking about you," he stuttered.

"Oh, thank you, Nicolas. Have they been here long?" I tried and failed to control my heartbeat.

"No, only a few minutes. He gave *Desmond* a bottle of *Scotch*." Nicolas's tone dripped the sort of awe usually reserved for a miraculous sighting of royalty.

I raised an eyebrow. "Yes?"

"You didn't tell me you knew Gabe Miller," he whispered, as if afraid to say the name.

"Should I have?" I asked, puzzled. *What was going on?*

I began to walk out of the kitchen and collided with Beverly rushing in as I flung the door open.

"Oh dear!" Her green eyes, gleaming like emeralds, peeked out from behind a gigantic bouquet of rainbow-colored freesias. The sweet scent drowned the food aromas.

"Beverly! Did I hurt you? I'm so sorry! I didn't mean to bump the door like that."

"Porzia! Gabe Miller is out there shaking hands with Frank. He brought *me* flowers!" She shook my arm with the flowers. "We need to do something!" She looked possessed.

"OK . . . ," I said warily. "What would you like me to do?"

"Oh dear! I don't know! Would it be too rude to ask him to autograph some of the wine bottles?"

"Beverly! What's going on? Why are you all so agitated about Gabe being here?" I demanded.

Nicolas looked at me suspiciously. "Porzia, how long have you known him?"

"A bit—"

"So I reckon you have no idea how famous the man is, do you now?" Nicolas's tone didn't help my confusion at all.

"Gabe? Famous? *Ma che caz*—?" I snuffed the last word to a muted snort at the last second.

"Gabe Miller is only the most famous driver of off-road racing that Australia has ever produced. He's a legend in the international circuits. He's won the Paris–Dakar a couple of times. Once with your fellow countryman Tonacci coming in second, eating dust. *And* he holds several records," Nicolas ended *tremolo*, with feeling cracking his voice.

Merda! I knew the name Tonacci: Italian billionaire, heir to the Tonacci Engines empire, painfully handsome heartthrob, and excellent off-road racer. And Gabe made Tonacci eat dust? It's like saying he walked on water with Jesus and Jesus sank halfway there.

I needed an explanation. I rushed out of the kitchen, then slowed down and struggled a second to regain my cool before Gabe's eyes met mine—and the rest of the world dissolved.

His serious eyes caressed every inch of my skin while his heart told me silently he was happy to see me again. I heard his voice beneath the loud thumping of my own heart pulsing against my inner ears. I shook my head, blinked—twice—and found my hand in his. Nothing had happened. Nobody seemed to have noticed the intimate moment he and I had just shared.

"Porzia, thank you for including us in such a special occasion," I heard him say, breaking the spell. "Frank was telling me tonight is the first time his Shiraz is to be enjoyed by mortal palate."

Oddio! Did he have to say "Shiraz" like he was reading it out of the Kama Sutra? I smiled wickedly.

"Well, I guess that would make the few of us who tried it yesterday perpetual souls." *Merda! Would that make Desmond immortal?* I drove frightening thoughts of eternal doom in the company of such a belligerent ogre from my mind. I smiled at Gabe, less wickedly this time. "I'm glad you were able to join us. Beverly was delighted to know I had some friends I wanted to invite. But not as delighted as when she found out who you were," I ribbed smoothly.

I didn't just say that out loud. Mamma mia, please tell me I didn't say that!

"It doesn't matter who he is, Porzia, dear lass. What matters is that he brought my Scotch, and he'll be sitting next to me at the table. So maybe he'll be asked to say grace this evening instead of poor old atheist me," Desmond intervened. He waved an aged bottle of Scotch under my nose and walked away.

I shook hands with Clark, looking smartly at ease in evening wear. For some intriguing reason I felt profoundly grateful for his presence.

Beverly, likewise having regained her perfect-hostess composure, made the introductions among those who didn't know each other and proceeded to seat us. I ended up in a cozy blanket between Gabe on my left and Madame Framboise as head of the table. The family, sitting at the table to enjoy the fruit of their extensive labor, reminded me of childhood celebrations at harvest time back home.

Dinner turned out to be a superb success. Seldom do I find myself in such an environment where business and pleasure hold hands so gracefully, enabling me to reach that plateau where my ever-working mind takes a step back and my emotional passion for gourmet is unleashed in the harmonious ambiance. The excellent Shiraz was the table's undisputed protagonist, complementing the assortment of foods offered by the various courses like colors on a painter's palette, creating a symphony of excellent flavors. I particularly enjoyed the cooked-to-perfection chicory risotto, a perfect partner to the smooth bouquet of the Shiraz. *A' la Carte* should expect one hell of an article, Australia and eventually the rest of the world, one hell of a wine.

By the end of dinner, the impact of Gabe's fame had been digested and Australian camaraderie reigned. We opted to take coffee by the fireplace in the cozier living room. Clark offered his arm to a delighted Madame Framboise, her personal "Two of Cups" for the moment. Desmond, having used at least three rolls of film already, decided to take a break and opened the Scotch. He began spiking coffee left and right, reminding me of a jovial priest dispensing holy water. I chuckled at the sacrilegious thought.

I finally managed to have a moment alone with Gabe. We stepped out on the covered porch where the chilling winter night drove me straight into his warm embrace.

"I've been thinking about this moment ever since I left you the other day," he whispered, breathing deeply in my hair.

"Hmm—" I barely murmured, snuggling even closer to him.

"You look beautiful in this dress." His hand caressed my back. "I love the way you're wearing your hair tonight." He tugged a handful of it, pulling my head back. His mouth inched toward mine as I arched my back and parted my lips. His hands found the side of my face and held me still, a breath away from his mouth. I could smell the heat radiating from his skin. His eyes sought mine and held me prisoner, waiting, searching my eyes for something he needed to feed on. Anticipation built and a thick core of undiluted lust began to melt deep inside me. I begged him with a silent plea to his eyes, then closed mine and felt his lips grant my wish. I exploded behind my shut eyelids into absolute raw hunger. Nothing mattered but to keep on drinking from his mouth as if my own life depended on it. I could have spent the rest of my life dancing with the tip of my tongue against his, tasting the fullness of his lips, brushing the harsh five o'clock shadow with my sensitive skin and hearing him whisper my name from behind a thick curtain of desire.

"Porzia—"

I kept on kissing him. He tugged my hair again, pulling my head aside to kiss my left ear. "Porzia, luv," he whispered, kissing my neck. Shivers ran through my body in vibrating echoes of pleasure.

"Hmm—"

"I was just thinking that I could do this forever but they might wonder about us inside." He raised his head, leaving a wet, hot trail on my exposed neck. I felt it steam away in the cold night air. I opened my eyes and looked at him. *How can he be so beautiful?* I marveled, gazing at him in fascination. I couldn't even blink, so intent was my contemplation of his perfect features. He smiled, showing me his chipped tooth. I stood on my tiptoes and lightly kissed the smile. I felt like crying, I was so touched by the moment. He must have sensed my reaction because he took my hands in his and brought them to his mouth to kiss my open palms. "There is no room for fear in this perfect moment." He folded my fingers over his kiss, sealing the warmth of his words.

"Thank you."

"No worries." He cast me an inquisitive smile I would soon learn to recognize. "What was the bet about?"

I sighed, "This isn't my first assignment with Desmond. I've worked with him in the past. Last time we saw each other he told me my boyfriend was having an affair and I was an idiot for not having noticed. He bet me the Scotch to go home and catch him."

Gabe brought my hand to his lips and kissed it. "How long ago was this?"

"Over a year ago."

He observed me silently for a while, then, keeping my hand in his, he led me back indoors.

The rest of the night flowed smoothly around wine production chat. Clark astonished us all a few times by revealing a deep knowledge of grapes and, surprisingly, French. At about midnight, the Dassaevs said their farewells, signaling the end of a great night. Gabe got the hint and took a special moment to say goodnight to Madame Framboise, Frank, and Beverly, promising the boys to have them come down to his shop for some off-road talk. Clark hugged me warmly, shook hands with the men, and kissed the ladies on both cheeks like a perfect European gentleman. Lori giggled like a teenager, and Beverly's freckles blushed into an ecstatic peachy glow. Madame Framboise actually accepted Desmond's arm and slowly walked upstairs, laughing softly at something he was telling her.

As Clark walked away to get their car, I was left alone to say goodnight to Gabe.

"Thank you again for asking us to join you tonight, Porzia."

"You're welcome." I smiled and handed him his jacket.

"Are we still on for tomorrow night?" he asked, bundling up.

"Yes, of course. How about I call you in the morning?"

"Great." His voice was a barely audible whisper as he bent his head to kiss me.

Just the brush of his lips is enough to set me ablaze, I thought, tasting his lingering scent.

"Goodnight."

"Goodnight." I caught a sparkle in his eyes. It blended with the night as he turned and walked out.

I closed the door, leaned against it, and caught Nicolas walking up to me.

"I need to say I'm sorry for the stupid way I acted earlier in the kitchen. I was just bloody stunned to find a legend walking in and shaking hands with everybody," he blurted all in one breath. "I mean, those hands have raced the best off-road circuits of the world, and here he is just using them to do regular stuff with, eating and drinking." Still amazed, he looked at his own hands as if they ought to perform miracles as well.

"Do you think he should unscrew them at night and place them in a safe?" I teased. "Or maybe have a regular everyday pair to do daily things with and then, when he races, he'd screw his special pair on?"

"Don't you know? He hasn't raced in a while."

Hair rose on the back of my neck. "Oh! He hasn't?"

Nicolas shot me a cryptic look and moved closer to me. "So it's true, you just barely know the bloke." He suddenly looked older than his seventeen years. "Porzia—it's not my place to tell you. It's late and you need to go to sleep."

Then all of a sudden he grinned broadly, dissipating the moment's heaviness. He grabbed my hands in his and smashed me against himself. With my boots on we were almost at eye level, but he was a lot stronger than I expected.

"Nicolas, you've got the power of a boa constrictor," I choked.

"Would you like me to *ssserenade* you, my dear?" he hissed, imitating a snake.

"How much Scotch did you slurp tonight, Mr. Boa?" I chuckled.

"*Ssscotch?* You *insssult* me, my dear, I'm a wine *sssnake*." He wiggled as if to emphasize his wine preference. I took advantage of his wiggling to do some of my own and set myself free.

"Well, Mr. Boa, it's way past my bedtime, so I gracefully ask you to forgive my yawning in your face and accept my goodnight."

"Goodnight accepted." He bowed, kissing my hand. "Porzia, how long are you staying with us?" he asked, on a more serious note.

"A few more days, Nicolas. Why?"

"You're going to need a lot longer than that to get to know a legend," he said, slowly turning and walking away.

Bloody hell! Here comes reality disguised as a wine snake to smack me in the face, I thought as I climbed up to my bedroom. *Measly mortal recently turned witch, am I up to getting to know a legend; furthermore . . . date a legend?* The sweet scent of flowers interrupted my brooding thoughts. A small lamp illuminated a fragrant bouquet of white freesias in a crystal vase on the dresser. I smiled thinking of Gabe, took the delicate vase in my hands, and buried my nose in the intoxicating blooms. I inhaled deeply and my heart opened. Nicolas's words suddenly shot through my core, "He hasn't raced in a while."

I got ready for bed and snuggled under the covers wondering why.

CHAPTER 10

I woke up extremely early after a dreamless night, refreshed for a change; my nocturnal activities often exhausted me more than my waking life. I lingered in bed listening for a few seconds. The rest of the house was silent. I yawned, stretched, and decided to take advantage of the early hour. With a sudden burst of energy, I kicked the covers aside and padded barefooted to a small desk. This kind of magic I felt comfortable with, this kind of magic I could perform. I lost myself in the craft of writing, spent a few hours working on my article, and time dissolved. Outside my window, dawn broke through darkness, tearing an orange seam through a violet sky. I paused in my work, watching raptly until the light show was over. If anyone, it's Mother Nature who excels effortlessly in magic.

I took a quick shower, tied my hair in a wet ponytail, and went downstairs to see if I could help with breakfast. I found Lori alone in the kitchen, busy lighting the fireplace. She smiled and offered me some coffee, freshly brewed in a French press. Bless her. I poured myself a cup, adding cream and sugar. Pleased with the happy fire, Lori wiped her hands on her immaculate white apron, leaving a trail of perfect black streaks a zebra would have killed for. "How about some pancakes for breakfast?"

"Sounds good to me, Lori, but you'd have to show me how you like to make yours." I smiled sheepishly.

Impalpable sunrays filtered through the lightly frosted courtyard doors as if beckoned by Lori's softly hummed tune. I set my mug down and went to work under her skilled direction in the warming kitchen, pouring, measuring, grating, and mixing. We used flour, eggs, sugar, buttermilk, grated Granny Smith apples, pinches of nutmeg, cinnamon, and fresh orange zest.

"Fluffy pancakes require a bit more skill than the thin, flat ones," she masterfully instructed me. "The secret is to not over-beat the batter and not add too much of the liquid ingredients. When the batter is lumpy and thick enough that you need a ladle to spoon it onto the skillet, stop right there. If you keep on messing with it, you might as well settle for the thin kind of pancakes you were trying not to make in the first place."

We made batches of both—intentionally, that is. As Lori worked on the pancakes, I got busy with the simpler tasks of apple and chicken sausages, maple-cured bacon, fresh tea, and more coffee. She excused herself and went to dress the table, leaving me with a fresh refill of coffee, a jar of homemade blueberry marmalade, fresh butter, and a warm loaf of walnut bread. I dropped the last strips of crispy bacon on the absorbing paper, wondering if they would be interested in adopting me.

Dom's appearance interrupted my daydreaming. He walked into the kitchen from the garden door and went straight to the fire. While he rubbed his hands together and slapped his shoulders, I poured him a cup of coffee. "This might help you warm up a bit faster."

"Splendid! Thanks." He accepted the cup gratefully. "We had a great time last night. Wouldn't you agree?" he asked.

"It was a very special evening. The new Shiraz is an excellent wine. I won't be surprised when the awards start pouring in."

"Your mouth to God's ear. It takes a lot of dedication and hard work to reach these levels of quality, but the results have this magic effect of making one forget about the hardship and just enjoy the outcome." He paused to take a sip of steaming coffee. His eyes lit up as Lori walked back into the kitchen.

She gave him a sweet smile. "Dom—Mr. Tanier is in the living room asking if you could go out with him and show him the American oaks we make the wine barrels from?" She paused, her eyes dancing to both of us. "I have no idea what he's talking about."

"Oh, no worries," Dom smiled, "Frank and the boys are pulling his leg. I reckon he had a lot of questions about unoaked wines. There was an award-winning Chardonnay produced in Tasmania a few years back. He wanted to know how we managed to win our award for the Cabernet. So Frank told him we mate Australian grapes with imported American oak barrels that we build right here using our own trees, especially brought over from the United States." He grimaced at me, "I reckon somebody ought to tell him the truth."

"Oh no! Let's see how much longer we can fool him," I suggested, recalling how I felt at the site of my ex and the other woman.

"Fine with me," Dom said.

"He might get upset about it and queer the review," Lori worried.

"No, he won't," I said. "Especially if he leaves not knowing."

Dom laughed at that and left to find Desmond. God knows what he was going to tell him.

The rest of the family came down shortly, and we gathered for breakfast. They were pleasantly surprised to learn that I had helped with the preparations. Desmond led them into a critique of my sausages and bacon with ranking scores and all. Behind a neutral façade, I kept thinking *American oaks* as I stole a smug glance at Desmond. Frank came to my rescue. He thanked me for my kitchen effort and ended breakfast by dragging the male population outside with him, Desmond included.

Lori busied herself with cleaning up and declined my offer of help. I took advantage of the quiet moment and told Beverly not to expect me for dinner.

"Well, dear, we'll sure miss you. Have a great evening." She paused, pensive for a moment. "What are you going to wear tonight?"

"You mean for the date?" I asked, surprised at the question. "I don't know yet. I don't even know where we're going."

"Well, whatever you do, honey, don't shave your legs." She winked.

My eyebrows arched. "I beg your pardon?"

"If you don't shave, you'll think twice before you get naked," she laughed.

"I see, but I don't think you need to worry about my virtue here," I told her, amused. "Let me go ahead and give him a call to see what he has in mind. Then I can decide accordingly." I stood from the table and headed toward my room, leaving Beverly to her tea and thoughts.

Once in my room, I got comfortable on the bed and dialed Gabe's number. When his voice came on the line I let go a long breath. "Hello? Gabe? It's Porzia. How are you this morning?"

"Just great, thanks. How about yourself?"

"I slept well. And you?"

"Not as well as I did on the plane with you in my arms." I sensed a smile in his voice.

I smiled myself. "You know, that would make two of us. I usually don't sleep well on planes."

"I guess we're looking at either starting to travel together or settling with the idea of getting no sleep," he said.

"How about not travel at all?"

"It would suit me just fine, but you'd miss running around looking for that perfect wine."

"You have a point."

"What are your plans for the day?" he asked, changing the subject.

"I need to work on my article and talk to Desmond about the photos, but besides that not much."

"Is he still fossicking for American oaks?" he asked.

I couldn't believe it! "You're in on it as well?"

"I heard Frank set it up, and I actually believed it myself for a second or two, then Clark told me they were mocking around."

I had never heard "mocking" used that way but the meaning was clear.

"Listen, about tonight . . ." Hesitation crept into his voice.

"Yes?"

"I'm afraid I'm going to have to cancel."

No! I was never going to see him again! I would leave Australia with the eternal wondering of a passerby that eyes a pastry in a bakery window and does not stop to eat it. All that I thought in the blink of an eye, and all that came out of my mouth as my card tower of whimsical expectations collapsed tragically was "Oh!"

"Porzia? Are you there?"

"Yes. I'm sorry, I'm here."

"Just kidding, luv," he said.

Bastardo. "You're lucky I don't have you in front of me," I hissed through clenched teeth.

"So how about I pick you up around five? Or is that too early?"

"I don't know if I want to go anymore now," I lied.

"You don't? I guess I deserve that. But I know you're not serious."

"No, I'm not. Five sounds good, but I'd like to know what we're doing so I can dress properly."

"Dress comfortably. I'm taking you to a local steak house, and it's a casual place."

"OK, sounds great. I'll be ready at five." My mind leaped ahead to the limited wardrobe I'd brought with me.

"Great. See you soon then."

"Ok, Gabe. Thanks."

"No worries. Bye."

I hung up wondering if I should rush into town for a serious once-in-a-lifetime-occasion shopping spree. Then I reconsidered thinking I would have to ask someone to drive me and what an encumbrance that would be for the family. I did not feel comfortable imposing for such a trivial reason as shopping. I remembered I'd brought some of my favorite pieces and resigned myself to making the best of the situation with what I had. I jumped off the bed, grabbed a jacket, and went looking for Desmond. Anyone would look better than such an ogre. Next to him my spirits and confidence ought to be restored, or else irreparably crushed forever . . .

I found him outside on the driveway shooting photos of the Jourdain dogs.

"At last! There you are, dear lass. How about a couple of piccies with the puppies right here?"

"Is this just for fun, Desmond?" I asked, kneeling to pet one of the dogs.

"Yes, yes, just fun. No hidden agendas here. Now be nice and say 'Foster's.'" He knelt and shot me an arrogant smirk. "That was a mighty fine bottle of

Scotch your mate brought over last night." He closed one eye and brought the camera up to his face.

"He's not my mate," I declared. Uncomfortable, I shifted my pose as his camera whirred and clicked. "Foster's . . . Foster's . . ." I managed to remain gracious; for how much longer, I had no idea.

"Yes, I must admit I'm rather impressed with your choice of *label* lately."

"Are you, now? Foster's . . . Foster's . . ."

He straightened and rummaged around in a camera bag looking for different lenses. "Porzia, dear lass, need I remind you about the piece of crap you called boyfriend last time we saw each other? It takes one loser alcoholic to smell another." He pointed a finger at his own chest. "Gabe Miller is a bloody legend," he chuckled. "A *sacred* legend that has managed to remain single, much to the disappointment of the Australian female crème de la crème." Satisfied with his choice of lenses, he crouched and resumed his snapping.

"*Accidenti!* Desmond, I just happened to meet him on the plane here and asked him over for last night. I'm not going to marry him!" I glared, indignant. "Sorry, I've run out of Foster's."

He stopped shooting and took a long look at me. "Porzia, you might spit the dummy after I'm done talking, but you happen to have an incredible mind behind those dazzling green eyes of yours. And I have known you long enough to not waste time with fatherly advice. Hell, that's almost incestuous thinking, for I'd love to trade places with our fellow racer here. And mine are definitely not fatherly thoughts." He chuckled again at my stunned look. "Here, here now, no worries. There's no need to look like I lifted your skirt up. Thanks for the Scotch, and I'd love to shoot the wedding."

Without even thinking, I yanked a boot off and threw it at him. He ducked and caught it in midair.

"You have a gift, Desmond: You piss people off. Mother Teresa would get pissed off after talking to you for a couple of minutes. Gimme my boot back," I snapped at him. Hopping over on one foot, I snatched it out of his hand just as he tried sniffing at it. "Beast!"

I sat on a rock to pull the boot back on. He took more photos of me as I tugged it up, and I took the opportunity to find my composure.

Finally, I stood, saying, "Just let me know when the photos will be ready." I bit my lower lip and added, "Better yet, just send them directly to *A' la Carte*. You have the address. I trust you won't be late? And if I don't see you before you leave, have a great trip, wherever the hell you're going." I spun around and strode off. His soft laughter echoed in my burning ears.

Still annoyed by the conversation, I stalked back to my room. For whatever reason, despite his overbearing demeanor, I valued Desmond's friendship and opinion. He's probably the only professional contact I can truly say I trust unconditionally to never harm me. In spite of his past or reputation (and crass jokes), I know he honestly cares for me and has demonstrated such care often in the past. In addition, I've learned how to canvass through his words for the real gold; among all those vulgarities he pretty much said I was like a daughter to him.

After thinking all this through, I sat down at the small desk and resumed work on my article.

I got so absorbed in typing that if it were not for Beverly softly knocking on my door to ask me if I cared for lunch, I would have kept on going forever. It always happens when I write; time seems to fly, the only proof of its passing is in my printed words.

She handed me a heaping tray and told me to just return it downstairs later.

With trepid anticipation, barely controlling my watering mouth, I set the tray on the desk and tucked into a delectable lunch. For a few precious moments I cared only about the incredible taste of the food in front of me. I loved the smooth texture of the grilled eggplants layered in the thick, basil-infused *ragù* and the aged *Parmigiano* cheese. Melted, runny mozzarella stretched into strings as I cut another bite with my fork and moved back in time to my family's kitchen, where my mother used to prepare a dish very similar to this particular one. Echoes of my father's delight rang in my ears, as I tasted the Shiraz with it. Here I was once again, fascinated by the intense color this wine seemed to exude no matter what light it was subjected to. I took a sip, then another, and swirled the glass, admiring the wine's legs, an old habit to break. Such legs (or "tears") that run down the inside of a glass of wine are one of the most fascinating visual components of the tasting experience but have nothing to do with the wine's quality, instead relating directly to the alcohol content. Simply put, and in my father's own words, a very general rule of thumb is that wine with a higher alcohol content will have a higher viscosity—and therefore, more legs. This is known as the Marangoni Effect.

I wiped my plate clean with a piece of wheat bread. (Not too posh, I know, but you would have to be an idiot to leave such a treat at the bottom of your plate. Just refrain from this stunt at any elegant restaurant.)

Munching on my last piece of bread, I put on my goose down jacket and returned the tray to an empty kitchen. I wanted to go for a walk and clear my head a bit.

A frost front had rolled in since the morning, and the temperature had dropped severely. Throughout the courtyard water puddles had frozen over, and an icy hoar dusted the landscape. I took a right turn to a path behind the main house and followed it, heading toward a wooded hill in the distance. Fields of arthritic vines sloped on both my left and right. My feet crushed fine gravel while the scent of leaves mixed with dirt tickled my nostrils. I noticed one of the caramel-coated dogs trotting behind me, and I stopped to let him know it was alright to keep me company. He shook his thick coat and quickened his gait to pace mine.

I'm a fast walker, and I warmed up as I climbed the gentle slope. Here the air smelled of wet wood and rich soil, clear and brisk. I could see my breath as I exhaled and glanced at the dog to check if I could see his as well. I was tempted to strike up a conversation with him but felt foolish even with no one around me. I cast a sidelong glance at him, wondering whether he was debating conversing with me as well, but he seemed content to just trot at my side. We soon reached the woods where silence hit us in a thick, engulfing fog. Paralyzing. It was so absolutely quiet I could hear my heartbeat pound in my ears when I stopped, crouched down, and listened. High, fluffy clouds chased one another across a vast gray sky, reminding me that changes are never permanent. Rather, permanence resides in the fact of change.

The key to change is to let go of fear, the Baci quote had read, but if change is not enduring, then how many fears does one have to shed through the course of a life? And in my case, lives?

Nothing. Absolute stillness. Even the dog seemed to sense the magical forest peace and quietly settled next to me, patient, as if expecting something.

The rich underwood scent brought back memories of another distant forest. The sharp cold stung my cheeks. I closed my eyes and drowned in yearning. A similar wintry breath hit my face as I ran, surrounded by darkness, toward a candlelit window and—Xavier.

I have never made love like that in this lifetime.

I blinked back tears and raised my eyes toward the sky filtering through the thick vegetation. I looked around me, recognizing acacias and maidenhair ferns. Focused ahead, enchanted by the dapple of light shining through the thickening foliage, I wondered about adventuring deeper into the core of the forest. Breathing quietly, I cast my magic gossamer net and gently tried to sense if I was being invited in. Waiting, I remained still for a few moments. Then I felt it: a distant rhythmical pulse, a visceral breath of energy. The enchanted forest inhaled and then, eternally slowly, almost undetectably, exhaled.

I thought of a riddle I remembered as a young girl: *Se ne fai il nome, scompare. Cos'?* If you name it, it disappears. What is it?

Silence.

And who was I to break nature's desire to be quiet?

Feeling like an intruder, I turned on my heels and headed lightly back out of the woods, followed only by my soundless, four-legged companion. A smirk broke my serious focus. I had felt the forest's wishes; I didn't get invited in, but I felt it, nonetheless.

CHAPTER 11

When I got back to the main house, I saw I had barely an hour to get ready.

Invigorated by the brisk walk, my body welcomed the luxury of a warm shower. I quickly toweled myself dry and moved on to blow-dry my hair straight until it fell in a smooth cascade down my back.

I rewrapped the uncooperative towel around my body for the hundredth time and critically eyed my limited wardrobe selection.

Gabe had said casual. *Hmm . . .*

After a distressfully ridiculous amount of consideration, I decided to go with the chocolate suede trousers, the gypsy flowered blouse and the black boots. *Casual, but . . .* I thought, pleased with my decision. I dabbed some amber oil in all the places I would like to be kissed as Coco Chanel used to say. I finished with extra mascara, leaving my lips bare with just a coat of lip balm. I puckered my mouth and blew a kiss at my reflection in the mirror.

I heard a light tap at my door and went to open it. Nicolas stood in the doorframe looking a bit sheepish.

"Hi! What's up?" I smiled.

"Gabe is downstairs."

"Thanks!" I swirled around. "Well? What do you think?"

"You smell great." His face twisted and exploded into a powerful sneeze.

"*Salute!*" I laughed.

"Thanks! No, I really mean it. You smell great and you look fantastic." He smiled. "Here are my keys. The long gold one is for the main door." He dropped them in my hand.

"Nicolas, are you sure? How thoughtful."

"Yep, no worries." He hugged me. "Have fun."

"I will." I grabbed my leather peacoat and my bag, and we headed downstairs together.

Gabe waited in the foyer talking quietly to Beverly. He looked sinful in dark jeans and a black leather jacket.

"Porzia, you look great." His eyes caressed me slowly, lingering for a second longer than I anticipated on my smiling lips.

"She smells great, too," Nicolas added, and barely suppressed another sneeze.

"Yes, she does. Nice to see you again, mate," Gabe said, laughing. He shook Nicolas's hand.

"Pleasure's all mine, sir," Nicolas replied.

As I fumbled with my jacket Gabe stepped forward to help. I nearly melted when he took the extra moment to lift my hair from under its collar. Quickly, I hugged Beverly and winked at Nicolas, and we left the house.

Right outside, Gabe stopped for a second, brought my hand to his lips, and lightly kissed it. "You look stunning this evening," he said. He kept my hand in his.

Heat rose to my cheek, and I was thankful for the surrounding darkness. "Thank you."

When we got to his car, he opened the door for me. It was roomy and yet cozy inside. I reached over to open his side with my nostrils tickling at Gabe's subtle scent lingering in the cabin. A feather hung from his rearview mirror.

"Did you have a good day?"

"Yes, not bad. And you?" I said, distracted. My eyes lingered on his golden hair reflecting pale moonlight that filtered through the smoked sunroof.

"Good, but I'm glad it's over," he sighed. "It's always really busy for a time whenever I get back from a trip."

"So . . . you didn't mention you race when we met."

"No, I didn't."

"Oh, I see. You were waiting for me to recognize you."

His midnight-blue eyes left the road for an instant and brushed my face.

"No, I wasn't, but I'm sort of glad you didn't."

"The Jourdain boys were absolutely ecstatic to have you over yesterday. Not to mention the women."

"And you?"

"I was very happy that you were able to make it. It was nice to see Clark again, too." I tried to sound neutral.

"Happy. Very happy. But not ecstatic."

"Yes, I was. I'm not good at fibbing," I mumbled, feeling myself blush in the darkness. "Are you still racing?"

"No. I crashed seven years ago."

I leaned forward and touched the feather. "You had a key chain on the plane with a similar feather."

"Roight here," he said, pointing at the ignition. "You're very observant."

"What kind of bird are they from?"

"Eagle. From an Aboriginal tradition."

"An eagle like the one I saw when I first arrived?"

He took a moment to answer. "I wasn't there to see, but I reckon it might have been *exactly* the same bird. They roam around the Adelaide hills, by Morialta Park." He switched the subject in that unexpected way of his. "What's hanging from your key chain, Porzia?"

"Dice." Well, I lied. I hadn't attached them to my keys yet. Soon, I would.

"How many?"

"Two," I answered as my mind remembered something. "Isn't Morialta Park by where you said you live?"

"Roight. Great memory."

"So—the restaurant is in your neighborhood?" I asked.

"You could say that."

"And you eat there often?"

"Almost every night." He glanced over.

"Oh! You must know the chef very well then?"

Gabe laughed. "You're looking at him."

"Do you own a restaurant or are we going to *your* place?"

"We're going to my place."

"And *you're* cooking *me* dinner?"

"Hey, no worries, I'm an excellent cook," he declared. "Plus, I figured we don't have much time, and I want to share some special things with you. Things that we wouldn't be able to enjoy if we went out to eat at some crowded place. Like talking, getting to know each other better, cooking some good food with a glass or two of your favorite beverage: wine; sharing a quiet evening away from curious eyes and noisy people." He pressed his lips together tightly. "So you get to know the man, not the celebrity."

I hadn't even considered the possibility of dealing with the media if we had gone out to a restaurant. *He does have a point, but I shouldn't have shaved my legs.*

We stopped at a red light and he turned to look at me. "I hope you're not offended about tonight. About my plans."

"No, of course not. Now I know why you said casual, but you could have said something. I would have brought dessert."

His eyes dropped, following the curve of my chin down my neck, pausing on the swelling of my breasts. A slow, sensuous grin spread on his lips, sending shivers down my spine. "Oh, but you have." He sped through the intersection looking like the wolf from *Little Red Riding Hood.*

Oh, great.

Unable to control the effect he had on me, I had to force myself away. I tried to concentrate on the unraveling darkness interrupted by the occasional streetlight and oncoming car headlights.

Gabe drove with confident skill, focused on the road ahead. Against the rare splash of lights, his eyes constantly shifted, like they hadn't made up their minds which shade to settle on yet. I hoped they never would.

He slowed down and the engine labored as we began to climb a winding road. Adelaide's night lights glimmered down below in the distance.

"I know it's dark and you can't see much but it's a pretty sight in daylight," he told me. "We're almost there."

"Oh, that didn't take long." I glanced at my watch: almost six. "I take that back, I can't believe it's been almost an hour."

"Perfect timing. I hope you're hungry." He dropped gears and gently rolled the car in front of a tall gate already opening.

"I can wait a bit longer," I admitted as we passed the gate. As it closed behind us, my heart skipped.

The house hid behind the massive silhouette of a tree I couldn't recognize in the darkness. I caught sight of a stone porch and a few steps leading to an oak door framed by cheerful stained glass. Dim light filtered from large windows lining the porch.

"Here we are," Gabe announced, pulling up by the front steps to park right near the entrance.

"Looks quiet," I whispered, getting out of the car. I took a few steps before finding my legs.

"It is," he answered, walking up to me to take my hand.

With contact, current flared like an overloaded switch, fire ignited between us. We barely made it to the front porch where we impatiently found each other. His hands slid inside my jacket as I backed into the front door with the length of his body pressing against mine. He smelled so good I felt high on it. My hands curled around his leather collar, and I lifted my face to gently kiss the corner of his mouth, brushing stubble and soft lips. He adjusted his head just enough for our lips to meet fully. Molding to my body, his hands found my hips and pulled me even closer. The heat of his fingers seared my skin through the thin lace. His tongue sought mine, and I parted my lips to welcome his intimate stroking.

I raised my hands to caress the sharp line of his jaw and held him even closer to me, smelling his leather jacket, tasting his desire for me. I wished to feel his hands on my bare skin. As if reading my mind, his fingers slid around my waist, found the scalloped edge of my blouse, and ducked beneath it. The kiss deepened with the growing intimacy of our touch, enveloping us in timeless devotion. His tongue stole a moan that escaped from my lips as my body responded to his exploration.

It could have gone on forever. I think it did, for I lost track of time in the privacy of his embrace. He brushed his mouth across my cheek, his hands relaxed on my waist, and he exhaled against my ear, "Come on in, luv. Before we decide this is where we're spending the evening." His voice dripped with arousal. Pulling away from me he opened the door.

I smiled at the effect this man had on me.

We stepped inside, and he closed the door behind us. "Do you want to give me your jacket?" He took his off and raked a hand through his hair.

"I always do that to you," I said, handing him my own jacket.

"What? Make me forget reality?" He raised an eyebrow.

I blushed. "No, I meant mess up your hair. But I like what you said better."

He looked right at me, his eyes clear and undiluted. "You can mess up my hair anytime, as long as I get to kiss you like that." His voice fired an irresistible temptation.

"Sounds good to me." My hands itched with the urge to start all over; I reached for my pockets instead, only to remember I didn't have any.

"Here, let me show you the place." He turned some lights on. I looked around, taking in the spacious entrance. Through large windows a panoramic view below of Adelaide by night bracketed a stone fireplace on the far wall. I bet in daylight one could see all the way to the ocean.

"We must be pretty high to be able to see so far," I observed, half to myself.

"We *are* pretty high. Not many houses above us," Gabe whispered in my ear. He had moved quietly right behind me.

Two comfy-looking sofas faced each other in front of the fireplace. An interesting array of handmade tribal rugs dressed the polished hardwood floors. Several pictures hung on the columns of exposed stone that separated the windows.

"The kitchen is this way." He showed me the way through an open hallway. I followed him into a spacious pinewood kitchen with stainless steel appliances.

"Do you need any help with dinner?" I offered, feeling instantly at ease in a familiar environment.

"I believe I have it all under control, but you could open the wine. If you don't mind..." He pointed at a couple of bottles on the counter. The label looked familiar.

"Gabe, this is the Jourdains' Cabernet!" I exclaimed, surprised.

"Yes, it is. Frank gave me a couple of bottles last night. He said the Shiraz would be just as good but you might have been tired of it."

"Frank offered you the Shiraz? Before it hits the market?" I was stunned.

"I guess there are a few advantages to being me." He winked and handed me a brand-new wine opener with a price tag still hanging from it. I smiled and felt all fuzzy inside; he went out of his way to please me. "So, what did you promise them?"

"Nothing, yet. But I invited the boys to come down and take a look at the shop."

"Where is your shop anyway?"

"That way." He tilted his chin toward the window pointing to Adelaide.

"Will I get the honor to take a look also?" I uncorked the Cabernet in a few practiced moves.

"You'd like to see my work?" Gabe handed me two wine goblets and I poured.

"Why not?"

"I didn't think you'd have the time to bother with it."

I shrugged. "I might not have much time left but seeing where you work is something I'd like to do before I go back." I raised my glass to toast his.

"Cheers."

"*Salute.*" I leaned forward to touch his glass with mine.

"That's almost like '*salut*' in French." He sipped his wine.

"Just add an *e* at the end to get the Italian version."

He peered at the ruby liquid and swirled it in his glass. "I have no clue if this is a good wine or not, or why it would be selected to win a prize."

"Do you like what it tastes like?"

"Yes."

"Do you like the flavors it leaves in your mouth after you swallow it?"

"What sort of question is *that*, Porzia?" he asked, raising an amused eyebrow.

"A *wine* question, *Gabe*," I replied, keeping a straight face.

"I guess it's not bad. It's as if my mouth has been coated with something woodsy and earthy."

"I guess you've got your answer right there."

"You mean it's as simple as that? Just a matter of personal taste?"

"To make it easy, yes; it's just like most things in life."

"You got that roight." He set his glass down, reached for containers in the fridge, and began dinner preparations.

We worked hand in glove, Gabe orchestrating by the stove while I set the table and refilled our glasses. By the time dinner was ready, a warm, relaxing blush lingered on my cheeks. I needed food. The steaks sizzled on the hot grill, smelling delicious. Gabe had roasted potatoes; the inviting aroma of rosemary and sage diffused through the kitchen. A colorful salad of spring vegetables waited to be dressed in an orange and ginger vinaigrette. Soft music played in the background from a hidden stereo.

With a little effort and a pinch of pleasure, a cooking experience often turns into one of the most intimate moments a man and woman might share. The brushing of fingers when cooking tools change hands; a juicy morsel of fruit fed with teasing fingers; hips colliding in the restricted space; arms reaching; eyes locking behind raised glasses while sipping wine; kisses exchanged over mouthwatering scents and tickling aromas—these are all essential ingredients to a perfect foreplay recipe.

We laughed and joked throughout dinner. He asked about my writing. I told him about leaving home after having won a full scholarship in journalism to a renowned college in the States and how I went back to Europe for culinary and sommelier schools during my summer breaks. I shared with him my passion for wine and gourmet cuisine, the challenge of making a career by believing in and living that passion through writing, my decision to move to Florida, never once regretting it. I got quiet for a moment, thinking about my choices and what had motivated me. He sensed my mood and held my hand, giving me the time to find a melancholy smile.

He talked about his first car and how he melted the engine racing toward the sunset, surrounded by endless desert dunes, a reminder that we are only grains of sand against the bigger picture. He laughed as I repeated Aboriginal words he tried to teach me. I fed him a cherry tomato, our eyes locked, and I wished for time to stop right then and there.

Gabe had grilled scrumptious steaks. He told me how years earlier, while racing in Northern Africa, a friend had shared his Japanese family's marinade recipe with him as they talked the night away next to a warm fire with a bottle of sake under a blanket of stars.

After dinner, he suggested I pour the rest of the Cabernet in our glasses and move to the living room.

"I'll clear the table and meet you there. It won't take long."

"I could help," I said.

He shook his head. "No worries. You're my guest. Go ahead and get comfortable. I'll get a fire going as soon as I'm done here." He shooed me out of the kitchen.

Above the fireplace hung a picture of Gabe on a pristine tropical beach next to a huge fuzzy bird and a golden retriever. The dog had deep chocolate eyes, massive wet paws, and sported a blue bandanna tied around its neck. The bird felt strangely familiar and was staring at me, perched on a lower branch of a gorgeous tree, its talons twice the size of the dog's paws. Gabe's hair was the color of pale, sun-kissed straw in September. His body glowed with a deep tan, and his left arm held a spear. He looked like a native god.

"That's me up in the Northern Territory, and the bird is a *Dhamala*, that's what the locals call it. It's a white-breasted sea eagle."

"That's a pretty big bird, Gabe," I said, repeating the word Dhamala under my breath.

"Actually, this one wasn't quite mature yet." He patted the sofa cushion for me to sit and crouched in front of the fireplace to start a fire. I sank in the surprisingly soft cushion and managed not to spill my wine.

"That day, I went for a walk on the beach you see in the photo. It's a beautiful beach with casuarina trees overhanging it. I was walking along with my dog, Tess, and carrying my '*garra*' and '*galpu*,' the first being an Aboriginal spear and the second a spear-thrower I took in case I saw fish. I was about fifty metres along the beach when I saw the sea eagle sitting in a lower tree branch, watching me. I whistled to it, calling it the local name, Dhamala. I set my camera on a piece of driftwood and rushed to stand as close as I dared to the bird to take the photo. Then I started walking away. Next thing I knew, she had spread her wings, tried to take off in flight, and tumbled at my feet. Right beside Tess and me. Hurt, but with no fear at all.

"I could see she had a damaged wing, so without really thinking, I bent down and picked up this huge eagle and carried it, squawking and clutching me with its talons, back to my four-wheel drive where I found my first aid kit and tried to assess the damage. That's when I realized she was horribly injured. Her left wing was just about to snap. I brought her back to the casuarina tree I had found her in and cowardly left her there." He cast me a painful look. "I didn't have the heart to—kill her."

"I continued walking along the beach, hoping to spear a fish to give her to eat and caught her hopping painfully. She followed us, struggling on her talons as we walked along. But I had no luck. I didn't see any fish. When I got to the creek at the other end of the beach I gathered some shellfish called Pointy Bums. I put my spear and spear-thrower down on the sand and started shelling them to feed the eagle. She watched me with bored disinterest, and although I told her it was food for her and the best I could do, she wasn't impressed. Instead, she picked up my *garra* in her claws and hopped away. She spread her wings trying to take flight, and that's when her damaged one snapped broken.

"So now I'm running back down the beach, yelling at this bloody Dhamala to give me back my *garra*, when I froze and stared into her wretched eyes." Gabe shook his head.

"It must have looked completely insane. I knew she'd taken the *garra* to show me. To put her out of her misery, Porzia.

"I struggled with her eyes for a while. It was quite a fight. Tess kept barking encouragements to me, but every time she got too close to the eagle she'd bounce backward and run away, tail between her legs. From a safe distance she'd resume her barking until I finally freed my *garra*. I begged the Dhamala for forgiveness and..."

A crackling fire now glowed in the fireplace.

Gabe stood. "That's the end of the story. I have some scars to remember her by and a couple of feathers." He sank next to me on the couch. "Deng Ming-Dao says that 'upon completion comes fulfillment, with fulfillment comes liberation.'"

I offered him my glass. I hoped I'd never have to face such a task. "So—the Dhamala had fulfilled whatever task she'd been born for?"

He shook his head and accepted my glass. "It was the first step I took to learn a lesson. Liberation allows one to go on. Even death is not a true ending." Once again, he changed the subject abruptly. "Do you have any sisters? Or brothers?"

"A younger brother, Alexander," I told him. "And you?"

"None, I'm an only child. Sole heir to a greeting card empire." He looked dead serious.

I cracked up.

He leaned over and kissed me. "I love your laughter."

The laughter died in my throat. I couldn't help it. He had this incredibly intense effect on me. He made me want to peel the world off my shoulders, to burn Prudence and her god-fearing siblings in the fire of the ancient goddess reawakening within me.

I looked at him and caught glimpses of my own heat rising, reflecting in the deep blue of his eyes. He took my left hand in his and brought my fingers up to his lips to nibble at my thumb. Watching my reaction, his mouth, teeth, and tongue worked around my nail and ... lower, down the sensitive curve between thumb and index finger and the inside of my palm. The slow dance of the tip of his tongue pulsing against my skin absolutely fascinated me. A surging tide of heat rose in me like madness, trying to burst my seams. My dry lips begged for moisture. I raised my eyes and met his. He was watching me with such intensity his eyes had shifted to a darker degree of liquid storm, reflecting the flames dancing wildly in the fireplace behind me. He took the tip of my index finger in his mouth and worked his teeth around it, biting. His hand, darker and stronger, held mine, lighter and thinner. His sensuous mouth worked every single one of my fingers, melting reason and resistance one teasing bite at a time. I watched through glazed eyes. He paused and turned to set my wine glass on the coffee table. Smiling just enough for me to catch a quick glimpse of teeth, he leaned back on the soft cushions and pulled me down with him. I hesitated and braced myself. His hands slid slowly across my back, caressed my hips, melting me, molding me against his legs. I felt the roughness of his jeans through the soft suede of my trousers and lifted myself up with my hands on his strong chest. Mistaking my move for retreat, he quickly blocked my legs against his, moved his left hand to the nape of my neck, and drew my face to his. Unleashed need spilled from his eyes, and I sank in it, willingly surrendering.

I felt his breath on my mouth. "We stop whenever you want, luv, but not yet," he whispered, kissing me. "Not yet . . ."

I raked my hands through his thick hair, parting my lips to welcome his teasing. His tongue ran along my lower lip, searching, exploring, tasting. His right hand found the bare skin of my waist, and I moaned against his mouth, helpless against the surging pleasure my body yearned toward. Giving in to the pressure of his fingers, I arched my back and felt him hard against my thighs. His hands found the round swelling of my hips and pressed. I plunged over the edge, crazy to know I had stirred such desire in him and met it with mine. I pulled his hair with my hand, turning his head, exposing his neck. I trailed soft kisses all the way to his right ear. With the tip of my tongue, I traced the shape of his ear; his fingers sank into the round softness of my butt.

My teeth found his earlobe. "I love the way your skin tastes," I murmured in a breath. *Oddio*, I was melting between my legs. The shadow of a pleased smile appeared at the corner of his mouth. He tilted his head and kissed me. My right hand blindly inched down his waist, my fingers twisted cotton, pulling, tugging his T-shirt clear of his jeans until the ripples of his taut stomach flexed beneath my fingers. He responded, shifting us on the sofa. With his hands guiding my hips, he leaned me against the pillows. With a lithe push, he got up to add more wood to the fireplace's scorching embers. Through a sexually infused fog, I watched him; his shirt untucked, his hair a tousled mess, his scent an irresistible spell. Without a word, he sat back on the sofa, lifted my feet on his lap, and took my boots off. His shirt followed, and I bit my lips, fighting the urge to lean forward and dig my nails along his chest. In the firelight his skin flexed like smooth ancient gold. His arms were strong and chiseled with fine honey-colored hair combing the dark tan of his skin. He sealed the distance between us by sliding on top of me. I couldn't resist anymore and trailed a hand along the sculpture of his chest; from his navel, my fingers traced a thin path of dewy hair that disappeared below his belt. He brushed a lock of hair off my face.

"Stay the night, luv." He held my gaze from behind dark lashes. "I just want to sleep with you in my arms again." He lowered his mouth to my forehead and lust bled into tenderness. The fire had warmed his skin to the point it released an intoxicating blend of male power and animal energy I found irresistible. I thought about spending hours licking every inch of his body, feeding off his scent.

Insidious rising mist dissolved reality.

His knee parted my legs, his mouth kissed, nibbled, sucked the pulsing vein at the base of my throat, making me forget what surrounded us. His strong hands reached behind my back, cupped my thighs, and squeezed me against him. His mouth found the plunging neckline of my lace shirt; his teeth pulled, exposing the curve of my breast. I tilted my head back and inhaled the hot scent our tangled bodies exuded. His left hand found my waist once again and, slowly moving up my burning skin, unfastened the trail of pearly buttons, exposing my navel to his warm breath. I sank into the soft cushions, a captive of sensation as his tongue ran along the edge of my bra. His hands brushed the thin straps down my arms. My body became a tangle of violin chords; liquid melodies begged silently for release. The budding tips of my breasts ached with exasperated anticipation.

"Gabe, please—," I whispered, pulling his head, parting my legs under the pressure of his. I felt moistness spilling, wetting me.

"Please what, luv?" he asked, unfastening my bra in one expert snap of fingers. He cupped my breasts in his hands and rubbed the hardening tips with his thumbs, sending pure pleasure shocks coursing down my spine. My hidden button began throbbing between the wetness of my inner lips; the first pulses of climax lapped, drummed between my legs.

"Please don't—stop—," I begged. *Oh!* My body tensed, inching slowly through his skilled touch. I became hot honey in his hands, a slave addicted to the pleasure his mouth inflicted on my body. A tide of lust swept through me, drowned me, possessed me, and I sank, surrendering. Not for one single instant did I doubt the power of the feelings washing over me.

"Tell me what you want—"

"Kiss me—," I moaned, an instant before he lowered his mouth to replace his thumb. Sucking and biting me, he teased until pleasure became ache, and the ache became an agony of emptiness, and I wished him deep inside me as a spasm of ecstasy shook my entire being.

He lifted his head, slid on top of me, and kissed my throbbing mouth. I ran my fingertips along his back, feeling the sinuous strength of his muscles tapering at the waist. I felt his belt.

I opened my eyes and met his about to melt into liquid silver. He reached for my throat. My speeding pulse barely veiled by transparent skin beckoned his fingers; his right hand traced the base of my collarbone. "You've got this bloody power over me. It's almost absurd." Yearning choked his voice.

"Yeah? Well that makes two of us," I whispered, running my hand through his hair. "I love your hair, Gabe." A multitude of golden highlights spilled through my fingertips.

"Are you cold?" he asked, worried.

"No," I laughed. "I'm everything but cold."

"That you are." He leaned on his right elbow.

"About spending the night—," I began.

He put a finger to my mouth. "No worries. I shouldn't have asked."

I felt his pang of disappointment pierce my own core.

I surprised myself by whispering against his finger, "I was going to say that I don't have my jammies with me and if I could borrow yours . . ."

His wicked smile interrupted my rambling. "I have no clue what these *jammies* are, but if it means you're staying, hell, you can have my firstborn son."

"At the rate things are going, Gabe, I just might." I lifted myself up, laughing.

I called the Jourdains and spoke to a sleepy Nicolas, who mumbled a drowsy "no worries" and hung up the phone on me.

I sat the phone down and noticed Gabe busy rekindling the dying fire. I took a moment to observe him from a distance and wondered if it was such a good idea to stay the night. Never before in my life had I moved so quickly into a relationship, but with him I crossed the river, barely brushing the stepping stones, finding my feet confident and sure on each pause in the crossing, neither wondering how I got there nor worrying how I would get to the next one. *You're learning to live in the present,* a whisper told me. It faded in the moment as Gabe got up and caught me gazing at him.

"What's the matter, luv?" he asked softly.

"I just had one of those timeless moments—," I told him, refocusing my eyes. *How am I going to know? Are you Xavier or not? I need a sign!* I yelled silently, but continued on with words, "The moment after the blow, when time dissolves but we know the pain will flare any given instant now. One of those times when you're afraid if it lasts a second longer you might end up trapped in the wastelands forever. But it might not be so bad there after all, if all you've got to look forward to—is pain."

"Yes, I've been there." His response penetrated my entire being. I couldn't believe he understood.

CHAPTER 12

I told Gabe that "jammies" were slang for pajamas. He answered with a puzzled look that made me believe his indigenous bunch slept au naturel. He offered me a makeshift camisole from a loud selection of T-shirts touting his off-road business. I turned them down. I couldn't imagine the sort of dreams one might conjure slipping into Morpheus's embrace wearing such abysmal fashion statements. I finally settled for one of his plain white T-shirts. I brushed my hair and rinsed my face of any trace of makeup and slipped the T-shirt on. I took my trousers off and was thankful the shirt reached below my hips. *Sort of a way-too-late chaste behavior, considering how I had responded to him earlier,* I blushed. I folded my clothes into a neat pile and, holding the bundle against my chest, walked barefoot on the plush rugs back to the bedroom. My shadows danced a wild gypsy reel as I crossed the room in the flickering light.

In Gabe's bedroom a massive sleigh bed faced a glowing fireplace, rising as a soft island from the barren sea of burnished wood floors. A cluster of potted cactuses loitered by the sliding doors. A wide bookcase leaned against one wall, heaving beneath the weight of well-read volumes. A collection of car magazines occupied the lowest shelf. Racing trophies doubled as bookends. The spear and spear-thrower he had mentioned in his story hung on the wall bracketed by Aboriginal paintings. An especially colorful one caught my eye, and I couldn't help but stare at it. A bright, radiant, feminine sun bathed everything in the painting with unconditional warmth, beaming life into creatures and supernatural beings. An extremely talented artist had captured movement on canvas in a spiraling nest of energy, creation, and genesis. The room felt warm and cozy. I dropped my clothes on a small wooden stool, sat down in front of the fire, and stared into the painting, enjoying the heat and silence.

Gabe walked in barefoot carrying frosted glasses of water. His belt-free jeans hung low, exposing sexy pelvic muscles. I thanked him for the water with a smile and took a long sip, welcoming the fresh taste. He sat behind me on the rug, stretched his legs around mine, and pulled my back against his bare chest. I noticed a tribal pattern of wings tattooed around his left ankle and asked what it was. He rested his chin on my right shoulder and nibbled at my earlobe before muttering something about a Cloud Dweller, an Aboriginal legend he was fond of. Then, still nibbling, he asked me if I was tired.

I relaxed against his chest, inhaling his masculine scent. I couldn't get enough of it. "A little," I said, "but it's nice to sit here by the fire."

I pointed at the sun painting and asked Gabe about it. He followed my gaze and in his deep, soothing voice began to tell me about it. His arms wrapped tighter around my waist, his soft breath brushed my neck like a desert breeze. His voice washed over me, spellbinding.

"The Dreamtime dates back—by some estimates—sixty-five thousand years. It's the way the Aboriginal culture explains the origins of the land and its people. It speaks of Earth's Creation by kindhearted and cruel gods and goddesses. In the Aboriginal worldview, a *jiva* or *guruwari*, a seed power, is deposited in the earth. Every meaningful activity, event, or life process that occurs at a particular place leaves behind a vibrational residue in the earth, just as plants leave an image of themselves as seeds. The shape of the land—its mountains, rocks, riverbeds, and waterholes—and its unseen vibrations, echo the events that brought that place into creation. Everything in the natural world is a symbolic footprint of the metaphysical beings whose actions created our world. As with a seed, the potency of an earthly location is wedded to the memory of its origin. The Aborigines called this potency the 'Dreaming' of a place, and this Dreaming constitutes the sacredness of the earth. Only in extraordinary states of consciousness can one be aware of, or attuned to, the inner dreaming of the earth."

I felt myself slip into a trance-like state as his words vibrated against my neck. He pointed at the bright sunshine in the painting.

"There once was a time on our Earth when nothing else but a beautiful woman existed. Her name was Sun Mother, and she lay fast asleep in a cave, deeply hidden below the Nullarbor Plain. The Great Father Spirit stirred her from her sleep. And as she rose and opened her eyes, she cast light upon the land, causing darkness to disappear. With her first breath she gave life to the sleeping seeds, and she began to walk, spreading life from north to south, from east to west, into every being, into every plant.

"Insects, grasses, trees, and animals all woke up to take their places and make their homes. Snakes began to slither, turning their paths into rivers of precious waters where fish teemed.

"She then brought balance, creating the seasons, and ended her long journey by disappearing below the horizon. Every creature held its breath in the darkness until the following morning when she reappeared again. And so she created the day and night, allowing everyone and everything a very well deserved period of rest."

Gabe inhaled a deep breath, stirring me gently from my spellbound state.

"That is a beautiful story, Gabe. How do you know so much?" I asked him dreamily.

"I don't know much. I'm actually a very selective-brain bloke. If it doesn't interest me, it won't stick." His lips kissed my neck slowly. "But I know I respect the people who've roamed these lands since the beginning of time, and I know they respect the land. So the least I could do was honor their sacred sites and not go trampling all over them when I raced."

It all made sense, but his last sentence held a deep bitterness I had never heard in his voice before.

"This is how we slept on the plane," he said quietly.

"This is a lot more comfortable than a plane."

"The bed would be ideal." In a quick, seamless move he swept me in his arms and stood. I wrapped my arms around his neck and swallowed a gulp. My feet dangled nimbly the few steps separating us from the bed. With a spark in his eyes, he laid me down, taking a quick peek at my panties.

"Gabe!" I exclaimed, pulling the T-shirt down.

"Sorry, luv," he said, grinning. "How about I show you mine and we're even?" he added, as he reached for his button fly.

"No, thanks." Turning away from him, I slipped under the cozy comforter.

His quiet laughter reached me, and just like on the plane, I was sprinkled with joyful, sparkly glitter. "That's just fine since I'm not wearing any."

My head snapped instantly, and I rolled over. My pupils widened, absorbing and reacting to the shifting light, flashing from cornered shadow to brighter, glowing flames to carry my gaze across the room to . . . Gabe's black boxers.

"Made you look," he said, getting under the covers.

I smashed a pillow on his head.

I was burning.

"Ouch." From beneath the pillow his muffled laughter stopped abruptly, then sudden stillness.

Did I kill him? I thought for a split second. *No way!* I bent to peek at him.

His blue eyes laughed at me just before he sprang with the soundless agility of a jaguar and pinned me to the mattress and began tickling me to death.

I laughed so hard tears streamed down my cheeks, my effort to fight back futile against his strength, my attempts to squirrel my body out of his reach confounded by his anticipation. I could barely breathe with all that laughter. I began to kick blindly, struggling to free myself.

"Gabe—you're going to kill me," I cried, laughing.

"Say please and I'll stop."

"No way in hell!" I incinerated him through tears with a withering glare. *Yeah, right.*

He just glared back and resumed his torture.

I jolted with laughter, shaking my head, and caught sight of his arm within striking distance, pinning mine down. I bit him.

"Ouch!" he said rather angrily. He released my arm.

Taking advantage of his distraction, I gathered all my strength and pushed against his chest with one free hand.

It didn't work. *Accidenti!*

He looked down at me with daring insolence, a confident predator toying with its helpless prey. I kept glaring at him and then realized he had stopped tickling me. His eyes shifted along with the energies around us, feeding off the heat of our intertwined bodies. His knee bent, insinuating its way between my legs. His hands released mine to cup my face, sealing the distance between our mouths. The tenderness I tasted in his kiss, after such intense wrestling, left me breathless.

Slowly he pulled away, holding my gaze. All resentment forgotten, I felt cold and snuggled deeper under the covers, pressing my body along his, one arm under the pillow, the other against his chest. He pulled me closer, resting his hand on the curve of my waist, and kissed me goodnight. I was about to close my eyes when I caught a quick grin creasing his cheek.

"Unless you'd like to play a bit longer . . ." He caressed my leg with his.

I smiled, leaned my head on his chest, and whispered him goodnight.

Comforted by the crackling fire and his steady heartbeat, I was asleep instantly.

*

The following morning I stirred and woke up slowly to the sound of rain pelting relentlessly against the garden doors.

Over Gabe's solid body, through the rain-streaked window, a glimpse of light peeked, announcing the break of dawn. Next to me, Gabe slept on his back, one arm bent by his head, the other above the covers. I propped myself up on my elbows and looked at him. In my mind, I overlapped his strong, present features with a darker, distant memory, obstinately searching for similarities.

Xavier's face faded against the living energy of Gabe's presence.

I didn't know what to believe. Life had taken matters into its own hands, and lately, I had confronted and ultimately accepted extraordinary events. Even Madame Framboise had confirmed this new path with her tarot—and Gabe as the next development.

Talk about a long-distance relationship. *Oddio!* This isn't even funny! He's living in the southern hemisphere, in a winter doomed forever to chase a reflected summer and vice versa; two parallel train tracks never meant to merge.

We were as Paolo and Francesca in Dante's *Inferno*.

Well, they had committed adultery, I thought, easing my fears. That's why they were punished.

Just like Xavier and you.

A heavy blow of despair swept me off my elbows, and I hit the mattress. This can't be it. I wasn't going to be punished for something which had occurred centuries ago.

That's why you have been made aware of it.

To break the pattern? I answered my own inner voice.

To go fearless through the portal. He leads by example.

I frowned, not understanding. Maybe I didn't see it all.

You have seen plenty, dear child. The path unfolds, and there is no turning back.

Well, since you seem to know it all, dear voice—is Gabe Xavier? I asked defiantly.

Gabe is magic, the rain whispered against the windows.

I knew that. I shifted my gaze to look at him.

He was staring at me as if he had seen a ghost.

"Bonjour."

"Morning," he mumbled, his voice thick with sleep. He rolled over, sank his head on the pillow, and went back to sleep, exposing his bare back to me. Two narrow scars ran along the entire length of his shoulder blades. I was surprised and frightened as a memory that wasn't mine, the memory of the pain that had carved such marks on his back, came to me. I wondered what it would feel like to touch the scars and why I didn't feel them last night. On the couch I'd had my hands all over his back.

I raised my head to take a better look. They were but a shade darker than his skin tone, barely visible. Ancient scars.

All of a sudden I saw him as vulnerable. I wanted to protect him from ever feeling pain again. I raised a hand to my mouth with the shocking realization that I was falling in love. My first impulse betrayed me. I just about threw back the covers, grabbed my clothes, and ran to the other end of the world. *Run home!* My second impulse wanted to throw back the covers, grab my clothes, and run back to Umeracha. *Not far enough.*

I took a deep breath and slowly exhaled through my mouth. I struggled with a dozen more slow, deep breaths until I felt the tight knot of terror begin to dissolve. With light fingers I traced the length of his scars. He stirred beneath my touch. I wasn't ready to face him with the realization of my growing love plastered all over my face. The last thing I wanted to do was wake him. I pulled away and lay back until I finally managed to churn myself into a troubled sleep.

Hours later, I woke up alone. The rain had stopped, and bright daylight filtered through the windows. The fire had been rekindled. From outside, the unfamiliar chirping of some sort of exotic bird reached my ears above the sound of crackling wood. I rolled over to Gabe's body imprint in the mattress and inhaled deeply, soaking up the warmth of his heat. The bathroom door opened quietly, and Gabe stumbled out, still half asleep. He smiled lazily at my body parked on his side of the bed, ran a hand through his hair, and sat right next to me. "Did you migrate?" he asked, pulling the covers off me.

"Sort of," I said. "Your side's warmer." Suddenly conscious of his T-shirt wrapped around my waist, I felt grateful for the covers hiding the rest of my body.

"Are you cold?" Gently, he pushed me over to lie back next to me.

"Not anymore." I snuggled against him. "Do you have to go to work?" I worried this might already be coming to an end.

"No. I called," he yawned. "I'm going to have a three-day weekend for a change."

"It's already Friday?" I choked on panic creeping up my throat.

"Yes."

I raised my head and locked eyes with him. "I leave tomorrow evening."

He looked at me seriously and pulled me closer. "I know, luv. But let's not think about it yet."

His hands slid under the T-shirt and caressed my waist. I closed my eyes. A flashing memory of him tickling me sparkled behind my closed eyelids, but I quickly realized that it wasn't laughter he sought this morning. I surrendered to his warm fingers.

He lowered his head to kiss and nibble at my navel. His hands lifted my shirt and peeled it over my head. His eyes echoed my own physical craving while my mind rebelled against such madness. "You're adorable in the morning," he murmured. My legs found cool sheets as I slid through his touch. He raised a hand to caress my face.

I kissed his fingers, then leisurely moved to his palm, tracing his life line with the tip of my tongue, tasting years gone by.

As if by silent agreement, lust bowed, gallantly acknowledging its victory over sensibility. I gave way to inquisitive desire to just explore one another. I sensed him relax against my touch. My hands slipped around his neck. I brought him to me.

He moved, bracing himself on his elbows, careful not to weigh down on me. I ran my hands through his hair, down the curve of his neck, and across the smoothness of his chiseled chest to his tapering waist, reaching around to his lower back. I drew them upward again to feel the definition of his shoulder blades. I remembered the scars . . .

Beneath my fingertips his body suddenly tensed up, reading my silent question. His predator eyes gathered clouds, darkening with unleashed thunders.

"That's where they ripped the wings off my back."

Amidst the crashes of thunder, I tasted the bitterness of lightning sear down my throat and had a fleeting look at an ageless struggle against eternal damnation.

He doesn't race anymore . . .

Gabe lowered his head, captured my mouth with his, and plunged his condemned soul into the kiss, seeking relief, forgiveness, hope.

And I knew I was falling in love. I would have given my life to heal his pain. *And I didn't even know who the bloody enemy was.*

We kissed until time stilled. I held him against me as if his life depended on it.

"I don't even know when I'll see you again, and at the same time I can't believe I've lived this long without you." He looked at me. "You're meant to wake up in my arms every single day of your life." He kissed me lightly on the cheek.

We both burst into laughter as my stomach chose that perfect moment to rumble. I pressed my hands against it to make it stop, but to no avail.

"I think we ought to fix breakfast." Laughing still, he pushed himself off the bed and stretched. My lungs drained of all air at the sight of his scarred back.

I shook my head. My life wasn't ever going to be the same. When and if he would decide to talk about it, I would listen, but until then I was going to honor his privacy, walking precariously along the wasteland's edge. *Careful not to drown.*

CHAPTER 13

I hurried through a quick, invigorating shower before joining Gabe in the kitchen. The inviting aroma of fresh-brewed coffee competed with the sight of him for my attention. I found him sexier than ever in jeans and bare feet.

We shared a delicious fruit salad, fresh yogurt, toast with honey, and a newspaper fight, all washed down with a pot of robust dark roast. We were sitting on the floor, totally engrossed in the Zen art of peeling strips of newspaper off my hair when we heard the front door open and held our breaths until we saw Clark walk in carrying a couple of grocery bags.

"G'day, lads." He took one look at us in disarray among the pages of the morning press. "Glad I bought my own copy," he said, waving a newspaper at us.

"G'day, Clark. Would you like some coffee?" Gabe pulled himself off the floor, extending me a helping hand. I took it and shot up, giving Clark a glowing smile.

"Good morning, Clark. How are you?" I asked, as if it was the most natural thing in the world for him to find me in Gabe's kitchen in such a disheveled state.

"Splendid, hon. How about yourself?"

I grinned at him. "Just peachy," I answered, pulling what I hoped was the last of the newspaper confetti from my hair.

He nodded. "You two got any plans for the day?" he asked, reaching for the steaming mug Gabe had poured for him. "They might need your help down at the shop after all."

Gabe looked at me and shrugged. "I'm sure they can handle it. What would you like to do, Porzia? When do you need to get back to the winery?"

"I don't really have to be right back. As far as my work, I have it under control. Now it's just a matter of wrapping up and sending it in. But I have plenty time left before my deadline and can finish once I get back home."

"Would you like to do some shopping?" Gabe asked in a tone usually reserved to herald death sentences.

"No. I need to pick up a couple of presents but can do that during my layover in Melbourne," I told him. "How about we just chill?"

"You mean relax?" Gabe asked.

"Yes, kick back," I said.

"Sounds good to me." Gabe pushed himself off the counter to browse in the grocery bags Clark had brought in.

"Well, I'll just head down to the shop since the boss here is going to—chill." That last word seemed to amuse him a great deal and Gabe got caught up in it.

I folded my arms across my chest, took Gabe's spot against the counter, and enjoyed the jolly clown show. Here they were, two fully-grown Aussies, up in stitches over American slang. Who would have thought? And I was falling in love with one of them.

Gabe must have read something across my face because he quickly sobered up and looked at me with such tenderness that I forgot all about Clark. It made me want to rush into his arms as our eyes locked onto each other's, lost in our own little abyss.

Clark cleared his throat, bringing us back up from the deep end. "Porzia, it was a pleasure to see you again," he said, shaking my hand. He went to open his mouth, thought better of it, and left shaking his head.

Silence fell like a discarded cape over the kitchen.

I moved to the counter to refill my coffee cup and raised the pot in a silent offer. Gabe shook his head and announced he was going to take a shower; I should make myself comfortable while I waited—unless I cared to join him.

"Tempting, but no thanks. I need a breath."

I grabbed my jacket and my steaming coffee and walked out.

A brisk ocean breeze had swept the sky clear of earlier rain clouds, leaving a stunning view of Adelaide and gleaming ocean waters down below. Against the pencil-thin horizon I spotted a couple of gray ships steaming off for distant lands. The biting cold air whipping my cheeks contrasted sharply with the coffee warming my stomach. I found a somewhat dry spot on the low stone wall bordering Gabe's property and sat down to enjoy the breathtaking sight.

Wearing a pair of stonewashed jeans and a troubled look, Gabe found me minutes later.

"What's the matter?" I asked him.

"Clark was right. Looks like I have to get down to the shop after all. Something came up." He shot me a worried look.

"It's no big deal," I reassured him. "I'd love to come with you, if you don't mind."

"It won't take long, Porzia." He sighed in relief.

"It doesn't matter. But be prepared for a lot of silly questions. I don't know anything about off-road racing, and I might exasperate you," I said, getting to my feet.

"No worries." He smiled. "You can exasperate me anytime you like."

I wondered if he really meant that. Would it survive a test?

We made it to his shop in less than half an hour, and I found myself catapulted inside a state-of-the-art garage and showroom equipped with every conceivable off-road extremist toy imaginable. Even my inexpert eyes registered as much.

Gabe introduced me to Gomi, his head mechanic, a young Japanese kid playing grown-up inside blue coveralls, his sleeves rolled over several times and kept in place by orange rubber bands that matched his streaked punk hair. One of those dazzling Hollywood smiles hung randomly on his lips.

Gabe escorted me to a spacious office at the end of the showroom where Clark talked on the phone, typed furiously on a keyboard, and added numbers on a calculator simultaneously. He glanced up and shot us a relieved look. He finished on the phone and offered me a seat. I sat, hoping to stay out of their way. They went right to business and I soon gave up trying to follow their conversation.

Gomi came in, poured himself coffee, and offered me some as well. I declined but asked him a couple of questions about some accessories on display as I had no idea what they were. He gave me an intrigued look, abandoned his coffee to grab my sleeve, and dragged me to the back garage where sparks were flying as someone welded metal on a far corner bench. Gomi told me they were customizing a white Land Cruiser. I had no idea what I had gotten myself into when I asked Gomi my simple question, but I soon found myself involved and somewhat able to follow his explanations. The vehicle belonged to Gabe, and it was being worked on for an upcoming desert rally. Over the loud welding noise I asked Gomi how long he had been working with Gabe. His answer left me gasping.

"About fifteen years," he stated, smiling.

"Gomi, how old are you? If you don't mind my asking." He must have been fresh out of the nursery when he grabbed his first wrench.

"I'm ready to bet I'm older than you," he said.

"Naaaw!"

"Let's just say that I never finished high school and met Gabe during an Australian Safari. See, he's got this *drive*, for lack of a better term. That no matter how tough it'd get out there, as long as you had a grip of your drive—this "need to go"—then you knew you'd make it. Only a handful of racers have it, and Gabe's got the meanest I've seen so far.

"He almost shut off once, that day . . ." he shook his head. "I'll never forget. Way deep in the outback, a couple of nights into the race, he crashed and got trapped under his vehicle. While we waited for the paramedics to show up, he kept on slipping in and out of consciousness. I held his head out of a ditch, but he was making no sense at all, mumbling something about following an eagle into the void."

His words brought chills along my spine. Suddenly I was afraid to hear more.

"I knew there was severe internal bleeding. He doesn't even remember any of this. But I kept him awake talking about the risks of life and the fact that we knew we couldn't live any other way." He held my gaze. The welder had stopped sometime during this conversation, and I was just finally aware of the silence surrounding us.

I read his eyes. "Why are you telling me all this?" My instinct told me that this was fair warning, not a rehearsed tactic to scare the enemy.

"He's never brought a woman to the shop."

"Ah!" I folded my arms across my chest and waited for him to continue.

He raised his chin defiantly. "To see if you're up to it."

I watched this kid and instinctively called upon my powers to pierce through the inscrutable façade of his almond-shaped eyes. Surprisingly, I reached his soul where the core of his friendship and bond with Gabriel Miller pulsed and glowed, alive.

"He's lucky to have you by his side, Gomi." Shook up by the force of the experience, I turned my trembling back to the dismantled vehicle in front of us. "So, what's next?" I asked, feigning control.

Gabe's voice answered as he walked up behind me. "We're going to chuck the standard engine in the scrap heap and put in a 5.0-litre that's been stroked to 5.7." He rolled his sleeves up, ready to jump into action. He hadn't even bothered with coveralls for himself, but he threw me a set.

Gomi smiled, waiting to see what I would do next.

I was all for it and didn't waste time. I just slid into the coverall, asked for a chew, settled for gum, and hoped for the best.

What was supposed to be just a quickie lapsed into several hours of hard labor. After 'chucking' the standard engine, a Holley nitrous Double Pumper went in for the extra boost when sand dragging, followed by thirty-five-inch BFG mudders and a four-inch suspension lift. By the time we took a break I was a starving, grinning, greasy mess. Gabe took one look at Gomi, who was covered in just as much slime, and called it a day. Besides a couple of greasy spots on his jeans, Gabe looked like he had just showered. And he had done most of the work.

How did he manage to keep so clean? I asked myself while sharing industrial soap with Gomi. He handed me a towel, then proceeded to tell me that I had a huge smear on my face and wanted to know if I was this messy when I cooked.

"But of course. That's the best part of it." I rubbed my cheek.

They both looked at me like I was some sort of extinct plant.

"What is it?" I asked. "Women around here don't get messy when they cook?"

"No, just don't know many women keen on jumping under a car hood, especially when the plan of the day was to just 'chill,'" Gabe said, reaching for my hair to free a piece of newspaper confetti.

And I thought I had gotten it all.

"Well, I'm sure there is plenty of time left for that," I said. I shrugged out of my coverall.

"Ready to grab some lunch?" he asked, offering an extended hand.

"Yes!"

We said good-bye to Gomi and Clark and stepped out into a bright sunny day. We decided to enjoy the fresh air and walk the short distance to a cozy restaurant just a couple of blocks away. We passed colorful fruit and vegetable stands, inviting coffee shops, and, incredibly, a couple of Italian grocers. Holding hands, we strolled down the sidewalk. At a flower stand Gabe bought a small bouquet of flowers to thank me for helping back at the garage.

I shrugged it off as we reached the restaurant. "I don't know if I did anything right," I told him. "But you probably would have been better off leaving me chained to the office chair."

He looked at me seriously and kept silent while the restaurant hostess greeted us and offered us seats. Delicious aromas tantalized my taste buds, and I realized that breakfast had been a long time ago. A blue and cream gingham tablecloth covered the inviting table. In a short crystal vase a cheerful bunch of yellow daffodils anticipated spring. A heaping basket of warm, fragrant bread appeared as if by magic.

"They only serve a couple of specials a day." Gabe pointed to a sun-kissed easel by the front window. It read *Daily Specials: French Onion Soup, Seared Tuna Steak and House Meatloaf.*

"The tuna is pretty good. But the meatloaf is excellent."

"Is that what you're having?" I asked.

"Yes. How about you, luv?" he looked at me, tilting his head to nod at the waitress approaching our table carrying glasses and a sweaty jug of chilled cider.

"The tuna sounds good to me," I said, smiling at the waitress. She smiled back her approval and switched her attention to Gabe, asking if he was going to get the meatloaf.

"They know me here." He cracked a grin.

She came right back with clay pots of steaming French onion soup and a tiny matching ramekin of whipped herbed butter.

I unrolled my cloth napkin to find a sprig of dried lavender scenting its core. *What a pleasant surprise,* I thought. I set the lavender aside, making a mental note to keep it for my journal.

I tasted the steaming soup. And wished I could make it like that.

Gabe handed me a piece of buttered bread and filled my glass with fragrant cider.

"I'm sorry it took longer than expected back at the shop," he apologized between gigantic spoonfuls of soup.

"No big deal. I had fun."

"That's what it looked like. It didn't seem to take you much time at all to figure things out."

"You mean you weren't worried about me messing up your vehicle?" I joked.

"Not really. I was a bit worried about you getting dirty and all, but you didn't seem to mind."

I raised an eyebrow. "How did you manage to stay clean?"

"I had you and Gomi soaking it all up," he smirked.

I had to laugh at that. He was a good strategist.

Our waitress replaced the too-soon-empty bowls with tuna for me and Gabe's meatloaf special. Both of our plates heaped with side orders of fresh veggies and juicy mango slices. She checked to see if we needed anything else and left us to struggle with the gargantuan portions. I knew I wasn't going to clean my plate, but Gabe offered to help me. I ended up sharing with him.

We definitely had no room for dessert and settled for espresso.

Over demitasses, we lost track of time and talked the afternoon away. Only when our waitress came by to light a small oil lamp on our table did we notice it was dark outside. "We should probably be heading back," I said, looking at Gabe.

"We should, but I don't want to."

"What would you like to do?" I murmured.

He smiled wistfully, pulling himself up. "Well, the ideal would be . . ." He sighed and rubbed the bridge of his nose. "Never mind, luv. This isn't the right place for this sort of talk."

I blinked sadness back and looked at him.

Conflicted emotions swirled the blue of his eyes. He sat back down and took my hand in his. The crown of his blond hair bent and he kissed my open palms.

I closed my eyes.

"I watched you sleep last night." His breath filled the lines etched in my palms. His words sieved through my closed eyelids and I tensed, waiting.

"In the darkness I believed I could tell you secrets I have told no one. And knew you would understand."

I barely nodded and closed my hands around his. In a whirlwind of spiraling emotions, I flashed back to the past life regression and the blood-caked wound of Xavier's chest. Madame Framboise's words echoed in my head, "Keep honesty and an open heart up front if you will . . ." And right now my heart was overwhelmed. I had kept it shut for so long I was afraid it would burst, unable to contain such an abundant amount of love.

This is not how I had envisioned it. I was falling for him.

Free falling . . . and the net will open.

But I was afraid. The meaning of my nightmare suddenly became clear. What was it going to take for me to leap? Into Gabe . . . into Magic . . . into my soul?

"How about I take you back to the winery, you pack your bags, and we go back to my place. I'll drive you to the airport tomorrow."

"You wouldn't mind driving me all the way to Umeracha and back to your home?"

"No, luv. What I mind is you leaving tomorrow." He let go of my hands and stood.

Another nightmare to face.

"I know. I'm sorry." I grabbed my flowers, added the lavender sprig, and readjusted my bouquet.

Gabe watched in silence. "No worries. Let's just forget about it and think *now*." He led me outside. His grip on my hand spoke a thousand words.

With the sun a distant memory across the dusking sky, it had suddenly turned cold. We walked arm in arm back to the shop, where we found Gomi all alone, busy locking up. He had changed into regular street clothes and looked even younger, disappearing inside an oversized fleece jacket and baggy jeans. He flashed us that breathtaking smile and smoked away on a chrome motorbike.

Gabe quickly checked to see if everything was in order while I gave the Jourdains a quick warning call.

We were both quiet as we left Adelaide and traffic behind us and began to speed up across the deserted country roads. The car smelled of dried lavender as I subconsciously gripped my bouquet with both hands. It didn't take long to get back to the winery. I guess it's true that time does fly when you're having fun. I couldn't believe how comfortably I shared silence with Gabe. I was content just to be near him. Too soon, we pulled into the driveway at Umeracha.

I love that about us, I thought, opening up my bottled, piled-up emotions. I rushed and tripped over my feelings spilling outwards as I climbed upstairs to my room to pack.

While the boys grilled Gabe about our work at the garage, Beverly joined me upstairs. I was sure she planned to do some grilling of her own, but she soon proved me wrong. Madame Jourdain wasn't feeling well and wasn't going to be able to say good-bye to me. She had written me a sealed note I was to read once I left, Beverly told me in a conspiring whisper. I thanked her for the note, for the great hospitality, and the unforgettable time I'd had in their company. She hugged me and helped me carry my luggage downstairs.

They were all waiting for me and I had a terrible time choking back tears. When Frank gave me a couple of bottles of Shiraz I lost it and began to cry. Then Nicolas grabbed me in a tight hug, hissed to me in his snake voice, and I cracked up.

"You idiot!" I choked, laughing through my tears and hugging him back.

"How about me, dear lass? How about hugging your favorite piccies taker?" Desmond's voice, sounding quite pickled, boomed from behind Nicolas's shoulder. I raised my head and noticed he didn't look in the least pickled, just his usual abominable self.

"Desmond! I thought you'd be gone already."

"And miss the chance to aggravate you a bit longer?" he quipped, squeezing me tight.

"You don't aggravate me, Desmond. You make my life *spicier*," I conceded leniently. A strangled whisper was all I had left after he depleted my air reserves with a single squeeze.

"Bloody hell! I can't imagine what sort of bland life you lead away from me, then!" He looked up at Gabe. "How about you help marinate the life of this *juicy morsel* from now on, mate?"

Oh great! I groaned.

"I don't know much about marinating, but she can count on me from now on," Gabe said quietly.

Dom and Lori helped me with my luggage, and I promised Beverly to send her a few copies of *A' la Carte* when the article came out. After another round of "good-byes," we finally left.

"They're great people. I see why you would want to write about what they're doing," Gabe said, maneuvering the car out of the driveway.

"What about you, Gabe? I'm sure you have had people writing about you ...," I tried not to think of the heavy sadness anchoring down my heart at the thought of leaving such a genuine and warm family behind.

"Yes, I have." His eyes shone black when he glanced over at me. "Especially after the accident."

I had suspected something of that sort. Did I want to go into it with him now? My instinct warned me about launching a serious, life-threatening debate. Oh, why not? Just like Gomi earlier, I decided to be straightforward. Now was as good a time as any.

"Is that why you have the shop now?"

"Yes. It's a way to still be part of it now that my body can't take it anymore." His voice had grown darker.

"Physically?" I was dubious; he looked to be in great shape.

"Partly."

"Mentally?" Had he lost the focus Gomi had talked about?

"Naw—mentally I've got it. More than ever, if possible."

"Then it's spiritual." It wasn't a question and of course he didn't answer. *Bingo. Here we go.* "But the fever is still brewing deep inside you." It felt like pulling teeth.

"I've learned to live with it," he justified curtly.

Oh, I personally knew this subject. I shook my head, "You've adjusted. Learned to live with the brewing intensity of it." I took his silence for agreement and pressed on. "What's going to happen the day the fever has gathered enough strength and finally decides to erupt?"

Gabe took a deep breath and slowed the car down. "How do you know?"

"I don't." *You tell me,* I gambled.

He saw right through it. "If I live to face the challenge—spiritual limitations and all—if the fever decides to fuel my dormant passion for racing, then I'll rise to the challenge and will give it all I've got, Porzia. And you should too. When your own Dreamtime erupts from the seed and you accept your own powers." The lavender-scented air in the intimate space of the car rippled with the force of his determination. He exhaled, easing off the subject. "You never cease to amaze me."

"Because I ask you questions about things you don't usually talk about?" I offered. Then I pressed hard, "And you like me enough that you'd rather answer instead of telling me to mind my own business?"

He shook his head, and his blond highlights caught flashes of the waning moon up above. "You haven't leaped either."

"No. I haven't."

The moon hid behind a cloud, and darkness fell around us like a spent mouth with nothing left to say.

Minutes went by in the dark silence and then something clicked in my mind.

"Is that why you said the quote in the chocolate couldn't have been about you? Because something binds your spiritual freedom?" Where the hell was I going with this?

"You're having a go at it again."

"Am I?" I smiled.

"You're not going to write about this, are you?"

"No, but I might tell your competition how you chucked the standard engine on the Land Cruiser and replaced it with a 5.0-liter stroked to 5.7—"

Illuminated by the headlights of an oncoming car, his profile creased with laughter. "That means that you're in for a tickle session that's going to leave you begging for mercy."

"Over my dead body."

"No . . . I might take you to the edge, but not over. I won't let that happen." He looked at me with amusement mixed with an edge of something I tried hard not to translate.

"You can't control death—," I breathed.

"How do you know?" he whispered in a voice I wasn't sure I recognized. "I've defied it once. I can do it again," he said in a thick Aboriginal accent.

Who the hell was talking to me?

"But it was your own body. We're talking about mine." Did I hear him right?

"Luv, do you think it makes any difference?" Controlling the steering wheel with his right hand, he reached over with his left to hold my hand. His voice had reverted to normal.

"I've got a few more hours and I promise, by tomorrow you'll be part of me. I'll fill your shadow with the colors of love. So no matter how far you are from me, you'll only need a bit of Mother Sun to remind you how close I am to you." His fingers caressed mine, sealing his promise with hot, liquid wax melting drop by drop, heating me up with every single stroke.

My instincts told me we wouldn't make it past the front door this time, my heart rate agreed, and the rest of my body couldn't have cared less. It was busy reacting to his scalding touch.

The car felt suddenly too small to accommodate my senses. Expectations mingled with my fears of rushing into something. I was quickly losing my grip on my own fate.

Through my shadowed eyelids I saw the burnished-gold speckles of his eyes focused ahead on the dark road. I shifted my gaze lower, to his strong forearm steady on the steering the wheel. I remembered how it felt to have his hands caress my skin.

Lost in my thoughts, I must have squeezed his hand inadvertently, for he looked over and instantly read me like he had written the words himself. He returned my squeeze and shot me an X-rated grin that left me breathless. I wished the road would never end, and I wished us already there.

CHAPTER 14

Gabe brought the car to a halt in front of his gate. While we waited for it to open, I needed to remember to breathe. Above us, on a field of velvet darkness, the moon peeked through lingering clouds. Just like me, she had yet to decide whether to show herself off or keep on behind the thin veil. Dreamily, I walked the few steps leading up to the front door. Gabe's steady hand on my lower back guided me inside where the cozy living room welcomed us. He turned on a couple of lights and headed for the bedroom with my luggage. I started to follow him but thought better of it; I was afraid to face the Aboriginal painting of Creation. Was I ready for my own Dreamtime? To plant a seed and hope it would blossom into the passionate death-defying love I sought? Was I ready to leap and trust the safety net of my magic to be there? To be left alone with my insidious ghosts in the dimly lit living room didn't agree with me either.

I sat on the soft sofa facing the silent fireplace. Gabe came back and stopped to trace his hand across my shoulder before moving on to build a fire. It didn't take him long, and soon bright flames echoed our beating hearts. I turned my face toward the dark window and caught my own reflection staring back at me, my eyes absurdly wide, framed by the thick curtain of my dark hair.

I looked afraid. Hell, I felt afraid.

I looked at Gabe's back and opened my mouth, ready to apologize only to realize I didn't know what for. I closed my mouth, kicked my boots off, and tucked my legs beneath me. Leaning forward I reached to touch him.

He turned to look at me; his eyes blazed with every shade of sunset, burning with flames trapped behind his eyelashes. In a blink, he was suddenly on the sofa next to me, running his hands along my bare arms. He drew me against him.

Brushing a hand on my hair, he settled my head against his steady heart and asked me if I would like to take a bath after such a long and labored day.

"That sounds like a marvelous idea," I whispered, relaxing against his chest.

"You're welcome to use either bathtub, but the guest bathroom is more comfortable than mine."

"What are you going to do while I take a bath?" I asked. I lifted my head and found his chin an irresistible temptation. I began to nibble at it.

"I'm going to shower and then, if you'd care for something to eat, I could fix us a snack."

"I'm not hungry after our late lunch. How about I meet you back here in a little while?"

"No worries, take your time."

With effort I raised myself off the sofa and went to grab my overnight bag, thinking that maybe it was a blessing I didn't have sexy lingerie with me.

Yeah! Like that was going to stop us tonight.

I filled the tub with hot water and added some of my own amber blend. Soon, the entire bathroom steamed in a fragrant cloud. I quickly stripped off my clothes and tied my hair in a high bun. I lowered my body into the hot water. It felt heavenly. I relaxed and exhaled, releasing all the worries roiling in my navel. I closed my eyes and allowed the gentle sloshing of the water to soothe me into a light meditation. Time drifted and I lost track of it.

I finally stirred when the bathwater had cooled down to barely lukewarm. Aware I had gained my confidence and strength back, I briskly dried myself. Surprised at the power I had drawn from the water, I mused with the idea that despite my skepticism, I might be turning into a liquid woman after all.

I wanted to join Gabe as quickly as possible. Someone inside of me had decided to trust him, to accept, *even if only for the moment.* I didn't think he was Xavier.

Was that an issue? I still felt torn between my soul mate in the abstract ideal and the vibrant man awaiting me in the next room. But I knew I was falling in love, and I wanted to be with him tonight. *No worries. No mental jerking off.*

I brushed my hair and slipped into a white ribbed tank top and blue flannel bottoms, and walked back to the living room with my own heartbeat echoing every step I took.

Gabe knelt in front of the fire wearing a pair of flannel shorts that almost matched my pants. I smiled. He heard me and turned, wiping his hands on the shorts.

"Nice pants," he said, taking in my pajamas. Pointedly, he glanced at his own shorts.

I chuckled. "I guess we just have the same taste in clothes we lounge around in."

He patted the carpet, inviting me to join him by the fire. I sat cross-legged right in front of him. He took hold of my ankles, spread my feet apart, and pulled me closer. He wrapped my legs around his waist. With his strong hands around my hips, I felt he could snap me in two if he chose.

The fireplace heat warmed my back, slowed my heart, and gave me confidence. I raised my own hands to caress his glowing chest. His skin felt smooth and warm to the touch. I felt the pressure of his hands tightening on my lower back.

I inhaled the need in his stormy eyes like a drug and surrendered to him. Sealing the distance between us, my chest collided with his. His hands slipped under my top, found bare skin, and began working their way up my back.

I lowered my head to meet his mouth. Willingly, I lost reality and cared not to find it ever again. I tightened my legs around his waist and raised my hands to his neck, cupping his jaw to deepen the kiss. I tasted his tongue, his teasing. His hands worked up my ribs, inching toward my pounding heart, and I moaned against his mouth when his thumbs finally brushed the yearning tips of my breasts.

His mouth left mine to work its way down my throat. I slid my eyes open, arching my back as my spine came alive in a current of liquid lust. My hard nipples ached, aroused by his teasing. Skillful fingers weaved my body with threads of rippling pleasure. While his eyes held my lustful gaze, his hands found the edge of my top and slid it above my head. He twisted the material to trap my arms behind my back. He lowered his mouth to nibble at my collarbone.

His hair glowed in the blazing flames, an unruly mess of golden silk I yearned to touch, but my hands were tied behind me. I wriggled to free myself, brushing my breasts against his chest. I moaned in agony and frustration. Spasms of thick, electric pleasure built inside the hard tips of my breasts and shot through my chest, down to my navel, lapped at it, and, with renewed strength, worked through my belly to rush between my legs.

Gabe chuckled softly at my struggles and carefully lowered me onto the rug as I tugged to free my trapped arms. He knelt at my feet and peeled away my pajama bottoms, smiling at the sight of my black lace panties.

I struggled with my trapped elbows trying to set myself free, but he shook his head and stretched his body along mine.

I looked at him. "Free me, Gabe—"

He propped his head on his left elbow and hushed me with a finger on my mouth, his eyes about to unleash a storm.

I couldn't resist and provoked the gods. I wetted my lips with the tip of my tongue and licked his silencing finger. I opened my lips a bit more and used my teeth to bite, slowly wetting his fingertip with deliberate, light strokes.

Gabe tensed. His eyes shifted to a darker shade of craving. His leg worked its way between mine, suddenly weighing me down. He dropped his head, replacing his wet finger with his eager lips, distracting me from his hand slowly sliding down my throat. His hand made silent love to my breasts, lightly traced my navel, and inched lower. Against my mouth, his tongue flickered, explored, sucked, demanding my undivided attention until I felt his finger slide under my lacy panties, dipping right into my own melting core.

At one single, confident stroke, my head jerked. I bit my lips hard to stifle a scream.

My body twisted like burning wire beneath his intimate strokes. I dug my trapped fingers into the rug, losing all sense of reality.

Slow and light at first, his touch intensified. Unhurriedly rubbing my sensitive fold, he brought me toward the aching edge of climax, only to stop instants before rapture became madness. Need ripened between my taut hips. My arms ached behind my back, and my voice swallowed pleading words he could read as easily in my unfocused, liquid eyes. *Oh! Dio mio!* What kind of torture was this?

My eyes dropped to his now still hand disappearing under my black panties. The visual image alone of his strong fingers cupping between my legs threw me into another yearning frenzy. I raised my hips to encourage his touch, to demand it. He held still, looking at my face. I held his gaze, licked my lips, and pushed up against his fingers.

Two can play this game.

Or so I wrongly thought.

He drove me crazy with yearning, holding still against my thrusting hips, allowing me to control intensity yet delaying my release. My breath raced, my heart wanted to explode.

Finally, he slowly resumed the stroking to meet my quickening rhythm. His fingers wet, coated with my sexual essence, dipped even deeper, searching for that secret spot . . . and found it. I felt his left arm slide beneath my neck to support my head just before I crashed against the last wave of surging pleasure. Exploding in a rush of ecstasy behind my trembling eyelids, I whispered his name.

*

He reached over to free my arms. His solid chest brushed my pounding heart, and he released me.

I rubbed stiffness off my wrists while Gabe grabbed some pillows from the sofa and looked at me, adjusting a pillow behind my head. "Are your arms OK?" He brushed a wandering lock of hair off my moist forehead.

It took me a second to cast myself out there to find my voice. I nodded. "Yes," I managed to whisper.

He knelt by my legs. With one questioning look he placed his hands on my hips, awaiting permission. I held no resistance. I looked at him, wordlessly lifting my hips.

He cracked a sensuous grin that held forbidden promises. "You're absolutely stunning, Porzia." Hunger, passion, and tenderness deepened his voice. "I don't want to do anything that you might have second thoughts about," he whispered, caressing my legs, pulling my panties down.

I raised myself on my elbows and looked at him, my love spilling out, reaching. *Beautiful, incredibly beautiful. Surreal.* "Do you want me?" I curled a finger over the elastic band of his shorts.

"More than life itself, luv," he answered, covering my hand with his.

"I want you too." So badly I couldn't think straight.

I helped him slide off his shorts and leaned back against the soft rug, adjusting my head on the pillow. I parted my legs to welcome him.

His breath brushed against my skin, his eyes ate me up, his scorching fingers branded my thighs when he lifted me up to meet him. The moment swept me off into a delirious, delicious spiraling of senses. I felt him ready, hard against my soft moistness.

He entered me, inch by inch, stretching me, filling me up, until my yearning became intense heat. Pulsing pleasure soared us to where nothing else mattered but fulfillment. Physical boundaries vanished. Our tangled bodies throbbed in unison, releasing an intensely intoxicating scent. It coated us in a sexual aura that fed us with each breath, each pang of pleasure that drummed out of us.

Wanting more, I raised my hands up to his neck and brought him down to me. I wanted to kiss him.

He held his head just inches away from my mouth, slowly sliding out of me, slowly thrusting back in, teasing me. I drowned in a pool of thick, undiluted lust.

He kept up his teasing rhythm, his mouth lingering over mine, his eyes intent on capturing every shade of pleasure my face reflected, feeding off the ecstasy he himself was conjuring.

I was soon ready to burst. "Please—" I begged, wrapping my legs around his, throwing my head back in total surrender.

He felt my hips tense against the built up reef, a helpless sea creature crashing with the surging tide. He lowered his mouth to mine, cupping my buttocks with his strong hands. With a few everlasting, hard strokes he drove us both over the edge, spilling release like scorching lava. Intense pleasure radiated from within, supporting our fall until he finally collapsed on me, heart against heart, still kissing me, still holding me.

We lay there, our glowing, entwined bodies warmer than the fire's embers. The soothing rhythm of our slowing heartbeats gently lulled us back to this side of life, a warm breeze supporting a dancing, descending feather.

*

I must have fallen asleep in Gabe's arms, for only vaguely did I remember him carrying me into the bedroom.

I woke up in his bed to my last morning with him. Our lovemaking lingered, still-wet tempera tenderly painted across my aching body. The memory of my intense pleasure churned in my stomach, wrestling with the rising dread of my imminent departure.

Merda! Talk about sweet and sour. I didn't want this to end so soon. I opened my eyes and took a second to adjust to the outside brightness invading the room. The insensible day sang loudly, sunny and bright, oblivious to my despair and miserable mood. I wished for a slingshot to deflate the sun to my sullen, gloomy level, to drag humankind down with me. I looked at Gabe asleep next to me and traded the slingshot for a Patriot missile. My sense of helpless rage rose dangerously the more I thought about the unfairness of the situation.

He looked so incredibly handsome wrapped in the safe embrace of sleep. Some people look more vulnerable when asleep. Gabe didn't. He still retained that strong masculine energy that so attracted me to him, as if even in his sleep the gods respected and acknowledged him as kin.

I wondered about his scarred back. *How long did he take to heal? Were there more scars?* The invisible ones were the ones I worried about. I had the feeling that just like mine, his healing wasn't quite over yet, and at the same time, a thin thread—a life connection—kept him in touch with whoever or whatever energies were responsible for saving his life. I could feel it threading just beneath his skin, like crystal water rippling through a rocky riverbed, following its course from source to ocean.

*

My plane left in the early evening, so I still had some time to share with him, and I resolved to make the best of it. Carelessly throwing all caution to the wind, I reached over and gently shook him, whispering in his ear a naughty request.

He stirred in his sleep, responding to my soothing voice. He stretched his arms above his head and smiled.

"I don't know about that," he mumbled, still half asleep.

"You mean I have to be more persuasive?" I asked, nuzzling his earlobe with my nose. I began to kiss him and moved my body on top of him. "Is this better?" I reached above his head to stroke his arms with my hands.

"We're getting there," he said. He blinked his sleepy eyes open to look at me. "What all did you have in mind?" His honeyed eyes told me that no matter what I thought of doing, he would be more than willing to agree to it.

"Uh—nothing. Just wanted to give you a quick good morning." I kissed his forehead and pretended to slide off him.

He quickly trapped my feet with his and sprang his arms to grab my wrists. "Tease."

I squirmed a bit trying to free myself and managed to arouse him even more.

"That's only going to aggravate the situation," he said.

A small dark place in me stirred alive, quite pleased. I found myself slowing down. I shifted my moves to a more seductive and insistent pulse to let him know I had every intention of finishing what I had begun. I used my hips and lower back to adjust myself in response to his swelling and braced myself against his chest.

He let go of my wrists, and his hands found my hips, guiding. His fingers sank in the curve of my butt, opening me up.

I plunged. I was more than ready and yet the impact of my aching, moist tenderness against his hardness stunned me. I crossed that line that marries pleasure to pain and cried out, bowing my back as he pierced his entire length deep inside me in one hard, agonizing thrust. He held me tight, giving me a chance to find my breath.

Like a surging tide, wet and foamy, my sexual impulse awakened, stirred, spread.

Slowly, I moved.

Physical craving manifested from age-old instinct. My senses burned, fueled by hunger and the advantageous position of being on top. I leaned in, flexing my inner muscles tight around his entire swollen length and sought sheer friction as I slid up and down, lingering on the edge of its larger tip. I swept my hips in a circular move and pushed back down, pulling him along, my pace quickened under the hastening pressure of his hands guiding my hips until blind raging bliss flared.

The initial pain faded, erased by the strong, magic strokes of our lovemaking. Pleasure thickened from a tiny flame flickering deep inside me to an enraged fire that consumed my whole body. It exploded, ricocheting madly against my skin from the inside out. With a sharp intake of breath, Gabe responded to my aggressive attentions. No longer capable of holding back, he shot me a sensuous look that flared pleasure through me instantaneously. Rising, rising, rising, the plunging rhythm of flesh against flesh exploded into a ferocious crescendo of excruciating pleasure, finally liberating us.

*

He rolled over and I stretched along his body. A single heartbeat drummed against our heaving chests. We lay quietly enjoying our fluffed-up auras until rigor mortis almost set in, and our stiffened limbs begged for mercy.

"I'd offer to cook you breakfast but I believe it's about lunch time," Gabe said.

"It's that late already?" I asked, looking around his bedroom for a clock.

"No, I was exaggerating." He watched me for a few minutes as if trying to memorize my features.

I held his gaze.

"Porzia, I don't know what's going to happen with this—," he began, combing a hand through his hair. His words held the hesitation of a newborn wave lapping at foreign shores for the very first time. "But I mean it when I call you 'luv.' This has all the roight signs to be the real thing." He looked at me. His soul spilled through dark lashes.

My heart skipped and made a run for my throat. I swallowed and pulled the sheet up my chest. I tried to smile, drowning shamelessly against surging tears.

"Gabe, I know—I feel it too." Forgetting all about the fact I had just tried to cover myself, I sat up to hug him tightly. The tears in my eyes made him a dreamy vision of liquid blue and gold, but the solid strength of his body told me he was real—painfully real.

"I know this is fast, and we don't have much time," he whispered in my ear, "but if you do have any time off soon, I want you to know that you need to get back here." He pulled back to see my eyes.

I bit the inside of my lip. I nodded, blinking tears away.

"You're absolutely adorable, Porzia." He wiped my tears away. "I'm my own boss, and as soon as I straighten a couple of things out, I'm coming over to see you in Florida. That is, if you want me to." He grinned, confident.

Delight burst through me. I smiled idiotically.

"How long is it going to take you to sort those things?" I asked, rubbing my nose with the back of my hand in an extremely unladylike manner.

"I'm not quite sure; no longer than a month, I guess."

"I'll work it out so I'll have time off to spend with you," I said, already making mental plans to shift a couple of imminent projects.

"Great. Then it's settled. I don't know how you feel about a long distance relationship, luv, but I'm diving into this head first." He caressed my cheek with the back of a bent finger.

I rubbed my face against his strong palm and inhaled the night just passed lingering on his skin. "I'm diving with you, Gabe." I planted a light kiss on his open palm.

We ended up sharing the shower, skipped breakfast, and worked toward an early lunch.

Why was I so concerned with food anyway? I wondered, once finally out of the bathroom. With hair wrapped in a thick towel, I rummaged through my luggage for fresh clothes to wear on the plane and involuntarily dropped the dice again. One and one: Two. Once more.

Interesting. I shrugged off the coincidence and a short-lived pang of discomfort and concentrated on my wardrobe. Flying back to summer, layers were in order. I set my sneakers aside, along with jeans, a short-sleeved shirt, and a periwinkle sweater. Gabe was still in the bathroom and didn't emerge until I had just finished getting dressed. I was tying my shoes when my towel decided to unwrap itself from my bent head. I was left sitting on the side of the bed, elbows resting on my bent knees, glancing at a very naked Gabe from beneath the thick, safe curtain of my wet, tangled hair.

He looked like something Atlantis might have left behind before sinking away forever beneath the waves, breathing proof that the gods still walked among us. Confident and strong, he moved about the room with the weightless grace and latent energy of a predator. He moved without hurry, as if air turned into clouds closer to his body, surrounding him. His body glistened with myriad drops of water.

The thought of kissing him dry, slowly, taking my time, became a yearning. I sighed; if only we had such time. His hair, still wet, was combed back carelessly in thick, sun-kissed wheat strands. In the back of my throat, I could taste his heat pulsing beneath the lingering fragrance of his shower soap. The sight of him getting dressed became my present focus. Black boxers went up, riding along his strong legs, followed by a pair of faded jeans that had seen better days and a black T-shirt I recognized as the one he wore on the plane when we met. He kept his feet bare.

"Hungry?" His voice startled me back to reality.

"Starving." I pushed my hair away from my face, combing it with my fingers. I tucked the dice in one of the suitcase's internal pockets, clicked the suitcase shut, and gave him a dazzling smile.

"Let's go see what we can come up with." He extended a hand to help me off the bed.

*

"Would you like some coffee?" I asked, hoping he would, knowing I did.

"Sure," his voice answered from inside the fridge.

He handed me a chilled coffee can, and I got busy setting up the coffee pot.

We quickly found bread, smoked salmon, eggs, tomatoes, and a ripened cantaloupe which I sliced and drizzled with lemon juice.

Gabe turned the radio on as I made a fluffy omelet. We soon sat to enjoy a nice brunch, good music, and each other's company.

"You mentioned a dog named Tess the other night when you told me the Dhamala story. She's in the photo with you and the eagle?" Saying the eagle's name gave me chills. I felt as if I was summoning her presence.

"Yes. Clark has Tess now at his place. I left her there when I went to Los Angeles. They get along, and he likes the company."

"He's alone?"

"Yes. Never remarried nor is he thinking about it."

"Still loves your mom?"

Gabe nodded. "He's come to terms with her death but doesn't seem to be keen on the idea of another woman by his side."

"And you?"

He shot me a quick glance, then focused on his mug. "You make outstanding coffee."

"Thanks."

"It doesn't taste like this when I make it."

"Do you usually have coffee in the mornings?"

"Yes. And toast. Sometimes eggs."

"Do you usually shower before going to bed or in the mornings?" I asked.

"Strange question. Why is it important?"

"I just want to know so I can imagine you once I'm home." I tried not to sound too sad.

"I do both but prefer the evening shower, usually. After having worked on a car at the shop all day."

"Do you ever take baths?"

"No." He smiled. "But we can change that if you'll take one with me—" He stopped as if he had just remembered something. "I take that back. I end up taking a bath every time I wash Tess." He smirked.

"I'm going to miss you," I confessed, looking up at him, riding on the tail of his lingering crooked grin.

He reached over the table to take my hand in his. "This was sort of unexpected."

"Tell me about it," I agreed, squeezing his hand.

"Even more precious because of it."

"How long a drive is it to get to the airport from here?" I asked.

"About half an hour." He pushed himself up.

"That doesn't leave us much time," I said, getting up myself.

He walked around the table to take me in his arms. I returned his embrace and leaned my head against his chest.

"Is there is anything you need to do before going back?" he asked.

"As a matter of fact, I need to stop by a florist and send some flowers to the Jourdains."

"We can do that on our way to the airport. Anything else?"

I took a deep breath and locked eyes with him. "I'd like to stop time and slowly enjoy every still second with you. I'd like to forget all about out there and allow only your arms around me to matter. I'd like to start over and re-live every delicious moment I've had the pleasure to share with you so far, from the way your hair feels through my fingers down to the tip of your toes wiggling against mine in bed."

That stole a smile from him.

"And only the fact that I know the future will bring me even more intense pleasure gives me the strength to go ahead and allow time to move as it ought to."

There, I said it! *Spelled*, like a true sorceress. Laced with only the purest of my intentions. I cast my wish out there, aware that by merely wishing, it would manifest. Was that the true power of magic? To shed all fears, to ride the power of pure love uncontaminated by obstacles we create?

"That's it! You're not going anywhere." He lowered his mouth to mine and kissed me ever so tenderly. I melted in his arms, as if becoming part of him would take care of all our troubles.

And so it was that time answered my plea, and what little we had of it lasted for what seemed like forever, and we had time to talk, make plans for the future, and even laugh as we held each other until it was time for me to go.

The drive to the airport and the stop at the flower shop were quiet, weighted by my imminent departure. And yet, a strong undercurrent—a certainty that all would be fine—kept us from drowning in sorrow.

How strangely the mind works when, in desperate situations, we make a point of focusing and remembering the simplest and least important details. I will remember forever the fact that the airport's waiting area was almost empty.

I turned to look at Gabe and opened my mouth to attempt a good-bye. I closed my mouth and swallowed my heart in a hard lump.

Gabe didn't look as though he was faring any better. He actually had a pair of sunglasses perched up high on his head. I knew he was going to wear them on his way out. His eyes were already fighting a red rim that reminded me of what happens to the moon when a cold front approaches.

I tried to smile. I looked up at him and rose on my tiptoes, resting my hands on his strong chest. "You were wearing this shirt on the plane," I said against his mouth.

His strong arms wrapped around my waist, and his mouth brushed mine. "Yes, I was."

Oddio, I was gonna miss his arms. "You were looking out the window when I sat down next to you. I couldn't wait for you to turn so I could see your face," I whispered.

"I had you there for a moment. When I asked you to hold my hand."

"Yes, you did." I smiled, thinking about how now it sounded so unusual. "I believed you for a second or two."

"When you looked at me with those bright eyes of yours and shook my hand, I didn't want to let go," he said in a breath that sent shivers down my spine.

"Then you gave me a rainbow and made me laugh. I felt totally spellbound. You fed me and let me hold you as we slept. Once we landed, I wanted to take you straight home. It was hard to see you go then." He took a deep breath. "It's harder to see you go now." He exhaled, but his grip tightened at my waist. "But I'll see you soon, and we'll have plenty of time to make more memories."

His words went straight to my heart. Carefully, I wrapped them with the strength of my love to cherish for the rest of my days.

CHAPTER 15

What kind of sins did I commit for karma to hit me like this?
My journey to Melbourne ended up being a sad affair of tears, nose blowing, and moans of despair.

I jumped off the plane the instant the door opened and sought a phone like a newborn seeks air after the slap.

I dialed his number. It didn't work. The wretched phone kept on swallowing coins like a black hole until I ran out of Australian change. I shoved my credit card down its throat. Exasperated, I finally managed to get hold of an operator and had her connect me to Gabe's home number.

The connection rang and rang until the machine picked up. No answer. *Merda!* I was about to leave a message when—dear heaven, if his voice didn't answer.

"Hey, luv! Where're you calling from?" he said, his voice sounding surprised and strong.

"Melbourne. I just landed and have a couple of hours to wait around for my connection to LA," I whispered, leaning my forehead against the cold metal of the phone box.

"I'm glad you rang. Are you OK?"

Tears welled up in my eyes. "I miss you, and I got really upset on the plane, leaving you like that and all."

"I know. It was hard." I heard him take a deep breath. "I miss you already, and I wish I could have you back here, never to leave my side." His voice faded behind the mad thumping of my heart. I panicked, afraid it would drown out his words with its furious drumming.

"Porzia, if you tell me to, I'll have a ticket for you to get back here instead of going home, waiting for you at the Qantas counter in fifteen minutes. Just say the word."

Is that what I wanted?

Yes! Yes! You idiot! my heart screamed, almost giving itself a stroke, killing me right then and there. I wondered about Australian funerals. I saw hopping kangaroos carrying my casket in the shadow of Ayers Rock with a blazing sunset behind the imposing, ancient monolith casting the surroundings in a deep, red glow.

Did they still burn witches in this country? I took a deep breath. "Gabe? Do you know how tempting that sounds? Thank you so much for even thinking of such a sweet gesture. I'd love to be able to with all my heart, but there are things that need tending to, and I am needed back home."

"I know. But I'll be damned if I care about responsibilities right now, Porzia, luv. You're still so bloody close I can taste you. And the thought of you getting farther away by the minute drives me bloody mad. I know you need to go back and take care of all you've got planned and that we'll see each other soon enough, but still I can't help wanting you back. You just have to leap, and I'll catch you, luv."

I held on to his strong voice.

I swept my head back, taking in the foreign, aseptic surroundings of the airport. A river of strangers coursed around me, an unraveling of unfamiliar smells, colors, and vibrations. "That's not the kind of leaping I'm struggling with," I whispered, closing my eyes. "Gabe, you're gonna have to tell me to be strong, and you're gonna have to be strong for both of us right now." I began to cry. "Because I can't." *Oh, merda!*

"We'll be there soon, luv," I heard him answer softly. "Hang in there, and we're gonna be fine, Porzia."

I wiped my eyes with the back of my hand and swallowed hard, choking back a tidal wave of tears. "I'll call you once I get home to let you know I've made it alright."

"Please, I won't be able to sit still until I know you've made it."

"OK, then—"

"Have a safe flight and remember everything, Porzia. Don't let distance dilute our present."

"I won't," I snuffled. "I have my multicolored shadow following me," I said, remembering his words. I heard him laugh softly.

"It's not as colored as I could have made it with a little more time."

I felt myself blush. I smiled, lifting my head, and opened my eyes, remembering where I was. *Melbourne. Airport. People. Civilization. Clock. Ticking. Next connection.*

"I need to get going, Gabe."

"OK, luv."

"I'll talk to you soon."

"I'll be here." His loving words revived my spirit.

My hands shook as I hung up. I looked for my shadow. It was right where it was supposed to be, stretched and angled at the waist, along the near wall. I stood still for a few moments almost expecting it to wave at me. Finally, I grabbed my carry-on bag and went looking for presents for Benedetta and Evalena. While I shopped for a boomerang, my mind whirred.

I can handle the magic of putting ingredients together and making a dish by following a recipe. Even Madame Framboise had tapped into that one. But I'm not used to abstract, esoteric forces. I'm not sure how to go at embracing them. So how the hell did I end up falling in love with a former Australian racer who shared lifetimes with gods and shadows of mysterious entities? He made love to me like he was tracing his own words along my pages, touching my inner core with the flame of his soul igniting mine.

*

I ended up with a boomerang, a hand-painted reproduction of a David Malangi Daymirringu painting of *Dhamala, Catfish and Brown Snake*, tea tree oil and soap, and sheepskin slippers for Benedetta, having remembered that her last pair had been stolen and probably buried by her Doberman in her back yard.

Laden with the goods, I looked like the typical American tourist boarding the plane. At least my eyes were finally dry.

Mercifully, I fell asleep, my last thought trapped between my crossed fingers as I wished for answers.

*

"When your *own* Dreamtime erupts," he had said.

*

Part of me—most definitely the French part—screamed at full volume that it was about time, and woke me up just as the pilot performed a landing as smooth as a perfect béchamel sauce. Although jet lag most definitely ruled my body, I lit up when I saw Benedetta stretching her neck like E.T. trying to see through an unexpectedly large crowd for such a late hour.

She shot me a huge grin and blinked twice behind her gold-rimmed glasses. "You look like something I'd flush after a binge on Mexican food," she said, hugging me.

"Nice to see you too." I returned the hug and planted a loud kiss on her cheek.

"Yeah? Stop the smooching." She pulled away, straightening her glasses. "People might think we like each other." She flashed a look that meant she didn't give a fig what people thought, she was just embarrassed by my affectionate display.

"Did you have a good time?" she asked, grabbing some of my shopping bags and poking through them. "What did you bring me?"

"*Siii*. I did," I replied dreamily. I clutched my laptop carry-on bag to my chest as we walked toward the luggage carousel.

"Oh, oh, oh! What's his name?"

I just smiled at her while the carousel burped luggage. I found my bag, swung it off the conveyor belt, and gave Bene a look that said, "Can't talk now, my hands are full."

Prancing around like an overjoyed puppy, she followed me outside and did her best at trying to coax the information out of me.

"Oh, come on now—"

"Let's get in the car, and I'll tell you all about it." The muggy Florida air hit me like a shower. I shed my sweater; I was way overdressed for such weather but bare skin would not have cut it either.

She found her car, deftly loaded my bags, unlocked the passenger door, and ran to the driver's side. We sped out of the airport parking lot merging into an almost deserted late-night highway.

What a difference. I had been gone only a week, and it felt like an eternity. The magic of flying and being catapulted to the other side of the world in just over the length of a day; it would never cease to fascinate me.

"So? I'm all ears," Benedetta demanded.

I reached over and vigorously twisted her right ear. "That you are."

"*Ahia!* That hurts!" She swatted at my hand, and the car swerved.

I forgot that it's dangerous to interfere while she's driving. I took my hand back and turned to look out the window.

"Gabe Miller."

"Wow! Sexy name! Sounds like something out of a sassy novel."

"He looks like he ought to be on the cover of one," I said.

"Maybe I read that one." She frowned. "His name sounds familiar. Hang on—" She turned her right signal on and sharply left Highway 110 behind. At the traffic light she realized she was in the wrong lane to turn right off the ramp and cursed in Italian under her breath.

Her hands fluttered at the traffic light and the general surroundings. "I hate this spot," she said.

Suddenly, two deep parallel tracks, respectively named *incredulous* and *suspicious*, creased her forehead. "Gabe Miller? Porzia?"

I nodded.

Her mouth opened, she blinked twice, and soundlessly, her mouth closed.

Somebody behind us honked.

She woke up from her stupor, shifted gears, startled the rearview mirror into life cursing the mother of the driver behind us in Italian, and cleared out of the intersection.

"*The* Gabe Miller?" she asked once she found her voice. We were almost at my place by then.

"Which one are you referring to, Bene—?" I tried to stifle a yawn but failed.

"How many Australians named Gabe Miller are there?" she asked.

"I didn't say he was Australian."

"You're exasperating me." She turned to look at me. "Is he that particular one or is he not?"

"He is."

She whistled softly. "He won the Paris–Dakar."

"Twice."

"No shit!" She gripped her steering wheel with a little more pride. "You're right!" For no apparent reason she jammed on the brakes, and I just about collided with the dashboard. Her ancient seatbelt stretched like worn-out chewing gum.

"How do you know so much about off-road racing?" I was impressed by the fact that she had recognized the name when I had not.

"I don't really know that much, but a guy I dated in college was really into racing and that was big news back then. I heard him talk once, on TV," she said dreamily. I knew what she meant.

"I know. He's got a great voice." I started thinking of all the other great things he was. I shook my head. "How's Peridot?" I asked.

"He's a sweetie," Benedetta smiled. "You'll see for yourself. I told him you were coming."

"You talk to him?" My eyebrows shot up.

"Don't you?" She cast a surprised glance at me.

The speed bumps of my driveway stirred my dormant brain marbles back into action. I would have hit my head on the car roof if it weren't for the fact that with Benedetta driving, I hung on to the seat with both hands.

"Welcome home!" She smiled, screeching the car to a stop beneath my windows. Gingerly hopping around, she grabbed all the shopping bags and left the carry-on for me. Despite everything, it's always nice to feel welcomed home where there are familiar surroundings and belongings.

I left Gabe less than a day ago. I glanced at my watch and mentally tried to compare Australian and Floridian time. I needed to give it a rest—at least long enough for me to get inside and get some sleep.

*

Peridot jumped off his bed by the sofa and ran to greet me. Purring loudly, he coiled himself around my legs and sniffed my sneakers. He was ecstatic to see me. After dumping the bags, I grabbed my cat and greet him properly. Peridot rubbed his nose against my chin and couldn't stop purring, kneading my shoulder with his strong tiger paws. I almost felt like purring myself, his joy felt so contagious. *Crazy to think how much a tiny animal can influence one's moods,* I thought. Carrying Peridot, I looked around and noticed fresh flowers on the kitchen counter and new candles scattered around. The place looked great, clean and neat.

"Bene, you did a fantastic job. My herbs are thriving!" I walked with Peridot still in my arms to the bathroom windowsill to sniff at the oregano box I keep there.

"No big deal. It was clean to begin with." She shrugged. "I just had to keep it."

Peridot started munching on some of the tender leaves but stopped as soon as the pungent flavor reached his taste buds. He looked funny, making faces as he tried to get rid of the bad taste in his mouth.

"I'd love to stay and grill you about the details of your trip," Benedetta said, jingling her car keys, "but it's indecent timing, and you need to rest." She pranced to hug me. "Call me if you need anything when you wake up tomorrow."

"I will. Thanks for everything." I returned her hug, squishing the cat between us.

I walked her to the door and waited on my threshold until her car bounced out of the parking lot. I closed my front door behind me and let Peridot down as I headed for the bathroom to quickly freshen up. Exhausted, I grabbed a pair of short pajamas and climbed into bed to call Gabe, struggling to mentally calculate the time difference once again. I tried his home first.

The first ring came and went, echoing in my ears; the second came and went, chipping a couple of my heartbeats away. He answered right in the middle of the third ring, settling my heart.

"Hi, it's me," I said, crushing pillows, releasing the familiar scent of my laundry detergent. Peridot jumped on the bed purring and sniffed my feet.

"Porzia. How you going? Did you have a good trip?" His voice sounded like he was right around the corner.

"Well, I was extremely upset about leaving you, but the planes were mostly empty all the way back here, so I managed to churn myself into sleep."

"Great, so you didn't meet any great-looking Aussies this time?" he asked, laughing.

"No. Nobody asked me to hold their hands," I teased.

"You sound tired."

"I am, and my cat is biting my toes," I said, pulling my feet away from Peridot.

"Smart cat," he answered in a sexy voice.

I laughed and blushed, remembering his nibbling.

"How about you get some sleep, and I'll ring you tomorrow sometime?"

"Sounds good." I slid deeper under the sheets.

"Thanks for letting me know you got there all roight. It's a long trip."

"I know, tell me about it." I yawned, almost locking my jaw wide open. *Oddio!* I was tired.

"OK, get some rest, luv."

"Goodnight. I miss you," I whispered.

"I miss you too. Bye."

I hung up with his voice still warm in my ears and pulled the sheets almost all the way up to my head. I fell asleep with Peridot purring contentedly at my now covered feet.

CHAPTER 16

The fluorescent-green digits of my nightstand clock diagnosed me with a bad case of acute jet lag. It's a bitch. The first concrete thoughts to blaze through my sleepy mind were of Gabe and what he might be doing at that exact moment. They fired my body like a torch set to parched underbrush on a torrid August day. Longing swept over me. An abrupt sense of unconquerable distance brought tears to my eyes. I rolled over and caught a glimpse of the world outside the window. In the breaking dawn, birds barely stirred. I had hoped for at least several hours of uninterrupted rest, but the fires burned too hot to stay in bed.

Spurred on, I thumped to the bathroom. A long shower washed away the remains of sleep and any traveling cosmic matter that might still be clinging to me.

Wrapped in my favorite oversized bathrobe I padded around my condo opening windows, smelling the fresh ocean breezes. The morning was about to explode crystal clear. Not a single cloud stained the little slice of purple-blue sky peeking through the Spanish moss draping the ancient oak in my back yard. I unpacked my clothes and hung the Dhamala painting in a corner of my living room. I stepped back to better take a look at it when a sleepy Peridot rubbed slowly against the hem of my robe. He yawned impossibly wide. I could see all the way down his tiny esophagus; it was empty. We set off for the kitchen. It was time for coffee anyway.

While Peridot attacked a breakfast of crunchy bits, I settled in with a double espresso with double sugar and wondered what time it was in Australia. I wanted to go for a run along the beach, then pop into the Napoleon Bakery for fresh *pains au chocolat*, and knock on Benedetta's door to get her out of bed.

I thought about it and decided to go ahead; my answering machine could trap any calls I might miss. I rinsed my cup, slipped into my running shorts, and grabbed some cash, Benedetta's presents, and my car keys. I ran out the door trying to get a head start on the rising humidity.

I live only about ten minutes from endless dunes of white sand, but since the last hurricane, the beach road I used to run on has been closed off, and who knows when it will be reopened. Instead, I drove over the Gulf Breeze Bridge where I parked at the entrance of the Sound National Park. I soon found myself running on a trail shaded by dwarf pines edged with saw palmettos, yuccas, and fiddlehead ferns. The pungent scent was almost alien, so different was it from the fragrant Australian acacias. I had Nine Inch Nails on my Walkman and a load of frustration to fuel my pace. Lost in thought, I left behind the sandy dunes and ended up in a somewhat familiar neighborhood behind Evalena's temporary dwellings. The jolly yellow paint I had irrationally resented on my first visit looked cheerful and warm. In a bathrobe that defied any sort of fashion sense, Evalena was happily watering some obscure bush. Three words: chenille, purple, daisies, and I am not describing the bush.

I paused, jogging in place. "Evalena?" I called from behind the short net fence.

She turned, raising her head. Her oversized watering can magically spilled a wet rainbow against the sunlight.

"Oh! Hello there! I was just thinking of you. When did you get back?"

I stopped jogging. "Last night."

She dropped the watering can, walked over to hug me—sweat and all—then asked if I'd care for a glass of tea. Evalena's sunshine tea is worth dying for any time of day. Formosa Oolong, dried Georgia peaches, candied orange zest, and something secret even my gourmet-trained taste buds fail to identify, all left to steep and brew in warm sunshine.

I told her I was going to be able to stay only a few minutes. Once we were settled in her sunlit kitchen, she asked me if I had a nice trip.

"Yes, I did have a nice trip. As a matter of fact, I met somebody interesting. I also had a true gypsy do a tarot reading for me, and I believe the magic has awakened." I shook my head. "I'm extremely confused by it all." I paused to take a sip of what the gods used to call *Amrita*, hoping its magic powers would actually stretch beyond quenching my thirst and give me answers.

"Have you ever thought about selling your secret recipe for this stuff?" I asked, pointing at the pitcher lazily soaking in the sun. Sweat beads trailed down the handblown, green glass.

"Yes, but then it wouldn't be a secret any longer." She gave me an enigmatic smile, sipping from her own glass. "What did the cards tell you?"

"Not much. By the time things started to get interesting Neige jumped on the spread and scattered my fate."

Evalena speaks French. She gave me a dumbfounded look. "It *snowed* on the cards?"

"No, that's the name of a fluffy white cat," I said, pleased with my little joke.

She shook her head and snorted daintily.

"The cards confirmed some of what I'd seen with you in the regression and announced the arrival of a new romance." I paused to sip my tea and frowned, remembering something disturbing. "I had the Magician as opposing brewing forces—"

"And a new love interest?"

"Yes, a Two of Cups?"

"Do you remember any of the cards that the cat disrupted?"

I was silent for few minutes, focusing backwards on that afternoon, but to no avail. I shook my head. "No, I don't."

"It could be that the Magician and the Two of Cups are inescapably linked," she said in a voice that made me think.

Gabe? A magician? Did she mean Gabe or did she have someone else in mind?

I suddenly remembered his scars and the way he recognized certain electric moments between us. *But then, why would he be an opposing force?* I looked up at Evalena who seemed again to have read my mind.

"He's intriguing," she stated.

I nodded.

"That's why you're attracted to him?"

I loved how she didn't even concern herself with taking the regular route of name, looks, business, and bank account info, all of which average women worry about. Evalena's intuition went straight to the core: Gabe's enigmatic energy.

"Part of it, I have to admit. He doesn't volunteer a lot of info, has this uncanny ability to switch the subject on a whim, but what he shared, like even a simple story of a wounded eagle, gave me a direct insight into what sort of man he is." I smiled. "The fact that I am *extremely* attracted to him physically doesn't hurt either."

"So this brewing force might not necessarily mean opposing. Perhaps it's just protection," Evalena ventured. She paused and looked at me pensively. "How much do you know about the Tarot?"

"Nothing."

"The suits are events and people in your life. The Major Arcana is higher awareness, ether. I would be keen on interpreting this Two of Cups as a terrestrial romance, while perhaps the Magician is a higher power. It could be that the Magician's influence obstructs the Two of Cups, for the latter is on a journey to fulfill his destiny, and you might change his heart. He might not be whom you're meant to be with. Remember the journey you now need to honor." She arched an eyebrow and then dismissed her own words with a quick hand gesture. "Anyhow, it's all speculation on my part. I shouldn't even plant such ideas in your mind. I wasn't there to feel the cards."

"It might or might not be," I said, with a pinch of my old skepticism. "But I've also experienced your intuition as a powerful weapon of divination. So there might be hidden truth in your interpretation of those scattered cards."

"What about the magic awakening?"

"Well, Evalena, when I promised Grandmother I had no clue how to harness the power. Once I arrived in Australia I was still questioning whether I wanted it or not. I can't honestly say when or how I consciously chose to dismiss my fears and inadequacies, or if the magic did it, but I played with it. Of course I tried with Gabe first but felt only a flutter of wings."

Evalena's eyebrows shot up. "You just gave me chills."

I continued, "Then, on another totally different occasion, I felt the heartbeat of a forest. And at last I was able to tap into the core of Gabe's bond with his mechanic Gomi."

"Not through Gabe," she stated.

"No. He's way too guarded. I sense that much."

"You need to honor his privacy, Porzia."

"Yes, I know," I smirked. "I just ask direct questions instead."

She shook her head. "What is your favorite fairy tale, Porzia?"

I shot her a wary look. "What does that have anything to do with all this?"

"Just answer."

"Can I think about it?"

She nodded. "And your grandmother's?"

I smiled. I knew that one. Joséphine and my mother shared a favorite: *The Little Mermaid*.

"Ah! Of course. Liquid women."

I laughed. "Yes, but you haven't told me why you're asking."

"Archetypes and women's transformation. You might consider it a fair warning."

Now that sounded extremely intriguing. I'd always had a feeling that Joséphine regretted trading her mermaid tail for legs. Metaphorically speaking, she had given up her elements—even her magic—to be with *Grand-père*. And just like in the fable, he turned out to be a prince with flaws.

My mother on the other hand . . .

Speaking of grandfathers, Evalena's majestic clock rang the hour and I realized how late it was.

"Evalena, I'm afraid I need to run, but I'd like to talk about this archetypes business some more." I gave her a quick hug and promised to come back soon for supper with one of the Shiraz bottles I'd brought home.

As I jogged back to my car, I thought about her words. I didn't particularly want to focus on a journey that would eventually empower me to be with a potential soul mate who wasn't Gabe. My feelings for Gabe grounded me. The idea of making my choices based on the hands dealt me by a deck of strange icons didn't appeal to me, especially since I didn't even get a complete reading. My misgivings made my mind up while I drove to the bakery downtown.

I dodged the pastry chef's sappy flirting with practiced skill. Etienne is otherwise known as Pepé Le Pew, not because he has an *odeur*, but because he acts like the little overly affectionate cartoon character. The white streak crowning his otherwise jet-black coiffure might have something to do with the nickname too. Benedetta always gets a kick out of visiting him.

I'm gonna start kicking, I thought as I stood in front of Benedetta's front door with a wrapped tray of chocolate pastries warming my left hand. I knocked for the third time in ten minutes. Another human would have given up. I knew better. *We've been through this before,* I thought, while a huge plant of rosemary, usually engaged in defending the front door from evil spirits, prickled my legs. I remembered that much about rosemary and its powers from my first interview with Evalena. Later, on a trip to visit Joséphine, I noticed how she had gigantic bushes by the left side of her garden entrance.

I heard a noise. Moments later a disheveled, crooked-glasses Benedetta opened the door.

"About bloody time!"

"Oh, it's you." She yawned in my face, opening the door wider to let me in.

I took one look at her and . . . *Good Gawd! What was wrong with everybody's clothes this morning?* "Is that what you sleep in these days?"

She swirled around to better show me the effect of the nightie barely covering her behind. "Do you like it?" she asked, coming to a precarious stop, whirling for her balance like an ice skater after a triple jump.

"Oh, that's why you're wearing it. For *me* to like?" I laughed. "Looks like something you'd wear to audition for a brothel."

"You're just jealous because they don't make them big enough to fit somebody your size." She pointed at my chest.

I raised an eyebrow and silently looked her up and down. The flabbergasting piece of flimsy material and too-little lace defied gravity and broke several laws of decency all in one short fall. It shouted in a ruby shade of red with black trimming and strategically placed cherries. I kid you not. Cherries. Not just printed ones. We are talking of plump red appliqués the size of marbles. Two at a time, hanging here and there.

"Those don't hurt to sleep on?"

She took one in her fingers and squeezed. "No, they've been pitted."

That's Benedetta for you.

"I don't think what I've got in the car will match your negligee," I said, thinking about the lambskin slippers I'd bought her.

Her eyes lit up. "It doesn't matter—whatever it is, I'll love it. Now, go get it." She shoved me out the door but snatched the pastries. "I'll start coffee!" she yelled.

As I ran back to my car, I mused that at least she hadn't offered to go get it herself. There must be laws against such public display of cherries.

We ended up on her patio sharing *pains au chocolat* with cappuccino for her and ice cold milk for me. She loved the slippers and slid them on, stretching her legs—not too far, given their length—admiring them and commenting on how soft and comfy they were. Her Doberman, a sleek, sexy beast she aptly named Eros, came by to sniff at her feet but soon lost interest when she engaged him in a game of catch with the boomerang I had just given her. She had no clue how to throw it to make it come back, so it was just as well she had Eros to retrieve it.

"So, are you glad to be back?" she asked, licking chocolate off her fingers; never mind the streaks on her cheeks and the handlebar moustache. But then, I had my own smears to worry about.

"It's nice to be home with you, with Peridot. To sleep in my bed and drive my car." I looked at her. "But I haven't been back long enough for it all to register."

"What's going to happen now?" Her look told me she worried I would move to Australia.

"I'm going to take it one day at a time and see what develops." I paused and took a long breath. "I like him a lot, Benedetta. But I know it's not going to be easy." I leaned back in the chair.

She shrugged, moving cherries I had not yet noticed. "It's going to be what you make of it. As difficult or as easy as you'll let it." She smiled and petted Eros, who had just brought the boomerang back. "Are you falling in love?"

"I think so." I felt all warm inside as I said it.

Both she and the dog tilted their heads and nodded in sappy agreement. I guess with a name like Eros, he believed himself an expert in such matters, therefore entitled to express his approval or lack thereof. Maybe he was just trying to snatch the boomerang from Benedetta's hands.

It was getting too hot for philosophical matters. Jet lag had begun to descend on me like a dull guillotine, hitting my neck right between head and shoulders.

"Bene, I'm going to go ahead and get back home." I stood and began to clear the table.

"You look like you could use a nap," she said. She followed me inside, carrying the rest of the dishes. "Just leave everything in the sink. I'll take care of it in a minute."

I did as she told me and quickly hugged her.

"I'm happy for you, Porzia," she said.

"*Grazie.*"

"I'm happy for myself. If you found somebody then there is hope for the rest of us," she chuckled.

"Let's just hope your cherries won't rot while you wait." I squeezed one of her cheeks and barely managed to avoid her kick.

*

I meant it when I told Benedetta about being happy to be back. There is a certain serene quality in coming home to find things as they were left, a strength and comfort in the idea that no matter what, there is a safe haven waiting with familiar, welcoming warmth.

All those loving feelings disappeared once I got home and noticed that there were no messages. I picked up my phone and listened to the dial tone, idiotically hoping it would explain why he hadn't called.

I hung up.

I grabbed the phone.

I shook it a couple of times.

I dropped it back on the cradle and pushed all the buttons on it, each and every one of them—repeatedly. I managed to erase my own answering message, messed up the time, and almost called 911 on the re-dial.

Then it rang.

I jumped out of my skin. *Merda! Maybe I did call 911.* They have a way of getting back at you. I saw it once on one of those TV cop shows. In the rush to answer, I knocked the phone to the floor. I knelt to grab the receiver with one hand, the phone with the other, and managed to crawl back into my skin. "Hello?" I said rather breathlessly.

"Porzia—" His voice rose from way down . . . way past that spot where the sun suddenly falls off the horizon.

"Hello, Gabe." I stretched my legs, sitting on the floor with my back against my bed.

"How you going, luv?"

"I'm fine," I exhaled dreamily. *Now that I'm talking to you,* my heart told him silently.

"Did you get some rest?"

"Not as much as I would have liked. I'm sure I'll sleep well tonight." There was no way I would be able to take a nap after this. *Thump. Thump. There went my heart.* "How are you?"

"I'm OK," he said. "Went to get Tess back from Clark. It was sort of empty here, especially after having you over for the last couple of days. Hard to sleep, too. It's almost three thirty in the morning here, but I wanted to hear your voice."

My thumping heart swelled and I closed my eyes, smiling to myself.

"Is she happy to be back?" I asked.

"Yes, like she never left. But I wanted to tell you that I had a great time while you were here and can't wait to spend some more with you."

"Even if I ask a lot of questions?"

"You've got more, eh?"

Smart man. "Of course I do. Of the introspective kind."

I believe I heard him groan. "Shoot. But I've got time for only one."

"What scares you the most?"

"Your questions, Porzia."

I burst out laughing. "I hope you're not serious."

"Roight. I've got one for you. What have you got goin' for the week?" he asked.

Amidst the laughter I had to think for a moment. "I'm driving to Georgia this Friday to write about beans for a different publication." I wondered if Benedetta would care to join me.

"Beans?" he asked.

I chuckled. "Yes. Beans."

"Sounds like fun, luv."

He had said he would only have time for one question. "Do you need to go?"

"Yes."

Dear God! This was going to be an intense ordeal. "Thanks for calling me. Sleep well."

"No worries. I miss you, luv. Cheers."

"I miss you too. Bye." I heard the soft click of his phone as I hung up my own receiver.

My bedroom's billowing blue curtains reminded me of his ever-shifting eyes. A week ago they were just meaningless curtains. And if the relationship failed, I'd resent them, find them impossible to stare at any longer. I would have to get rid of them.

Dropping my head I raised my legs and rested my cheek on my knee. As the curtain filled with the marine breeze, I silently asked for strength and guidance. I really, really liked the blue.

CHAPTER 17

Beans in Georgia; My next assignment after I polished, printed, and filed a copy of my Umeracha article for my records. I faxed and e-mailed the other copy to an eagerly awaiting Helen in Miami and moved on to the next adventure.

Benedetta ended up being quite taken with the idea of a weekend getaway before school started. The afternoon caught us driving up north, leaving the ocean and the pets safely lodged at the pet sitter's place.

I had spoken to Gabe earlier in the week, and although the distance between us was a stretch, it seemed we both had our minds set to make it work.

I did miss him. A lot. Every time I heard his voice over the phone, I questioned my reasons to come back home. A tiny, resonant voice kept on telling me to throw all caution to the wind and pack a bag to join him in Australia for the rest of my days.

I knew I was going to get the phone bill from hell. We used e-mail as well, but it didn't cut it. I didn't like the impersonality of it. I have a weird phobia about electronics and modern gadgets—I just don't trust them. I even call the magazines every time I fax my articles to let them know my stuff is on the way. Call me old-fashioned, but I like the sound of another human being's voice replying to me instead of a metallic beep-beep. I don't even own a cell phone. I refuse to.

Gabe, on the other hand, didn't seem to mind electronics at all. And here I was, struggling with the several phone numbers and e-mail addresses he'd given me. He was getting all sorts of semi-funny, frustrated messages, loving every single one of them. He asked why I didn't have a *mobile* and how would he get in touch with me while I was on my way to Georgia. I gave him Benedetta's cell phone number, and she began calling it a mobile as well. She got all worked up at the thought of receiving a phone call from the legendary Gabe Miller.

"How should I answer?" she wondered aloud as we drove through green pastures where cows lazily brushed flies from their sides, sending us pungent whiffs of country life.

While fidgeting with the radio, I shot her a puzzled look. "What do you mean, how should you answer?"

"Oh, just kidding. I'm a little apprehensive at the prospect of talking to him, though." She looked out the window. Low vegetation and straw-scented pastures edged the way. "How are we gonna know that we're in Georgia? It all looks the same to me."

"They should have a sign that says welcome to Georgia," I told her. I smiled as the wheels in my brain clicked with the idea of a potential prank. "By it they're going to have a little stand with a person offering peaches and information to folks driving up. Just like when you come to Florida they give you oranges . . ."

"Wow!" she said. "I sort of knew about the oranges, but I didn't know they did that in all the states."

I nodded. "But of course. Cheese in Wisconsin . . . corn in Kansas . . . barbeque in Missouri . . . suntan lotion or avocados in California—they've got to be different over there. Mardi Gras beads in Louisiana . . ." *Hmm, what else?* "Potatoes in Idaho . . . clam chowder in New England . . . lobster in Maine . . . peyote in Arizona . . . chilies in New Mexico . . . salmon in Washington . . . lines of credit and condoms in Nevada . . . hair spray and steaks in Texas—"

She hit me.

"*Ahia!*" I yelled, rubbing my leg where she had smacked me with her flip-flop. I noticed her toe polish. "Benedetta, that's a nice color," I said, admiring a pretty shade of pearly coral that set off her tanned feet.

She forgot all about me fibbing and lifted her foot up on the dashboard, gingerly admiring her pedicure. "It's called Vulva Peach."

Who was kidding whom here?

We drove in silence for a while, munching on some dried-fruit mix and listening to some depressing honky-tonk whining. I wondered if playing the songs backwards would make things better for the poor country fellow who lost dogs, women, jobs, and precious belongings; all in less time it would take them to spit a pinch of chew.

Benedetta opened a bottle of water and noisily gurgled some. I laughed, pointing at the approaching road sign welcoming us to Georgia. "Look." I slowed down. "We can stop and snap some pics if you'd like."

The water bottle gurgled and bobbed in agreement with her head.

The sun hung low in the western horizon beyond a grassy field where a distant pine forest ran endlessly along the road. Spectacular hues of purples and oranges streaked the sky against the solid black wall of trees. On our right, a waning moon rose, dragging along a darker mantle of dusking skies. We parked on the side of the road, and I snapped several photos of Benedetta hugging the Georgia sign. She does everything with the enthusiasm of somebody who almost died and was given a second chance. I love her dearly. I love her even more knowing that a few years back I might have lost her forever.

While in college she worked at a convenience store. One evening, during a graveyard shift, an idiot decided to rob the store. He hit Benedetta in the head with a jumbo beer can. He hit her really hard. She lost consciousness and was left for dead until a customer walked in and called an ambulance, saving her life. They caught the robber with the help of the security camera. He wasn't new at this; third strike and he was out. Benedetta followed the trial from her hospital room. Nevertheless, even knowing that he had been locked behind bars, she still struggled with safety issues for months afterwards. Hence, Eros, her trained Doberman killing machine. Once in a while she gets horrible migraines, but most of the time she's busy feeling, tasting, absorbing life, and hugging Georgia signs. And she discovered Wicca.

"Ready?" I asked her, before she would decide to get frisky with the sign and start licking it.

"Yeah," she said.

She jumped back in my car and landed on the forgotten water bottle on her seat, smashing it. "Uh—I think I just had an accident," she whined in a childlike voice. A dark stain spread like a shadow under her yellow shorts.

"Have you got a change of clothes?" I asked, assessing the damage.

"Yes, in my bag in the trunk." She hopped out of the car, dripping water as she went.

I popped the trunk open and heard her rummage through her stuff, whistling softly under her breath. She's an incredible whistler. We would have to hurry or the entire Georgia state bird population would soon show up to accompany her.

*

She was still whistling when we pulled into the well-lit parking lot of Aunt Delilah's Roadside Café.

The place buzzed with lively energy. I had to drive around the ample parking lot twice before I finally managed to squeeze my car in between two monstrous pick-ups, one of them sporting a huge rebel flag and a bumper sticker that read, "Fight violence, shoot back." Indeed.

We stepped out of the car, filling our lungs with the breezy evening air and a strong whiff of whatever was cooking inside. With watering mouths we walked up to a spacious front porch where customers chatted. One tickled a guitar and lazily rocked on a swing. I couldn't tell if they were waiting for tables or if they liked the food so much they had separation anxiety issues. Just like me a week earlier in Adelaide, but I was supposedly leaving the love of my life behind. These people had bean soup issues; but then, I hadn't tasted the soup yet.

Framed in ancient wood that must have been painted light green circa the Civil War, a mosquito screen introduced itself to us as the front door. Amazingly, it didn't squeak when we opened it. But who would have heard it anyway? The kind of southern blues that grips your soul reached our ears while our nostrils filled with the teasing aroma of smoked ham swirling weightlessly, directed by several ceiling fans working overtime.

The dining room was full. Packed.

As we entered, the entire room turned to look at us, and we stood there, a bit uncomfortably, taking it all in. I was wondering where to go from there when an older man wearing a stained apron welcomed us with a genuine gap-toothed grin. With a strong hand on my shoulder, he moved us to a table in the back of the restaurant by an open window.

"Welcome to Aunt Delilah's. What cannah get you to drink?" A crooked smirk hooked his ageless face, reminding me of a well-tanned Popeye.

Benedetta often and randomly reads my mind. "Nice to meet you, *Pop*. My name is Benedetta, and this here is my friend Porzia." She introduced me with her hand. "What do you recommend?"

Pop smiled. He patted Bene's head lightly and mumbled something about leaving it up to him. In less than two minutes he reappeared, out of nowhere, with two jumbo, frosty mugs filled to the rim with ice-cold beer, and a platter of fried okra.

He winked at Bene, then turned to me and asked if I was there to meet Delilah.

I nodded, dipping my nose in the beer head.

"She's in the kitchen, brewing tomorrow's stock," he said. "After you eat, I'll take you back there." He left us to tap our feet to the crescendo rhythm of the music.

I sipped my beer. *Caspita!* One of the best I'd had in a while.

By the time Pop came by, we had drained the mugs. He placed two bowls of the renowned bean soup in front of us along with a basket full of corn muffins and a crock of whipped butter.

It smelled heavenly, if heaven smelled of smoked ham and hearty beans.

He grabbed the empty beer mugs. "Ready for another round?"

We nodded.

In no time Pop brought us the second round and grabbed a chair from a nearby table. He sat on it backwards, using the chair's back as a support for his elbows, wiping his forehead with his stained apron.

"How'd you like it?" he asked, pointing at the mugs.

"It's excellent," I answered. "What is it?"

He grinned and balanced the chair closer on two legs. A conspiratorial look spread across his face. "Delilah's own secret brew." He shifted his shrewd eyes to Benedetta. "So—your parents thought you were a blessing?" he asked as if it were the most natural thing on the planet to find an old grandpa at a truck stop able to translate Benedetta's name.

"Yes, they did." Benedetta lifted her head to answer. The soup had steamed up her glasses.

One would probably think we were nuts to eat hot soup on a sticky, warm August evening, but with my job's deadlines I'm used to it, like models get used to wearing bathing suits in January. Besides, an entire dining room agreed with me this evening. The ice-cold beer married superbly with it, like *Parmigiano e maccheroni*.

Benedetta took her glasses off to wipe off the soup steam and smiled at Pop with her nearsighted, angelic blue eyes. She's cute with her glasses on. She's not of this world when she takes them off. I suspect the gods made her nearsighted so humans could handle looking at her, and vice versa.

"Hey, Dad, are you so busy charming these pretty young ladies you've forgot the rest of the room?"

Pop turned his head to look at an incredibly handsome man with chiseled features.

Did he just say "Dad"? I wondered. My eyes darted, all unglued, between Pop and the black Adonis towering right behind him. It was like thinking of Geppetto manifesting the David instead of Pinocchio out of a piece of wood.

No way.

Benedetta's glasses dropped in her soup.

"Ladies, may I introduce to you my son, Jason," Pop said, grinning proudly, not without a hint of sarcasm. "Named for the leader of the Argonauts and Medea's main love disaster." Pop tugged at Jason's shirt trying to make him take a bow.

I was speechless. *Pop a mythology expert? Oddio, what next?*

Jason swatted a rolled kitchen towel at his astute father. He then shook hands with us, offering Benedetta another bowl of soup. She nodded, hastily wiping her glasses so she could take a better look at him.

Pop got up with a look that told us he wouldn't be long and followed his stunning son into the kitchen.

"Benedetta, stop staring at his butt."

She turned around. "Can't help it." She grinned and reached for her beer. She took a long gulp and smiled at me, curling up a white, foamy moustache. "This is a hell of a place." She cast her arm out in a vague general direction. "Your mailman told you about it?"

I nodded with chipmunk-size cheeks grinding beans. "Uh-huh. He always has great tips."

"I bet Pop's real name is Aeson," she said knowingly.

"Why do you say that?" I asked, busy counting the different varieties of beans in my bowl. So far I had recognized seven—no, eight—I had just noticed the black-eyed peas.

"You know I'm fascinated by Greek mythology. The Argonaut Jason, his father's name in ancient mythology was Aeson, then the Medea disaster and blah, blah, blah . . ."

"When did you start learning all this?" I interrupted, curious.

She reached across the table to dunk half a corn muffin in my soup. "I was taking it in college when we met. Then continued researching on my own, among other things. Did you know that the philosophers called their narrations *myths*? Look how we've distorted the meaning of the word now and relegated it to something invented, fable-like." She brought the soaked muffin up to her mouth and took a bite. Amazingly, it didn't crumble. It made me want to do the same. I reached for the breadbasket as Jason approached the table carrying a professional camera and Benedetta's soup.

"I should have known you were from *Gusto*. Dad just told me." He extended his hand. "I'll be taking the photos for your article," he added, smiling.

I raised an eyebrow and shook his hand. "You're the photographer?" I asked, not quite believing him.

He nodded. "They should have told you at the magazine that Delilah doesn't allow strangers to take photos in her establishment."

I liked that word: establishment.

I suddenly recalled my conversation with Oscar, the editor in chief of *Gusto*, the magazine that commissioned me for this article. He *had* mentioned something about Delilah's voodoo belief that pictures could steal souls.

"So here I am, at your service." Jason bowed gallantly.

"So why are you so special?" Benedetta asked him.

Jason grinned somewhere up around a thousand watts and made matters even more intriguing, telling us that Delilah not only was his mother, but also his generous benefactor. She had paid for his art school tuition.

Benedetta and I exchanged a look. That made Pop Delilah's husband. I couldn't wait to meet her.

Skimming the livid glare of a row of Carmen Miranda look-alikes at the bar, Jason escorted us into the kitchen through a multicolored beaded curtain that tinkled like chimes as we passed through. We stepped into a spacious kitchen with industrial-sized appliances. On the walls chilies and garlic garlands held hands, festively hanging between wooden shelves stacked with jars of spices, herbs, legumes, and rice. I believe I saw frog legs and lizard's tails. Or maybe a hint of voodoo fueled my imagination.

A back door opened onto a small courtyard allowing a cool breeze to ventilate the space and tousle the beaded curtain behind us. On a miniature altar, a porcelain Virgin Mary looked down on a tiny vase of fresh daisies. A fake snake coiled by her feet, strangling a shot glass filled to the rim with what I suspected to be spiced rum.

Holy Mother, may I introduce to you Damballah?

The mouthwatering aromas of steaming bread pudding tickled my nose, and my eyes landed on an ancient black woman standing on a small stool stirring a large pot. She smiled at us as we approached her, then, without missing a beat of her stirring, she called over her shoulder in a raspy voice, "Delilah! Your guests are here!"

Framed by the open back door, a silhouette appeared. A ghostly line of smoke rose off a cigarillo hanging from the naked lips of Ezili's human manifestation. The Haitian goddess stood in front of us dressed in a brightly flowered sundress. A jet-black braid crowned her head, and yellow tiger-eyes smiled at us warmly above flawless mocha cheekbones so high and sharp they could cut through glass. She pushed off the doorframe, extending her arms. Now I knew where Jason got his looks.

"Welcome," she purred, taking both my hands in hers. "You must be Porzia."

"It's a pleasure to meet you, Delilah." I wondered if I ought to curtsy.

"And this must be your . . . *blessed* friend." She let go of my hands to take Benedetta's.

"Hello," Benedetta said in her cool, friendly voice.

"Hello," Delilah answered. "I dreamed about your visit." She stared at Benedetta. "Evil has been lingering. I dreamed a blessed soul would come and restore balance."

Delilah's words sent shivers down my spine.

"This night calls for a celebration. Aeson, honey, would you fetch some of Mama's *agua*?" she asked her husband in a purr.

I gasped silently. Benedetta had guessed right about Pop's name. *What the hell was going on?*

From beans I had been catapulted into Congo Square. I could feel Marie Laveau oozing in from the afterlife. It was happening quite often lately; I kept finding myself in the midst of some sort of esoteric endeavor. I shook my head and trailed behind Benedetta and Delilah out the back door into the small courtyard.

Aeson followed with a tray holding three small shot glasses and an old bottle filled with a foggy liquid. He left us as we sat around a cast iron table on matching chairs covered with floral-print cushions.

Night jasmine and honeysuckle sweetly scented a gentle breeze. A tall brick wall surrounded the courtyard, giving us a sense of privacy and the feeling we were all alone.

"Gerome called. He said you'd be coming up to write about some of my recipes," Delilah said as she poured the liqueur. "How is he?"

Gerome is my mailman and second cousin to an innumerable amount of culinarily dedicated relatives sprinkled throughout the Bible Belt.

"He's doing pretty well," I answered distractedly. My eyes widened as she lit a match and set the contents of the glasses on fire.

"What are you doing?" Benedetta at her best, mincing no words.

"This is Mama's *aguardiente*. A distilled, mystical concoction I won't divulge." Delilah looked at us. "Once the excess alcohol burns off only the concentrated essence remains. That's when you drink it, but we must wait until it has cooled a bit. Patience is everything."

We settled thoughtfully to wait while the ethereal flames danced and died.

An irreverent breeze tousled my hair, bringing the notes of a blues guitar to my ears as if from a distance. High above, the moon had reached her peak and lingered, curious, to wait with us before resuming her descent.

Benedetta is not good at waiting. "So, what am I supposed to do for you?" she asked Delilah bluntly.

Overhead, I thought I heard the moon sigh in exasperation. Maybe it was me.

Delilah's amber eyes swept us. She frowned, struggling to find the right words. "Evil has been meddling with my ingredients, spoiling things up." Her subtle accent told me Jamaica wasn't that distant in her past.

Benedetta pushed her glasses up her nose. "Uh—could you be a little more specific?" she pressed.

"Humidity. This year it has been impossible. My saffron, for example." Delilah paused dramatically, making a rubbing movement with her thumbs and two fingers, like sprinkling a pinch of salt on a dish. "Or my cayenne. Or cinnamon. Not silky dry, but pasty." She paused again, dramatically. "Fungus-like."

Her words had such vivid impact I actually visualized the saffron clotting.

"An oath has been spoken," Delilah whispered, as if saying the words out loud would enhance the evil powers. Her eyes sparkled like topaz. She picked up her shot glass and gulped the agua down, throwing her head backwards. Amazing how her braid remained in place against such a sudden jerk.

We tried to follow her example. She had made it look so easy, like a shot of regular water.

It was fire. It burned down my throat. It stung my eyes and seared my lungs. It blazed in my stomach. I had just swallowed liquid lava. I coughed, I cried, I grabbed my stomach. I wanted to roll on the ground in agony. I wished I were a dragon to spit fire back at her.

Benedetta fared no better. Her nose ran mercilessly, and her eyes glowed red. Her entire face was red. Smoke came out her ears.

"*Oddio!*" I wiped my eyes.

"What the hell was that?" Benedetta choked.

"You said it right, *sistah*." Delilah looked at Benedetta. She refilled our glasses and lit them up once again.

Was this woman out of her mind? Frantically I searched for an acceptable reason to refuse the second shot.

I have faced difficult situations before, mostly in foreign countries where etiquette requirements differ and where offending your host is a matter of *professional* life or death, but to cross a voodoo believer in her dwellings—even though she offered us liquid hell—called for extreme caution.

"Here, the second one is a lot smoother," Delilah said, raising her tiny glass to toast us. There she went, throwing her head back again, enjoying every drop of it.

Benedetta had more guts than me. She took the second shot and held a napkin on her face, crying into it. Screaming into it. Biting it.

Oddio! I thought she said the second one was supposed to be easier.

"This was as painful as losing my virginity," Benedetta mumbled into her napkin.

"Not as bad as childbirth," Delilah observed, settling back in her chair. She lit a thin cigarillo and looked at me, waiting; her friendly tiger-eyes glittered, bemused.

I pinched my nose, lifted my glass, and drained it. My tonsils burst into flames, and I closed my eyes for fear my eye sockets might detach like parts of the space shuttle skyrocketing into the universe. They were going to make a saint out of me after this. I momentarily toyed with thoughts of people crawling from far away to witness my miraculous remains, preserved in a crystal case for posterity, defying decay thanks to the agua I had been pickled in. The devoted pilgrims, totally unaware of such chemical mysteries, would babble *miracle* in a cacophony of foreign languages I couldn't hear in the safety of my crystal cocoon.

Devotees *un corno*. It was Benedetta's babbling. She was trying to shake me back to life by shoving a glass of water down my throat.

I drank like there was no tomorrow. I hoped tomorrow would never come. I couldn't begin to imagine how my stomach would punish me come morning.

"Are you back, Porzia?" Benedetta asked. She cradled my head in her hands.

"Yes. I'm fine," I lied. I focused on her and noticed that, other than her flushed cheeks, she looked normal.

How come?

I must have asked that out loud because she answered me. "You'll be fine in seconds. The effects fade really fast."

I looked at her and decided I wanted to crawl back into my crystal case. I wanted to trade places with Sleeping Beauty or Snow White, either one, it didn't matter . . . and then my head cleared. *Poof!* The fog lifted. Miraculously, I was back in my skin, in Aunt Delilah's courtyard in Savannah, Georgia. All was cool, the night air included. I suppressed a shiver. I glanced at my watch; it read midnight.

"Come, sisters. Let me show you my spices," Delilah said, tipping the ashes off her cigarillo. She pushed off her chair and led us back into her kitchen.

I stood and followed her, somehow managing to keep my dignity. I glanced at Benedetta; she seemed fine, actually enjoying herself.

Compared to the courtyard's breeze, the kitchen tickled and moistened my nostrils like an aromatic yet stifling sauna. By the main sink, Jason wiped sweat off his brow with the back of his hand and continued stacking a dishwasher, while the raspy-voiced older lady Delilah introduced as her *mama* cleared the counters.

"Dad's got it under control out there. He's closing down," Jason said, pointing toward the dining room with his chiseled chin. Frowning, he cast a disapproving look at his mother. "You shouldn't bother these ladies, Mom—"

"Thank you, hon." With firm authority Delilah silenced her son and reached for a jar on one of the shelves. She pulled the cork lid off and sniffed the contents. Disgust twisted her features. She offered me the jar to sniff at. "See what I mean?"

I took a look inside and noticed how the cinnamon had clustered into wet spots resembling melted wax. Its pungent odor tickled my nostrils, bringing to mind the early stages of autolysis; that jolly revolt—post-death occurrence—when the digestive juices begin to break down the gastrointestinal tract. *Odd for cinnamon*, I thought, it being a spice with one of the longest shelf lives.

Delilah continued on, showing us her spoiled vanilla beans coated with a gray fungus; her saffron, carefully wrapped in cotton gauze had stained the pure-white material with red, bleeding streaks. Her cayenne had lost all its zest. Her bottom lip quivered and her eyes welled with tears.

I had no idea how to help her. The only thing I could think of rationally was that the cork lids might have caught some sort of moldy virus that had spread to several of her jars. I suggested that she toss out the affected jars and buy brand-new ones. Jason seemed to agree with me. He wiped his hands on a kitchen towel and told me he had already suggested something similar to her a few weeks back.

Delilah believed it was a curse from an envious acquaintance. She had asked for divine intervention and dreamt about a blessing soon to be delivered.

The blessing in question was busy entertaining naughty mythological thoughts with Jason as the unquestionable protagonist. Jason certainly seemed to be enjoying the attention.

Oh, this ought to be interesting, I thought. I had never seen Benedetta practice The Craft. I crossed my arms and leaned against the immaculate stainless counter. I kicked Bene's shin, bringing her attention back to the present. She shot me a resentful look, recovered quickly, and asked Delilah if she knew the name of the person who had started all the trouble. Delilah nodded. Benedetta pushed her glasses up her nose and cleared her throat. "Well, it's an auspicious time to get rid of negativity, for the moon is indeed waning out there . . ."

I had no idea what she was talking about but felt awed and afraid to interrupt.

"Delilah, you'll need to write the name of the person in question on a piece of paper. You then fold the paper four times to have the sealing of all four elements: earth, air, water, and fire. Then, you take the ruined spices, jars and all, and you go out there." She pointed toward the courtyard and tugged Delilah's arm, drawing her closer. She cupped her hands around Delilah's delicate ear and whispered the rest of her spell.

Delilah kept on nodding as if what was being told to her made perfect sense.

". . . And make sure you're beneath the moonlight the entire time," Benedetta finished, stepping back. A look of satisfaction spread across her face, like light returning to the dark sky after a lunar eclipse.

Jason and I had been completely forgotten.

Delilah hugged Benedetta in gratitude and asked me if I would now care to talk about the recipes I came to write about. I told her I was ready and asked her if my work would intrude with her curse-riddance plans.

"Oh no! Now that I know what to do I can take care of it later when everybody's gone." Her eyes moved up and left, as if repeating a well-memorized lesson.

Jason invited Benedetta to follow him into the dining room to take photos, promising to return to shoot the display of ingredients Mama was setting up for us on the spotless counter. I began to take notes of her Smoked Ham and Bean Soup and Traditional Corn Muffins recipes.

"The secret of the soup is to make sure the ham hasn't been de-boned, and I usually sauté some of the juiciest morsels with a little butter and onions, until the onions are translucent. About ten minutes on low heat," Delilah told me. "That releases the ham flavor and infuses the stock much quicker." She paused, running her hands through a heaping bowl of multicolored dried beans, her crimson-varnished nails a vivid contrast.

"How many varieties of beans do you have there?" I asked, still writing.

"About fifteen. I soak them in cold water for at least eight hours, but it's best to allow them to soak overnight. You have to change the water at least three times." She moved to another bowl where beans of all shapes and sizes swelled happily in a water bath. Delilah drained the bowl and refilled it with fresh water, covering the beans by at least two inches. "Another secret is to use cooled ham stock to soak the beans with. When you change the water the third time, replace it with the stock. That allows the beans to absorb the flavor." *It makes perfect sense,* I thought, jotting notes down.

I suddenly realized that we were alone in the kitchen. "Where is everybody?"

"I don't know," she answered. "Mama?"

Mama appeared from behind the counter dragging a twenty-pound sack of corn flour. "Yes, dear?" She reminded me of a tiny ant struggling with an oversized cargo.

"Where is everybody?" Delilah asked, glancing at a big clock on the wall. "Did Aeson close down?"

"He sure did. He's counting down at the register," Mama croaked.

I wondered how much agua it took to reach such a hoarse timbre.

"Jason and *The Blessing* are outside taking photos of the front porch by moonlight," Mama said teasingly.

Aeson raised his head from his bookkeeping and silently pointed out the windows.

Benedetta and Jason sat on the swing. He sang, softly tickling a guitar along, while Benedetta followed the melody whistling. The combination of his smooth, low voice and the lightness of my dear friend's whistling coiled around the anguished notes of the guitar. And then she switched from whistling to singing in that low Astrud Gilberto voice of hers. The effect sent chills through me, stretching my human abilities to grasp such a heavenly melody. Emotions replaced the flow of my blood, boundaries faded, and time vanished.

We stood motionless, Delilah and I, listening in rapture.

The slow notes pierced the silent night like the cry of a tormented soul. It crushed my heart and squeezed ancient drops of undiluted pain from it.

Behind me Delilah sobbed quietly. I thought of Gabe so far away yet so close, deep in my heart. I shed my pain and metamorphosed it into pure love, and cast it to him on the wings of the poignant music. Such magic was bound to find every enamored soul out there.

Eventually, I had to tear Benedetta away from him. Morning was fast approaching, and we still had to drive into town to get to our hotel. I asked Delilah if it would be possible to resume our interview the following day. Both Jason and Benedetta lit up at the thought of being able to see one another again. Delilah invited us for lunch, and we agreed to be back at the restaurant by noon.

A feeling of melancholy drove away with us knowing that the evening had drawn to an end. The entire family waved good-bye from the front porch; I watched them getting smaller and smaller in the frame of my rearview mirror.

I gave Benedetta time to recover, then asked, "You OK?"

"Yes. Thank you, but I'm fine. I guess that *agua* stuff had a weird effect on me."

"Bene . . . how did you know how to help Delilah? I mean, what was that business with elements, waning moon, and so forth? Which goddess did you invoke?"

"Why put a human face to magic?" she frowned. "You know I've been learning about The Craft for a while now. Even as a solitary practitioner, I knew how to help. It sort of came naturally."

"Wicca and voodoo mix?" I asked rather dumbly.

"Magic, when used in love, has no boundaries."

Maybe I ought to introduce her to Evalena. "What is magic, Bene?"

"Magic is willing energy operating on a level that our minds know nothing about. It streams from our hearts, Porzia."

"And Jason?"

"He didn't drink any agua," she yawned.

"That's not what I meant," I said, stifling a yawn myself.

"I know what you meant. But I'm too tired to talk about it."

"What was he singing out there, Bene?"

"I have no idea. He said something about a lullaby, and I just made up words to follow."

"It was beautiful, but you're right, that agua did have a weird effect."

Dark shapes of gnarled, arthritic oaks shadowed the moonlight with their heavily mossy branches, looking like stylized souls ready to stir and jump on us at the first provocation. The dashboard clock read 1:00 A.M.

I caught myself breathing more softly than usual. Next to me, Benedetta was just as silent until rounding a corner we, skimmed a graveyard. Talk about spooky. I heard her intake of breath and her shoulders sank lower in the passenger seat. "I can almost feel the Confederate ghosts' mournful laments," she murmured.

"Confederates? I'm thinking of pirates."

"The pirates wouldn't be mournful. Their victims might." She had a point.

"We're almost there," I told her, recognizing the street sign for our destination on our left. I turned, passing a lonely bench, and saw a lit sign straight ahead. I drove head first into a parking spot in front of the main entrance.

Our room featured a garret ceiling sloped all the way to the floor. Two full-size beds beckoned us, inviting us to jump on the multi-flowered, quilted bedspreads. Open, round windows allowed the cool night breeze to flow in. Our feet sank in a plush maroon carpet.

Benedetta jumped on the far bed by the windows. "Ahhh, I'm so tired," she sighed, tilting her glasses on her forehead to rub her eyes.

"I guess that's your bed choice?" I pulled my suitcase onto a chair and began to look for my nightclothes.

"Yes, it is. You sleep close to the door in case the pirates decide to pay us a surprise visit. They'll get you first, and I'll have time to escape through the window."

"You'll end up stuck like Winnie the Pooh." With my cosmetic bag, I headed for the bathroom. An antique claw-foot bathtub stood by another round window, this one large enough for Benedetta to climb through. Loads of fresh towels were piled up on a pine table next to a wicker basket stuffed with a selection of herbal products. I took a quick bath gazing over endless Savannah roofs and the occasional patch of trees. The moon lay low on the western horizon, resigned to the imminent arrival of a brand-new day. Lazily, I wondered if Gabe ever looked up at the sky and realized that, no matter the distance, we did share the same firmament. I slid underwater and held my breath like I used to when I was a child, when I still believed wishes may come true. With my eyes shut tight and my lungs ready to explode, I tried to last until my effort materialized my hope into reality: "*Gabe will be sitting in the tub with me when I open my eyes.*"

I emerged from the water gasping for air, my rush of breath louder than the water's splashing. I adjusted to my disappointment in the darkness of the empty room. *If only I could have lasted another second or two.* I almost tasted Gabe on my tongue. I turned toward the window and blew him a silent kiss before I finally grabbed a towel to dry off and get ready for bed.

CHAPTER 18

Driving through Savannah in blazing daylight restored our courage. Even the graveyard looked a little less intimidating. We found a decent radio station and made it back to Delilah's a little before noon. The place looked more peaceful than last night, and I found parking right away.

Jason must have been hanging on the ship's crow's nest, for even before I brought the car to a halt, he was lunging off the front porch grinning from ear to ear.

He had eyes only for Bene, which proved essential when she almost fell, tripping on her own feet as she got out of the car. He managed to catch her right before she went *splat*!

Maybe she did it on purpose so he'd have to hug her. Stars shot out their eyes and violins started playing.

It wasn't violins instigated by their passions, but violins we heard undeniably, as Benedetta's cell phone screeched for attention like a newborn demanding a feed. It was my turn to get all worked up. Benedetta answered, discontentedly dislodging her limbs from Jason's. She handed me the phone, smirking.

Gabe, from Australia. *Gulp!*

"Hey, luv!" he greeted me, melting me. I sprouted wings, taking a chance at fluttering on the spot; I batted my eyelashes, found solid ground again, and blushed.

"How are you?" I chirped.

"Not bad. Where are you?"

"In Savannah with Benedetta. We're in the parking lot of the restaurant I'm writing about." I plugged my free ear with a finger to hear him better.

"So the fun hasn't started yet?"

I thought of last night and smiled. "The fun has already begun. Ever since we left home we've been busy."

"I actually meant to ask you about that." He paused. "When are you due back home?"

"We're leaving later tonight, after supper. We should be back in Pensacola tomorrow morning, early."

"Great, because I'm sending you something, and I wanted to make sure you'll be home for it."

"What is it?"

I heard him laugh softly. "You don't know what I'd give to see the look on your face right this moment."

"Well? What is it?" I asked again, rocking impatiently on the balls of my feet.

"Just wait and see."

"You're making me want to jump in the car and head back right now." I was seriously intrigued. I stopped the swinging; I was getting motion sickness.

"No, don't do that. I haven't sent it yet. I was thinking about you last night, and I felt you closer than ever. But it was so bloody frustrating, luv. I don't know how you're managing to hang on. So I figured I'd ship you something to close the distance a bit." He was really fueling my curiosity.

"I was thinking about you too," I said, once again amazed at the connection between us. "I was taking a bath before bed and wondered if you ever—"

"Look up at the moon and ask if you're staring at the sky as well?" he finished for me.

"You know—you take my breath away." I smiled softly.

"How long you think you can go without it?"

"At the rate we're going, not much longer."

"Hang in there, luv. In a few minutes you'll have forgotten all about it, busy with delicious food and other important matters."

"No. What's going to happen is that I'll be so busy trying to figure out what you're sending that I won't be able to write anything sensible. Give me a hint," I pleaded.

"Hint, eh?" He paused to consider my words.

How great it was to talk to him again, even to just play and tease one another like this. I felt an adrenaline rush, and my emotions stirred, responding to his energy.

"No. Sorry. No hint. You're going to have to just wait. It won't be long."

I gave up. "OK, then. I'll try. But it better be good," I laughed.

"I'll call you again tomorrow evening once you get home..." He lowered his voice, "... when you'll be alone and I can tell you how much I miss you and all sorts of other things that might really distract you from your job."

"Great. At least I've been warned and can now plan on fighting back."

"Fighting back is healthy."

"OK then, I'll look forward to tomorrow evening."

"Me too. Bye, luv."

"Bye, Gabe," I said, hanging up.

I found myself standing alone in the parking lot. Gabe's voice still sizzled in my ears. I pocketed the cell phone, grabbed my notebook, and walked up to the restaurant. Delilah greeted me at the front screen door looking even more stunning than she had the previous night. She wore a simple wraparound dress the color of glowing amber. Her hair shone raven-black, braided high on her head and coiled, held in place with multicolored pins. I felt rather homely in my cargo shorts and yellow tank top.

"How are you today, my dear?"

"I'm great, Delilah," I answered. I still basked in the afterglow of Gabe's phone call.

"Ready to continue our conversation? Or would you rather eat something first?"

I told her I would prefer to finish the interview first, and she nodded in agreement, leading the way to the kitchen.

Benedetta and Jason had evaporated. I soon forgot about them as Delilah and I began to go over her corn muffin recipe. She handed me an oversized apron and tied one around her body as well and then proceeded to show me how she soaks Silver Queen corn kernels in warm milk for several hours until they are plump and moist. She added them to a smooth batter of corn meal, eggs, maple syrup, unbleached flour, whole milk, salt, and baking soda.

"The secret is in the soaked kernels," she told me as she buttered a large muffin pan. She set it down, satisfied, and began buttering another.

"You seem to use the soaking technique a lot," I commented, remembering the ham soup.

Delilah nodded. "I find it does enhance the flavors. Fresh herbs added at the last minute to soups, stews, and salads is another one of my favorite kitchen secrets. For example, the bean soup is excellent when I serve it cold with chopped, fresh cilantro."

Now that was an innovative idea. I asked her if I could mention it in the article, and instead of answering, she told me she would like me to try some. She finished buttering the last muffin pan and quickly prepared a bowl of soup for me. She handled the sharp knife to chop the cilantro with confident skill. With the knife blade she scooped the finely cut herb and dropped it into the bowl. She wiped the blade against her apron. "Doesn't it smell heavenly?"

I lowered my nose closer to the bowl. "Yes, it does, Delilah. Sometimes I wish that when I write about something, the readers could actually inhale the aromas I try to describe. Writing can be so—limiting, so two-dimensional."

Delilah nodded. "I understand what you mean. Most of my clients—many of the faithful ones—were drawn in by the mouth-watering aromas from my kitchen or by the guitar playing on the porch. Just driving by they had to stop and see what it was all about." She grinned over the huge bowl as she scooped the batter out to fill the muffin pan up to the rim. Lost in the sweet memories, she absentmindedly dripped batter onto the floor. I didn't have the heart to tell her, but I quietly moved her arm so the dripping would continue harmlessly back into the bowl. She regained consciousness and resumed her task. "How do you like it?"

I took a moment to savor the spoonful I had taken. The soft texture of the beans and the freshness of the cilantro exploded together in my mouth. The flavor of the ham stock danced at the back of my tongue.

"Wow, Delilah! I think I like it better cold than hot." I took another spoonful. Maybe I was afraid the second one wouldn't be as good as the first, so I hurried before my taste buds would get used to the flavors, but it didn't happen. I contemplated tilting my bowl in order to get what was left of the delicious soup.

Delilah came to my rescue, handing me a muffin fresh from the oven. "Gerome was right when he told me I'd enjoy talking to you as much as you'd enjoy my food," she told me.

Still busy chewing, I looked at her for a moment. "Is that what he said?"

"He said you're special, that you'd be inquisitive but respectful, and a pleasure to watch when you eat a dish you appreciate."

Aeson chose that instant of perfect timing to walk into the kitchen, sporting a smart golf outfit and a huge grin. He waltzed to Delilah's side, took her in his arms, and swirled her around to silent music, not forgetting to wink at me over her shoulder. I cupped my chin in my hands and enjoyed the sight thinking about how timeless love is just absolutely beautiful.

He bowed and kissed her hand. She regally curtsied just as Jason walked in from the courtyard door and snapped a photo of them. *That would make a great article introduction*, I thought. The beginnings of an idea stirred to life, my brain gears meshing against one another like a huge clock movement.

Benedetta walked in right behind Jason, still in one piece, and I asked her if she was ready to go.

I dreaded the thought of having to watch Benedetta and Jason say good-bye to one another, expecting some sort of high drama, but my dear friend handled it pretty smoothly. They'd exchanged phone numbers earlier and were happy enough with that.

Phew!

I thanked Delilah and her family for their hospitality and wished her my best. We exchanged hugs and sincere promises to keep in touch.

*

Benedetta and I spent the late afternoon in downtown Savannah browsing through small, off-the-beaten-path bookstores where we bought several books featuring recipes for me, haunted house and folklore tales for Benedetta. We found a great kitchen store where I bought new spice jars to be delivered to Delilah's restaurant the same day, as a way of thanking her and helping her replace the spooked ones she was "fixin' to get rid of."

We headed back to the car after a light seafood supper that we washed down with a bottle of crisp Sauvignon Blanc. It was such an excellent wine we didn't even mind the tall African American fellow who chased us from outside the small restaurant for several blocks trying to sell us tickets to a voodoo ritual later that evening. Benedetta finally stopped, straightened her glasses, and told him that if he wouldn't bugger off, she would *ritual* him right then and there. He walked away crossing himself.

"You know, you're beginning to scare me," I told her, resuming our walk.

"About time," she said enigmatically.

"You want me to fear you?" I grinned. She couldn't be serious.

"No, but made you think," she said, giving me a little shove.

"You'd be good at this voodoo business."

"You think I ought to quit my job and embrace my true vocation?" She stopped and raised her arms in a voodooist pose, holding her shopping bags aloft. It totally ruined the effect.

I looked at her straight blond bob, her clear blue eyes, and sincere expression. I shook my head. "No way!"

"Let's go home, Porzia."

"No worries." I had a delivery to look forward to.

*

Once back in the car with Savannah behind us and the countryside ahead, Benedetta looked up from her book of Savannah haunted houses and gave me a blank stare.

"What?"

"No worries. You said, 'No worries.'" She smirked.

"'No worries' is something Gabe says a lot," I told her.

"That's odd."

"What's odd about Gabe saying 'no worries'? He *is* Australian. It's a typical Australian phrase."

"I'm aware of that. The oddity of the situation lies in the fact that, dating *you*, he ought to be at least concerned, if not downright *worried*."

I recognized the academic tone she usually reserved for her classroom.

"I'm hungry," she announced suddenly, sitting up. "I could use a snack."

"Check to see if we have any dried-fruit mix left. I'm getting hungry myself."

Munching on some pineapple I drove us through darkness. Benedetta was humming softly. I recognized the tune. "So, how about Jason?"

Silence...

"Benedetta?"

"He's something else, Porzia," she answered dreamily.

"Yes?"

"It's not only his looks. It's the way he sang on the porch and didn't mind my whistling or my goofiness." Her voice tingled with captivation.

"I love your whistling. And I don't think you're goofy. At least not as much as I am. So, if you'd like to tell me more..."

"I don't know what's going to happen." She looked out the dark window. "I mean, he's got such a different life, shooting models and glamorous photos. He could have anybody he wanted. Why would he choose me?" She sighed.

"I've never heard you talk like this." I was stunned at how candid she was about her fears.

"What about you and Gabe? Don't you worry about stuff like that?"

I was silent for a moment thinking about her question. No, I wasn't worried about other women or trust matters. I was worried about a past-life-regression soul mate interfering with what was happening in my present.

"I need to tell you something, Bene."

And I spilled the beans.

I told her everything. I spent the next hour confessing all I had on my mind, all that weighed on my heart, from my promise to Joséphine to the past life regression and what I had seen. I told her of Xavier and the love we'd shared and how strongly I felt about it. I told her of Evalena's advice and how I had met Gabe right afterward. And I told her of the intense physical attraction he and I shared on the plane. I told her of my inability to calm the confusion in my head at first and then finally loving again after Steve. I told her about the magical feeling surrounding the entire escapade: signs, omens, Madame Framboise's cards, and, finally, my constant wondering if Gabe was or wasn't Xavier and whether I should even bother with the entire thing or just stand up on my own two feet and surf the wave.

"But I'm not worried about other women," I concluded as we left Georgia and crossed back into Florida.

Benedetta was silent for a while.

"Are you asleep?" I glanced over.

"No. Would you like me to drive?" she offered.

"I'm fine. But I'd like to know what you think."

"I think you're *afraid*. So this mental jerking-off thing that you're engaging in is not really because you're worried about him being or not being Xavier. You're worried about him not being the one because *you're* not ready to be with the one. Full stop."

What did I tell you about her way of speaking? And she wasn't even done yet. "You don't even worry about normal insecurities like other women, like why me? Or is he for real?

"Are you listening, Porzia? You're spending so much energy building insurmountable obstacles that it's insane! Why not use such ill-spent energy to create an enormous amount of healing magic instead?" She shook her head. "I guess I'm doing the same about Jason, just on a smaller scale, eh?" She pushed her glasses up her nose.

"I *am* listening!" I said, frowning. "What's more, I think you're right."

Accidenti! She was. "I don't know how to harness the magic."

"Of course you don't." She smiled. "Magic finds you as soon as you stop building obstacles. Don't worry. When are you going to see him again?"

"In a couple of weeks, I guess. He's got some things to take care of and then he'll be flying over to see me here." Right at that moment I realized how much I missed him. The distance between us stretched my emotions like vibrating, colored threads extended to their limits, threatening to snap at any minute. And what of the effort he was making, hating to fly as he did and leaving his beloved Australia—to see *me*? "He told me he's sending something I should be getting any day now."

"No wonder you're hauling ass," she laughed.

She was right again, I thought as we drove on through the night.

CHAPTER 19

In the company of a breathtaking sunrise, we woke the pet sitter and her charges. We paid her in the midst of warm effusions, wiggling tails, purring, barking, panting, and hugs, recovering Eros and Peridot. They were so relieved to see us they diplomatically ignored one another and continued to respectively purr and pant happily in the small cockpit of my car.

I dropped Benedetta and her beast off and waited until she reached her door. What an adorable sight: my lithe friend in her olive green sundress and her dog, sleek and sinewy, at her side.

On a whim I called after her, "Bene—what's your favorite fairy tale?"

She spun around and yelled back, "Fairy tale or myth?"

"Fairy tale!"

"*The Ugly Duckling!*" she yelled back.

A smile stretched across my face as I drove the short distance to my place. The sun slowly spread its arms and reached out to weaken the grip of darkness. Alone at last, I wondered about what Gabe had sent me and sped up.

*

There is no place like home. Peridot agreed with me at once. I dropped him inside and closed the front door with a kick. I set my bag down and followed him into the kitchen. He sniffed at his food bowl, made a disgusted face, and sang protest right by it, giving me a look which I translated accurately: *You wouldn't dare do anything else until after you've dumped this old crap and refilled my bowl with something that better be worth my having spent a few days at whatchamacallit pet-sitter purgatory. Thank you very much.*

I set aside my own priorities and microwaved a bowl of cream for him, just enough to take the chill out of it. He didn't even blink; he just dismissed me with a tail flick and sank his nose into the freshly warmed cream.

I leaned against my kitchen counter in silence, lost in thought. I stared at Peridot lapping at his bowl without really seeing him. I felt tired after the long drive and the many adventures and went over to collapse on the couch, falling asleep almost immediately.

I awoke after an hour or so of napping, still a bit bleary but with a feeling nagging at me about the recent culinary experience. I wanted to get the feel of Savannah into words while they were freshly brewing in my mind and got up to make some coffee.

Sitting down with an espresso and a croissant, I worked through my notes, incorporating them into the basic outline for my article. I became so immersed in my writing, the hours slipped by before I finally took a break to unpack my bag and freshen up a bit.

After a quick shower, I laid down again for a while. I didn't even notice as a very satisfied Peridot curled up at my feet, and the gentle woop-woop of the ceiling fan lulled me into a dreamless sleep.

It must have been early evening when a buzzing noise pierced my slumber. What sort of suicidal idiot could be so stubbornly leaning against my doorbell? Groggily, I stumbled out of bed, not caring that I was in my pajamas. I cracked the front door open, rubbing my eyes, yawning shamelessly, wishing—with every bit of my heart, soul, inner child, and future lives' personas—this idiot to be felled by one of those fatal lighting strikes that randomly roam the Florida Panhandle beaches.

I smelled lavender. A second before I opened my sleep-cemented eyes, struggling to focus on the idiot, I smelled lavender.

"Hi, luv. You forgot this back home."

Omadonnasanta!

Gabe waved a sprig of lavender under my nose, and my stupor evaporated. I leaped at him, straddling his waist with my legs crossing behind his back, kissing every exposed bit of his skin I could reach.

"Wow! What a welcome!" he said, kissing me back, laughing through that lethal, crooked grin of his. "And who's this?" he asked, looking down behind me.

My eyes followed his gaze to land on my cat. Peridot stared up at us, an amused look on his face, his tail flicking to an invisible rhythm.

"*Micio*, get back inside," I ordered my cat, thinking that if I were he, I wouldn't listen to me either. I wasn't in any position to impose disciplinary rules at the moment, precariously hanging from Gabe's waist.

But who cares what my cat was thinking? I was dangling from the waist of my beloved. His strong hands cupped my thighs, holding me firmly against his solid body. I finished drowning him in kisses and now inhaled his delicious masculine scent. My limbic brain reacted swiftly to his pheromones, sending one single, solid pulse through my feminine channels. Reaching deep down it lit a flame, melting me from the inside out. Liquid need, pulled like a high tide, glazed my eyes. I lowered my eyelids to whisper against his mouth, "I want you so bad it hurts."

His sharp intake of breath, followed by a smooth, stealthy move, brought us inside. With a kick, he shut the door and landed us on the sofa. I closed my eyes and plunged into the kiss. His indecently sexy lips devoured me with a hunger that matched and incited my own.

Oh, the pleasure! To taste him again was overwhelming.

I couldn't believe it. I kept running my hands all over him, making sure he wasn't some sort of conjured manifestation of my frustrated need. "Gabe, *amore mio*, you're for real?" I said softly, dreamily.

"Yeah, luv, real—," he answered. His voice, a beckoning caress thickened by yearning, his hands quick against my shorts, pulled and tugged, tearing the thin material away from my hips. I kicked my legs free and hurried to pull his shirt up from his jeans and above his head. I felt material rip and his fresh breath on my exposed nipples a second before I screamed his name out loud as he took my breasts in his hands and captured the aroused tips with his mouth. My hands caressed his neck and crawled up his hair—thick, luscious silk beneath my fingertips. I yanked hard when his mouth sucked along that thin line between pleasure and pain, weaving me in and out. I felt every shade in between; from one extreme edge of pleasure to the opposite, red tips dipping in ache, matches waiting to be stroked, latent fire waiting to ignite.

"I missed you so bloody much," I heard him say through the dense cloud of pleasure fogging up my senses. I blinked and found myself drowning in his deep blue eyes, liquid pools of ever-shifting, stormy waters.

"I missed you too, Gabe," I said as I lowered my hands to unfasten his belt. "I want you inside me." I lifted my hips and quickly unbuttoned his jeans. I saw him grin, pleased with my feral urgency. His arms swept me up and the world spun upside-down for an instant. He stood, turned, and laid me back on the couch. I settled against the pillows and watched him, holding my breath. He kicked his shoes off and got rid of both his jeans and boxer shorts in one single move.

Dear gods, thank you for creating such a masterpiece. He lowered himself onto the sofa and pulled my legs around his waist. With a sinful light twinkling wickedly beneath his dark lashes, he held my gaze.

"This is how real I am," he whispered. I felt him enter, slow and hard, working his way deep within me, radiating pleasure pulses so intense I couldn't help but moan his name as I raised my back and pulled him down to me. I kissed him deeply. My hips pounded against his in a hot, passionate rage that involved all senses. Swept away in the blissful moment, I was barely aware of my surroundings. His eyes, locked into mine, showed me how much he needed me. His arms wrapped around my body held me, shifting me ever so slightly to intensify the already unbearable pleasure. He slowed his pace, withdrawing almost completely, coming to a full stop.

"Oh, you're not going to do *that* to me again." I remembered how his teasing drove me crazy the last time. I managed to pull myself up against his chest without losing our intimate connection and pushed his body with my entire weight. It carried us both up until he sat upright and I straddled him. I relaxed, lowering myself down his hardness, holding him tight, in total control of every move. Or so I thought. I felt his hands on my hips guiding me, sliding himself slowly in and out, building up my level of pleasure as the rhythm became a crescendo of thick bliss. It ignited every cell of my body, filled it to its rim, and pushed it overboard to peaks of shuddering climax that spilled in a cascade of throbbing spasms, vibrating against the limits of my human form. And I realized that I wasn't alone in my rapture. Slowly, I opened my eyes and inhaled his bliss. I exhaled my own, allowing him to breathe me in.

*

With my head against his shoulder, his heartbeat reverberated in my own chest as it slowed with mine. Wrapping my arms around his neck as his hands rubbed my back, I allowed myself to return to this dimension. Our bodies, breathing in unison, rippled the fragile silence. My feelings began to shift from a tangible present to cherished memory; the flavors weakened with every swallow of fading aftertaste. I looked out the window to catch the day sneaking away.

I stirred in Gabe's arms and turned my face up to look at him. "I can't believe you're actually here with me." I kissed him lightly.

"Would you like me to show you all over again?" His tongue darted softly between my lips. I almost felt like biting but only smiled instead.

"How much time do we have?" With one day already ending I was afraid it would never be enough to show him how much I cared.

"A few days. I need to get back for the Australian Safari. I know this was kind of sudden, and I know you've got things to do. But I wondered if you could work around the fact that I'm here and maybe we'll be able to spend some time together."

A few days? Merda! Not enough, but better than nothing.

"I have a few assignments on deadlines, but I can work with you being here with me." I thought about it and smiled. "You could just be my Guinea pig and bear with me through all the food and wine I have to deal with."

"No worries, luv. I'm sure whatever you feed me will taste great." He didn't even bother to stifle a huge yawn. I slid away from him.

"You're tired." I stood and walked slowly toward the front door where he had abandoned his bag in the heat of the moment. I knelt and picked up what it took me only a second to recognize as the sprig of lavender I had unrolled from my napkin in the small restaurant by his shop where we'd had lunch.

"I can't believe you brought me this all the way from Australia." I walked back to him with both his bag and the lavender. "Thank you for remembering it."

"No worries," he mumbled a second before drifting into sleep.

I spent a few minutes watching him drift, breathing quietly so as not to disturb his descent into dream realm, still not quite believing my eyes.

My nostrils tingled, inhaling an ocean-scented essence streaked with the syrupy aroma of sex. My body ached pleasantly, still pulsing with the aftershocks of our lovemaking. My skin glowed magically in the same hue as his, telling me my eyes weren't mistaken. He was with me for real.

Making the least amount of noise possible on my bare feet, I walked to my bedroom where I found my journal tucked in the first drawer of my writing desk and opened it randomly. I laid the sprig of lavender between the crisp white pages, wondering for a second where I will be in my life when my pen finally touches those immaculate, blank pages. As I closed the drawer, I noticed my brochure from Umeracha folded with my airline itinerary and a small sealed envelope. I frowned, trying to remember where I had last seen it. Picking it up, I realized it was Madame Framboise's farewell note. I had forgotten all about it until now. With a fingernail, I ripped the envelope open.

My dear Porzia,

It has been a pleasure, even if short-lived, to finally meet you. I apologize for my absence at your departure, but I assure you, your grace and charm are things I will long treasure in my heart.

I wish you a warm and brilliant future. I wish you success and rewards in your career, personal gratifications, fulfillment, and an enchanted, unrestricted love, free of earthly boundaries and human expectations to fill your warm, loving heart. Never forget life is a mystical journey, 78 steps to transformation through the Minor to Major Arcana and ultimately, fulfillment.

Framboise

I read it, twice. I understood exactly what she meant. Her simple words shot straight to my heart, and I felt her sincerity from across the world reach a special place within me, where light hadn't shone in eons. *I'm on my way, Madame Framboise . . . I'm on my way, Joséphine . . .*

Peridot chose that moment to come by and sniff at the paper; he actually attempted to take a bite. Perhaps he smelled Madame Framboise's cat or perhaps he was just being his old nosey self. I folded and tucked the note in my journal next to the lavender. Casting a glance over my shoulder, on the couch in the living room Gabe was sound asleep. On tiptoes I walked into my living room, closed the sliding doors and pulled the curtains. Peridot had jumped on the sofa and was staring at the phone as if willing it to ring with all the strength of his mystical feline mind.

As usual, it only took a second or two.

I answered on the first ring. Evalena's voice greeted me cheerfully. Gabe didn't stir.

"Hi, hon! Did you have a good time?"

Hmm, does she mean in Savannah or just minutes ago? With Evalena, one never knew. I chose to answer about the trip.

"We had a *blast*, Evalena," I said, thinking particularly about Delilah's explosive potion. "How's everything with you?"

"All is well, thanks. I won't keep you long. I'm calling to see if you'd like to come over for dinner tomorrow."

She does not particularly like to talk on the phone. Her calls are always short and to the point.

"Well, Evalena, Gabe is here. He just arrived this afternoon, and if it's OK with you, I'd like to bring him along."

"That would be great. How about seven, then?" She didn't sound the least surprised.

"Sounds good to me. I'll bring the wine."

"OK, see you guys tomorrow."

"OK. Thanks, Evalena."

"You're welcome, hon. Bye."

We hung up and after checking to see if Peridot needed refills, I got some fresh water and walked back to the couch to snuggle in Gabe's arms. I kissed him lightly on his strong chin. My body still ached pleasantly, satisfied and coated in that afterglow only precious lovemaking exudes. *What about a woman's body after climax? Before lovemaking with Gabe, did I ever take the time to stop and listen?*

In the dim light I closed my eyes and summoned all my senses to savor my body's tingling energies. My skin smelled heavenly of warm spices carried along by sirocco wings moving across the parched sands of the North African deserts. My hair was a tangled darkness of fragrant, damp silk. The hollow of my throat, where my heartbeat purred like an expensive engine after a great ride up a winding mountainside, tingled and echoed where Gabe had bitten it. On my fingertips the intensity of his scent lingered like a shadowy prisoner. I wondered if men felt it as well. Are they able to understand—for one instant—to grasp the concept, to taste and feel the magic like we do?

Gabe stirred in his sleep, moving his arms to encircle my waist. He whispered something about me smelling good and went right back to sleep. I kept on munching on his chin for a while. I admired the sharp profile of his straight nose, the fullness of his sensuous lower lip, and the curve of the upper one, speckled by a day-old shadow. His mouth barely parted to reveal the whiteness of his teeth. I loved the thin laugh lines fanning at the corners of his eyes and the sharpness of his cheekbones, his eyes shadowed by long, dark lashes. Two thin lines extended across the smoothness of his forehead, interrupted by long rebellious strands of golden hair, longer now than when we met weeks earlier.

I remembered how the first time I saw him his thick, luscious hair had mesmerized me. I had yearned to run my hands through it, and now I was able to do so. From an unreachable horizon, he had transformed into the incredible love that filled my heart.

I gently woke him and suggested we go to bed. Holding my hand he followed me, half asleep, and just about collapsed onto my bed. I pulled the sheet over his body and stretched out next to him. With one last butterfly-wing kiss I settled into his arms, exhausted.

Dreams whispered, riding the warm night breeze. My curtains swelled against the pressure, trying to contain the questions brought on by Ether. It was a night when one could hear Peter Pan chase Tinker Bell around; a night when shadows broke free of their supporting roles to become prima donnas in dramas played silently on the stage of my unconscious.

Beaded with sweat, Gabe groaned in agony. Peridot cowered, a lonesome spectator of the frenzy, the madness, the mystical music, the beckoning of shadows. His ears flexed backwards as the keening sound rose from the camouflage of the chorus of cicadas and summer crickets, silencing nature. The howl coiled slowly at the foot of the bed, raising a shadow against the moonlit wall. It gained strength, piercing through the deafness of sleep to insinuate its echo in my waking mind.

As Gabe's scream died, I awakened in time to see a form withdraw hastily out the window. Distant drumming faded and finally ceased.

I sat up with a start, pressing the palms of my hands against the mattress' heat. I blinked sleep off while my mind questioned what had just transpired. Gabe settled back in his sleep like nothing had happened. I took a second to look at him. Finally, his face relaxed and my heart skipped a beat.

At the foot of the bed, Peridot purred and the curtains settled gently as the breeze withdrew. The chorus of insects resumed their serenade to the rising moon. I wondered if the lingering panic that drummed in my heart was just the echo of a nightmare I couldn't remember.

What now? Are we sharing nightmares? Overwhelmed by sleep, I did not pursue it. I leaned back into Gabe's arms. I banished the monsters as I drifted back into sleep, sure the rest of the night would be quite peaceful.

*

With the sun high up in the sky, all the fright and fears of the previous night seemed a distant mirage. Being in Gabe's embrace sure helped make things all right. I wished I could wake up in his arms for the rest of my life. I felt his body slowly stir from sleep; I readjusted myself against him and smiled.

"Morning," he mumbled against my neck.

"Hmm—"

"Do you always feel this good in the morning?" He nibbled at my earlobe.

"Yeeesh," I managed to respond as I stretched my limbs and arched my back like a lazy cat. I purred in contentment.

Thump!

"*Meow!*" Peridot complained loudly. The real cat had just fallen off the bed. I must have hit his sleepy body curled at the foot of the bed when I stretched my feet, pushing him off the edge. I swear I didn't do it on purpose.

"Ow! That must have hurt," Gabe said. He raised his head to see where Peridot had landed. His strong back emerged solid against the fluid blue sheets. I felt an irresistible urge to reach over and touch him.

He tensed against my fingers as they trailed along his scars. He turned to stare at me, wide-awake. His eyes clouded over, filling with something like despair.

"I'm sorry I'm not flawless. Those scars are a part of me, and there's no bloody turning back," he stated defiantly.

"Why are you so defensive about it?"

Gabe exhaled his frustration. His shoulders collapsed back on the pillows. "I didn't mean to sound so harsh." He blinked, looked up at me, shoving his clouds back inside, and closed his eyes. "It's something I can't really talk about."

I could feel a palpable turmoil behind his shut eyelids. "You can't talk about it because it's painful to remember or because you promised not to talk about it?" I asked softly, frowning.

He opened his troubled eyes, betraying, exposing the intensity of his distress. Yet he managed to raise a hand to caress my cheek. "Both."

Am I supposed to just let it slide? Wait until he's ready to explain? Why does it matter so much?

I can put two and two together, and I knew he had gotten those scars in the near-fatal accident that put a stop to his racing career and kept him from starting over. I could only begin to imagine how painful it all must have been. Not only the physical aspect of it, but he had given up what he loved to do most in this life.

He hadn't been given a choice. Fate had chosen for him. That was probably the hardest part of it all. For someone as headstrong as Gabe, it must chafe to bow to fate and admit defeat. Still, I had the feeling this wasn't over. I shook my head. I had no idea how to deal with it. Evalena would have been much better at it.

"Never mind, Gabe." I rubbed my cheek against the palm of his hand. "No matter how many scars you have, I still love you with all my heart."

Oddio! Did I just tell him I loved him?

"*Fair dinkum?*" he asked quietly.

I nodded, not trusting my voice.

"You're in love with me, Porzia?"

I looked straight into his crinkling eyes as he broke into a huge grin. "Come here and let me show you how much I love you, Mr. Miller," I whispered. I smiled softly as I lowered my mouth to meet his lips.

He pulled me closer to him. His fingers wrapped around my hair, tugging. A second before losing myself against the softness of his mouth, his eyes captured mine and allowed me a glimpse of his infinite blue. I tasted his breath against my mouth as he whispered, "I love you too, Porzia."

I closed my eyes and literally collapsed against the strength of his chest, feeling his love wash over me and merge with mine. Our mouths joined in a slow, passionate dance; our first kiss to seal our love. How many had we shared until that moment? How many yet to come? Each kiss had been different in taste, but all were essential stitches quilting the mantle of our growing love.

*

"*Meow?*" Peridot, his fall forgotten, leaped back onto the bed and butted his way in between us. He purred loudly as he kneaded his huge paws in the small space between Gabe's chest and my waist.

"I think your cat loves me too," Gabe said, smiling against my lips.

"Then we know you're not going to want to go anywhere, with both of us head-over-heels for you." I lifted my head up and smiled at him.

"Is food part of the deal?" he asked.

"Of course it is. I only have a little time to spoil you, and I'm going to make the most of it." I cast him a sultry glance. "Would you like help in the shower scrubbing your back or would you rather I started coffee?" I teased him, jumping out of bed to grab my robe.

"Tough choice but I guess it's going to be coffee since you're already getting dressed."

In the kitchen, the radio chirped something about another gorgeous summer day in heavenly Florida and don't forget sunscreen. The first notes of Shania Twain's latest hit reached my ears. We had a light breakfast; I didn't have much in my fridge to play with after having spent the past few days traveling.

While Gabe touched base back home on his laptop, I took a quick shower and then put on a sundress. My damp hair trailed refreshingly against my back. I pirouetted and curtsied in front of the full-length mirror, excited and ready to enjoy the rest of the day with him.

We drove down to the coast, passing Gulf Breeze and the Sound, to the sandy white shores of Pensacola Beach, where we spent the morning walking lazily hand in hand. Emerald water lapped shyly at our feet. Seagulls swirled above us, and a gentle breeze tousled my hair. We kissed, laughed, and joked, teasing one another with the salty water, splashing as we chased each other to breathlessness. I pointed out dolphins jumping out of the water in the distance and, closer to shore, the shadow of a huge manta ray gliding like a dignified mother superior in the penumbra of a convent.

We stopped for lunch at a small bistro with a terrace overlooking the water. We ate grilled amberjack sandwiches, homemade coleslaw, and refreshing lime sorbet and talked the entire time about everything new couples talk about: our hopes and dreams, our families and friends. It was too early to talk of our future, but our pasts were presents enough for the day.

To open up came naturally. He stared at me with rapt attention as I shared the experience of my trip to Georgia with Benedetta and then burst into laughter when I mentioned the fiery agua and Bene's summon of magic to bail us out of trouble. His mood shifted as he listened to my description of the intense feelings unleashed by Jason's guitar and Bene's whistling. I told him a little about Evalena; without going into much detail I could see that she intrigued him.

We made our way back to my place for a short nap before we headed out to dinner. Away from the water, the day hung limp with humidity; the air heaved thick and nearly liquid. My hair clung to my neck, still impossibly damp as we reached my front door and stepped inside. We closed the windows and turned on the air conditioning for respite from the oppressive heat. It was the kind of suffocating heat that builds before a storm.

On the answering machine, Oscar's voice from *Gusto* welcomed me back home after my Georgia adventures. If he only knew . . . He wanted to know if I could fax him Delilah's article before the end of the week, as they were expecting Jason's photos to be ready by then as well.

Benedetta had also called, and I dialed her number while Gabe stretched on the bed and pulled his shirt above his head.

I kicked my sandals off and sat on the bed waiting for Bene to pick up. No answer. No machine. *She's probably at work,* I thought and hung up. The room was finally beginning to cool off. I reached for the fan to switch it to low and gasped when Gabe grabbed my waist and pulled me down on the bed against his chest.

"This is a really nice dress you're wearing. You've been teasing me in it all day long." He tugged at my dress straps. "What's even nicer is what's beneath the dress." He slowly unfastened the few buttons on my back and sneaked a warm hand onto the bare skin of my waist.

"I thought you wanted to take a nap," I said, turning to face him. I kissed his chin.

"That's roight, but where does it say we can't have a nap in the *nik*?"

"Nowhere." I reached down to unzip his jeans shorts.

"The problem is I don't think you'll be able to sleep if I'm lying naked next to you."

"You think I'd be the only one having a problem?"

"No, but I can handle it. The question is, can you?" His voice trailed off as he adjusted himself against the pillows and was soon drifting off into sleep.

I struggled to find a way to sneak into his dreams. I finally gave up and settled into his arms. *This is how it should always be,* I thought as a sharp pang of panic reminded my heart it was only for a few days. I decided to just ride the wave until it crashed to shore. *To live the present is to live a gift.* I drifted into a soothing sleep. Gabe breathed quietly right next to me.

CHAPTER 20

We drove to Evalena's house with the windows down, the radio music snatched away by the wind twirling around us. The day's torrid heat had given way to a bearable evening breeze. Gabe sat next to me looking toward the bowing sun. He propped an elbow on the window ledge, lost in thought, his eyes hidden behind dark lenses. He had changed into a pair of shorts and a navy button-down shirt with tiny yellow palm trees printed all over it. I'd bought it for him earlier that afternoon, more as a gag gift than anything else. Leave it to the gods; he wore it nonchalantly, as if he had just stepped out from the freshly printed pages of *L'Uomo Vogue*.

"I wish I'd brought my camera." His deep voice brought me back to the moment.

"I've got one at home." I smiled at him, taking my eyes off the road for a moment.

He reached over to caress my chin. "You've got such a lovely smile, Porzia," he said quietly. "I wonder if capturing it on film will be enough once I head back."

"Maybe with a panoramic view you might be able to fit it all in." I grinned broadly to show my point. "Did you want to go somewhere special while you're down here?" I considered places to visit, places to take pictures of.

"No, not really. I came to see you." He brushed a rebel strand of hair off my cheek.

I shook my head. "And what an incredible surprise! I still can't believe you're actually here."

"I'm here." He pulled his hand away and turned to look out the window again. We drove the last few miles to Evalena's place in silence. It wasn't the right time to get into such a serious subject.

We parked and walked hand in hand up the few steps leading to the front door. I was about to knock—with my arm midway up—when Evalena opened the door.

"Hello, dear." She hugged me tightly, then pushed away and held me at arm's length to better inspect me. "You look fantastic!" Her eyes drifted up to Gabe standing quietly behind me. For a moment, time froze. My intuitive abilities struggled as Gabe stiffened and Evalena perceptively bowed as if to give due respect to a higher power.

Now, that was interesting.

Evalena tilted her head to one side, breaking the spell. The energies shifted as she offered a hand to Gabe.

"Glad to meet you, Evalena." An edge of wariness tinged his tone.

"Pleased to meet you too, Gabe," Evalena answered. Her smile lifted the last veil of caution like warm sun dissipating lingering fog. I felt Gabe relax behind me as Evalena motioned for us to step inside. The smell of barbeque hit my nostrils. We followed it toward the back of the house, past the kitchen, and out into the back yard. There we found Rex fussing over succulent racks of baby back ribs. He glanced over at us and grinned wide. He managed to hug me with one hand gripping long tongs while the other held a sweaty bottle of Corona.

"It's great to see you again, Rex," I said. "This is Gabe." I turned in his arms to properly introduce the two of them. Gabe shook hands with Rex and promptly received an offer to dig into the fridge for a cold beer.

I told Gabe I would fetch him a Corona and left the two men talking about that stuff men talk about in front of blazing barbeques. In the kitchen I pulled a bottle of Shiraz from Umeracha out of my oversized bag and showed it to Evalena. She brushed her hands clean against the apron hugging her hips and took the bottle. She read the label and raised an eyebrow. "So, this is the famous wine you flew halfway across the planet to write about?"

"Yep."

"And that out there is your Two of Cups?" She pointed the bottle's neck in Gabe's direction.

"Yep."

"He doesn't know about the past life regression." It wasn't a question, so I didn't answer. She whistled softly under her breath. "Do you know what a *nurrullurrulla* is, Porzia?"

I frowned. "No."

"A sorcerer, an Aboriginal sorcerer." She waved a hand in midair. "Enough said. I'll explain later, when we're alone and we have more time. I can't say more and I need to be around him a bit longer. Would you like a beer?" she asked without missing a beat.

"*Merda*, right about now I could use a keg." I shook my head, wondering what had just hit me.

"How about lime?" She handed me two Coronas with lime wedges stuck in their necks. I grabbed the two frosted bottles and headed back to the patio, my hands gripping the bottles' necks in a futile attempt to absorb some of their coolness.

"Here's your beer," I offered, handing one of the bottles to Gabe.

"Thanks, luv." He brushed my hand with his fingers.

"We're about ready here," Rex announced, piling the barely blackened, caramelized ribs onto a serving tray and covering the barbeque with a lid. I usually adore barbeque but for once the charred meat scent hit my nostrils all wrong, and I felt queasy. We made our way back into the kitchen. Too busy swallowing the surging nausea, I still hadn't had a chance to sip my beer. I glanced over my shoulder as I stepped over the threshold leading back into the house and noticed enormous clouds gathering, obscuring the scattered pattern of stars that sprinkled the heavens. I couldn't see the moon anywhere. I blinked and readjusted my eyes to focus on the candlelit dining table.

"Porzia, would you sit by me tonight?" Rex pulled a chair out for me and motioned Gabe to the one next to me.

Evalena placed heaping bowls of potato salad and baked beans on the table and took the seat between Gabe and Rex, smiling like the Cheshire cat the entire time. Come to think of it, that was her usual smile.

"Is this your first time in this neck of the woods?" Rex asked Gabe, putting a small rack of ribs onto my plate with no formality whatsoever. He then tossed some to everybody else, nearly missing Evalena's plate.

"Yes. I've never been to Florida before," Gabe said. He eyed the baked beans suspiciously. They might not cook them like that in Australia.

"They're really good," I encouraged him.

He scooped some onto his plate, mildly alarmed by the juices running dangerously close to his meat. I handed him the breadbasket and the potato salad. He knew what to do with those.

I concentrated on my own plate and finally managed to push the lime down the neck of my beer bottle and take a sip. Nothing beats cold beer on a hot, muggy summer evening. I closed my eyes and swallowed, following the bitter taste. It went down my throat to the mouth of my stomach and farther, crashing against the cliffs of my stomach like high, foaming surf. *Exquisite!*

It didn't take long for the mounting surf to reach my brain. I relaxed my back against the solid wood of my chair and exhaled deeply, realizing that, until that moment, I had been holding my breath. I took a slow, lazy look at Evalena and then shifted my eyes to Gabe. He seemed relaxed, easily chatting with Rex about cars and engines. Evalena followed the conversation, taking dainty bites of her ribs and toying with her potato salad. I didn't know if it was an effect of the beer or if the motes above both Gabe's and Evalena's heads were actually sparkling. I shifted my eyes onto more solid sights: my plate. The runny baked beans didn't look at all appetizing. I was no longer hungry. I wondered what the hell was happening to me. I took another sip of my beer and shook my head, trying to make sense of whatever it was that had suddenly crept up on me.

"What's wrong, honey? You're not hungry?" Evalena asked me, pushing her own plate away.

I'm not the only one having problems eating tonight. I remember thinking that just before the room started spinning into solid darkness and I lost consciousness.

*

Two cards danced in front of me. The Magician and the Two of Cups. My hand reached out. And in the darkness I rolled a set of dice. Two.

*

Soft voices called me back up as a pungent smell hit my nostrils and made me wince. A strong hand held my neck, and I relaxed against it; intuitively I recognized and trusted the source of that strength.

"Porzia, luv, can you hear me?" Gabe's concerned tone reached through the fog, gripped my will, and pulled me out slowly.

"What happened?" I mumbled, keeping my eyes shut. *What was I afraid of looking at?*

With enormous effort I blinked slowly, absorbing the lamplight, clutching Gabe's hand tightly.

"You had a dizzy spell, honey," Evalena said. She brought a glass of iced water to my dry lips. I lifted my head to take a sip, helped by Gabe's hand still supporting my neck.

I blinked again to adjust my focus and tried to pull myself up; I realized I was lying on the same couch I'd had my past life regression on. I was suddenly uncomfortable. As if lying on burning coals, I sat up quickly, swung my feet onto the floor, and tried to get up.

"Whoa! Not so fast, luv!" Gabe said, standing up himself to support me.

Grateful, I hung on for dear life. Confused and disoriented, I tried to toss a few words out there; "I'm OK," I managed. "I'm sorry. I didn't mean to ruin the evening. I don't know what happened."

"Perhaps you're just tired," Evalena ventured.

"Maybe we should head back home." Gabe's eyes shadowed with concern.

"I think that's a good idea." Rex spoke his first words since I had regained consciousness. "How about you give him your keys and let Gabe drive you home, Porzia?"

I looked at Gabe. "Can you drive on our side of the road?" I felt reluctant to hand him my car key chain. Not because I didn't trust his driving abilities.

"No worries," he said, taking charge. He apologized to Evalena and Rex for not being able to stay longer. As he carried me out to the car, he promised them he would take good care of me. Before I knew it, I found myself sitting on the passenger side, seat belt strapped tightly across my chest. He sped off into the night.

"What happened back there, Gabe?" I whispered. Quietly, I observed him.

"What do you mean?"

"I'm not psychic, but something definitely took place between you and Evalena." I relaxed against the car seat. "Something did. Even an obtuse mind like mine was affected by it."

"You're not obtuse." A shadow of a smile flickered across his face.

"I am when it comes to things not of this world." I don't know any better way to get straight answers than to ask direct questions.

"You didn't tell me Evalena was an Intuitive," he said matter-of-factly.

"I didn't tell you Rex was retired Air Force either." I pressed him. "How do you know Evalena is an Intuitive?"

"She's also an Initiate."

"Pardon? A what?"

"Initiate. She's capable of recognizing the strength of medicine work." He paused. "I bet she's capable of a lot more than that." He took his eyes off the road to look at me. "If I didn't know you better, I'd think you were trying to test me tonight."

"What the hell are you talking about, Gabe?" I spat, tasting bitter anger in my own words. "Test you? Test you on what? And how do you know so much about all this hocus-pocus business? I thought you raced cars for a living." *Oh no! Merda! I hadn't meant it to come out like that.*

"I did."

"I'm sorry, Gabe. I didn't mean it like that." I took a deep breath. "Listen. The last thing I want to do is argue over something I don't even understand. Please forgive my rude remarks and help me make some sense of all this." I reached over to squeeze his hand.

He sighed. "Are these the dice you've been rolling?" he asked me, pointing at the two shiny cubes hanging off my car ignition.

"Yes. But what do you mean—?"

He shook his head. "This isn't the right time. Not while we're driving."

"OK then, when we get home." I wasn't going to let this one slide. I needed answers. But, ever cautious, I wondered how much flour I would have to spill from my own bag to make it a fair trade.

CHAPTER 21

"Gomi pulled me out of the car. Nothing new. I'd had accidents in the past, and he would always be the one rescuing me. That's how we actually met in the first place." Gabe glanced over at me to see if I followed.

I had kicked off my shoes and sat cross-legged on the sofa right in front of him, but without touching.

His eyes shifted, narrowed, and stared at the Aboriginal Dhamala painting I had gotten in Melbourne. "Where did you get this?"

"At the airport in Melbourne, coming home. Why?"

He shook his head. "No wonder . . ." His voice cracked, remembering pain. He turned his head away from me and time drifted. "As I was saying, I was told Gomi found me, but by the time he and the rescue team got to me, night had fallen; temperatures had dropped drastically. Several hours had gone by since the crash, and I'd lost consciousness. See, I'd driven away from the designated course and lost my way in the bush. While I was trying to figure a way to turn back and get on track something cut across in front of me. I think a dingo, but it could have been a bunyip for all I reckon. I couldn't say. In order not to hit the animal, I chucked a yewy, swerving to the right. I smashed the bull bar into a massive boulder at about eighty clicks; that's about fifty, fifty-five miles an hour. The car flipped and rolled about twenty metres to the bottom of a canyon where it stopped, upside down, with me trapped in it, hanging by the seatbelt.

"I don't remember exactly how long I was out altogether. Clark won't say and Gomi just shakes his head when I bring it up. Anyway, I woke up in the hospital a few weeks later after being in a coma. Doc said if it weren't for the helmet, I wouldn't have woken up at all." He closed his eyes and relaxed his head against the blue of the sofa.

Somehow, I found myself with him, trapped behind his shut eyelids. I spiraled backwards against the blue of his eyes and fought the surging wave of claustrophobia closing in on me. His eyes slit open, and I was suddenly free, back in the room, breathing again. My own heartbeat immediately screamed for attention. I shook my head, stunned with what had just happened. No one told me magic could be this painful. I focused on his familiar features, struggling to anchor myself on solid ground. The strength of his sharp profile reassured me. The silence thickened around us as if to tangibly shield me from what he would say next.

"I don't agree with what the doctor said," he ventured at last. His eyes cast a doubtful look at me, searching to see if I would be open to hear more.

"Porzia, this time Gomi wasn't the first one to get to me," he let out in a breath. "Someone else got to the accident site before he did and helped me to not give up." His eyes glazed over with memories still vivid, the brush strokes not yet dry on the canvas of life.

I felt my mind go empty. I knew deep down inside, without knowing *how* I knew, that we would never be the same once he told me what he was about to share.

"I didn't know for the longest time whether I'd dreamed the entire experience or if it actually happened. Just like you at Evalena's tonight, being out of consciousness can be disorienting and even scary. There's nothing to hold on to, no sense of direction, not even a hint of what choices and possibilities might lie ahead. I saw it all in an instant: the halted, failed courage of eternal, unaccomplished dreams. Not to mention the fact that your past has been completely erased. Wiped away." He smiled wryly. "Talk about feeling bloody vulnerable."

Accidenti!

"I'd been in a coma for so long I was having a hard time grasping reality. To this day I remember images, dreams or whatever you want to call them, that

I had while I was unconscious. But I can't tell you honestly what was true and what I made up in my mind as I spun farther and farther away from reality.

"I was shown this to be a positive thing; something not to be afraid of. It was this state of pure potential that existed before the universe was created. So I was taught how to be into this . . . nothingness . . . into the silence between the worlds. I learned to watch the void between outgoing and incoming breaths and to treasure each empty moment of the experience. As time goes by, it seems I remember more and more, but it's still bloody confusing."

He paused. With a deep breath, he gathered courage to finish. "But in order to save my life, I had to pay a price. *Liberation* walks hand in hand with *Loss*, Porzia. You must promise me you'll remember these words. Evalena, being an Intuitive, could tell you more. But not much more than what I'm saying to you right now; she senses the ordeal I've gone through. She respects the silence as part of the bargain I honor in order to be here today. I'm bound by the pact, and I am trying to keep up my end of the deal even if it means giving up my wings."

Chills ran down my spine. I pictured his scarred shoulder blades. *Did he bloody sell his soul to the devil?* "Your wings, Gabe?"

"My wings, luv." He leaned forward to kiss me. He meant to speak no more. With that kiss, he sealed his words. "Am I scaring you to death?"

I knew better than to press the matter. "No," I said, resting my forehead against his lips. I searched myself for fear or uncomfortable feelings, but all I found was peace and acceptance. "Are you in pain?"

"Not the physical kind," he said after a second. "Not anymore."

"You have nightmares." I thought about his scream and the shadow slithering away in the shattered stillness of the night.

He stared straight into my eyes, "Yes. But, you do too."

"My nightmares are a joke compared to what you must have gone through."

"No nightmare is a joke. I learned that a long time ago, luv. You need to learn to respect your fears. That's the only way you're going to be able to conquer them."

"I need to worry about my own monsters and you'll take care of yours?" I asked quietly.

"Yes."

"Where does all this leave my love for you?"

"In my heart, Porzia. I've put my life on the line but my heart is free to love as I choose."

I cupped his face with my hands and drew him closer. I smiled a soft smile and kissed him. "This love I've got for you . . . well, it's sort of out of control . . ."

That night our lovemaking reflected the newly acquired reassurance that no matter what the past had been or what the future held, *we* were going to happen. Surrounded by silence, as if nature respected our decision, our movements had a liquid slowness, an unhurried, smooth rhythm, a stillness that held its breath. It lingered along with darkness right outside my windows until mounting pleasure shook every cord of our beings, rippling against the hot summer air, stirring a surreal breeze one shade darker than night itself. The profound connection of our bodies and souls in that velvet darkness reset the matrix of our destinies.

I woke up in the night stillness with my mouth parched. Gabe's arm weighed heavily across my lower waist; for a second, I felt trapped by it in the darkness. With both hands, I lifted his arm so I could get up. I walked silently to the window to stare out at night itself. Nothing moved out there. The sky, in its impossible vastness, struggled to accommodate my heart. Right after the past life regression, Evalena had said that the immensity of my soul would be capable of embracing knowledge, and yet I struggled with the mystery surrounding Gabe's accident.

Bulging storm clouds pushed against one another like giant, confused pachyderms. A few raindrops fell; slowly at first, as if not quite sure falling from the sky was their intent, then faster and stronger. The seams tore and the rain crashed down all at once.

Peridot's tail coiled around my ankle as lighting struck, giving shapes to darkness around me. I knelt to pick up his soft body and held him in my arms. At the flash, I counted mentally: *uno . . . due . . . tre . . . quattro . . . cinque . . . sei*

. . . sette . . . otto . . . nove. The thunder arrived. I divided nine by three, figuring the storm to be about three miles away.

"The gods are tilting buckets up there, *micio*," I whispered to my kitty. It was an old expression Joséphine used when thunderstorms like this struck back home.

In the tear of another lightning bolt, Gabe appeared. Face down, sleeping undisturbed with a sheet wrapped carelessly over his lower back, and a bent arm supporting his head half-buried beneath the pillow, he faced away from me. I left the window and walked in darkness until my knees found his side of the bed. Above the rain, his peaceful breath filled my ears. Oblivious to the storm outside, the rhythm of his breathing stilled my heart. I waited for the next burst of lighting and used that instant of brilliant illumination to look at his back. I didn't see the scars. I waited for another lightning flash and tried again, but it didn't work. The flash didn't last long enough for me to even focus. It came and went; thunder walked toward us in the sky above.

I wondered why I was so set on looking at his scars. I wasn't going to get answers from looking at his back. I pondered what he had told me earlier. How much it must have meant to him to share such a painful part of his life with me. My heart bled in pain at the thought of him trapped in the metal wreck. I imagined him coming out of the coma to face what had happened, having to deal with it, to ultimately accept it. I knew that, except for the thin scars along his shoulder blades, he was in perfect physical shape. He had proven it to me. Whatever kept him from racing now must be something entirely spiritual and extremely profound.

Was I relieved he wasn't racing anymore? How would I feel knowing he would be going off for weeks, risking his neck at every turn? I honestly found no answers to such questions. All I knew was that racing was what he loved the most and that I would not be the one keeping him from it.

No. No matter how dangerous.

I followed the edge of the bed to my side, balancing Peridot on my left arm. I took a sip of water from the glass on my nightstand and waited a second, holding my breath, listening for Gabe's.

"Xavier?" I asked softly.

Peridot's purring was my only answer. I scratched his chin.

Sleep eluded me and I didn't feel like laying back down. I fumbled in the dark to find my robe, all the while holding the cat. Barefoot, I walked into the den to work a little. I sat at my desk, slipped into the robe, and readjusted the folds along my bare legs. Peridot jumped off my lap and went to sit on his favorite chair, fascinated by the rivulets of rain streaking the dark window. He completely ignored me. I flipped open my laptop and hit the on switch. Oscar wanted the article by the end of the week so I went to work. I barely had to glance at my notes, picking up where I left off; as my fingers flew over the keyboard I recalled the magic of Delilah's recipes from memory and captured Aeson's charming hospitality and the intriguing energies of their restaurant.

Rain poured relentlessly as night collapsed under the weight of a gray dawn. My brain begged for coffee. I made a cappuccino and sipped at it as I re-read my words, correcting here and there, stifling yawns. I stretched my aching body and went through the motions of saving the article, e-mailing and faxing a copy to Oscar. The sleep that so eluded me earlier now filled up my brain like a wet fog. It was still raining cats and dogs when I crawled back in bed.

*

For being a gourmet writer/critic, my fridge was looking pretty depressing, I thought a couple of hours later as I poked through the rubble of yogurt and San Pellegrino mineral water for something more substantial.

Gabe fidgeted by the stove with the Moka. "I can't believe this bloody thing is supposed to make coffee."

"I can't believe I have such an empty fridge." I stared straight at a jar of salted capers on the top shelf next to some clarified butter. Empty fridge, but still gourmet.

"Never mind." I shut the refrigerator, giving up on breakfast.

I walked up to him. "It's an espresso machine, *amore mio*," I explained, tickling his bare toes with mine as I filled the lower part of the Moka with fresh water, set in the filter, and added the ground coffee. He folded his arms against his chest and watched every move I made. I screwed the top part of the machine back on and fired the stove burner.

"Once the water boils, it percolates through the little funnel filter, soaking the coffee up, making magic happen . . . *et voilà*! Espresso shoots up from the tiny chimney into the top chamber." I wasn't done speaking yet when the little Moka, as if prompted by my words, began to huff and puff, letting us know it was happily doing its duty.

I took two small cups from the cupboard and asked Gabe how much sugar he would like.

"One." His arms were still crossed against his chest.

I scooped one spoon for him and one for me into a small stainless steel creamer. I then added a little steaming espresso from the Moka and, using a small spoon, beat the sugar and coffee, whipping up a frothy cream in a matter of seconds. I added the remaining espresso to the creamer and stirred gently until a thick, sweet, creamy foam rose to the top. I poured the espresso into the small cups and handed one to Gabe.

"Am I supposed to drink this with my little finger standing at attention or what?" he asked, taking the cup.

"You do whatever, just let me know if you like it or not." I raised my cup to my lips, anticipating the pleasure of the flavor that already intoxicated my sensitive nostrils.

"This is great!" He licked the frothy cream from his lips.

"Of course it is," I said, laughing at his surprise.

"Can I have another?" He looked to see if there was any espresso left in the Moka.

"Be my guest. Now that you know how it works you can make your own while I watch." I handed him the coffee can and sugar bowl.

"Do you want another?"

I shook my head. "No, thanks." I hugged his waist and planted a kiss on his bare shoulder.

"So, what would you like to do today?"

The phone rang. As I reached for it, the doorbell rang, too. I motioned to Gabe to get the door as I picked up the phone.

It was Oscar calling from La Guardia airport, all twitters and delights over the article and the excellent photos Jason had just sent him.

Chirp . . . chirp . . . he went on . . . and *pardon* for such short notice, but would I enjoy an invitation to the grand opening of Chez le Chat, an old New Orleans brothel just turned restaurant, scheduled for tomorrow evening? It could turn into a great piece . . .

How could I refuse? Oscar is such a colorful creature, a real pleasure to work with. His bubbly enthusiasm is not only contagious, but also so powerful he can turn water into champagne just by giggling.

I turned my head to ask Gabe if he would like to see New Orleans and caught him winking at me. Still wearing only his boxers, grinning from ear to ear, he pointed to a stunned and entranced Benedetta now standing in my kitchen. Above Oscar's tweeting I heard him tell her to have a seat as he left to grab something to wear. I waved at Benedetta from where I stood, but she didn't notice me. Her busy eyes followed Gabe as he walked away. Her already impossibly purple cheeks darkened even more.

I finished my phone call and walked back into the kitchen. I put my left hand under Bene's chin and my right on the top of her head. With a quick professional move—one of those you struggle to follow when they happen in karate movies—I shut her mouth, forgetting that her tongue might have been hanging out. I did hear the gritting of tooth against tooth, so I assumed her tongue was safely tucked out of danger.

"*Buongiorno!* Would you like some coffee?"

She blinked, looked at me, scratched her head, and nodded. I poured half of the fresh espresso Gabe had just made and stuck a cup under her nose. I pushed the sugar closer to her, too. She shook her head and looked at me. "That's him?"

"Nope. That's the holy ghost, Bene."

"Wow!"

"Drink your coffee before it gets too cold."

She picked up her spoon and added sugar to her tiny cup as Gabe walked back into the kitchen. He stopped in his tracks when he noticed what Benedetta was doing.

"Is that the fresh espresso?" he asked, raising an eyebrow in that sexy way of his.

"*Si.* Yes. She likes a bit of coffee with her sugar in the morning," I teased, watching Benedetta stir her syrup. My affection for her spilled outward, as if summoned by my friend's silly, sugary habit.

"I like it really sweet," Benedetta confirmed, smiling as well. She tapped the spoon on the rim of the cup to make sure it was clean of any sugar and drank her coffee. She pushed her glasses up her nose and smirked at me.

"Is it alroight?" Gabe asked, pouring the rest for himself.

"Yes, it's excellent. I didn't mean to bother you guys, but she didn't tell me you were visiting." She shot him a shy look.

"She didn't know I was coming until I showed up."

"And you never bother me," I assured her, still basking in my idyllic state.

"I was wondering if you could check on Eros for a few days next week."

"You're going back to Georgia, aren't you?"

Benedetta's plum checks were just about ready to be picked and made into jam . . . This was the most I had seen her blush in such a short time frame. "Yes. Eros didn't like the pet-sitter place much. It will only be for a couple of days."

"And school?"

"School's fine, I'm only taking off two working days. The other two I'd have free anyway."

"Are you driving?"

"No, I was thinking of manifesting myself *Star Trek*-style, Porzia."

Gabe chuckled.

"Look, if it's too much trouble because you've got company, I understand."

"No, he'll be back home by then." I looked at Gabe for confirmation. He nodded.

"Of course I'll check on Eros. It's the least I can do after you took such good care of Peridot and the house while I was in Australia." I reached over to hug her.

"Not to mention the countless times you were out there somewhere stuffing your face," she said, returning my squeeze.

"OK then, it's settled. Now, let's have a bit of feed," Gabe said.

"I'd love to feed you two but I've got no food. The cupboard is bare," I apologized.

Benedetta stood and brought her cup to the sink. "It's OK. I'm off to work anyway. But I wouldn't want to be in *your* shoes." She looked at Gabe. "But then, you've got no shoes." She grabbed her bag, chuckling, and hit the door waving good-bye.

"That's your best friend?" he asked as he walked over to hug me.

"Yes, that's Bene all right."

"You're from two different planets."

"Maybe that's why we get along so well." I lifted my lips to kiss his chin. "How about I get dressed and you do too." I tugged at his quickly thrown on shirt. "And we hit a good place I know for breakfast; then we go grocery shopping."

"Roight." He kissed me. It took a while to find clothes.

*

We had breakfast at Napoleon Bakery where Etienne waltzed around us with fluffy truffle and brie omelettes, warm baguettes, fresh orange juice, and fruit salad.

When I introduced Etienne to Gabe, he said, "Breakfast is on the house," and then sat down next to me. With a deep sigh he asked Gabe how it felt to beat Tonacci.

I tensed waiting for Gabe's response. I wasn't sure he would be comfortable talking about his racing days with perfect strangers.

Gabe set his fork down to give Etienne his full attention. "Piece of piss, mate," he said. "Roight before start-up, Tonacci had actually come up to shake hands. To wish something like 'break a leg.' Gomi, my head mechanic, whose blood is worth bottling, actually thought Tonacci wasn't fair dinkum and accused him of coming up to check things out, to see what we were up to. Gomi told him he stood Buckley's of beating us this time.

"Since we'd be his most difficult opponents, and he wasn't inclined to share the limelight, he didn't take it nicely. We'd heard he'd been too busy circulating in the VIP's scene to actually get a solid ride. So this time, the bloke was driving a bodgy car not up to his usual standards and began having minor trouble with his performance soon after we crossed over into the Northern Africa territory.

"I had to give it to him; up until then, he'd been as cunning as a dunny rat and had stamina to sell. Nothing to jeopardize his pozzy quite yet, then he still had a fair go. But once things got heated up, he started spewin' and I gained distance until he wasn't within cooee of beating me to the finish line. He got as mad as a cut snake."

"*Mon Dieu!*" Etienne exclaimed, raising his hands to heaven as if having just witnessed a miracle.

Stunned by the way Gabe's colorful speech whirlwinded me into a vastness of speed, control, focus, endurance, and Oz slang, I felt his rush, his fever brewing, his adrenaline pumping through the challenge, and a flutter of wings erasing it all in the blink of an eye.

Etienne went off to find a menu for Gabe to autograph.

"You don't mind people recognizing you all the time?"

"It doesn't happen so much anymore," he said, finishing his food in two forkfuls. "I used to have to do it to promo the business, especially when sponsors got involved—TV appearances and newspaper interviews. I never did media endorsements, though. I remember when I first started and was scraping to put a vehicle together, I told myself I would never do commercials. I never did."

"So, when you were a little kid and adults asked you what you wanted to be when you grew up, what did you tell them?"

"A driver," Gabe said, cracking a grin. "Clark gave me a pedal car when I was about four, I reckon. I drove it everywhere and parked it at the foot of my bed every night before going to sleep. It drove my mother bonkers. By the time I was six, I had outgrown it. I asked Clark to help me mount the lawnmower engine on it so I wouldn't have to bloody pedal all the time anymore, and we opened up the frame, turning it into a go-kart. The rest is history."

"That's amazing. You were able to fulfill your childhood dream and become a racer."

"It took a lot of hard work. But, yes, you're roight. I made it happen." He took a long look at me. "Did you tell people you wanted to eat for a living when you grew up?"

"Very funny," I smiled, knowing he was teasing. "I got traumatized by kindergarten food."

His raised eyebrow invited me to explain.

"Minestrone with big veggie chunks; spinach leaves bigger than my spoon, dripping dark broth; chicken bits with more fat than meat on them." I shivered just thinking about it. "Family food, on the other hand, has always been a big part of what I considered comfort in my childhood."

"And the wine?"

"The wine? Oh, well, that's familiar territory. They say the apple doesn't fall far from the tree? I guess in my particular case, the grapes didn't fall far from the vine. On special occasions my father would pour just enough in my glass to stain the water a light-pink blush. He says that no matter how rough life gets, as long as there is wine on the table, problems can be solved."

Gabe was still laughing when Etienne returned with a brand-new menu and a fountain pen, which he handed to Gabe with a bow and flourish. Gabe signed it and shook hands with him. As we walked out, I wondered, feeling a surge of relief, if this would finally free me of *Monsieur Le Pew*'s sappy flirting.

With full tummies we headed for the grocery store. On the drive over I told Gabe about Oscar's invitation to Madame Magdalena's new restaurant and asked him how he felt about driving over to New Orleans. Then wondered how *I* would feel to be back there with Gabe. New Orleans drips of memories of times I had shared with Steve. I hadn't gone back since. I had even turned down a few assignments because I didn't think I could handle it. *Look at me now. Facing my own fears.*

"How far of a drive is it?"

"About three hours, depending on if we take the highway or the scenic route along the Mississippi coast. Have you ever been to New Orleans, Gabe?"

"I like the way you say my name with that accent of yours. No, I've never been."

"Gabe . . . Gabe . . . Gabe . . . Gabe," I repeated slowly, teasing him. "Would you like to go?"

"What I'd like is to be alone with you somewhere I can take your clothes off roight now. Yes, I'd like to go. Later."

I brought the car to a halt just in time for Gabe's arm to wrap itself around me. My right hand let go of the emergency brake and worked its way up his strong chest, found the back of his bare neck, and grabbed onto his golden hair. His lips fed hungrily off mine. I felt desire build up deep within. The emergency brake painfully stabbed my hip as I inched myself closer to him, then I forgot all about it as his tongue slipped inside my mouth, searching, teasing. I moaned throatily against his lips and opened my eyes slightly to meet his. Soulful blue eyes sparkled at me through thick lashes, his simmering lust clearly visible. A surge of thick desire built up within me.

To feel the strength of his need reflected in his melting eyes drove me crazy with power. I couldn't stop looking into his half-slit, blue-shifting eyes as I teased his tongue with mine, as I nibbled at his lips with my teeth, as I ran my hand through the thickness of his luscious hair and pulled it downward until my wet mouth found the stubble on his chin. I kissed and kissed and kissed . . . I lost track of time, space, boundaries.

He pulled away from me just before I lost total control. Breathing heavily, he bored straight into my eyes and asked me, "Who's Xavier?"

"My soul mate," I blurted before I had time to think, my lips still wet with his taste.

Merda!

CHAPTER 22

"Your—bloody what?"

I didn't like the frown creasing his usually smooth brow, not one bit.

"My soul mate." I took a deep breath, took my eyes off his troubled face, ran a hand through my own hair, and dared to look at him once again. The frown had deepened.

"According to Evalena—" I stopped abruptly. *Accidenti!* Why was I blaming her? And how much was I willing to share? I had begun to believe what I had seen during my past life regression, and a small part of me wanted desperately for Gabe to be Xavier. The rest of me, the real me I've grown up with and knew well, was telling me to shut the hell up.

But I knew better. It would be only fair, after what he had told me about his accident. So I took a big breath, cast a sidelong glance at him, and as usual, as of lately, questioned my choices. Treading on unfamiliar territory, I had no idea how to go about it. Italians have an expression for such a feeling: *Brancolare nel buio*—dwelling in darkness. That's exactly how I felt: about to jam myself against unpredictable sharp corners, walking ever so slowly, afraid to step into *and* be swallowed by a bottomless hole, keeping my arms wrapped around myself, jeopardizing my balance in the process, but too scared to extend my hands out and touch . . . the monsters of my own devising.

Exhaling painfully, I decided I would risk it. I knew no other way: honesty before all, even loss . . .

With difficulty, in the small space of my car, I told him about losing Joséphine and my promise at her deathbed. I wasn't looking for sympathy or excuses. Fully aware of my decision, I briefly described my past life regression and how Evalena had helped me.

Gabe's face darkened, quickly clouding over.

Xavier's essence flared alive, beckoned by my words. Like a genie impossibly manifested from a magical lamp. Out of nowhere, I smelled dry hay.

The sky had gone gray again; the early afternoon sun had given way to rain-laden clouds. Drops hit the fogged-up windshield and brought me back to the present.

"You reckon I'm him?" Gabe asked, after a moment of silence.

"No . . . Yes . . . Perhaps? *Merda!* Gabe, I have no idea."

"Do you want me to be him?"

"I thought you *were* him a couple of times. When you told me you spoke French . . . when you understood about me having lost track of dimensions and mentioned the wastelands . . . almost a reflection of what I saw to be real. '*To let go and believe it fully.*' Hell, I'd like to believe it fully, but reality is a different matter. You're so real, and I feel *you* so strongly that it's difficult to worry about someone else in another life. The intensity of you and me as *us*, building a relationship . . . making memories with you is erasing my doubts. You take over and I stop thinking about it. Until something you do or something that happens triggers the thought. But I am obsessing—"

He interrupted me. "To let go of what?"

"Fear." I looked at him.

He understood.

Xavier or no Xavier—Gabe Miller was my present, not only as present in time, but as a gift as well.

"I'm not him."

"How do you know?"

"I don't, but I won't do a past life regression to find out either." He ran a hand through his hair, then leaned over and flicked at the dice hanging off the car ignition. "You're gambling, Porzia. On *two* dice. And I only have *now* to believe in." He held my gaze. "I hope it's enough, luv."

Like a puppet whose strings are magically pulled by invisible hands, I could only nod. And *Pinocchio* is not my favorite fairy tale.

*

It was still raining when we arrived back home. I hoped the weather would clear up by next morning when we'd have to hit the road. Highway 10 to New Orleans is a boring drag in good weather but with rain it would be the equivalent of a never-ending funeral sermon.

Keeping in mind we were going to drive to New Orleans, I had bought mostly breakfast items, plus bruschetta ingredients, new potatoes, and tenderloins for dinner.

While Gabe unpacked the groceries, I marinated the tenderloins with extra virgin olive oil, added salt and pepper, and stored them in a covered container in the fridge to marinate.

"Would you mind peeling some potatoes while I check New Orleans to make hotel reservations?" I handed him the peeler.

"No worries."

I left him in the kitchen and walked to my computer desk where I sat down to check my calendar. In about two weeks I would most likely be in Oregon for the wine aficionados' publication *Grape Expectations.*

Gabe walked into the den with a glass of white wine.

"This is where I might be going next." I blew him a kiss and accepted the wine.

"Looks like fun." He peered over my shoulder at the screen. "How long will you be gone?"

"About a week all together."

"I'll be done with the Australian Safari by then."

"When is that?"

"Last week of August through the beginning of September."

"So you're heading back just in time for it."

"I should be there now, luv. But Clark and Gomi have things under control, so no worries."

"I won't worry if you don't." I took a sip of chilled-to-perfection, crisp wine and clicked on the hotel's link to make a reservation at Le Moulin, my favorite, just outside the French quarter, with the façade opposite a cemetery and all the rooms tucked away around a picturesque courtyard.

"I'll go fix a bag." He kissed the top of my head. "Join me when you're done?"

I found him minutes later, standing over his suitcase with a worried look on his face. "I don't have anything formal, Porzia. I wasn't planning on attending anything ceremonial."

"No worries. Oscar has fashion connections everywhere. I'm sure we can ask him. You'll be fine. I'm not planning on dressing up either." I scanned my wardrobe.

"We sound pretty domestic, don't we, luv?" he observed as he stretched himself out on the bed beside the folded clothes waiting to be packed.

I stopped pawing through my panties and bras to look at him. "Yes, we do."

"You're OK with that?"

"Yes." I dropped my lingerie pile and crawled onto the bed to press myself against him. I gave him a light kiss on the nose and snuggled until I felt his arms wrap around me. His breathing eased into sleep. I remember thinking how luxurious it felt to nap like that before falling asleep myself.

*

Time faded. Sleep took over until Gabe stirred, waking me up.

I stretched and sat on the bed, taking in all the clothes still patiently waiting to be packed. Peridot had followed our cue; he snoozed among bras and panties, his nose buried in a lacy cup.

Gabe followed my stare looking at the kitty cat happy in dreamland. "That's a place I wouldn't mind falling asleep myself."

"Weeell, the bra does have two cups . . . ," I teased. I got up from the bed and stepped into the bathroom to wash the leftover sleep from my face. I couldn't hear any rain hitting the skylight so I guessed it must have stopped. Feeling pangs of hunger, I walked back into the bedroom where Gabe was finishing his packing. I reached for my cherry-red overnight bag, a graduation present from my brother and faithful companion on many adventures. I began to stuff it with clothes and things I chose quickly for the trip. "How about dinner?" I asked.

"Sounds good. Will you need help or can I jump in the shower?"

"No help, but company would be nice once you're done," I told him, zipping my bag up. I'm a fast packer.

"No worries."

I retrieved my empty wine glass from where I had left it by the computer and walked into the kitchen where I poured myself a short refill. I hit the light switch, turned on the radio, and set to work while the jazz station coated the kitchen with the sultry voice of Astrud Gilberto. Humming along, I opened the fridge and thrust my face in.

I planned to make seared tenderloins in horseradish butter sauce, *smashed* potatoes, as Bene loves to call them, and a light spring salad. For a starter, I had bought some crusty baguettes that morning at the bakery. I grabbed stuff from the fridge and looked around for the bread, my arms barely holding all the ingredients. What did I do with it? *Ah! Eccolo!* There it was, right there on the counter, waiting to be sliced, toasted, and spread with imported caponata. I couldn't resist and sampled it with the tip of a knife, savoring the rich taste of eggplants. I topped the sliced bread appetizers with freshly crushed black pepper and turned the broiler on. Filling a cookie sheet with the small crostini, I threw them in the scorching oven to warm up. Yummy!

I pirouetted in my kitchen and wondered *what next*? How about the smashed potatoes? I'd leave the tenderloins to the last minute so they'd be still sizzling. I filled a pot with cold water, added sea salt, and cubed the peeled russet potatoes Gabe had left soaking in a bowl of cold water. I switched the burner on high, dropped a lid on the pot, and decided to set the table.

This is my favorite part of a dinner party. I chose a light yellow tablecloth and matching napkins. I added rustic blue plates and salad bowls I had bought in Provence a couple of years back while visiting Joséphine. I rummaged through the silverware drawer to find knives and forks, and finished with water goblets and Riedel wine glasses. Gabe walked in looking refreshed. He smelled delicious, and I almost dropped the oil and vinegar cruets on the table. Phew!

"Wow! It already smells great!" He hugged me from behind and planted a kiss on my neck.

"It doesn't take long to make miracles." I turned to face him and return the kiss properly on his lips. I inhaled deeply. Good heavens! He smelled fantastic! Fresh soap mixed with his intense masculine scent which was becoming so familiar.

"You smell great. My food is a distant second." I inhaled his essence again. I could get high on him.

"Can I help you with *anything*?" he teased. He was clearly aware of the effect he had on me.

"Just hold me and stay still so I can keep on breathing you in."

"For how long? Whatever you're making smells really good."

"You're hungry?"

"Yes."

"Me too," I agreed and nibbled at his neck, working my way up to his earlobe. With extra effort I pried myself away and went to open the oven. Using a cactus-shaped oven mitt Benedetta had given me for a birthday a while back, I took out the cookie sheet and showed Gabe the crostini. The mouth-watering aroma of baked eggplants suffused the kitchen. Holding the sheet like a serving tray with my right hand, I rested the left on the curve of my hip and leaned forward. "Is this what you wanted?" I smiled; the perfect Italian waitress flirting with a patron.

He laughed heartily. "You're absolutely impossible." He reached for a crostino.

"Watch out. It's hot."

"I bet." He sank his teeth into the crunchy bread, his eyes still laughing. I set the cookie sheet on a wire rack, transferred the crostini to a real serving tray, and poured Gabe a glass of a delicious full-bodied Napa Valley Cabernet; time to switch the wine. He settled by the tray with his glass and kept on munching while I resumed my work on the rest of dinner. I tossed the salad, peeled and sliced cucumbers, added fresh olives and orange slices, and then remembered the potatoes. I rushed to drain the pot and sighed, relieved it hadn't all turned into a starchy mush. From the colander I nonchalantly transferred the salvaged potatoes into a cobalt blue terrine, added butter, a bit of hot milk, a pinch of salt, a twist of freshly ground pepper, and whipped it all up until the potatoes got creamy and fluffy, still steaming hot. I brought the bowl to the table, careful not to burn my hands.

At last the tenderloins! I anointed them with a fresh coat of olive oil and sliced them lengthwise using my hand to guide me. They were so thick I got five slices per tenderloin. I sprinkled on fresh pepper and lightly floured each side. I then set a heavy skillet on a burner and turned the gas on high. I dropped in a tablespoon of clarified butter that impatiently sizzled immediately. Carefully, I added the meat, half a cup of cream mixed with horseradish and extra pepper, and allowed it to reduce for a minute or two, turning the meat only once. Gabe silently watched me as I finished everything up. I let the tenderloins rest a second in the skillet and filled the goblets with sparkling San Pellegrino water, sliced more bread to bring to the table, and checked to see if Peridot needed anything. I presented the meat right on the skillet I used to cook it in. As I grabbed the salad, I cast him a sultry look over my shoulder and silently invited him.

"You're ready?" he asked.

"Yes, just grab the wine and whatever crostini you've got left," I said, taking a seat.

"This looks great." He refilled my glass.

"Thanks. I hope it will taste as good as it looks." I unfolded my napkin to rest on my lap and raised my glass. "It's heavenly to have you here with me."

He touched my glass with his and leaned over to kiss me lightly on the lips. "Thank you for doing all this tonight. Even if it didn't take you long at all," he teased.

"You're welcome." I passed him the bread basket and then quickly moved it away before he could reach a slice of bread.

"Now, Porzia," he laughed.

I handed him the bread basket one more time, and again, as he went for it, I moved it away. But not fast enough. He grabbed one side and pulled at it until he got his bread and then snatched the entire basket out of my hand, moving it closer to him where I couldn't reach.

"May I have some bread?" I asked, grabbing the salad bowl. "I'll trade you some salad."

"Oh, now we're bargaining?"

"Please?" I pinched an oil-glistening slice of cucumber with my fingertips and fed it to him.

"OK." He passed me the bread with one hand and held the salad bowl with the other. I guess he didn't trust me.

The tenderloins had cooked to perfection in the creamy, rich sauce and the tanginess of the horseradish complimented the smoothness of the fluffy potatoes and the fresh texture of the salad. It turned out to be a scrumptious dinner.

"So how do you keep the feeling of sampling a dish vivid enough for you to write about later on?"

"That's an excellent question, not easy to answer. I usually take notes as I eat. Especially if it's a dish I've never had before. But honestly, my appreciation, exuberance, and enthusiasm for flavors seem to always find a way to permeate my words, soaking them until the essence of the dish I'm writing about is almost palpable."

"And the wine?"

"The wine is a personal taste option. If you had to be professional about it, you'd end up serving a different bottle with each course. I know chefs that end up with a selection of seven or eight bottles per dinner." I smiled at his raised eyebrows. "I prefer Italian and French wines just because of my background and my personal experience growing up surrounded by those particular grapes. Australian and California wines are great choices as well. Champagnes I use only on special occasions. New Zealand and South American wines are something I've yet to spend a lot of time discovering."

"Do you believe they lose flavor with traveling?"

"It's more than that." I struggled to find a good explanation. "Many times you find that a wine just tastes better when it's consumed in its native area, enjoyed with the local foods it was designed to complement. Even the air seems to make a difference sometimes."

He nodded agreement, but his eyes clouded over. "Tell me about New Orleans." He got up and began to clean up the table while I filled the sink with water for the dishes.

My heart skipped a bit but I found my love for the city unblemished by my past.

"New Orleans exudes a spice-infused essence, addictive and intoxicating. Her heart beats to its own rhythm. She's a decadent cornucopia that never tires, just keeps on giving with a visceral soundtrack of rich blues, jazz, and Cajun-French ballads. The past rules, spilling into the present. Caribbean, French, African-American beliefs wind around your soul, dripping superstition into your heart like thick, warm honey."

"You sound like a tourism ad for an intrepid thrill seeker."

"Do I?" I laughed, piling dishes in the sink. "Then you're gonna love it." *Almost as much as I do,* I thought. I had truly missed the primeval energy of the place. "You'll understand once we get there. It creeps under your skin." I finished the dishes, cast him a coy look, and sprinkled him with soapy water. That, of course, started a water fight that ended up with both of us completely soaking wet on the kitchen floor, smelling strongly of Palmolive and kissing madly.

He swept me off my feet and carried me into the bedroom where the mattress welcomed our tangled bodies. He kept on devouring me with kisses, until kisses were no longer enough and skin became necessary. Caught in the momentum of rising heat we tore our clothes off. The speed it took him to light me on fire left me breathless, and I jerked my head away from his, gasping for air, for some sort of restraint, my entire body begging me to resume the kissing, *screaming and why the hell did I stop! Was I out of my mind? Oh, Madre mia, what is he doing to me? This is insane.*

I fought to slow down, to grasp control, but the mere brush of his fingers against my skin sent shivers down my spine, webbing me back in. Through half-parted eyelids I caught sight of his mouth inching in on mine; it drove me wild with anticipation and melting pleasure rippled through me, took over, and dissolved reality.

The following morning I woke up aching pleasantly and stretched my sore limbs. I blinked, focusing on Gabe's dark silhouette standing stark naked by the bedroom window, blocking daylight. I didn't think he knew I was awake, so I took a moment to adjust my eyes to the light that exploded like an aura around his solid body and simply observed him.

From my angle, he looked taller than ever, more solid, especially the width of his shoulders, the strength of his back tapering at the waist, where it curved to his chiseled buttocks, thence to the sinewy muscled length of his legs.

"*Buongiorno.*"

He turned slowly. That was something I had noticed about him. When he turned, he did it unhurriedly . . . he moved his head, neck, and shoulders simultaneously.

"G'day, luv. Did you sleep well?" As he walked away from the window, sunrays fanned around him. The effect was stunning—Apollo of the Shadows.

"Yes, I did." I stifled a yawn. "What time is it?"

"Not quite seven yet." He sat on my side of the bed, pulled the sheets away to expose my bare breasts, and bent his head to kiss them. I relaxed against the pillows and raised a hand to comb through his hair.

His kisses held the gentle breeze this morning. He worshipped my breasts unhurriedly. I felt devotion, respect, and appreciation pouring through the heat of his lips as they explored my skin. My hand, trapped in the tangle of his luscious hair, slowed down, then stilled while he continued to kiss up my neck and finally reached my lips.

"You're so unbelievably beautiful in the morning, Porzia." His lips vibrated along mine.

"*Merci.*"

"I'm bloody afraid I'm going to wake up any time now and you'll disappear like a mirage in the desert."

"You're afraid, Gabe?"

"Yes." He rested his head on my chest.

"I'm real," I reassured him and resumed combing through his hair. "Have you had many?"

"Mirages?" His voice spread through my entire body.

"Yes."

"No, but you sure feel like one." His eyes met mine.

"How do you know what a mirage feels like if you haven't had any?" I asked softly, wandering into his deep blue.

"I didn't say that, luv." He closed his eyes and turned, resting his head back on my breasts.

I sensed he didn't really want to talk about it anymore. I kept on running my hand through his hair and wondered if I considered him a mirage. *No, not that,* my aching limbs told me.

"I don't think you're a mirage, Gabe. But I've got a question for you."

"Yeah?" I sensed a smile tingeing his passionate voice.

"Yeah." I pulled him up until our mouths met. "What's your favorite fairy tale?"

Abruptly, he jerked away from my lips. And for once he didn't change the subject but was purely honest about it. "It's not a happy one, luv. I don't think you're ready to hear about it." In a flutter of long, blinking eyelashes, his eyes refocused and saw me.

I let go of my fear and tasted his.

"You don't know how it ends . . ." I whispered, choking on surging bile.

He dropped his head and shook it.

I needed to get away. All I could think of was survival. I was about to fling myself out of bed, but he pulled me back and pinned me down. No matter the advantage, I wasn't ever going to win with him. Then he surprised me and, scooping me into his arms, lifted himself up. "Let's not ruin the day with sad stories, luv . . . let's live the present."

CHAPTER 23

We shared the shower. He made me coffee. I buttered his toast and he fed me fruit salad. I did the dishes. He brought the luggage to the car. I filled Peridot's bowls. He opened my car door and I drove out of the parking lot. Direction: New Orleans.

The glorious morning helped lift our spirits. Not a cloud diluted the azure sky, a perfect summer day for people to play hooky and hit the beaches. If everything went according to plan, we'd have time to stop somewhere along the coast and have a nice lunch.

"We're going to pass welcome signs at every state border?" he asked.

I considered teasing him with local products as I had with Benedetta but thought better of it. "Yes."

Garth Brooks sang at the top of his lungs about friends in low places, and Gabe whistled along with the radio almost all the way through Mississippi. My eyes swept the surrounding sights. The Deep South breathed heavily, echoing the ocean waves eternally crashing against the shore on our left. I slowed down, adjusting our pace, and cast a silent prayer out there. *Enough secrets for now—please let this be a magical getaway.* Ahead of us I imagined the Goddess of New Orleans spreading her arms wide open, ready to receive us. Beyond her sultry silhouette, wings fluttered briefly, clashing with my wish.

I maneuvered the car through the thick midday traffic. Salty moisture weighed heavily around us. My back, sticky with perspiration, was just about glued to the car seat.

"How about a drink?" Gabe asked as we left behind the busy center of Biloxi, with all its casinos, and headed toward Gulfport.

"Sounds good, but if you don't mind waiting a little longer, Gerome told me about a place on the other side of Gulfport famous for its seafood salads and incredible lemonade." I winked. "*Hard* lemonade."

"Hard?"

"*Si*. With a 'kick'," I told him, quoting my mailman.

The thought of a nice refreshing drink in this hellish heat sounded heavenly. We found the place right off the highway in no time, and with no traffic at all. Just outside Pass Christian, a bright yellow sign steered us in the right direction, and with a swift turn—sharper than expected—we found ourselves in the crowded parking lot of Tante Louise's Joint.

We parked beneath a scrawny oleander that I felt sorry for; breathing the highway fumes throughout its life, the poor thing didn't stand a chance. I found myself caressing the knobby trunk while Gabe stepped out of the car and gave me an enigmatic look.

"Ready?" His eyes shifted from tree to me.

"Yes." I reached to take his hand. We walked through the small parking lot hand in hand up to the restaurant's screen door. A cacophony of loud music and laughter burst through the tattered netting as we pulled it aside and entered. A plump woman with skin the color of caramel, hourglassed in gingham, greeted us warmly. Her Rubenesque hips rolled like a galleon in a gale as she escorted us to the last free table. I followed, amused, as the dangerous swaying of her stern threatened to knock over several full tables. Despite the crammed space, it was refreshingly cool in the restaurant.

"Are you Louise?" I asked, sitting down.

"Yes, I am." She smiled at me and winked at Gabe. He winked back.

"Gerome told me about you," I said. "I'm Porzia."

Her face broke into an enormous gap-toothed grin, and I found myself swept up and engulfed in folds of warm skin and gingham.

"You're not on official business are you?" She dropped me to wave a plump, admonitory finger at me. "You should have given me a fair warning."

I fell back on my chair. "Uh, uh—no," I said in a tiny voice.

"Great!" With a huge smile she told us she would be right back with a pitcher. I tilted my head to better follow her hips, like over-inflated balloons raising the back of her skirt several inches higher than the front, where it draped past her knees.

Gabe leaned back in his chair, reached for a worn-out, plasticized menu wedged between the ketchup and mustard, and looked at me. "What are you going to have, luv?"

I grabbed a menu as well and took a quick glance. "I think we should ask Louise."

"OK with me."

She came back with a full-figured pitcher filled to the brim with thick lime-green lemonade and two frosted glasses.

"Here you are." She set the glasses and pitcher down on the table. "Y'all wanna be careful about brain freeze." She smiled, touching her third eye with a chubby finger. "I'll be right back with your food." With a whoosh of hips smacking against chairs, she made it clear we were at her mercy.

I shrugged. "I guess she'll take care of us."

Gabe carefully poured the lemonade. "Is this going to get you pissed?"

I reached for one of the glasses. "You mean drunk?"

"Yes."

"Probably." I touched his glass with mine. "*Cin cin,*" I said and tasted the lemonade. *Mmmh... icy... bitter.* My eyes cringed and my stomach contracted. Thick, most definitely thick, and absolutely loaded. I loved it. I took another sip, careful not to ruin the effect with brain freeze, and felt a buzz creeping up already. *Uh-oh!*

"It's a straight shot from here to New Orleans, anyway," I offered. "You could drive the rest of the way."

"I didn't see you taking many curves up to this point." He shot me a quick grin.

"We really didn't, huh?" My nostrils twitched in anticipation of something delicious approaching our table. Louise juggled two heaping trays and plates on her arms and didn't quite make it; one of the trays slipped out of her grip. I caught it in time with relief; my reflexes were still working.

"Thanks, hon. I'll be back with bread." She gave us the plates and handed Gabe a serving spoon she magically manifested from the folds of her apron.

On the first tray tottered an abundant serving of grilled garlic tiger prawns. I inhaled the inviting aroma of garlic and my mouth melted. On the second tray, Louise had brought us a baby green bean salad with cucumbers, peeled strips of yellow and red bell peppers, mango, and wedges of aged cheddar. The bright colors glistened with olive oil.

"This looks incredible," I said, holding my plate up for Gabe to fill.

"Wait until you taste it," Louise said. She handed me a basket of fragrant French bread, sliced lengthwise, and a jar of thick honey. "The honey we make ourselves: Lemon-Verbena. It marries well with the bitterness of the lemonade." She smiled and winked at Gabe again. With an auspicious "Enjoy your meal and holler for refills," she left us to our food.

We dug in. I took a bite of the salad and told myself I needed to buy Gerome a gift. I tasted a prawn and the gift got bigger. I took a sip of lemonade and forgot all about what I was thinking and stared at Gabe who was quietly peeling prawns. His nimble fingers glistened with buttery juices while his head swayed in rhythm to Elvis's voice oozing out of an ancient jukebox; he seemed enthralled by the atmosphere.

"*Très bon, n'est pas?*" I asked him, lapsing into French, but never got an answer. Louise's laughter reached us from where she sat at a nearby table filled with patrons who looked like they knew her well. Relaxed people enjoying the excellent food occupied the remaining tables. The lemonade must have been the drink of choice, for there were pitchers of it everywhere. I wondered if everybody would get as drunk as me.

"Yes. It's pretty good feed," Gabe finally replied. He drizzled rich honey on one of the peeled prawns. "Would you like a bite?" His fingers extended the juicy morsel.

I leaned across the table, reaching for it with an open mouth, brushing his fingertips with my wet lips as I took it, and caught his eyes shifting to that darker shade I recognized. I smiled at him and pulled my lips away from his fingers. "Thanks," I said, resting my back against my chair. Slowly, I chewed the heavenly bite.

"I think we should dance," he announced, taking a sip of his drink. He pushed his chair back and stood, offering me a hand that I took with the first notes of Van Morrison stroking my ears. I found myself in his arms, barely swaying to the music, oblivious to anything else but his solid body pressed against mine. Tante Louise's walls faded; the tables, chairs, and the laughter of the patrons receded from my awareness. At the small of my back, the heat radiating from Gabe's left hand worked magic, and the gentle pressure of his right fingers at the back of my neck transported me into a timeless cloud of unconditional safety and warm love.

It seemed like an eternity elapsed.

Finally, when the music ceased, he walked me back to the table. I sat and blushed when he kissed my hand. I closed my eyes to bask in the moment. Gabe took his seat and asked me if I wanted more prawns. I nodded lightly and with effort opened my eyes.

"How'd y'all like it?" Louise asked us, placing a bowl of fresh seedless watermelon chunks on the table.

"Excellent," we choired.

"Great! Try the watermelon, we grow it ourselves." She smiled. "Tell Gerome that he needs to come and visit more often. We haven't seen him in over a year."

"I sure will . . . along with the many thanks I owe him for telling me about your place."

She bent over to give me another bear hug and blessed me with enough good wishes to wipe half of my purgatory sentence off my record.

Soon it was time to leave. I excused myself to go to the ladies' room and came out shortly to see Gabe talking quietly with Louise by the main counter. She nodded when he folded a piece of paper into his wallet.

"It would really mean a lot, Louise," I heard Gabe say as I approached them.

Louise smiled. "Consider it done." She caught sight of me walking up and went quiet.

Gabe turned from her to look at me. "Ready, luv?"

"Yes, but I think you'd better drive."

"That's some powerful stuff, young lady," Louise said.

We exchanged good-byes and I gave Gabe the car keys. We left the coolness of the restaurant and walked into the brothy day outside. It felt like diving into a pot of chicken stock.

Set on the sinewy curves of the silver-watered Mississippi, New Orleans appeared on the horizon. Gabe drove silently, tapping his fingers on the steering wheel to the slow rhythm of blues songs that droned from the radio. We glided into the French Quarter—the goddess' core.

At Le Moulin we checked into a luxurious room overlooking a typical courtyard the city is so renowned for. The bed was king-size, and the bathroom had a marble tub the size of the Colosseo. A mossy fountain gurgled three stories below, reaching our ears like throaty laughter. I loved it.

Gabe seemed to be pleased with it as well. He stretched out on the bed and bounced a couple of times to test the mattress. Satisfied, he adjusted a quilted pillow behind his head and grinned at me. "What would you like to do, luv?" He crossed his arms behind his head, flexing biceps that stretched the short sleeves of his T-shirt.

I'd like to lick and bite your arms right there where the muscle flexes and follow that disappearing vein with the tip of my tongue . . .

"Besides that, Porzia." He must have read my mind from my lustful expression.

"Wash the road off my body and go for a walk before sunset?"

"OK."

"I need to touch base with Oscar and see if we can find you something to wear for tonight. Then come back and get ready for dinner. But first . . ." I headed for the bathroom with my beauty case. I shut the door behind me and took my time washing my face, combing my hair, putting on some extra mascara, and making a face or two at the mirror. I stepped out, giving Gabe a chance to freshen up. Opening my luggage I looked for a fresh sundress to wear for the walk. I had brought a yellow, calf-length silk one with an empire waist that I knew would keep me fresh even in such soupy heat. I matched it with cork wedges and a pale yellow hair band. I sat on the bed and rang Oscar to tell him we'd made it and asked if he could suggest a tailor that could help us fit Gabe for the evening. He said he would just need Gabe's measurements and he would have someone send a suit to the hotel. I thanked my twitty friend and chatted with him a little longer until Gabe walked out of the bathroom, then handed him the phone so they could discuss the fitting details.

Gabe changed as well and traded his white T-shirt for a black one and baggy denim shorts with loads of pockets. He looked comfortable and at ease. Holding hands we walked down the three flights of stairs to the courtyard and out into the streets of the French quarter. We skirted the main district, taking the outer streets to make our way toward the Mississippi River. We meandered hand in hand, stopping here to admire Mardi Gras masks in a window display, and there to watch a mime tease passers-by, and later to listen to a sax player outside Saint Louis Cathedral. We made it to the Mississippi River bank and walked though the park, all the way to the aquarium. At the levee we admired the riverboats gently hugging the bank down below.

We crossed the street and walked into the French Quarter where a party brewed; a crowd was gathering to celebrate the night away. Music blasted out of the bars and restaurants. Lights were coming on. The air cooled down as the day gave in to night.

Strolling back toward the hotel, we passed a small boutique window where a stunning dress beckoned me. I stopped to look at it. A crimson shade darker than blood, it was cut like a nightgown with thin spaghetti straps, a plunging V neckline, and a long narrow skirt. *It must have a slit in the back to permit walking,* I thought as I moved to the side of the window to peek at the back of the dress. *Oh!* There was no back! The straps looped back onto the sides of the dress under the arms like a professional swimmer's bathing suit, leaving the entire back open. It was breathtaking.

"Wow!" I tried to whistle and failed.

"They're open, Porzia. Go try it on—" Gabe opened the boutique door and stepped aside to allow me to walk in first. A French-knotted, sophisticated blonde greeted us.

"Welcome! How may I help you?"

"The red dress?"

"Of course." She walked to the window, pulled a curtain aside, and stepped up to undress the mannequin.

Gabe leaned nonchalantly against the counter, taking in the boutique décor, all pink velvet and satin. "It's like being inside a lolly."

"Gabe? Where am I supposed to wear such a dress?" I asked him, worried about how sexy the thing was.

"At dinner tonight, luv." He folded his arms across his chest. "Here she comes."

"It's the only one left," she said, taking a good look at me, "but it's perfect for you." She led me to the dressing room and asked me what size shoes I wore. While I changed, she went off looking for heels more appropriate than the ones I was wearing.

I shut the dressing room door, awestruck at my own daring behavior. To even consider trying on such . . . sin . . . I mean—Venere would have traded her shell for something like this. *Oh!* There I was once again, on the threshold of becoming a liquid woman.

A light tap on the door announced the blonde's return. I cracked the door open and thanked her. I smiled at the sight of black patent leather sandals with heels so high there should have been a warning against vertigo on the side of the box. I set them aside and took the dress in my hands. The pure silk felt smooth and light against my fingers. A seamless thong was the only thing that would go under such sheer luxury. I wasn't wearing one.

Excited, I untied the straps of my sundress and slipped my bra and sandals off. I gingerly held the dress against my body, tilted my head to one side, and finally slid it on. I didn't want to look in the mirror until I had the black sandals on, so I turned away to face the wall, noticing that besides the sandals there was a tiny black G-string in the shoebox. *Clever girl,* I thought, slipping off my average cotton panties. I sat down in a mauve velvet chair to tie the sandals' thin straps around my ankles. Finally, I stood. Slowly. I found my balance on the high heels and turned.

I gasped at my reflection in the full-length mirror. Cinderella ready for the ball! And it wasn't even my favorite tale.

I looked stunning!

Well, besides the yellow hair band I had forgotten. I quickly removed it and passed a hand through my hair. I turned to look at the back of the dress. It fit me like a glove; it clung to my curves, slid smoothly off my hips, and hugged where it was supposed to hug. The back yoke plunged down to a slit climbing up the back of my knees. The open back showed off a couple of dimples I have at the small of my back.

I grinned. I felt beautiful. I felt seductive. I felt sophisticated.

"Gabe..." Softly, I cracked the door open. My index finger curled, beckoning him.

"Well?" he asked, approaching the dressing room.

I put on a sad face, blinking the mischief from my eyes. "It's too small. It doesn't fit."

"No way." He raised an eyebrow. "Let me see."

"I can't even zip it up."

"There *was* no bloody zipper, Porzia. Let me see."

I let the door fall open and stepped languidly in front of him. I raised an arm against the doorframe and leaned my head in the curve of my elbow. My hair fell across my face.

"*Buona sera,* Mr. Miller. *Se non ha altri impegni si potrebbe cenare insieme—,*" I purred in my lowest Italian accent, turning a simple dinner invitation into a hell-bent adventure.

"Bloody hell, Porzia—," he whispered, closing in on me with supernatural speed. His hands slowly stroked down my nude back, striking a match the length of my spine's nerve endings. The tips of my breasts responded instantaneously, pressing against the silk of the bodice. Gabe's eyes widened and he stared without blinking, his lips parted slightly.

A tiny cough rising from behind Gabe's imposing frame broke the spell. "I believe we have a nice fit?" the blonde asked neutrally. She acted like having Aussie hunks drooling over her clothing selection was an everyday occurrence.

"Yeah! We'll take the dress, the shoes, and whatever else she's *not* wearing as well," Gabe answered her without even turning, his breath warm on my exposed neck.

"Are you sure?" I asked. "I didn't even look at the price tag," I worried all of a sudden. I mean—it was one thing to play with him in the boutique dressing room, but to buy the dress . . .

Oh, why not? What was I afraid of? To live up to my full, magical potential? The look on Gabe's face when I stepped out of the dressing room would be something I would never forget. I've never had a man look at me with such intense desire.

What the hell, I told myself, *you only live once.*

"I'll be right out," I whispered to him. I kissed my index finger and touched it to his lips. I shut the door and quickly stepped out of the dress, the thong, and the strappy sandals. Back in my own dress, hair band, and wedges, I sighed. *From goddess back to mortal.*

I stepped from the dressing room to hand the collection to the blonde. Quickly, she packaged all three items in a pink-handled bag and gave it to me. I reached for my wallet.

Gabe stopped me. "It's been taken care of, luv." He thanked the blonde and, with a hand on my lower back, directed me toward the boutique door.

"What do you mean it's been taken care of?" I asked him, my brain not quite yet registering.

"Consider it your birthday present."

"My birthday has passed already," I objected.

"A belated birthday present, then. My apologies for being late." He smiled and took a more serious tone. "You're a vision not of this world in that dress,

Porzia. Please allow me the pleasure."

Tears welled up in my eyes, and I looked at him; in my arms the precious bag almost choked with me. "I'm going to wear it tonight, feeling like the luckiest woman on earth just because I have you in my life, *amore mio*." On my tiptoes, I kissed him.

CHAPTER 24

Back at the hotel, we found the suit Oscar had sent over for Gabe. We showered together and got ready for the evening. I decided to wear my hair up in a French knot with a few loose strands flirting down my shoulders, to enhance the daring lines of the sin I was about to slip into. I wore only eyeliner and mascara on my eyes, leaving my lips bare. A natural blush lingered on my cheeks; it would deepen with the excitement of the evening. I daubed a little amber oil by my earlobes and the pulse point at the base of my neck. I was ready.

Gabe looked stunning in a pair of dark charcoal trousers, a white silk shirt and—surprise, surprise—smart-looking suspenders. Leave it to Oscar to be fashionably daring. His blond, unraveled looks contrasted with such elegance, provoked my senses, and made him irresistible. He caught sight of me and I pirouetted.

"I think we should skip dinner," I teased.

"And waste a perfect chance to have every man out there wish me dead?" he teased back. "I don't think so."

"The restaurant is within walking distance." I rummaged through my clothes for a fringed black silk shawl I had thrown in my luggage at the last minute. "How about an evening stroll to work up our appetites?"

"Roight." Gallantly, Gabe offered me his arm, and we left the hotel room. I felt like Cinderella and begged the gods to preserve me from ankle injuries.

The night had wiped away the mugginess of oppressive heat. A cool breeze insinuated itself under my thin shawl to caress my bare back. My heels echoed on the cobblestone sidewalk in an otherwise silent, still milieu until we rounded a corner and smashed against a solid wall of crowd.

The French Quarter is like that at night. Deserted side alleys dump you suddenly upon a main vein, and it's like lights on a stage being clicked on simultaneously. As if on cue, the play begins.

We inched our way through the thick mob of sweaty tourists, blasting music, pungent smell of spilled beer, and brash invitations from half-naked dancers Gabe silenced in mid-hip sway with his intense glare.

"You can be extremely intimidating," I observed as he led us away from the crowd.

"I know." He squeezed my hand as if to apologize. "It doesn't seem to bother you."

I thought about it for a second. "No, it doesn't." I knew his heart and how it spoke directly to mine. Intimidation wasn't something we shared.

We crossed the road to the front door of Chez le Chat. There, an incredible creature—a head taller than Gabe—towered among the valets attending to guests' cars. Wrapped in a fantastic cat costume of black velvet and sequins, she greeted us in a voice a tenor would sell his soul to the devil for. Sparkling in the night with diamond glitter, the tips of sheer wings peeked from behind her massive back. I wondered if Benedetta would dare to touch those wings. I smiled at the thought.

"*Bonsoir et bienvenu Chez le Chat.*" She curtsied, showing a leather ankle boot no smaller than a size ten and a calf that spelled testosterone in upper case.

"Cheers, mate. Gabe Miller and Porzia Amard," Gabe said, totally unfazed by the bizarre creature towering above him like a bad case of doom.

"Ah! *Oui*, you're with Oscar of the *Gusto* party." She warmed up, switching to English, and complimented my dress.

"Thank you," I answered and did touch her wings. *For Benedetta*, I thought, my fingers sparkling in twinkling glitter.

She re-adjusted her tail and opened the vaulted front door for us. We found ourselves in a spacious parlor lined in heavy oak. A middle-aged couple chatted quietly with a woman I was certain to be the owner of the establishment, Madame Magdalena. Her looks must have been stunning once, not long ago. Her flawless skin still retained that incredible peach smoothness some women are just blessed with. Heavily done in dark emerald shadows and black eyeliner, her eyes shone; jewels in the candlelight. I admired her jade evening gown. Unquestionably *haute couture*; in fact, I was quite sure I recognized a Valentino. It complimented superbly an egg-sized emerald nested happily on her ample bosoms. I thought of pirates and fantasy treasure hunts.

When the older couple in front of us disappeared into the dining room, her attention shifted to us. A spark of recognition ignited in her sultry eyes. Suddenly she smiled, wiping decades off her face.

"You must be Porzia." Extending both hands to take mine, she kissed the air by my earlobes. "I'm Magdalena, Magda for my friends." She swept her head in a grand gesture in the general direction of the half-hidden dining room— "Welcome to Chez le Chat. Oscar has already arrived. He told me all about you, and I am to escort you personally to his table." Still smiling, she eyed Gabe with a hint of curiosity.

"Magdalena, this is Gabe Miller. Thank you for having us tonight."

She let go of one of my hands and offered it to Gabe to shake, not kiss.

In the opulent dining room crystal chandeliers hung low on chains from the vaulted ceiling. Booths and tables were scattered in a pattern skillfully designed to guarantee undisturbed privacy to the diners. I noticed the heavy wood panels separating the different areas were made from the original headboards of sturdy antique beds. So far, that was the only detail giving away the origins of the building. Everything else just spelled restaurant.

Several pairs of eyes followed our progress across the dining room. I could feel the stares of men appraising me with unquestionable interest, and I knew Gabe was getting his fair share of looks from the women. At the small of my back Gabe's strong arm reassured me. Magda escorted us to one of the bigger booths where Oscar and a few other people were engaged in lively conversation. Like an evanescent longing, Edith Piaf's voice coiled its way around the chandeliers, singing throatily of a nostalgic French *époque*.

Oscar greeted us warmly. In his particularly vibrant style, he introduced his friends, making everybody feel instantly at ease. In front of everyone, knowing I would be a good sport about it, he whistled softly and complimented my dress, bowing his head in a perfect *baciamano*, his moustache lightly brushing my knuckles. Still holding my hand, he made me pirouette so he could have the total effect, until I blushed and gratefully took the seat Gabe offered me.

The menu was to be a total aphrodisiac experience, Magda explained: each selection a tantalizing invitation to the next, a choreographed seduction from the spicy appetizer to the passionate dessert and sparkling entremets. She excused herself with the promise to join us for a toast later on and left us in the capable hands of the sommelier. He began to pour what would turn out to be an endless flow of inebriating bubbly.

Muscadet de Sèvre et Maine Sur Lie paired the steamed oysters that arrived as an appetizer along with side servings of Red Savina sauce.

Red Savinas are habaneros' evil cousins. They've made the Guinness Book of World Records they're so hot. Originally of the Yucatan peninsula, they range from a scale of 350,000 to 500,000-plus Scoville units. The Scoville scale measures hotness of peppers, named for Mr. Wilbur L. Scoville, a pharmacologist who in 1912 set out to measure the heat of various peppers. If you can imagine that a typical jalapeño is about 4,500 Scoville units (that means that it takes 4,500 parts of sugar water to 1 part jalapeño to dilute the heat until you can no longer taste it), imagine how bloody hot a Red Savina is. What power ancient civilizations must have attributed to such heat!

Now, combine it with oysters and the Muscadet's slight prickle of fizz ... and that was only the appetizer. Fortunately, everybody at the table was familiar with the little pepper's exuberance, and we all took care not to exceed our tolerances in smothering the oysters. Sometimes exaggerating is not a good idea.

Saffron *pappardelle* in creamed crab followed, with a Prosecco di *Valdobbiadene* as the surprising sparkling choice; not a champagne, not a spumante, but a *mosso*: a 'moved' wine. If you ever have the pleasure of a close encounter with a Prosecco, please, take the time to admire the smooth, wavy dance the released bubbles entertain themselves with as they rise to the top of the flute. It's as if the bubbles, already inebriated—drunk, dare I say—after having spent such a long time in the bottle, are not in a hurry to get up there. They're taking their merry time, dancing along the way.

In the tradition of excellent service, the plates were removed by phantoms and more wine poured. I asked Oscar about the history behind the place.

He wiped his moustache and took a sip from his flute. Then, casting a slow look across the booth to ensure everybody's undivided attention, he told us about how Magdalena's grandmother's career as a theater *meneuse de revue* at the turn of the century escalated to mistress of a shipyard mogul who was killed mysteriously during an alligator hunting excursion in a nearby bayou, his body never to be recovered. Miserable days followed, for the legitimate wife of the deceased mogul inherited the wealth, leaving Magdalena's grandmother exposed, vulnerable, and without protection or resource.

Oscar interrupted his narration at the arrival of the next course: steaming servings of alligator tail medallions with grilled polenta, thinly sliced and dressed in truffle shavings. A black bean sauce had been drizzled lightly over the polenta as a subliminal reminder that we were still in Cajun country. It's not easy to pair polenta with champagne, and Oscar wondered out loud about the selection to be served with the amazingly rich dishes steaming in front of each one of us. Leafing through the evening menu for clues, he seemed puzzled. I waited expectantly as well, mentally going through several bottles I would consider or not . . . until the sommelier pleasantly surprised both Oscar and me with a chilled-to-perfection bottle of Taittinger Prestige Rosé NV.

A few precious minutes of silence followed as we all took the time to savor the delicious food, and then Oscar resumed his tale. Enthralled by the scrumptious flavors exploding in my mouth, I struggled to attend to his words:

"Apparently, it didn't take this resourceful woman long to come up with a plan of revenge. Engaging the services of a *voodouienne*, she threatened the mogul's widow with nightmares. Menacing images of horribly painful death afflicted the miserable wife until a generous payment for services rendered was finally established. Magdalena's grandmother used the money to open Chez le Chat, catering to the New Orleans gentlemen-elite until her own death put an end to it. Magdalena turned the establishment into an upscale restaurant, still catering to the bizarre needs of New Orleans's elite, just—," he paused dramatically and swept the table with his intense glare, "*via une route différent.*" Oscar concluded his tale by telling us he would leave it to Magda to share with us some juicy details of growing up in such an atmosphere.

The waiters cleared our table and presented dessert: passion fruit and sabayon crème crêpes. A bottle of Pol Roger Rich Demi-Sec NV paired the decadent dessert.

I had been cautious and mostly just tasted each sparkling wine selection, but with dessert I finally surrendered. I would willingly kill for sabayon and judging by its creamy texture when I sank my fork in, this particular one would take care of any eventual feeling of post-murder guilt. Delicious! I sipped the champagne and took another bite.

Magda joined our table, daintily sipping off a flute I suspected to be her choice of nourishment for the evening. Under Oscar's jovial pressure, in a voice as smooth as the champagne she was drinking, she shared with us the 'Bell Room' tale.

"Grandmother decided after the death of her beloved ship mogul to just manage the business and never again take a man to her bed. She held her vow true until a handsome stranger sporting a deadly grin under a well-trimmed moustache walked in one wet winter evening and told her how he couldn't afford to pay but, if given a chance, he would be worth the risk. Unfortunately, the young fellow had no idea whom he was dealing with. With disdain, my grandmother took one look at the puddle of water from the handsome stranger's shoes soaking into her beautiful Persian rug and decided to set a trap. She hated presumptuous people. She would teach this one a lesson.

"Merciless, she told him that if he could stir a bell hanging from a headboard in one of the upstairs chambers, he would have not only one night, but as many as he wished. If he couldn't, then she would take his life.

"He agreed to it on one condition: she would have to be the woman in the bell bed with him. She consented, knowing she had won, for the bell was merely painted on the headboard. Ready to teach the arrogant stranger a lesson and do as she pleased with his life, she ended up accepting an extremely pleasant and fulfilling defeat, married the man, and never regretted giving him his chance." Magdalena raised her flute to salute the portrait of a distinguished, dark-haired man hanging above the regal fireplace on the dining room's far wall. "*Mon grand-père.*"

It had indeed been an incredible gourmet soirée. My head felt pleasantly light with bubbles, my palate purred with the delicious flavors of the exquisitely prepared dishes, and my stomach was satiated just short of excess. Gabe's strong leg pressed firmly against mine, reminding me of his strength, to combine it all into a single, flawless moment.

We spent a while longer savoring the incredible richness of the passion fruit crêpes, chatting about food, wine, and life's pleasures in general.

We joked about the aphrodisiacal powers of the meal we'd just finished and Oscar asked me if I would be interested in doing a piece on the restaurant. Smiling at the idea of mixing work with pleasure, I looked at Gabe, squeezing his leg with my hand under the table. "As long as you wouldn't mind reaping the benefits of such labor," I whispered.

"Not at all, luv," he said, cracking one of those breathtaking grins of his.

Amid laughter, handshakes, and light air kisses, we untangled ourselves from Oscar and the rest of the party. Graciously, we thanked Magda for her hospitality and finally walked out of Chez le Chat.

"Do you get the double meaning of Magda's grandmother's choice of name for her business?" Gabe asked me, once outside. I turned around to read the elegant red sign humming softly above the stained glass door.

"Yes," I chuckled. I wrapped the shawl around my elbows, loving the feeling of the soft material against my bare back.

"That was one hell of a meal," Gabe said, offering me one of his arms. I took it, not only for warmth, but for balance on my high heels. All the fizz I had consumed was finally taking effect.

We skirted the French Quarter to stay away from the swarming crowd. Taking a few side roads, we were able to stroll at a lazy pace and play *innamorati* along the way, kissing at every chance we'd get, stopping to inhale the sweet scent of night jasmine shrouding tall iron gates. Hidden doorways stirred our curiosity. We discovered silent courtyards where unseen fountains mumbled prayers to the devoted, surrounding darkness. New Orleans summer nights have such a piquant quality about them.

A block away from the hotel, we heard music seeping through the open shutters of a candlelit window. Sheer white curtains billowed with melody, swaying sensuously to the rhythm. Without a word, as if by unspoken agreement, we stilled for a moment, allowing the music to truly reach us, and then we danced in the deserted alley. Embracing tightly, I rested my head against Gabe's strong shoulder. He brought my hand up his chest and held it there while his other reached the small of my back and drew me closer to him. With my lips only a breath away from his throat, I brushed his steady heartbeat pulsing from within. We barely moved; our hips just swayed as we rippled through darkness, seaweed abandoned to the will of the tides.

We reached the hotel and decided to enjoy the fresh air a while longer. In search of a quiet spot, we walked into the courtyard and sat on a wrought iron bench facing the fountain. Coiled in a fragrant flowerbed, a Creole cat slept in the otherwise deserted courtyard. Bothered by our intrusion, he woke up and cursed us with an extremely annoyed stare but remained where he was.

"We're disturbing him," I murmured to avoid aggravating the tawny cat's incensed stare.

"I bet we are," Gabe replied under his breath.

"I wouldn't be surprised if he opened his mouth and told us to piss off."

"He doesn't need to speak, luv. He's already telling us. I've heard it before." Gabe stared at the cat.

The tiny feline's glare was enormously unsettling. In its depth, a glimmer of what Joséphine would call *le mauvais oeil*, the evil eye, stirred. A chill ran down the length of my back, and I snuggled closer to Gabe. "How about we leave him be and go upstairs?"

"Just a sec, luv—" Gabe stared at the cat in some sort of unspoken contest. Neither of them blinked. They seemed hypnotized with one another. Their breaths slowed to barely vital. Not a single muscle of Gabe's body twitched; the warmth radiating from his body was the only detectable sign of life left in him.

Then, as if nothing had happened, Gabe broke eye contact with it. He turned to look at me, blinking away the moment of eeriness. Golden, iridescent sparkles faded quickly into the recesses of his blue eyes.

"Ready?" He stood, offering me his hand. Still chilled, I wrapped the shawl tighter around my arms.

"Yes." Struggling to my feet on the illegal stilettos, I looked back to the flowerbed. The cat had disappeared.

Upstairs, opaque wall sconces lit the paisley-printed carpeted way to our room door. In the pitch-black darkness, the time display of the TV warned us that the witching hour neared an end. I fumbled, running a hand along the wall for the light switch. I was about to turn the lights on when Gabe's hand pulled mine away from the switch.

"Don't," he whispered on my bare neck. His fingers entwined with mine, and he drew my hand to rest on my own navel. Through the thin silk barrier my own warm pulse drummed, and I gave in to his gentle pressure to lean back, shaping my hips against his hardness. His other hand found the chopstick holding my French knot together and pulled, releasing my hair. It tumbled free in a fragrant fall down my bare back.

"I've been waiting all night to do this," he said. He wound the thickness of my hair around his fist and tugged at it to expose my neck for his lips. He brushed a pulsing vein and bit gently.

I melted against his body with weak limbs, surrendering. His hot breath, a prelude to his mouth, brushed along my neck, by my earlobe, and down to my shoulder where the thin dress strap offered no defense against his searing touch.

In one fluid motion, the black shawl slipped away from my elbows to crumple weightlessly at my feet. His right hand abandoned mine to work its way to my hip where it explored the contours, then plunged between my legs and traced the edge of my G-string. The warmth of his fingers felt like a wish about to come true. How slowly his hand moved to gather silk, inching the dress up, ever so gently . . . *Oddio, what sweet agony!* I held my breath . . . until his fingers found the bare skin of my thigh. In a quick move, his hand slipped confidently under my G-string and stroked me . . . once.

Behind shut eyelids my pleasure became a vivid image of his two fingertips, wet and slick, dipping in between my moist lips to tease me, to coax me into climax. My own desire mounted like foam on a wave about to crash ashore.

I wanted more. And he obliged.

*

It took us a few minutes to finally move again. Moisture soaked my forehead, not to mention the rest of my body. Gabe, spent beneath me, struggled to slow down his breathing, his body as wet as mine. The grin on his lips told me he didn't care. His hair shone in the darkness, a shade darker with perspiration.

"We should take a shower." Then I grinned. "Better yet—a bath." I slid off him carefully.

"Yeah . . . you go ahead," he said, adding that he would get up once the water was ready.

I padded into the bathroom on wobbly legs, turned the hot water on, and adjusted the temperature to warm but not toasty. Clary sage bath salts I found by the edge of the tub stirred an idea. I poured the entire container into the churning water and lowered myself into the not-yet full bathtub. The warm, scented water felt heavenly against my sore limbs and hot body.

If Gabe could outstare a cat, no matter how eerie the feeling was, I could do this. I spread my arms and thought about magic. I shut my mind and lit my heart. I visualized Xavier, overlapped Gabe's features, and tied the image with a ribbon the color of love.

With my whole being radiating sexual energy, I summoned the powers and challenged, daring them to bring it on. Whatever I was to encounter or face along my path, I was ready. Still basking in the glow of our intense lovemaking, and inebriated by my own arrogance, I had no idea how much was at stake.

Gabe joined me moments later. We enjoyed the bath, quietly rinsing each other off. I accepted the silence he offered. The magic of the night hummed along in our slow movements when, tired after such an overwhelming day and evening, we climbed into bed without even bothering to dry ourselves off. I fell asleep as soon as my head hit the pillow with enchantment slowly drying on my skin.

CHAPTER 25

Dreamless sleep can be so deep and restful I believe sometimes it's all the medicine a tired soul needs in order to heal.

I woke up with Gabe next to me, still deeply asleep. Daylight filtered through the shutters, making it difficult to guess the time. My body told me perhaps eight o'clock, but it's seldom right about time of day. I turned to look at the TV display and saw that it wasn't on. *A sign I wasn't to bother with time today?* I decided not to worry about it and rolled on my back to give Gabe a kiss on his shoulder. His left arm folded across his eyes as if to shield them from the intruding daylight. I peeked under the arm to see if he was really asleep and met his blue eyes wide-awake, laughing at me.

"*Oh! Ma vai!*" I hit him.

He rolled on his stomach and pinned me down.

"I can't believe you're awake!" I mumbled with my face smashed against the pillow.

"Why not?" he asked, curious, letting me go.

"Because I thought you were asleep. I mean, it looked like you were sleeping deeply."

"I was," he said. "But I felt you stir and woke up."

"Just like that? In a matter of seconds?"

"Sure. I've slept out in the desert many times. There's no room for mistakes out there, luv." He looked at me with his clear blue eyes.

I could lose myself in such deep blue vastness. I lowered my lips to his and kissed him instead.

We faced the drive back to Pensacola and our last night together. I didn't want to think about it, not yet. I ignored the painful grip tightening around my heart. I still had time, still had air to breathe to keep my heart from writhing with sorrow.

We rang the concierge for a typical New Orleans breakfast in bed, chicory coffee and beignets, then got dressed and checked out. I made a point of having the desk clerk order flowers to be delivered to Magda with a thank you note for the ambrosia of the previous evening. I mean, if everybody at the restaurant last night felt a tiny bit like we did after such a scrumptious meal . . .

Gabe surprised me by asking to drive on the way back. I gave him the car keys and took the passenger seat. We sped off, leaving New Orleans behind.

As we neared the exit for Tante Louise's Joint, Gabe told me we needed to stop for gas. I remembered a gas station right next door to the restaurant, and we decided to fill up there. We pulled into the station, and Gabe got busy filling the car up while I went inside to pay. I grabbed a bottle of water since it was getting pretty hot out, and bought a scratch-off lottery ticket with a bunch of grinning alligators stamped on it. I briefly wondered what the hell they had to grin about, but when Magda's grandmother's tale of the lost ship mogul came to mind, I decided they had loads to grin about.

Once outside, I got so engrossed with scratching the alligators off with a quarter that it took me a moment to notice the car was no longer at the pump. I immediately scanned the surrounding area and exhaled, relieved. Gabe had driven to Tante Louise's Joint next door and was fighting with something that didn't seem to fit in the trunk. I walked the short distance, happy to have won the incredible amount of two bucks with the lottery ticket, pondering whether to go back to the gas station and cash it in when I saw what Gabe was struggling with. Standing right by him, Tante Louise sported a huge gap-toothed grin spread like gossip across her cheeks.

I almost dropped the water. I couldn't believe my eyes.

"Hon, you've got yourself a real man here." She winked at me, pointing her chin toward Gabe.

The oleander I'd felt sad for when we stopped on our way to New Orleans was now hanging out of my trunk, its roots packed in a potato sack full of dirt and tied off with a rope.

"Make sure you give it a good watering when you get home," she admonished me, as if it were an ordinary event for her to pack her trees up and give them away.

"No worries, Louise. Thanks heaps again for having it ready." Gabe pulled the trunk down to almost shut and secured it with a bungee I keep for emergencies.

"You're welcome. Have a safe trip. I need to get back to my customers." She turned to head back inside, then thought about something, and turned again to face us. "You're sure you don't want to come in for some food?"

I was about to open my mouth and say whatever might come out when Gabe thanked Louise again and told her we'd best be on our way. I thanked her, too, and followed her hips swaying back into the restaurant.

I turned to Gabe. "I can't believe you," I said, emotion cracking my voice.

"It didn't stand a chance in this parking lot, luv." He pushed down on the trunk to test the cord that kept it from jerking wide open. "I figured it would look great in your front yard."

Uh, I don't really have a front yard. I hugged him tightly. "Thank you, *amore mio*," I whispered against his chest. A silent tear ran down my cheek.

"You're welcome, luv. Let's get you home." He tipped my face up toward his and wiped the tear away with his finger. He kissed me lightly on the nose. We drove back to Florida with the oleander's crown sticking out of the trunk, sprinkling a trail of pearly petals along the highway.

A light drizzle welcomed us home in early afternoon. Peridot greeted us at the front door, all happy purring. His circumlocutions around my legs almost tripped me on my way to drop the overnight bag in the bedroom. Oblivious to my stumble, he kept drawing eights around my legs. Giving up, I set the bag down in the hallway and picked him up to properly greet him at eye level. His purring got so loud that Gabe, walking right behind me with his bag, made a comment about wasting top-of-the-line Ferrari engines inside pussycats.

Smartass.

Knowing that the drizzle would actually help the oleander, we grabbed a shovel from my storage shed and walked back downstairs to plant the tree. In the excitement, I even allowed Peridot to stand on the landing by the front door, away from the rain, to enjoy the show.

Since I live in a townhouse, I don't really have much of a front yard. There is a small strip of grass by the stairs, but still, it would be much better than where the poor thing had been until now. I told the oleander all about its new place while Gabe dug the hole. I freed the roots from the potato sack. With Gabe holding the trunk straight, I lowered the root ball into its new home, filling the hole up with the freshly dug dirt and patting it down hard to make it stand on its own. It took less than ten minutes, but I could tell the tree was already happier. We watered it in a bit and then decided the rain would do the rest. We stood for a few seconds under the light raindrops to admire our work. I didn't mind getting wet; I was just too happy. Now, every time I would see the tree growing and blooming, content in my front yard, I would be reminded of Gabe's precious love gift.

His arms encircled my waist, his chin rested on my right shoulder, and with the rain as a humming choir he began to recite:

Tree
he watching you.
You look at tree,
he listen to you.
He got no finger,
he can't speak.
But that leaf...
he pumping, growing,
growing in the night.
While you sleeping
you dream something.
Tree and grass same thing.

They grow with your body,
with your feeling.

I turned to Gabe and cupped his jaw with my fingertips. Dirt crusted my nails. "That was beautiful, Gabe. What is it?"

"Aboriginal cave-painting poem."

I stopped on the landing to scoop up Peridot and took one last look at the tree. It seemed to have extended its branches, welcoming the light rain to wash off the exhaust fumes from its erstwhile home and the grime of the highway trip that brought it here.

"I'm hungry." I closed the door and let Peridot jump out of my arms. "How about you?"

"I could eat," Gabe said. He walked away toward the bedroom—to unpack and then re-pack.

I followed him. "How about something light to keep us from starving until dinner?" I leaned against the doorframe and inspected my dirty hands.

"Anything, luv. I'm sure it will be tasty." He opened his bag.

"I had a wonderful time, Gabe." I crossed my arms against my chest. I tried to keep my emotion from my voice, from unraveling right then and there, I guess . . . but, as usual, something in my voice gave my feelings away.

He looked at me for the longest time, then just opened his arms. I crossed the short distance between us and wrapped myself inside his safe embrace. I closed my eyes, wishing to stay there forever. I wished to be a painted bell on a headboard trapped with him as my sound forever.

Then my stomach rumbled.

"Was it you or me?" Gabe chuckled.

"Me." I unwrapped myself from his arms. "I'll go make something to eat."

"Do you need help?"

"No, but company's welcome."

"I'll be there in a sec, luv."

I washed my hands under warm water and dried them with a red gingham kitchen towel. I checked to see if Peridot's bowls were OK. They were both almost empty. I refilled them and got a thank-you rub against my legs before he started eating.

Perusing the fridge I found some prosciutto and a very ripe cantaloupe. A bottle of Galestro, my favorite Italian white, had been chilling on the top shelf since before we left for New Orleans. The thought of a nice plate of *prosciutto e melone* with a fresh glass of wine doubled the rumbling of my stomach, and I set to work. It didn't take long at all to peel and seed the melon and slice it into juicy moon slivers. I wrapped the prosciutto slices around each melon wedge and arranged them on a colorful Spanish serving tray. I set the table with indigo place mats and bright yellow cloth napkins. I added a pitcher of fresh water, yellow plates, thick Spanish glasses, forks, knives, and salt and pepper shakers that matched the serving plate. Gabe walked in as I uncorked the wine.

"Would you like a glass of wine?" I asked him, pouring myself some.

"Yes, thanks. What kind is it?"

"My favorite: Galestro."

He laughed. "Do you have a wine that you don't like?"

I thought about it for a second, holding the Galestro bottle in midair. "Yes."

"Well? What is it?"

"Chardonnay."

"Chardonnay?" he asked, incredulous.

I noticed how his face had a deeper tan and a few freckles bridged his elegant nose. "I don't care for *young, un-oaked* Chardonnay. Too crisp and tart. When it is aged in oak barrels and then aged in the bottle for a while it becomes creamier—buttery."

"Now, since we're on the subject of likes and dislikes . . ." I paused, tried to look dead serious, broke into a smile, and then resumed, "what is it that you like about me?"

He cracked a grin. "What is there that I don't love about you would be easier to answer. You're the sexiest goofball I've ever met, Porzia, and, unfortunately for me, that's a deadly pairing, luv." He burst out laughing. That laughter sprinkled over me like joyful confetti.

"Sexy goofball?" I could not believe it. *Did he even know the meaning of "goofball"?*

"That's roight." He leaned over and took my right hand in his and kissed my palm softly. "You're the sexiest woman I've ever met. Every action, the way you look at life, is with the strength of a mature woman, the purity of an uncontaminated soul, and the sense of humor of a compulsive prankster." He smiled at me. "The only thing I don't like about you is how far away you live from me and how much better you look in high heels than me."

I cracked up. I was laughing so hard I couldn't stop. Through teary eyes I saw him take a sip of wine, watching me, totally amused. He took another sip of wine, cast me an enigmatic look, and grinned. "I don't like your favorite wine, either." He reached for my glass and poured the contents of his into it.

That sobered me up. I got up from the table and got him an ice-cold beer from the fridge.

"Better?" I asked him once he had taken a sip.

"Yes, thanks." He toasted my glass with his bottle. "Cheers, mate," he said, turning his attention to the tray of *prosciutto e melone*. "This looks good."

"Have you ever had prosciutto?" I asked him, handing him the tray with one hand while I wiped tears off my face with the other.

"Yes, you gave me a panino on the plane I liked a lot, but I'd had it before that a few times."

"Great!"

"I like it with eggs in the morning instead of bacon." He helped himself to several prosciutto-wrapped wedges of melon.

"This here we usually serve as antipasto back home. But people have it as a main course as well," I told him, filling my plate. I took a sip of wine and wished him bon appétit. Laughter aside, it was time to eat.

And it was complete: a quiet early afternoon meal with great music in the background, drizzle outside, and the perfect setting inside. We shared the last wedge of melon and then I peeled an apple that we shared as well.

We were just finishing up when the phone rang. I went to answer and Gabe got up, telling me he was going to clean up the kitchen. Peridot followed me to the phone; it could only mean one thing: Evalena. As I picked up the phone to answer, I noticed it had been blinking with several messages I hadn't realized were there. Busy with planting the tree, I had forgotten to check the phone.

"Hello?"

"Hi, hon, it's Evalena."

"Yes, I know."

"Oh, you do?" She sounded amused.

"Peridot told me."

"Sweet kitty."

"How are you, Evalena?" I asked, smiling at Peridot. His duty accomplished, he left me to amble back into the kitchen. I sat on the sofa armrest.

"I'm well, hon. How's everything with you?"

"We're doing great. We got back from New Orleans and just finished a late lunch."

"Oh, well, I won't keep you. Give me a call when you get a chance sometime in the next few days."

"OK, I sure will. Say hi to Rex."

"Yes, hon, I will. Bye now."

She hung up, barely giving me a chance to say good-bye back. I hung up the phone and checked the rest of the messages.

Grape Expectations had called as well to follow up with their instructions for the Oregon assignment. I felt a bit apprehensive. I didn't know this magazine well; however, I knew their reputation for being one of the toughest wine reviewers in the nation, employing master winemakers and international sommeliers ruthless in making or breaking a name. Fancy how they'd ask a novice like me to contribute an article.

And that is exactly what they told me over the phone when I returned the call. In a scholarly British accent, the *voice* said that, despite my inexperience, they would like me to submit a piece. The editor in chief, tired of reserve and vintage opinions, had expressed the wish for a *vino novello*, as we say back home—a young wine. Would it be possible for me to be ready in two to three weeks? Of course, I answered as my brain translated the conversation to: None of those *vintages* could bother traveling to the Northwest to discover grape pioneers making great wines in a region that has all the qualities, if not more, of some of the best wine producers of the world. *Just give them time.*

I told the posh voice on the phone I would do it.

"Excellent," he replied. "We'll be in touch."

I hung up with a lingering feeling that the voice sounded somewhat familiar, but I shook it off.

Gabe walked into the living room and we decided to go enjoy the sunset at the beach. We drove fast across bridges, against evening traffic, and made it to Perdido Key Beach with a few minutes to spare. We parked in the main parking lot and found a secluded spot on the beach among virgin dunes and salty mist. The sand, warm with the day's heat, massaged the bottoms of my bare feet.

Gabe laid out a blanket. In silence we held each other and watched the sun go down, stroking the sky with confident swirls of purples and blazing oranges. Everything around us held its breath.

"It must feel incredible to be the horizon," I whispered.

"You mean to receive the sun at the end of every day?"

"I mean to be worthy of such an honor." I turned to face him. I raised my right hand to caress his jawline.

"That's how I feel when we make love, Gabe," I told him. "I feel like the horizon welcoming the sun."

"I can't bloody believe you just said that," he whispered.

I looked straight into his candid eyes and showed him my soul.

This love was to know no boundaries, no limits. I shed my veils of defense and allowed Gabe to reach me completely. I unburdened my soul and, with my eyes, I offered it to him with my hopes for our future surging like a high tide.

The sun faded away. A cool breeze stirred, creeping up from the eastern sky, already dark and fast spreading to herald the arrival of evening.

CHAPTER 26

Our last day together.

We had fallen asleep on the sofa where, alone with miserable thoughts as my only companions, I wondered what had awakened me. It must have been the sound of water running in the bathroom. My brain didn't want to think. It was like trying to hold back an avalanche. The past week had been heavenly; I didn't want it to come to an end. Not quite yet. Hell, not ever. But Gabe's bag, packed and stowed by the door, heralded a different end to this chapter.

Why in the world was I even considering dipping the quill of my thoughts into the vivid ink to write of what my life might be like if distance weren't an issue? I mean, what if Gabe lived *here*? Not even with me, necessarily, but close enough so we could do this anytime.

I wondered if I could live in Australia. Then I realized we hadn't even talked about it. So why even consider it? *Because I was in love.*

How could a flower not bloom? Imagine this seed of love tucked in warm soil, feeding slowly on water and energy. In the darkness, life stirs; from the downward-curled fetal position, the tender head of unborn foliage straightens itself on a fragile stem and breaks through compact dirt. It's impossible to defy nature. To not go ahead and live? Absolutely impossible!

My own Dreamtime had begun.

The shower was silent. Gabe walked out of the bathroom in a cloud of steam, a white towel wrapped around his hips. With another towel he was drying his hair and almost walked into me as I reached the door.

"G'day, luv," he said, bending to kiss my forehead. Drops of water still clung to his chest. I wondered if he'd mind if I licked every one of them off.

"I'm going to jump in the shower myself." I looked over my shoulder to smile at him as I closed the bathroom door behind me with every intention of taking a long shower and shedding all my tears, but decided I wasn't going to waste precious time like that. If I needed to cry, I would do it later, after he had left that evening.

I stepped out of the bathroom with my robe on and my hair in a towel. The delicious aroma of eggs and something else sizzling tickled my nostrils. Freshly brewed coffee was in the mix too. I walked into the kitchen.

Gabe handed me a small espresso cup. "I hope you don't mind, but I've made us breakfast."

"Mind?" I laughed, taking a sip of the hot coffee.

"I've used up the rest of your prosciutto with the eggs." He handed me a plate with toast and sunny-side-up eggs on a bed of pan-fried prosciutto.

I sat down at the well-laid table, a carafe of orange juice in front of me, and waited for him to join me with his plate.

"Thanks," I said, pouring us juice.

"No worries." He took the glass I handed him.

We ate, talking and making plans for the day. I wanted to take it easy and not do too much. He wanted to pack a picnic, go to the beach, and spend the day in the sun. He reminded me that back home it was still winter, and I gave in. He told me he could rest on the plane, making a point to comment that he wouldn't be able to sleep without me.

We cleaned up the kitchen, packed a light lunch, and headed downstairs to the car. The morning was refreshingly crisp. After the rain of the day before, the humidity hadn't had a chance to thicken yet. We admired the oleander for a few moments on our way out to make sure it was OK. It seemed to be doing fine. The few blooms it had possessed we had sprinkled along the highway, but I had no doubt it would bloom stronger and fuller than ever once it settled in.

We had a blast of a day. Besides a pair of cut-off denim shorts, I wore only my yellow bikini and almost lost my top a few times as I pretended to be a mermaid and frolicked in strong, agitated waves. Gabe couldn't believe how warm and clear the water was, even when the tide rolled in, threatening our sprawled junk: towels, suntan lotion, bottles of water, a Frisbee, and a picnic basket. He finally dragged me out of the ocean, literally pulling me away from the waves by my braided hair. What can I say? I just love to swim and play in the sea.

I joined him by the towels, grinning and dripping wet. I felt deliciously fresh against the blazing midday sun. "I want to be a mermaid in my next life." I laid on my towel inches away from his face and noticed his nose was beginning to burn. I reached for the sun lotion, squirted some on my fingertips, and massaged his face gently.

"Mermaid." He closed his eyes as I spread the leftover lotion onto his forehead and then down his neck. "Is that your favorite fairy tale?"

My eyes pierced him. "You don't forget a thing."

"You'd give up those gorgeous toes?"

"Maybe," I told him. I shifted on my back to lie down on my towel. The sun felt great against my cool, wet skin. "But that's not my favorite tale."

"Your bathing suit's sheer, luv," Gabe said in a breath. Against the blazing sun I slit my eyes open and stared down my chin to my chest. My breasts were up at full attention against the thin yellow material of my bikini top. The outline of my nipples was totally visible. I looked around us; we were alone for miles. I rested my head back on the towel.

"If I were home, I wouldn't even bother with it."

Gabe gave no answer.

I relaxed. With my eyes closed, I tilted my nose up in the air. My lips tingled with salt drying on my sensitive skin. I was too lazy and comfortable to reach for lip balm in the beach tote. I thought of asking Gabe but...

No movement. No stirring. No breathing. No sign of... anything. *Perhaps he's asleep*, I thought, opening my eyes and turning my head to look at him. Suddenly a cold chill ran the length of my spine. A shadow shielded the sun from my still-wet body; I needed the sun back to warm me up. Gabe was no longer lying on his towel. He had quickly and silently shifted on top of me, bracing himself on his hands and knees with the sun a glowing aura behind his solid frame.

It took my breath away.

I swallowed hard. "You scared me," I told him once I was able to talk again. *How in the world did he do it? What kind of life teaches you to move at the speed of light?*

"Didn't mean to." He lowered his sun-warmed body against mine. And the dripping meltness of a burning candle hit the coldness of a marble slab. Only this marble slab molded itself to welcome the heat radiating from Gabe's body.

We lay there for the longest time. The sunrays hit Gabe's back and through him they reached me slowly, not as intense, but still hot and soothing, tinged with my lover's energy. It warmed me up, not only with heat but with passion as well. My emotional batteries slowly charged up with his love, to keep me from cold and solitude in the days to come. It was an incredible feeling I had never experienced before.

Not in this lifetime, for sure.

"How do you do it?"

"Do what?"

"So fast and silently and yet your movements are of such a frugal nature."

"You should have felt it. I blocked your sun."

"Actually, that's *all* I felt, just a drop in the temperature."

"Cooler, roight?"

"Yes, but that's not what I asked." I looked straight into his eyes. "That's not the first time you've done it."

He was so close I noticed his eyelashes fading from dark brown into blonder tips. His crystal blue eyes stared right back at me for what seemed like an eternity. "It won't be the last either." He lowered his head to brush my lips.

"So how do you do it?" I whispered against the softness of his mouth. My eyes never left his.

"Salty."

"Pardon?"

"Your mouth is salty."

"I bet I'm salty everywhere," I teased.

"Close your eyes."

"What for?"

"It won't feel the same if you keep them open."

The mere brush of a feather was all I felt at first. I struggled to keep my eyes closed and concentrate on the lightest shift of heat to follow his movements. On my neck at first, he barely caressed the moist skin with the tip of his tongue. My skin rose to respond, my breath quickened in anticipation, and red swirls spiraled behind my shut eyelids. A trail of warm sand tickled the inside of my right wrist and softly rained all the way up to the tender spot where the elbow bent. It felt warm and grainy and left me totally unprepared for what followed next. His lips closed in on the tip of my left breast, sucking slowly through thin, wet cloth, the warmth of his lips a definite contrast against the coldness of the fabric covering my nipple. Soon it all melted into a heated throb of pleasure as my breast responded to the teasing and blood rushed to answer. Involuntarily, I parted my mouth and moaned, only to be silenced by his firm finger on my parted lips.

I licked his fingertip lightly, tasting salt. I closed my lips around it, sucking deeper. As if on cue he bit the swollen tip of my breast and dipped a finger under my bikini bottom, stroking through my wetness ever so slowly. So entwined in the heated pleasure building up I barely heard him whisper, "Look at you."

My eyes slit open, and I was suddenly blinded by the intense sunlight. Tears streamed down as I made an effort to adjust my eyes to the brightness. Gabe stretched next to me, supporting my head in the bend of his elbow while his other hand disappeared under the triangle of my bikini bottom. The veins streaking his wrist moved with the rhythm of his fingers stroking me until, almost hypnotized, I arched my hips to meet his touch. Quickening the pace, I rubbed myself against his finger, climbing, building up. I held my breath and covered his hand with mine, pushing his fingers to thicken the intensity of my rising climax. When light burst all around me, I threw my head backwards and called his name, breathless.

His mouth plunged into mine, feeding off the ecstasy I was exhaling.

I held on to him as my breath calmed.

*

Much later a shift in the breeze and lengthening shadows told us it was time to head back.

We packed our stuff and drove back home. Gabe fell into a silent mood, not much different than mine. We gnawed at the same thought: his plane left in less than four hours.

"Are you hungry?" I asked, sounding like my mother. *Food: her universal answer to every ailment.*

"No, luv. Thanks, but I don't think I'll want anything before I go."

His preoccupied look told me he was already distancing himself. I recognized that look. It appears on my own features on the threshold of every imminent departure. Half the mind is already there at the destination.

I left him to finish with his luggage and jumped in the shower to wash away the salty patina the ocean foam had left on me. My skin came alive under the invigorating shower jet. A slight sunburn blushed between my breasts, and I took care not to scrub myself too harshly. I was about to suds up my hair when the bathroom door opened, and Gabe asked if I would mind if he joined me. I slid my hand past the shower door and beckoned him with a crooked finger. Without words I handed him the shampoo and turned so he could wash my hair. I closed my eyes and relaxed. His hands worked the scented shampoo into lather; his strong fingers massaged my scalp soothingly, relaxing me. He turned me to face him. My body pressed against his while both his hands worked slowly through my hair. He cupped my face and bent to kiss me, getting his own hair all wet. I took the bottle of shampoo and, just as silently, washed his hair, combing my fingers through its smooth silkiness, wiping his eyebrow of lather. I caught his eyes watching me. I returned his stare until he closed his eyes. He threw his head back under the shower jet, rinsing off the shampoo. I watched, mesmerized; the streaks of foam ran along his wet body, tracing every muscle, defining his shape only to disappear finally down the drain. I pressed myself against him and felt his hands wrap around me, holding me tight. Water drenched us. It cleansed us, drowning the world outside.

We took turns drying each other. Our mood shifted; this was our last chance to imprint our memories, like reading a classical poem for the very first time, absorbing every profound line.

Wrapped in towels, we walked back into the bedroom hand in hand. There we sat on the bed with his bag nearby, a symbol, an arrow aloft, a separation foretold. I closed my eyes, rested my head against his chest, and tried to forget about time.

"Luv, we need to get going."

"OK." Mechanically, I walked to the closet and found a dress to wear. As if on autopilot, I grabbed panties, a bra, and sandals and got dressed.

He wore a black T-shirt, jeans, and sneakers. He'd gotten so tanned in such a few days it was amazing. Then I caught my own reflection in the mirror and noticed I was just as dark. I managed to manifest a smile, a rainbow during a downpour. "Ready?"

"Yes."

"I'll get the keys." I reached for my bag, turned, and realized I was alone. "Gabe?" I called.

No answer.

My heart stopped, and for an instant I wondered if I might have dreamt the whole week with him.

I blinked. And stood there, incapable. I found myself devoid of will, vaguely aware of missing something but for the love of God couldn't recall what.

As if awaking from a coma, with inadequate control of my limbs, hoping my brain functions would eventually kick into gear and follow, I walked into the living room where silence met me.

Then the sliding door's drapes swelled in the light breeze, and I saw him out on the deck. His bag lay abandoned on the sofa.

I walked to the door and saw that he had Peridot in his arms. He was quietly whispering something that my cat must have found seriously interesting. Peridot was all ears.

". . . Roight, mate?"

Peridot nodded, blinked agreement, and then turned, giving me away. His pupils shifted from perfect rounds to pinhead-size.

"What's going on?" I asked. They both looked like I had interrupted some sort of male-bonding moment.

"Just telling him to take care of you while I'm gone," Gabe said, handing me my cat. Peridot looked at me with new interest, as if suddenly I had turned into a precious commodity he'd never considered of value before.

"Thanks."

We made one last pass to make sure Gabe had packed everything, and we drove to the airport.

We had just enough time to park and check in before it was time for him to board.

My eyes finally lost the battle. Tears welled up and spilled down my cheeks. Everything blurred. Gabe looked at me and his smile quivered. He hugged me for the longest time and kissed me deeply. *How can the body produce so much water?* I wondered with streaks of tears streaming down my face.

I couldn't see the end of it. No matter how hard I tried to stop crying, I could only sob uncontrollably. I clawed the stretchy cotton of his T-shirt and dug my nails into his back. Pain and tears mixed into a mushy whirl, quickly draining me. Madonna Santa, *why does it have to hurt so much?*

"This is the last time I leave you behind, Porzia." With the tips of his fingers he wiped my tears. "There is no way in hell I'm going to see you like this ever again." His eyes told me he meant it.

I looked at him, trying to smile. "I know. It hurts too much."

"Come and see me when you get back from Oregon, and we'll work it out," he said.

"OK. Call me when you get home." I choked on my own sorrow.

"I love you, Porzia."

"I love *you*."

He looked at me for one last second and walked away. The connecting tunnel swallowed up his form as the echo of the last boarding call faded into silence.

Motionless, I sat on one of those absolutely hideous airport chairs and watched his plane take off. A fist squeezed my heart until I physically cringed and gasped for air.

*

I slammed into darkness outside the airport. My eyes had puffed up so badly with all the crying that I could barely keep them open, and I was so out of it that I ended up driving away without my headlights on until I registered the oncoming cars' warnings, flashing theirs repeatedly at me.

Once home I parked and leaned my forehead on the steering wheel. It vibrated with the engine buzz. I reached for the keys, switched the car off, and closed my fist around the dice. I hoped my heart would shut off, too, but no such luck. It still hurt infernally.

Outside, barely visible by the light of a rising moon, the oleander stood; a dark silhouette against the night sky. I reached to touch the smooth trunk and told him quietly to give me the strength to walk upstairs into a silent house. I felt the urge to cry again, so strong it made me queasy. Holding a hand over my mouth I hurried upstairs to open the front door. I scooped Peridot up in my arms, kicked the door shut, stepped out of my sandals, and ran barefooted to my bedroom. I collapsed on the bed and cried myself stupid against my pillow until it turned into a mushy mess. I rolled my head onto the other pillow. My heart stilled as I inhaled Gabe's scent lingering on the soft pillowcase. I buried my nose, breathing deeply, worrying if I took it all in at once it might not last. The thought caused another rush of tears to sting my already burning eyes.

Peridot settled himself at my feet, purring.

I pulled the dress over my head. Bra and panties followed, randomly hitting the floor in the darkness. Naked, I hugged the pillow and tried to focus my breath, to empty my mind, and to shut down my heart. I didn't even bother to slide under the sheets. It took just about an eternity but I slowly calmed down and finally drifted into sleep thinking how blessed I was to have an entire night in front of me while Gabe had to endure a sleepless journey all the way back to Australia. Tonight . . .

*

I floated into darkness. Eerie. That's how I felt.

Warm ocean waves engulfed and lulled my body. All around me the waters met a black sky sprayed with stars that sparkled and randomly winked at me.

The warm water soothed and dulled my senses, making me believe that everything would be alright. I immersed my entire body underwater; I remember thinking that's how opium ought to feel.

Then the waters turned into sand and I struggled to free myself.

With conscious effort, I walked to shore where I felt warm and comfortable. I turned to look at the wide reach of dark sand, not quite believing that a few seconds earlier it had been an ocean supporting me as I floated. Incredibly, the sand still moved in slow, relentless waves as if it believed itself to be water. It inhaled and exhaled each breath slowly, following the ancient rhythm of waxing and waning tides.

No moon shone above me, and the weak twinkling of stars was no help in casting light to penetrate such darkness.

Suddenly, without a warning, Gabe stood right next to me. With my heart welled up with joy, I reached out to him, but before I could say anything he walked into the sand until I could see him no more, and my heart told me he was gone forever.

Just as despair took over and pain burst to light the sky, a powerful, dark figure separated from the darkness. Far in the distance, as far as where the stars met the horizon, the figure grew, barely distinguishable, yet solid.

The sand shifted back to water, shyly lapping at my toes. I was sinking in wet sand.

Xavier walked up to me. He smiled and handed me one single die. One.

*

I awoke from the dream parched, my throat so dry all I could think of was water and how much I wanted to drink some. I reached for the glass I usually keep on my nightstand and remembered the way I had fallen hastily asleep. I swung my legs off the bed thinking I might land on sand. Relieved that my toes found hardwood floors instead, I groggily got up, walked to the kitchen, and poured a cold glass of water. I gulped it down without breathing, then poured another and drank it more slowly, down to the last drop.

I walked to the bathroom and washed my face in the darkness. I pressed a towel against my cheeks, went back to the bedroom, and crawled back into bed. I begged for no more dreams. No more heartache.

Peridot snuggled against my back. I rolled on my stomach to pet him and asked him quietly if he missed Gabe too. He didn't answer; he just settled against my hand and resumed his purring.

I laid there in the darkness, hoping to fall asleep right away. My mind whirred with everything that had happened to me in the past few weeks instead. From a normal life of work, friends, and family, I was now soul-deep in esoteric mysteries, true love, and unknown paths. Worst of all, I seemed to have no control whatsoever over any of it. My past life regression under Evalena's guidance seemed to be the catalyst unleashing all these forces. Even my work seemed to be part of the conspiracy. From Madame Framboise's tarot reading to Delilah's voodoo issues, the strange forces were coming out of the woodwork. Then Evalena tapped into Gabe's secret and who knows what else was to come? I wondered if Oregon would be full of clues or simply generate other mysteries.

Of one thing I was irrefutably certain: This treasure hunt had my attention.

So, what was my inner intuition telling me this time?

In the darkness of my bedroom, with Peridot breathing next to me and Gabe up above, flying farther and farther away with each passing second, I thought of rivers of tears running to become ocean. I rubbed my eyes. There would be no more crying, I decided. It was time to set things straight and put an end to all this nonsense.

CHAPTER 27

"*W*arrawarra,*"* Evalena stated flatly, making an impressive job of rolling *R*'s and pouring coffee simultaneously. She took a look at me. I had shown up at her door unexpectedly—well, sort of, since she always knows anyway—earlier that morning. I had barely managed to take a shower and put on some jogging clothes and sneakers. I had tied my wet hair into a braid, hidden it under a ball cap, glanced one more time at the phone, wondering where Gabe could be at the moment, and rushed out the door in search of answers.

The fact that coffee came with Evalena's advice was a pleasant extra bonus. I scooped three teaspoons of sugar and added cream to my cup. "You were saying?" I asked her, bringing the cup up to my lips.

My question seemed to startle her back into the now and she shook her head. "Yes, I was saying . . . A *warrawarra* or *nurrullurrulla* is an Aboriginal witch doctor, perhaps a shaman or medicine man. I'm sure you've heard of Aboriginal people going on their merry ways with life, having a family, a career, an established routine, and all of a sudden, *poof*! They're walkabout." She stared at me as if she was about to wander off herself.

I had heard of that happening and nodded at her.

"Well, this walkabout practice seems to go a lot deeper than what white folks think. It's a matter of following ageless spoken and unspoken traditions and about being in tune with ancestral patterns enough to be able to hear them calling when the need arises. Some shamans are known to borrow the spirit of an animal to travel."

"How do you know all this?" I asked, frowning.

"I just do. The terms I am using are from the Kaurna people language, so I am not sure I am giving the due respect here. But trust me on this one."

Her words held that certainty I wasn't about to stupidly slam against once again. "OK."

"Your man seemed to have some sort of extreme bond with one such spiritual figure. There goes your connection between the Two of Cups and the Magician."

"What?" I wondered if Gabe was going to go walkabout on me, just like that.

"You know I have this gift of being able to tap into energy fields and auras, Porzia," Evalena reminded me.

I nodded, sipping my coffee silently. This I could do. Coffee I knew how to handle.

"Well, the night you two came over for supper, I tapped lightly and—I must add—involuntarily, into such a connection and found a strong resistance. It wasn't only emotional but also impressively *physical*. Gabe is not Aboriginal, but he has been exposed to their traditions and he has an undeniable bond with one of their powerful warrawarra. I didn't register anything negative about this bond, but Gabe has been given a second chance at life and someone is working hard at making sure he's breathing." Evalena stopped, lost in thought again.

"And?"

"And nothing." She shook her head. "I've told you everything I sensed. Gabe is the only one that could explain more, but I have the feeling he has exposed himself to you because he wants you to understand. He loves you. But I have reservations regarding—"

I interrupted her. "You know he loves me?" I asked, stunned.

"Yes."

"It has to do with his accident," I said almost to myself.

Evalena just nodded silently.

I had one more question to ask but, as usual, she was prepared.

"I don't know the answer to that one, Porzia, honey. We spoke about it when I brought you back from the past life regression. Only you can answer that. Only you can recognize him for whom he really is. But, as I was saying, I do have reservations."

I blinked tears away. All of a sudden, no amount of sugar in my coffee was going to sweeten the bitterness I felt.

"What if I can't distinguish between the feelings of recognizing him to be the true one and wanting him to be it so bad I'll trick myself into believing it?" My own words frightened me.

"That's not what you should be concerned with," Evalena said. "What should worry you is do you love him to the point he's dissipating a bond you carried on with someone else through the barrier of death? Or is he a teacher along your path? And if so, why? What lesson is Gabe teaching you?"

"Evalena, I love him." I bowed my head.

"He leads by example, Porzia. Beware."

*

Instead of answers, I had gotten myself tangled up deeper in questions. Don't they say when in quicksand, be still? And there I was kicking up a storm.

A true storm had gathered up from the horizon and was working its way to shore, looming over me like an impending guillotine. I could taste salt in the wind picking up speed around me when I said good-bye to Evalena and walked to my car. Around me, arthritic pines and a few frayed palms still stood, forlorn and defeated by the continuous attacks from the ocean's strong winds. They bent, sway-backed, all the way down to the ground, resigned to their fate. Still, they struggled to live on. Amazing when, doubtful of our course of action, we suddenly scout our surroundings and label nature's regular occurrences with the official title of signs meant purposefully for us. Not that I have anything against such trees, but was I actually trying to read omens and draw strength from crippled pines?

The first drops of rain hit my windshield as I slammed the car door shut. By the time I sped across the Gulf Breeze Bridge, the storm had surged, chasing me like the pressure of wasted time. With my windshield wipers dancing wildly in front of me, I thought of Gabe up above the rain. I was glad at least one of us was away from such bad weather.

I wondered if someday we'd both be above the storm.

*

The blinking of my answering machine greeted me like a mad heartbeat. Under the wet ball cap, my hair had turned a sticky mess. My clothes clung to my skin. I peeled layers away and hit the play button.

Benedetta's voice came on. She sounded sad and strained. Her trip to Savannah had been cancelled and she wanted to know if by any chance I wanted to get drunk. *Merda!* So early in the morning? It didn't sound good. I wondered what had happened to Jason as I speed-dialed her number.

No answer. *Where could she be in such awful weather?*

The following voice was Helen's, executive assistant to Camille Weir, *A' la Carte*'s editor in chief in Miami. Camille had something serious to discuss with me and wondered if I could squeeze in a visit to Miami by the end of the week; the magazine would cover all expenses. My instincts told me I had better check this one out. What could be so important to require my *physical* presence? I put the rest of the messages on hold and called her back. I told Helen I would fly down and to send me the info. In a grateful tone she told me an envelope would arrive by morning.

Right after I hung up, the phone rang again.

Oscar, from *Gusto*.

Chirping joyfully, he asked me for a piece on Chez le Chat.

We ended up chatting for quite a while. He'd been summoned by Camille as well and was keeping his visit hush-hush. But, as he lightly put it, even if she is the competition, more importantly, she's an icon in the business. Simply put, you don't say no to Camille Weir. I told him I couldn't wait to pinch him in Miami and he laughed, quipping something about birdcages that I didn't quite get. The doorbell was ringing as we said good-bye.

*

Benedetta stood in front of me with Eros on a leash, both soaking wet, her glasses fogged up, and with the saddest look plastered on her face like an obituary notice. She looked like a dunking clown after the show. I hugged her and dragged them in. She sighed and took a seat in the kitchen. Eros hid under the table.

As I put on the teakettle my mind scoped any possible reason why she would look so upset. I tried my best to keep quiet and give her the time she needed. I found two mugs, the loose chamomile jar, honey, and teaspoons. Finally, I sat myself in front of her. I watched her use my gingham kitchen towel to wipe her glasses clean.

Silence unfolded, disturbed only by the hard rain tumbling against the roof.

"It's over," she blurted and began to sob uncontrollably into the kitchen towel.

"*Why?*"

"Delilah did the spell and I was right. He got spooked."

"*What?*"

"Accused me of witchcraft."

Peridot and Eros both sensed her distress and rushed into one another trying to console her. I, on the other hand, struggled to suppress my anger. I physically seethed.

"Pretty pathetic, eh?" she said. "And he was raised by a *voodouienne*." She sniffled and blew her nose in the kitchen towel.

"Oh, *Cristo!*"

"You *should* say 'Oh, Goddess'!"

I leaped off my chair to kneel and hugged her, squishing cat and dog, letting her cry against my shoulder.

"I called you, then decided I didn't want to be alone and drove straight here." She looked at me over the edge of red-rimmed eyes filled with the wet debris of a devastated heart.

Peridot meowed from between us, and we shifted so he could jump off her lap.

The teakettle whistled and I got up to make us some chamomile tea. I added honey and a drop of lemon juice, then handed Benedetta a steaming cup. She thanked me, looking a bit better. At least the crying had stopped. We sipped our tea in silence and then I told her she should stay with me for the night.

"Thank you," she said. "I don't want to be alone."

"No worries."

Benedetta took a long, silent look around. "He's gone back?"

I nodded, not trusting my own voice.

"Oh, *merda*! I'm sorry. How selfish of me to just puke all my stuff on you and you're dealing with your own load."

"Do you still wanna get drunk?" I glanced at the clock. Way past noon. We could have a drink. Or *two*.

"No, thanks," Benedetta declined, cracking a small smile. "I'd rather do something else."

I thought about it for a few seconds and then got up.

"*Vieni*—," I called her, extending my right hand to pull her off her chair. We walked into the living room where I dug out some old Italian comedies.

We spent the afternoon watching silly movies on TV. We ordered pizza and listened to heavy rain ricocheting off the roof. She fell asleep, her immaculate, vulva-peach-painted toes curled up on my sofa. I brought a blanket out for her and told Eros if he wanted to it would be OK for him to sleep with her. He seemed to understand me, for he jumped on the blanket and settled behind Bene's curled knees. I removed her glasses and tousled her hair goodnight.

I had just barely had a chance to walk back into my bedroom when the phone rang. I wondered if I should just let the answering machine pick up. I really didn't feel like talking to anyone, but it would ring several more times before the machine answered, and Benedetta was asleep in the other room.

"Hello?" I sat on my bed. Unconsciously, I began to rub my feet. My mother told me once I used to do this every time it was raining outside and I had to get ready for crib. Not bed yet—crib.

"Porzia." Gabe's voice, tired and distant, reached my ears.

"Hey!" *Oh! He'd made it safe and sound.*

"I'm home, luv. I miss you."

"You're OK?"

"Yes. Knackered, but OK."

"How was the trip?"

"Long. I didn't sleep at all."

"I'm sorry."

"I miss you."

"I miss you too. But it must be nice to be home."

"What's going on, Porzia? You sound upset."

"Benedetta. Her love adventure got nipped in the bud."

"How come? Where is she now?"

I took a deep breath "She's here, asleep on the couch. He didn't believe in magic."

"Not everyone does."

"Do you, Gabe?"

"Only the kind I'm capable of, Porzia," he sighed, exhausted. "Luv, I'd talk to you until the end of the world, but I need to go catch some sleep. I stopped by the shop on my way home. We're so bloody busy with the Australian Safari we're working hard to fit it all in before the start. I really wish I could race it. It's bloody hard to see everybody get ready. The excitement is absolutely contagious. Gomi hasn't been sleeping for the last three days. He's chewing some strange root, telling everybody that's how he keeps his energy going." His last few words slurred, thick with sleep. "I'm rambling and I should really get going to bed, Porzia."

"OK, Gabe. Thanks for calling and letting me know you made it safe."

My heart bled for him.

"Yeah! I'll ring you once I feel human again." He laughed softly. "Have I ever felt human?" he asked almost to himself.

"OK, Gabe. Sweet dreams."

"Not without you, luv."

"I love you."

"I love you too, Porzia." The phone went dead.

I sat there for a moment, then wandered into the bathroom and took a long, warm shower, trying to wash away all the sadness of the day. I braided my wet hair and went to bed after checking on Benedetta. She was deeply asleep on the couch. Eros gave me a reassuring look. *OK, buddy, I know she's in good paws. I'll leave her to you.*

*

The following morning, while Benedetta still slept cuddled on the sofa, Gerome brought me a pile of mail.

Peridot followed me around puffed up thrice his normal size to protect me from the beast still asleep on the couch with Bene. I made an espresso and walked to my desk to sort through the bundle, starting with Helen's thick envelope. I glanced at a round-trip ticket to Miami set to leave Pensacola first thing the following morning and returning the same evening. A business trip with no time scheduled to play around in sunny Miami. Helen had outlined a detailed itinerary, down to the limousine pickup and return to the airport—including a lunch break at Lumière, Camille's favorite restaurant in South Beach. She suggested an appropriate change of clothes.

Two copies of the issue of *A' la Carte* with my article were included as well. The front cover featured the Jourdains and their dogs with a background of stark vines. I remembered when Desmond took the photo; the massive brick porch of Umeracha blurred on the right, while a field of bare vines gently sloped up a hill to the left.

"*Umeracha Expands Their Award-Winning Portfolio with Shiraz*," the headline announced.

An envelope fell off the magazine as I leafed through its pages. With increasing curiosity I opened it and found a handwritten note from Camille Weir. Grateful for the excellent article, she congratulated me on my spirit and resilience for putting up with Desmond and hoped I would like the spread and article layout. In her editorial she mentioned my article, as she always does, with the magazine's main features, describing me as the up and coming, talented young writer the Jourdains had specifically requested. She went on to announce the impending release of what I described as strong wine laced with the eternity of Australian soil, traditional French harvesting methods, and phantom American oak barrels.

I smiled at my own words.

She had included copies of Desmond's photos—even those that hadn't made the cut. Apparently, he'd been stressing everyone out wanting to make sure I would get them. She concluded by asking me to get in touch with Helen for future assignments and, thanking me again, signed her note.

I looked at the pictures and had to admit that, even if a colossal pain in the ass, Desmond is one of the best photographers in the business. I loved the shots he'd taken of everybody around the fireplace, like a family gathered for a holiday. My eyes fell on Gabe standing tall right next to Clark, his muscular arm on my shoulder. My own eyes sparkled, alive with the gratitude I felt about their cozy hospitality (not to mention Gabe's arm wrapped around me).

Lost in the memories, Benedetta's voice startled me back into the present.

"Got anything to eat?"

"*Buongiorno* to you too." I stood and motioned for her to follow me to the kitchen where I patted a cushion of one of the table's chairs and invited her to sit. She plopped down, yawned, and rubbed her sleepy eyes.

I quickly got some toast going and washed and refilled the Moka. Just as I was switching the stove on for another round of espresso, the phone rang. I answered, keeping an eye on the coffee. Despite Eros's proximity, Peridot stood by the phone looking like a sleepwalker. He made me smile. It must be Evalena.

"Hi, Evalena!"

"You're getting better." I could feel her smile.

"My cat is—or has always been." Peridot blinked at me languidly.

"How are you, hon?"

"I'm fine, Evalena."

I took the brewed coffee off the stove and poured just enough to wet two teaspoons of sugar I had in a cup. Beating the espresso with the sugar, I made my thick cream base and then added the rest of the steaming coffee.

"Come down for lunch. We'll chat."

"Sounds great! Maybe in a little while?" I asked, glancing at Bene. I had an idea.

"Sure. I'll be home."

We made arrangements to see one another later and hung up.

I handed Bene a plate of toast and a shot of creamy espresso and sat down in front of her.

"So?"

"So what?" she countered, buttering a piece of toast and looking at me. "Why did you ask which was my favorite fairy tale when we got back from Georgia?"

"Evalena said our favorite choice is an archetype of the women we are."

Benedetta smirked. "Of course . . . *The Ugly Duckling*."

"Bene! What's going on with you?"

She pinched the bridge of her nose, sneaking two fingers under her lenses, and rubbed her eyes again. "You know," she began, "after my accident I had to deal with a lot of fear." She sat back and looked at me with grief-stricken eyes. "I had to learn to live with it. I mourned my ability to take my safety for granted and slowly took baby steps into this new, unfamiliar territory of ordinary tasks now mutated into potential dangers and perils.

"When they locked my assailant in jail, I relaxed but still dreaded the day he would be free. Eros and my beliefs have helped a great deal, but as I told you in Savannah, I'm a mere solitary practitioner. I'm learning to face the eventuality that I may confront him again, and I am trying to understand how to *deal* with that particular situation or any other similar and dangerous ones."

She sighed and I had a feeling I knew where this was going. "A life with The Craft, a choice that not many understand nor appreciate, allows me to be free, but in order to deal with my fears I am feared."

I leaned forward and took her hand. "Benedetta . . . you can't doubt who you are just because of Jason."

"I know. Remember how he insisted it was just an ordinary fungus? But where did the fungus come from? Where do our fears come from, Porzia? He's always been scared of his mother's Santeria ways and he's boarded the door shut on magic." A look of determination cracked the surface of her wretched features. "I mourn the fearless girl I used to be before I almost died. But this renewed inner strength sprouts from mystical, ancient beliefs that I have embraced and now honor. I shed my old identity and recreated this Benedetta from such enormous loss . . . I would never have made it. I would never have been able to help Delilah! Or scare that freak that tried to sell us voodoo tickets if it weren't for my belief in the Goddess. I have come such a long way and now, at last, I respect myself again." She sighed. "What I'm trying to explain here, Porzia, is that we're changing. As women we're honoring our true selves and we are taking risks; we're paying a price that I believe is worth it. Even if it means the Jasons of this world will refuse us. I only wish it wouldn't hurt so much."

I nodded somberly. "I feel it."

"I know you do. You're manifesting your own renewal. You wouldn't have embarked on this soul mate quest otherwise."

Later that evening, making a mental note of the time, I gave Gabe a call. After several rings his answering machine picked up.

I left him a brief message to let him know I was trying to reach him, hung up, and then dialed his work number.

Clark answered.

In an extremely distressed voice, he told me Gabe had decided on the spur of the moment to jump in a vehicle with Gomi and follow the *ute* they were sponsoring in the Australian Safari—literally. He told me Gabe hadn't called me because he knew it would have been the middle of the night for me and that although he doubted he would have a signal so far in the outback, he would call as soon as he got a chance. Clark concluded by saying that I shouldn't worry— he was worrying enough already. Something is his words held my smile back. I asked him how long Gabe planned to be gone. Clark said he thought it would probably be the better part of a week. He told me that because of unseasonable rain in the desert things were heating up. I imagined a muddy Gabe grinning from ear to ear as he pushed a sport utility vehicle stuck in sludge.

I tried to comfort Clark and thanked him before I hung up to try Gabe's cell phone, but I had no luck, not even his voice mail.

So, his fever was still brewing . . .

*

I drove across the Gulf Breeze Bridge to Evalena's house thinking that Benedetta had ended up giving *me* guidance.

She and Rex still lived at her jolly yellow bungalow in Gulf Breeze. Hurricane Erin had wiped away the connecting road from Pensacola Beach to Navarre Beach, and reconstruction was taking forever. How tired they must be of waiting.

I parked my car by a chubby blue hydrangea and walked up the porch to knock on the door. Evalena answered promptly, her hands green with bits of chopped up parsley. She pushed the screen door open with her elbow. "Come on in, honey. I'm making couscous." She smiled at me. "I would hug you but I'm sure you don't want parsley all over you."

"It's OK. I'll hug you instead." I gave her a nice squeeze, veering away from the green hands, and followed her into the kitchen.

Her table displayed a battlefield. A big ceramic bowl heaping with fluffy couscous waited to be dressed with a colorful palette of veggies and roasted chicken.

"Have a seat and excuse the mess," she told me, resuming her parsley chopping.

"Do you want a hand?"

"Sure. You could chop the tomatoes."

I took a cluster of ripe tomatoes still attached to the vine and rinsed them under cold water. "Would you like them peeled?"

"No, thanks, they're organic."

"This looks delicious," I told her. "I was with Benedetta and we just had some toast and coffee." I munched on a bit of chicken.

Evalena dumped a handful of fragrant parsley into the couscous. The bright green herb brought out the cooked grain's pale yellow color. She added the chopped tomatoes, roasted chicken, steamed carrots halved and cut in bite-size pieces, raisins plumped up in orange juice, and bright red slices of roasted peppers. A generous pour of extra virgin olive oil went in last. She tossed everything with a large wooden spoon, added salt and fresh ground pepper, and then scooped a heaping pile into a bowl for me.

"Thanks." I grabbed a spoon.

"Here." She handed me a glass of her famous iced tea, took a seat next to me, and poured herself a glass as well.

"We're home alone?" I asked, looking around.

"Rex went to check on the construction progress down in Navarre."

"I meant to ask you about that. How is it going?"

"Ever so slow. We don't even have a driveway yet." She took a sip of the tea. "How's the couscous?"

"It looks delicious." I took the first bite. I looked at her with my mouth full and gave her thumbs up.

She grinned.

Perhaps I ought to write an article about Evalena and the benefits of esoteric cuisine, I thought, taking a sip of her tea. *Don't get me started on her tea.*

"How's Gabe?" she asked after giving me a chance to wolf down almost the entire bowl.

"Fine. Made it home *knackered,* and his father just told me he's following the Australian Safari with his head mechanic." I took a long sip of tea.

"And what is your heart telling you?"

Accidenti! Talk about a straight-to-the-core question!

"My heart is worried at the moment." I looked at her, hesitating, wondering whether to share *all* my worries. "You mean I can talk to him through my heart?"

Evalena smiled. "Of course you can."

"How?"

"Find him in the space between heartbeats. Then fill that space with the message you want to send him. Cast it out there on the next breath, over and over until you believe it has reached him."

"Is this something you've done before?" I remembered, without knowing of the technique, I had tried something of that sort in Savannah. Perhaps magic is an innate quality.

"Ancient tribes didn't have e-mail, Porzia. Communicating with their hearts was—and perhaps still is—at the root of drumming. They used their hearts and their drums, beating in unison, to cast prayers, to send heavenly messages, to offer gratitude to the gods."

"At any given time?"

"Well, some moments are more favorable than others, but truly speaking, I believe when he's most present in your heart is probably the best. Don't you think?"

"What would I do without you?"

"Oh, you'd get there on your own," she said, refilling my glass. "So what's next?"

"I'm flying to Miami tomorrow to meet with Camille Weir, the editor in chief of *A' la Carte*."

"A business proposal?"

"I don't know, Evalena. I guess so," I ventured. "She's too professional to fly freelancers around just to impress them."

"Make sure to wear blue."

"Why?" I asked, mentally running through my closet.

"Soothing, calming, reflective."

"OK, I will."

"Plus, I read in *Cosmo* it increases your chances of getting the job by twenty-seven percent." She winked.

"Oh! You're impossible!" I laughed.

She shrugged. "Any other assignments after this trip?"

"Oregon and Washington, to check out some wineries up there."

"Ah! Now that's an interesting destination." She cast me a look that made me suspect she might have had one of her visions about my impending trip.

"Have you ever been?"

"Once. Mystical grounds all over up there. Great healing for a sabbatical." She sipped her tea silently for few minutes. And then she dropped the bomb: "Porzia, how is your friend Benedetta? I haven't had the pleasure of meeting her yet."

"Yes." I took a long breath and slowly let it out. "I think you two should talk."

*

Although I truly felt I had done the right thing, I drove home second-guessing my instinct.

I opened the door and pushed Peridot back inside with one foot. I kicked my sandals off and walked straight to my wardrobe. I saw the dress Gabe had bought me in New Orleans and for a second I toyed with the idea of shocking Camille. With Evalena's advice in mind, I pulled out an ocean-blue silk dress I'd bought in France last time I went to visit Joséphine. I eyed it critically. I had matching high-heeled sandals and a shawl that would work great with it.

I grabbed my overnight carry-on bag and began to pack. I set my laptop aside and made a mental note to remember to add it to the bag in the morning along with my toiletries. Peridot walked into the bedroom and jumped in my open suitcase. "It's only for one day, *micio*," I told him, scratching his chin. He looked up at me through emerald slits and meowed loudly. I chuckled at his unrestrained disapproval and played with him until we ended up with the old ritual of hide and seek. It was frightening how good he was getting at it; a couple of times he startled me to the point of screams. But I had him jumping as well, his tail all fluffed up as he scurried away while I chased him. I had crawled under the kitchen table trying to grab him when the phone rang, and in the rush to answer, I banged my head on the solid wood.

Mamma mia! Che dolore!

I massaged what I knew would soon turn into a huge bump as I answered the phone.

"Cheers, luv. Can you hear me?"

"Gabe!" My knees gave and I sank slowly onto the floor. "How are you? Where are you? Are you all right?"

His laughter reached me, warming up my heart. "I'm OK. We're OK. Gomi is here with me and besides some sore bones from going from airplane to sleeping bag on hard sand I'm OK."

"Where are you?"

"We'll be by Ayers Rock by nightfall, luv."

Just where I had imagined him.

His voice became an irritating sequence of hiccups. "Gabe? I'm losing you—" Static spread into my earpiece like a devouring disease. Finally, his voice cleared just long enough for me to understand he would call back soon and not to worry. I told him I loved him and then silence, without even the annoying static.

Relief and anxiety churned like tangled sumo wrestlers in my stomach. I made a conscious effort to breathe slowly and relax. As much as I detest interrupted phone calls, I hate even more the idea of the phone having the power to control my feelings. I poured a glass of fresh water and drank it. I leaned against the counter and felt a bit better. I switched the water for a glass of wine and decided to take a bath to help me relax.

Surrounded by softly glowing candles, I soaked, sipping the chilled wine. I let my mind wander but steered it clear of troubling thoughts. And then, remembering Evalena's words, I went deep within myself, searching. I found the steady pulse at the base of my neck and felt blood pump against my moist fingertips. I filled my heart with Gabe's name and laced it up with intense love. I unleashed it in the instant between pulses. The still waters of the tub rippled gently and I smiled. I repeated the meditation several times, noticing how the instant between pulses stretched to accommodate all the love I felt for this man and how my heartbeat slowed down in unison with my deep breathing.

CHAPTER 28

Wishful thinking accompanied me outside Miami International Airport and dissolved in scorching sunlight. Shielding my eyes from the brightness with a hand, I spotted Oscar casually leaning against a shark-sleek black limousine. His eyes crinkled behind miniscule dark shades, much more fashionable than functional, as he smiled and kissed the air around my cheeks. He pulled away to arm's length and twitched his nose in disapproval of my casual outfit. "What a sedate choice compared to New Orleans!"

"I have a change of clothes, Oscar," I assured him, waving my bag under his nose. "You're the only human I know who doesn't get wrinkled when flying."

He smiled and bowed as I got into the limousine. We sped off in the direction of the skyline.

"Do you have any idea why we're here?" he inquired in amusement, flaring a long-fingered pianist's hand at our surroundings.

"Not a clue," I answered, distracted. I had never been in a limo before. I pushed a button and the glass between the driver and us rolled down. He glanced at me from his rearview mirror. I tried another button.

"Uh . . . Ma'am? What can I do for you?" the driver's voice came through a speaker.

"Nothing! Thanks!" I said, finally managing to bring the glass up.

Oscar laughed, shaking his head. "You're absolutely impossible."

"I can't imagine why she called both of us." I opened the bar and saw it was loaded. I closed it and pushed another button. A TV flipped on with local news in Spanish. "Maybe she's into cannibalism." I smiled mischievously and switched the TV off.

"She would have to braise *me* for a long time." He touched his chest lightly with impeccably manicured fingertips strongly contrasting his charcoal Armani shirt.

I flipped on another switch and the sunroof began to slide open. I closed it. "I have to change so you're going to chance her alone."

"Oh, I see—feed me to the shark alone and then, once she's satiated, you waltz in. Sure she won't bite your head off?"

One last untried button sent Oscar's seat into rippling vibrations.

*

The magazine occupied the top four floors of a glass and steel skyscraper. It was my second time there and I couldn't wait to admire the incredible view.

Security had buzzed Helen and we found her waiting by the elevator. Poised like an Asian orchid, she showed me where to change. Camille was in a meeting and it would be a while. I had plenty of time. I made a face at Oscar and walked to the ladies' room. I had rolled the dress to keep it from wrinkling too much and was happy to see it had worked. I shook it a couple of times and put it on. I traded my sneakers for the thin-strapped sandals and looked at my toes, checking my pedicure. Great! Still holding. Humming softly with a mouthful of hairpins, I French braided my hair, securing it with an azure silk clasp and then applied light makeup. The dress brought out the deep tan I had acquired while Gabe visited. I looked sophisticated, professional, and not overdressed. I grabbed the silk shawl and folded it in my brown leather laptop case that in this instance would double as my purse.

Only minutes had elapsed when I emerged from the bathroom as if reborn. Helen smiled at me, offering me a seat and a cup of tea. I declined the seat and stood, catching up with her for a few minutes. I thanked her for the magazine copies she had sent of the Jourdains and asked what she thought of the article. She smiled and told me it was one of my best so far. Then, pausing for a moment, she said she thought in some of the pictures she had recognized Gabe Miller, the famous off-road racer. I told her she had been right and that the older gentleman was his father.

"Camille said it couldn't possibly be," Helen said with a twinkle of mischievousness in her almond-shaped eyes. "Are they friends of the Jourdains?'"

Oscar answered for me. "No, peach blossom. Porzia here is dating the fellow."

I blushed and Helen's eyes got so round that for a second she looked like Betty Boop. She regarded me with awe and a lingering skepticism, awaiting confirmation with her mouth slightly open. I nodded, smiling self-consciously. "I trust this is to remain between us."

"But of course." She recomposed herself. Then, as an afterthought, she looked up at me and smiled. "He won the Paris–Dakar."

"Twice," Oscar added succinctly.

Camille opened her office door, releasing a trail of somber editors and mournful graphic designers. She looked smart in a Chanel pantsuit with a price tag worth three of my assignments, and princess-cut diamond stud earrings. Her piercing gaze landed on us and she walked our way, her hands extended to shake ours simultaneously. She does not usually waste time with trivialities but seemed honestly pleased to see us. She told Helen to hold all her calls, led the way into her spacious office, and shut the door. We sat in comfortable leather armchairs facing a vertiginous view of the Miami skyline.

Camille glanced at her watch and corrugated her brow for a second before raising her cerulean eyes to us. "Reservation for lunch is for one o'clock sharp. With traffic these days we don't have much time, and decisions are often better pondered after a nice meal." She smiled at me as her vermilion-painted lips mouthed those last words. I felt like a child in front a carnivorous plant. Appalled, fascinated, terrified.

"I'll get right to the point," she stated, handing us large black leather folders. I took mine and rested my back against the fresh leather of the armchair. I opened the folder and glanced quickly at a magazine outline.

"*Scoop!*" Camille announced, snapping shut her thorn-studded petals. "I'm launching a new magazine. A quick glance at what's happening in the underground gourmet and spirits circles. The antithesis of *A' la Carte*'s grand presumption. A vibrant, eclectic guide to the rising stars, happening places, and hidden treasures that anonymously surround us."

She paused to appreciate the effect of her words on us. Pleased with our enthralled expressions, she continued, looking at Oscar. "I'm offering you the driver's seat: Editor in chief. Carte blanche on commanding the project and a five-year contract with a yearly bonus. I'd double what you're currently making at *Gusto* and move you down here. All expenses paid."

She turned to look at me. "You'd have your own monthly column and carte blanche as well, as far as who, what, where you'd like to feature. I would like at least four of these features to be our main ones throughout the year. Quarterly, that is, Porzia. You'd have monthly deadlines to keep up with, but you'd often have the choice to pick the photographer, the place, and the length of the piece, to be no more than three pages for your regular column and not to exceed five for the feature articles. And just like Oscar, all expenses paid. I'll double what we currently pay you for the *A' la Carte* articles as well."

She paused for a second to leaf through some papers in her folder. "I wouldn't ask you to move down here. I don't see it as necessary. You've proven to be extremely professional. So far we've been able to communicate and exchange information smoothly with you living in Pensacola. Also, I wouldn't require you to be ours exclusively. You'd be free to pursue your freelance career but, as a resident columnist, I'd ask you to sign a contract with *Scoop* nonetheless."

She turned to Oscar once more. Engaged in a fast-paced tennis match with a woman who held the power to make us or break us with a sweep of her hand, so far we'd only been able to absorb her strikes without a chance to return them.

"Oscar, I've followed your rise to senior editor of *Gusto* and have always admired your ability to keep a fresh outlook in a business that easily becomes trite. Of you I'd require, of course, that you resign from your present position and give me the exclusive."

With those final words she leaned back in her chair and smiled at us, sure, confident.

*

Game. Set. Match.

*

Camille's table at Lumière overlooked a picturesque marina. I sat down admiring the soothing water in front of me and the gently lulling boats content to just float moored next to one another. I had been in Miami once before, for my first meeting with the same woman now seated in front of me and who was about to make one of my dreams come true. At the time, I was trying to make a name for myself in the business and—being the arrogant European that believed she could skip the painstaking climb up the ranks—I went straight to her: one of the biggest icons in the publishing business. I remembered how she had slashed my piece here and there with a bright red marker, her legs crossed and a Chanel-clad foot swinging as she read. "Not bad for someone who hasn't even been weaned yet."

Her interest in me had been slow but constant. At the rate of two articles a year, we'd now been collaborating since I graduated college. I admired and feared the woman, but I was also grateful for her trust in me. I had learned priceless lessons—sometimes painfully, sometimes just by silently observing. And now she offered me this career-changing opportunity on the proverbial silver platter.

A waiter laid a linen napkin on my lap and startled me back in time to accept the menu.

She offered a dream come true. Subconsciously I began to make plans: locations, ideas, and the photographers—maybe Desmond would be interested. My business mind was spinning, high on adrenaline. But my heart told me to slow down. She said she would be fine if I stayed in Pensacola. *Could I run my column from Australia?* I shook my head. As my mother often said, I needed to wait until the wave had receded before stepping on shore. Gabe and I were sailing on full winds, but we hadn't really sat down and seriously discussed where we were going with this sweeping love. One of us would eventually have to move. And taking a realistic look at both of our careers, I was the one with less to lose.

Would I move to Australia if he asked me tomorrow? With Oscar's soothing voice in the background and Camille's slow steady tone, I closed my eyes and sought silence in my heart; *Yes*, my heart answered as Camille's hand lightly touched my arm. "What's the matter? Are you alright?"

"Yes, of course." I opened my eyes and smiled.

"Tired?"

I shook my head. "No. Inebriated."

Oscar laughed and Camille looked at me. "That's why I believe you two would do such a great job."

"Why?" I asked. "Because we get easily intoxicated?"

"It's the freshness. How you approach situations, events, perhaps even hardship and struggle." Her diamonds refracted brightness as she turned her head to Oscar. "She gets inebriated by a business proposal."

"I, as well," Oscar answered candidly.

"Oh, come on, Camille!" I said, finding my old self. "Of course this is exhilarating. It's not like you're offering peanuts here; we're talking about an excellent proposal. It's absolutely flattering that you thought of me with so many other talents in the field. I mean, if word got out, they'd be stampeding all over each other to get to you first. Who wouldn't want to be part of such a project? Especially with your name as a backbone. And you sought *us* out."

"Such colorful verbalization." She batted her eyelashes at Oscar. "Wouldn't you agree?"

"She compared your name to a backbone," he mused.

"A first, I must say."

I ignored their teasing and studied her for a moment. "What would be *your* position in all this?"

"I'm the financial asset required to develop such a project."

"Where's the catch?" Oscar asked for both of us.

Camille laughed lightly at the implications as if enjoying an array of colorful butterflies fluttering around her face as potential food. "Oscar, I just asked you to take an incredible leap of faith. Turn your life around and believe in this." She spread her arms in a theatrical, sweeping gesture. "The catch—as in all things that begin in abstract form—is that perhaps once concretized, it won't be successful." She wasn't smiling when she added, "Not all caterpillars turn into butterflies."

The sommelier approached our table and greeted Camille by name. She introduced us to the tall, balding man, and I found myself shaking a hand that felt more like an overcooked noodle. Oscar looked at me in amusement and gave the fellow a pumping handshake that almost made him lose his balance. Camille listened politely to the man's wine-pairing suggestions for a couple of minutes, then silenced him with a swift gesture of her hand and asked about a specific bottle of Pinot Gris in a way that made the sommelier walk away from the table believing the wine had been his choice. That's what I meant when I said I could learn by just silently observing her.

"Everything here is tasty, but I do recommend the eggplant, the lamb, the tuna carpaccio, and the goat cheese salad," Camille told us.

I read the description of the eggplant she mentioned, and my mouth began to water: roasted, thin slices to wrap asparagus, mushrooms, and, incredibly, scallops. The lamb was skewered and accompanied by fresh mango chutney. The goat cheese salad had walnuts, endive, and a honey dressing that made me think of dessert more than a side dish. I went for the eggplant, Camille ordered the carpaccio, and Oscar opted for a conch ceviche in lime, cilantro, and jalapeño sauce.

The sommelier came back and ceremoniously poured Camille a glass of wine to taste. She approved and motioned for him to fill our glasses as well. We had just moments to toast before a waiter appeared to take our orders. He brought us a basket of fragrant bread, olives, and a tin of herbed butter. The perfectly chilled wine tasted lush and ripe, and I found myself on familiar ground, sipping slowly to better savor it. I read the label and memorized the name; a label from Oregon I had never heard of. I wondered what else the vineyard made.

"This is excellent," Oscar remarked, sipping from his own glass.

"I agree," Camille said. "It's a small vineyard I literally stumbled upon while having car troubles over a decade ago in the Willamette Valley. They were gracious enough to accommodate my party for the night. The morning after, they called us a tow truck and sent us off with a couple of cases of their wine. I have never forgotten their kindness, especially since they had no clue about who we were. Their hospitality was genuine and heartfelt." She smiled, taking a sip from her glass. "And they make excellent wine."

"How does Lumière know about them?" I inquired.

"I told them," Camille replied matter-of-factly.

Our food arrived and we set about enjoying it, chatting lightly between bites. We barely talked about her offer. But I knew both Oscar and I had plenty of questions we would like answered.

The waiter came to clear the table and suggested a light passion fruit sherbet that would marry well with a flute of champagne. It was Camille's call and a quick one, indeed. She told the waiter we were game.

"I believe you still have questions to ask. And perhaps you need clarification on some of the details of my proposal?" she asked once the waiter left.

Oscar and I exchanged a glance, and I nodded imperceptibly to give him the go-ahead. He cleared his throat before launching the first round.

"I have a life in New York, a partner, and a mortgage. There is nothing I'd like to do more than trade cold New York winters for sunny Miami year-round. But I have to think this over and ask my partner for his opinion. It's only fair, considering he's moved once for me already. It's a matter of respect. I can't do otherwise.

"I'm willing to try my best and make this move as long as you give me plenty of time to settle everything back home and as long as my partner agrees to come with me."

"Certainly," Camille agreed. "I've asked you here today with plenty of advance time. I'm not ready to set things in motion until the New Year, even if everything goes smoothly. But, I must admit, I want to secure both your and Porzia's collaboration in this project before I even start. I won't do it unless you two say yes." She looked at me.

"I'm inclined to do it," I told her, "as long as you don't mind where I'm living and I get the freedom of traveling as I please."

"Planning on moving across the globe?" she asked. Her tone was only half joking.

"Perhaps," I said in the same tone.

"Back to Europe?"

"No."

"Australia? Porzia?" Oscar asked with a bit of surprise in his voice.

"I wish I knew," I said sincerely. "But I won't for a while. Just like you, I have to discuss it with someone." *A someone in the middle of the outback desert chasing sunsets.*

"Well . . . at least we've set foundations," Camille said, not in the least discouraged by our answers.

Dessert and champagne arrived, and we toasted to doing our best to make *Scoop* happen.

We returned to *A' la Carte* headquarters where Camille gave us each copies of the project outline and contracts. We agreed to stay in touch and to keep her posted on our progress. By the time we finished working out the details, all our questions had been satisfied. It was time for us to take leave. Camille said good-bye and thanked us for coming down; Helen escorted us downstairs to the limousine. A perfect example of absolute discretion, she simply told us it was a pleasure to have seen us and waved us off.

In the limo heading to the airport Oscar and I had a chance to talk freely.

"That was quite a shock. Don't you think?"

I nodded. "Totally unexpected."

"I wonder why us. I wonder why now. I wonder what prompted her idea." He looked at me. "I mean, I thought her position at *A' la Carte* satisfied her ambition."

"I guess she wants to do something new. Fresh. Inebriating. That's why she's asking *us* to help."

"So. You've pretty much decided you're gonna do it, right?" he asked me.

"Right."

"I haven't decided yet. I mean, if I were alone and didn't have to worry about

Joel, I would have said yes right then and there. But I have someone else I need to think about."

"I'm sure once you discuss it with him you'll both come to the right decision."

"By the way, the Aunt Delilah article was fantastic. I loved the pictures, too."

"Thanks. It was great fun."

"I can think of several photographers we could engage—"

"You're doing what I was doing earlier."

"And what is that?"

"Trying to reach the shore while the wave is still crashing."

"I know. It's impossible not to." His piercing black eyes held my gaze. "It's an addictive creative process. A challenge and a push to our best buttons."

"I agree with you. Camille Weir is good at getting what she wants and making it look like we're doing her a favor."

*

I boarded the plane and flew home following the curve of the sun dipping low behind the horizon. I worked on my laptop writing Oscar's piece on Chez le Chat, but my mind kept on going back to the day's events.

The flight took less time than expected; thanks to strong tail winds we landed in Pensacola almost half an hour ahead of schedule. I couldn't wait to get home and change out of the blue silk dress. I must admit it had remained fresh and wrinkle-free throughout the day.

CHAPTER 29

Every reunion with my cat is an event worth recording; a tear-jerking scene typical of the kind of movie where the heroine runs through green meadows, wild flowers blooming all around her, losing her straw hat to the wind a second before the camera zooms in on the valiant hero riding up on a white charger. Finally home after having proved his honor in some sort of Augean task, he sweeps her off her feet, reunited forever; enemies dueled, wars fought, deadly demons and witches finally trapped in the roots of ancient trees, until the next fool comes along playing a flute and trips, unleashing hell once again.

No matter if it's only for a day or an entire week, Peridot dives into spastic fits of joy every time I return. I'm always afraid he's going to die on me, overjoyed.

I finally managed to make it into the bedroom with Peridot tucked in the curve of my right elbow, carrying my bag with my left hand. I tossed him on the bed, stripped, and went to take a shower. He followed me to the bathroom and perched himself on the toilet seat, his purring so loud I could hear him through the thunder of warm water pelting my tired body. Like a desert flower, my skin welcomed the therapeutic drumming. It drank and drank and drank some more, gaining strength and life with every drop until I switched the shower jet to steam and sat on the tiled step. I breathed in slowly, relaxing, allowing the day's events to become opportunities to welcome and embrace.

I don't know how much time elapsed, but when I slid the shower door open, the bathroom had filled with steam and Peridot had fallen asleep, curled into a fur ball on the toilet seat, only his tail hanging loose halfway to the floor. I wrapped a towel around my body and walked to the kitchen for a glass of Galestro, leaving a trail of wet footprints on the hardwood floors. I checked the phone for messages and ended up with disappointment. Gabe hadn't called. I walked around drinking the chilled wine, making sure everything was as I had left it in the morning. I watered my herbs on the several window boxes I have; the basil smelled particularly strong in the evening breeze.

I had forgotten to retrieve my mail, and shrouded by darkness, I ran downstairs with just the towel on. I hugged the oleander on my way back up. Too enervated to bother with the mail, I barely glanced at it before tossing it on my desk and went to brush my teeth. I braided my hair and climbed into bed exhausted, scooting Peridot away from my pillow. He meowed a feeble protest and plopped himself right into the curve of my neck as soon as I switched off the light.

*

The following morning, refreshed, I went for a long run. It was still early enough that I breathed brisk air and not the dripping heat that marked a higher sun.

The path I chose follows a ridge through a lush forest of dwarf pines. I usually park my car at the park entrance and run the entire course of about five miles. The wood stretches along a pristine beach. I love the blue waters sparkling through the fragrant branches. Halfway through the path is a small opening where a lighthouse stands proud. Often, during the summer, I have to zigzag around meandering tourists.

At the end of the trail there is a marina where small boats lie at patient anchor and doze, lulled by the smooth waters. Once at the marina, I turn around, cutting a path down the virgin dunes, leaving the only footprints around for miles as I reach the beach and run back with waves lapping at my feet. It's an experience I wouldn't trade for a five-star meal.

After stretching for a few minutes, I climbed back in my car and headed home.

The blinking of my answering machine welcomed me as I kicked the sneakers off my drenched feet. I hit the play button and Helen's voice came on. She thanked me for making the trip and hoped that I got home all safe and sound, and that the night might have brought me sound advice. I knew it for what it was: her gentle reminder that Camille does not like to wait.

Benedetta's voice followed, wondering where the hell I could be at such an early hour and to please call her back, she had the day off.

I finished sorting through the mail and found an envelope from *Grape Expectations*. It held a detailed contract for the Oregon assignment with approximate dates set a few days ahead, a pretty hefty budget, and a phone number to call to confirm acceptance of the assignment. I tried the number and got a busy signal. I decided to jump in the shower and try again later.

The doorbell rang and Peridot zoomed by me to hide under the bed as I toweled my hair dry. I wondered who it could be to scare the cat like that. I put on my robe and went to the door, tying the belt around my waist as I walked. I peeked from the front window and saw Benedetta at my doorstep with Eros. I guess he didn't like the burdening sadness of their last visit; when she saw me looking at her she smiled and her dog barked.

"Hi! You're home!"

I opened the door. "Yes, come in."

Her dog slipped in and leaned forward to lick me. I let him nibble at my hand even though I had just taken a shower.

"How are you?" Benedetta asked me, stepping inside.

"*Bene*, Bene—" I shut the door giggling at my own pun. *Gabe must be right*, I thought, *I am a goof*.

She knelt to unleash Eros, and he sniffed the floor around her feet. We heard and felt Peridot's tail poof up like a static antenna. The hissing from the bedroom reached hair-raising intensity and turned into a throaty growl. Eros ignored him.

Benedetta handed me a brown paper bag. "I brought bagels."

"Great! I have cream cheese and salmon."

She followed me to the kitchen. "Capers, too?"

I nodded. "But of course."

Her face disappeared inside the fridge. I fetched plates and glasses to set the table, humming a catchy tune. I poured orange juice and toasted the bagels while she collected the cream cheese, salmon, and capers. As we ate, I told her about my trip to Miami and waited for an answer. She just kept on chewing pensively. Suddenly she stopped and inspected her bagel. "What's this?"

"What do you mean?"

She made a face. "It's a blueberry bagel."

"Blueberry?"

"Yes. Look." She split open her bagel and shoved the top half under my nose. My vision blurred with blue spots.

I inspected my own bagel. "Mine isn't."

She sighed. "I asked for whole wheat and nuts, not blueberry."

"I bet it's yummy with the salmon," I laughed.

"Heavenly." She reached for another bagel and inspected it closely. Satisfied, she spread cheese on it and added salmon and capers. Her chewing resumed.

"So?"

"So what?" she asked.

"What do you think?"

"Much better without the blueberries."

I shook my head. "That's not what I was asking."

"Oh! You mean about the Miami job offer."

"Right," I said with a hint of impatience.

She began to pick capers off her bagel, eating them one by one. "I think you should go for it, but tell her you might move to Australia first. And if that's not a problem then you have nothing to worry about."

"What about covering assignments from such a distance?"

"You mean to travel from there?"

"Yes."

"You don't seem to mind jumping on planes from here, Porzia." She found another caper. "You're making the step longer than the leg. You don't even know if this Oscar fellow is going to accept or not. You ought to stop the mental jerking off until you know more." She sank her teeth into her bagel and squinted at me.

"I think you're right. It's not that I am really concerned about it yet, but it's a tempting offer indeed."

"Have you discussed compensation yet?"

"She said she'd double whatever I get paid for my articles with *A' la Carte*."

Impressed, Bene whistled softly and Eros ran up. "That ought to cover the extra dough you'd have to fork over to travel. Especially if you end up moving to Australia. How's that going anyway?"

"I talked to him a few days back. He and his head mechanic are following a vehicle they're sponsoring in the Australian Safari. They were in the middle of the desert, somewhere by Ayers Rock."

"That's pretty cool." She frowned. "He's driving?"

"No. They have a different driver." I took a bite of my own bagel and chewed for a while. "Bene—after what you were telling me the other day, I think you should meet Evalena."

"What for?" She dropped the last caper. It tumbled on the place mat and rolled somewhere off the table. I almost expected it to hit the floor with the impact of a cannonball. Eros ignored it.

"Why not?" I countered.

"Why at all? I shouldn't have brought it up." She looked skeptical and afraid, just like me at the beginning of my endeavor. Evalena's fame is renowned in mystical circles. This could be compared to an ancient visit to the Oracle of Delphi, minus the cryptic divination. Evalena's visions are pure and crystal clear—and not for everybody.

"But I'm glad you did," I said. "I was afraid to see her, too, for my past life regression. But now I'm grateful. It opened up avenues I would have never explored on my own."

"We're not walking the same path. I don't need a past life regression." Benedetta's fragility spilled through her quivering lips.

I pursued nonetheless. "I know that. But I think you should at least speak to her. It might help you see things more clearly."

It took some persuasion, but Benedetta finally agreed. Somewhat reluctantly, she took Eros and left me to make arrangements. I phoned Evalena and asked if she might be available for dinner. Apologizing for the short notice,

I quickly explained the situation. I told her Benedetta was quite distressed. She understood the importance of the matter and agreed to come over around seven that evening. She told me she would bring wine. I sincerely feel for those without an Evalena in their life.

I spent the rest of the day organizing my assignments and tidying the place up. Never did find the cannonball caper that rolled off the table from Benedetta's bagel. I called Oscar and left him a message saying that I had the Chez le Chat article underway. Then I called Helen and briefly told her I didn't have any news yet but that as soon as a decision was made I would notify them. As gracious as ever, Helen told me Camille had sent a parcel, and would I please let her know when I received it?

*

On my way to the farmers' market to collect fresh ingredients for dinner, moist heat forced me to crank the air conditioning on. I cast a look at the somber sky where the end of summer, in one last, sacrificial effort, must have saved the best for last. Scorching humidity now unleashed a grand finale before leaving center stage to fall. I smelled rain in the air and wondered how long it would take for those heavy clouds gathering on the ocean to crash into the shore. At least the hurricanes had been sparing us . . . well, since Erin.

I parked my car next to an old Buick with Alabama plates. Dean's Market is the only organic one in the area. I grabbed a basket and headed toward the herb section to inspect fragrant bouquets of basil, chervil, sage, lemongrass, mint, and oregano. I picked a few bundles of basil and moved on to get garlic, organic pine nuts, and walnuts. At the last moment I added a couple of pounds of vine-ripened tomatoes, mozzarella, and Georgia peaches so fragrant I could have eaten one right there. I paid for my groceries and drove to the Awakenings Books and Gifts store where I bought white candles, some frankincense, and a bundle of Native American white sage to smudge.

A few years back I would have never thought of such ways, but frequenting Evalena had opened doors that I'd never have had the courage to peek through on my own. Especially after being raised—eclipsed from it all—by a very pragmatic Joséphine. Thanks to the mystic blood coursing through my veins, Evalena was sure magic would have found me regardless. And it did.

In an herb-infused car, I drove home thinking about how I had become so much more receptive to the metaphysical world. I remembered how doubtful I had been at first. I didn't feel comfortable to call upon the powers yet and had a strong, queasy feeling this lesson wasn't going to get much practice time. I somehow knew I would be catapulted, despite my own will, into a burning mosh pit where the only way out would be to summon magic or put my life on the line. I understood now that every woman is a reflection of the divine feminine; every one of us enchanting creatures has the potential.

I had opened a door.

Talking about doors, Gerome had left a parcel on my doorstep. The packing slip told me it was Camille's. I used a knife to cut the box open and found two bottles of Pinot Gris, the same brand we had enjoyed at Lumière. A short note, handwritten by Camille, accompanied the two bottles.

*

Dear Porzia,

From one wine appreciator to another, I trust you to enjoy this wine as much as I have since my fortunate discovery years ago.

Don't wait for special occasions to uncork . . . every given day should be celebrated as special.

*

Best regards,
Camille Weir

*

I cleaned up the packaging, made room in the fridge for the two bottles to lie down on the top shelf, and began dinner's preparation. Peridot poked around, curious about my purchases. I removed the candles and incense from a brown paper bag and dropped it on the floor for his enjoyment. He promptly attacked the bag, sniffing loudly, and finally crawled inside it and fell asleep. Meanwhile, I made a pesto so bright green and fragrant I couldn't resist a taste. *Perfetto!*

I turned the radio on and set the table with cheerful summer plates, a handwoven bread basket from South America, salt and pepper shakers in the shape of roosters I had found at a secondhand store in France, and generous wine goblets I knew we wouldn't have a problem filling with a bottle or two of Camille's Pinot Gris, deliciously chilled.

After a quick shower I changed into a loose sundress with a pattern of orange and red stenciled fish that I love to lounge in. I wrapped my hair in a French twist and moved on to make a *Caprese* salad with the fresh tomatoes and mozzarella I had bought at Dean's. I sliced the juicy tomatoes and the mozzarella into thin slices and alternated them on a serving platter into a red and white pinwheel. Not able to resist, I ate a slice of mozzarella so creamy and moist it practically melted in my mouth. I sprinkled the appetizing slices with salt and fresh pepper and drizzled olive oil here and there, ending with a few basil leaves I tore with my fingers. Basil easily bruises if cut with a blade. I always use my fingers.

The doorbell rang as I finished. I went to open the door and found Evalena standing there with a small bouquet of bright orange roses. She hugged me, saying, "I changed my mind about the wine on my way over here and got you these instead," and handed me the fragrant bouquet.

I took the roses, smiling, and was about to close the door when I caught sight of Benedetta's car pulling into the parking lot.

"Look, Benedetta is here."

Evalena turned and leaned against the wall to take her sandals off. "Great! I finally get to meet her."

Benedetta got out of her car carrying a long paper bag stuffed with a couple of baguettes. She wore her usual warm smile, a pair of baggy turquoise silk pants tied at her waist by a drawstring, a white ribbed tank, and a crown of sun-kissed locks that framed her delicate profile, exposing her exquisite neck and shoulders. She climbed the stairs and handed me the bread.

"Hi. I hope I'm not late." Pushing her glasses up her nose, she stepped inside and tossed her flip-flops into the corner in one kick. She met Evalena's inquisitive stare.

"Benedetta, this is Evalena. Evalena . . . Bene."

They shook hands. I read Benedetta's struggle in her strained features while Evalena silently took in my dear friend. She broke the silence first. "Nice to meet you, Benedetta. You have a beautiful name."

"Thanks. Porzia might have told you it means 'blessed' in Italian."

Evalena looked at me. "You did mention something after your recent trip to Georgia."

I nodded, motioning them to follow me to the kitchen. "It's almost ready. The pasta is boiling."

Benedetta knelt to check inside the bag. I had forgotten Peridot was sleeping in the middle of the kitchen floor. "What do we have here?"

Evalena settled into a chair and looked at the bag curiously.

Sleepy and disoriented, Peridot crawled out. He looked at Benedetta, arched his back in a stretch, and then saw Evalena. Totally ignoring Bene, he walked straight under Evalena's chair where he drew eights a couple of times until she scooped him up on her lap. He purred and we all laughed. I took a bottle of wine from the fridge, uncorked it, and filled glasses, feeling grateful for my icebreaker *micio*. I filled a carafe with fresh water and set it on the table, then got busy with the pasta and slicing the bread, allowing my two guests to make small talk and get acquainted.

With her soft embracing aura, it didn't take Evalena anytime at all to make Benedetta comfortable. Her face relaxed, her shoulders dropped, and her locks shook with laughter at a funny comment Evalena made about cats' faithfulness.

I drained the *trofie* and dressed them with pesto, mixing them swiftly until nicely coated, then added freshly grated *Parmigiano* in abundance. Mixing it all one more time I then transferred the pasta into a serving bowl, dusted it with extra cheese, and after taking the *Caprese* salad out of the fridge, refilled everybody's glass and announced dinner.

Evalena left to wash her hands while Benedetta sat at the table with me. Her smile reassured me; she would be alright. I reached over and squeezed her hand, not sure if she needed the extra comfort or not. I was just glad to have them both there with me. Silently holding hands we waited for Evalena to come back, then reached for our glasses and toasted friendship, old and new.

"Heavens! Am I glad I brought you flowers instead! My wine choice would never have matched this!" Evalena puckered her lips and took another sip.

"It wasn't my choice but a timely present from someone who knows how to enjoy every given day." I followed her example.

"This looks delicious," Evalena said as I filled her plate with a generous helping of *trofie al pesto.*

"Wait until you taste it! The stuff is addictive. I often wonder if she secretly mixes marijuana with the basil," Benedetta joked, eagerly handing me her plate.

"I know a few people who could use such a secret ingredient—" Evalena winked, skillfully using her fork to capture the first bite.

"It's illegal," I shrugged.

"Like that would stop you," Benedetta teased.

Evalena tasted the wine and gave us a piercing stare above the rim. "I read somewhere chocolate was close to being declared illegal as well when it was first imported to Europe from Columbus's expeditions."

Benedetta nodded in agreement. "It was the drink of royals, believed to have magical powers and therefore forbidden to the commoners. The Mayans used the beans as currency and as funereal offerings for fallen warriors and aristocrats."

I looked at her. "You'll never cease to impress me with your knowledge of arcane stuff."

She smiled and took a sip of wine. "I just like to know about the stuff I eat, and chocolate is one of my favorites."

I passed the *Caprese* salad around and asked Benedetta to help herself to extra juices to mop with bread.

"Good idea." Evalena made a colorful pile of mozzarella and tomato on a slice of bread and bit into it.

It brings the Italian out in me when friends gather at my table and truly appreciate simple flavors. I just love it. I poured more wine, and amidst small talk, laughter, and teasing, we enjoyed dinner, reminiscing about earlier times, how we met, and how easily acquaintance had given way to the stronger emotion of friendship. I shared with Bene the tale of my first encounter with Evalena and how many of her herbal remedies rang bells and brought back memories of childhood. Bene nodded her agreement to this or that balmy plant or soothing salve. Ever since she'd embraced Wicca she'd been devouring herbal manuals and had pledged to a healthy and respectful appreciation of Mother Nature.

CHAPTER 30

Benedetta helped me clean up. I asked Evalena to take the peaches out of the fridge and bring them to the table where only the wine and glasses remained. I handed her fruit plates and knives. We sat back and I refilled our glasses. Then, using the dull side of the knife blade, I took a peach and began to loosen the skin, making it easier to peel. Benedetta and Evalena watched me in silence while I sliced my peach and dropped a juicy sliver into my wine glass with a splash.

"My father often ends his meals like this when peaches are in season," I explained in answer to their puzzled looks.

"Getting his peach *drunk*?" Benedetta asked with one raised eyebrow.

"That's right."

"What have we got to lose?" Evalena mused, and dunked a slice of her own unpeeled peach in her glass.

"Bene, go ahead. It tastes great," I encouraged.

"Can't be worse than Delilah's *aguardiente*." She peeled her peach and dropped a small slice into her glass.

"Now what?" Evalena asked.

"You carefully pick it up with your knife and eat it." I demonstrated how to proceed; they both followed my example, and the delighted look on their faces made me smile.

"See? I told you it was good."

"Better than dessert," Benedetta admitted, daintily nibbling at her slice.

Evalena wasn't having much luck with her knife; she abandoned it and used her fingers. I thought of Camille: if she could see us now. I had the presumption to believe she would toss the knife to use her hands just like Evalena.

"I've never had a drunken peach before," declared Benedetta as she tilted her glass to drain the last drops of sweetened wine.

"Me neither," Evalena said. She paused for a moment and then looked straight at Benedetta.

I summoned a long breath. I knew what was to come and exhaled slowly as Evalena spoke. "Porzia has done a great job at making us feel relaxed and comfortable, but honey, I believe you have had questions since your accident that need to be answered."

Benedetta looked back at her. A sharp edge sliced her blue eyes. "Yes. I do."

I moved my chair back, away from the energy connection that was palpably forming, and gave them space. Evalena leaned forward in her chair. I noticed she didn't cross her legs. She never does. She's always grounded, with both feet on the floor.

"Emotional scars take longer to heal," she told Benedetta.

Benedetta bowed her head and murmured, "Why do you say that?"

"Because often they're not only scars, but portals for change. And you're changing. Through these scars you're empowering yourself. Along your journey you're gathering strength, knowledge, magic. Events confirm your growth."

Benedetta's head snapped upward. She looked at Evalena, then at me, then back to Evalena, and finally nodded, bowing her head in agreement but also defeat.

"Sort of like Greek myths," Evalena mused. "We've erased the nuances of the meaning of myth, reducing it to a dried pit of certainty—"

"All things considered, certainty of knowing gives us serenity. Knowledge, on the other hand, is a constant discovery . . . therefore always implying uncertainty," Benedetta concluded for her. She'd raised her head and her eyes now shone with awe, respect, and gratitude.

Evalena nodded and asked me to light a white candle and some frankincense. I stood to do as requested. My hands shook as I lit the candle. *How did she know of Bene's accident? And of Bene's love of Greek myths?* She had tapped into the core of my dear friend and brought up to the surface her issue through the comfortable path of her love of mythology.

Evalena's breathing rose and fell, steady, calm, while Benedetta's body hummed with a light tremor. She took a deep breath and reached across the table to lay her hands in Evalena's. "Is this the right choice—" My sweet fragile friend took another deep breath as if afraid to continue.

Evalena's voice rose like intoxicating plumes from a boiling cauldron. "It's an indispensable thread in the web of your dream-consciousness."

Benedetta, paralyzed with awareness, barely nodded. I myself was afraid to blink, fearful of disturbing the current flowing between the two women in front of me. I held as still as possible.

"Scars will flaw your skin only if you choose to view them as flaws. Change will occur and you'll never be the same if you choose to embrace it. But just like the ever-shifting sky, change is never permanent. Permanence resides rather in the fact of change," Evalena stated.

Evalena's words catapulted me back to Australia, behind Umeracha on the threshold of an enchanted forest when I first thought those exact words. I realized how far I had come in my own mystical journey.

I no longer stood on the threshold of my nightmares. I was *in* the water, feeling it shift into quicksand, and only I held the power to rise, to awaken. *Did I want the power? Yes, of course I did. I was about to need it . . .*

Benedetta's voice reached me from afar, interrupting my thoughts. "I know," she said in a tiny voice.

I spiraled back into my kitchen.

"Apparently we're causing a chain reaction." Evalena cast me an inquisitive look. "Are you well, dear?"

"Not quite," I murmured. "Perhaps I ought to leave you two alone. I feel I'm being pulled in." In a daze, I pushed my chair back and stood, ready to walk out.

Benedetta grabbed my wrist and squeezed. "I can't do this without you here."

I struggled to focus and met her pleading eyes. My entire being shook uncontrollably.

"I believe we've had plenty for one evening." Evalena sounded exhausted. "It's extremely tiring for me to summon such energies."

Her own exhaustion shrouded me as well, like constrictive ivy suffocating a tree.

"Benedetta, if you wish to continue, here's my card." She handed Bene a lilac business card and then got up with effort. I helped her, supporting her elbow, and asked if she needed to lie down. I knew *I* could sleep for a week.

"No, thanks. I'll be fine with fresh air on my drive back." She inhaled slowly. Her unfocused eyes gave the feeling she was looking within, but I was sure her sight actually cast outward, toward tomorrow's horizons. Exhaling, she regained contact with her surroundings. "Thanks for a lovely dinner, Porzia. This is to be continued."

"Do you dream?" Benedetta asked her.

"Of course I do. But, if you mean do I have premonitory dreams, I have to admit not as often as one would think. It seems that whatever connection I have works best when I am awake. I often have nightmares, but that's only because I'm a bit slow at perceiving hints, so in my dream state whatever issue I am struggling with recurs to get my attention. And what better way to motivate than with fear?"

"So you have pretty scary nightmares?" I asked her.

"The kind one never forgets." She looked at me. "Don't you?"

I thought about it for a few seconds. "I do. But not often, and I seldom remember them once I'm awake. But even if I don't recall what frightened me in the nightmare, once I finally awaken from it I'm paralyzed with fear." I shook my head at my own weakness. "I have been so afraid that I wouldn't get up to go to the bathroom until I could shake the bad feelings. Sometimes I'd hold it until daylight." I tilted my head toward the dark window behind Benedetta and shifted my gaze to address her. "Do you have bad dreams?"

Benedetta smirked. "I seem to have it all scrambled. I have bad dreams when my reality is peachy. Like, if everything is going well, then I dream of something catastrophic happening to disrupt the balance. When my reality sucks I sleep like a baby."

"A shrink would have a blast with you, sweetie," Evalena smiled.

"So I was told after the accident."

We escorted her to the door where she slipped her sandals on and reminded me to smudge with sage before she left us.

Benedetta left shortly after.

I cleaned up the kitchen, lit some sacred sage, and walked around letting the sweet smoke cleanse the atmosphere as I straightened up. By the time I was done my clock read way past midnight.

I got ready for bed wondering if Gabe might still call, but I knew he was better at calculating the time difference than I was and was sure he wouldn't call this late.

My bedroom faces in the direction of the Sound, so I pulled the blinds down but left the window open to welcome the fresh breezes then hopped into bed, switched the nightstand light off, and fell asleep with my fingers crossed against nightmares.

*

The phone rang, piercing through the buttery thickness of my sleep. I opened one eye and noticed the bright daylight outside.

"Hello?" I managed groggily. I shook my head, glanced at the alarm clock—not as late as I thought—and spoke again. "Hellooo?" *Maybe Gabe from out there somewhere?*

Finally, a formal British voice replied, "Good morning, Miss Amard. How are you?"

"Splendid," I responded, stifling a yawn.

"*Grape Expectations* here, Miss Amard. We were wondering if you had received our information. And if isn't too much pressure, if you'd agree to a tentative deadline for the end of October at the latest? It would force you to leave in a few days."

I shot out of the sheets and sat up straight. "Yes, good morning!" My brain wheels clicked into survival mode and my professional gears shifted in smoothly. Well, somewhat smoothly. I pulled the sheet up over my bare breasts and asked to whom I was speaking with.

The distinguished voice chuckled and then left me speechless. "Gilroy Wyvill, Miss Amard. At your service."

I opened my mouth, and then shut it; opened it again, stuttered silently, and closed it. After taking a deep breath I finally managed to tell my former professor that it was a pleasure to talk to him again.

"It has been quite some time indeed, Miss Amard. I have enjoyed your career's progress, and I must admit I have been looking forward to the day our paths would cross again."

"This is quite a surprise, Professor. How are you, sir?" I said, still shocked.

"I'm faring well, thank you. I have been contributing to this magazine for quite some time now, Miss Amard, and truly enjoy it. I'm retired from the academic world, and I do this now as a favor to an old friend. We were discussing innovative ideas at a recent meeting and I thought of you. Merely mentioning your name along with a couple of your recent publications stirred the editors' interest. I hope you don't mind."

"Of course not, Professor! I'm thrilled!"

"And how have you been?"

"I've been doing well. I'm pleased that you remembered me. I'm working steadily and slowly building a solid reputation. I honestly enjoy what I am doing. I don't want it to merely turn into a job. It has to be a pleasure first, then a living. And yes, I have received the itinerary."

"Interesting perspective, Miss Amard. Please feel free to browse through my suggestions, but if you have any original ideas don't hesitate to add your personal touch. Also, you need to contact a photography agency in Portland where one of our professional freelancers will join you."

I wasn't familiar with the name he mentioned and silently hoped this person would be friendly and not too overbearing. I hate to be stuck for days with someone too clingy. I told him I planned on about four days at the most, and he thought that agreeable.

"The phone number you have, Miss Amard, is the only one I have available here at the magazine. I do promise to be available if the need arises."

"Thanks. I'll call only if I have questions. If not, I'll get in touch once I get back from Oregon."

"Sounds good. Have a great trip."

"Thanks, Professor."

"You're welcome."

I took a deep breath. *Professor Gilroy Wyvill.* I couldn't believe it! Originally from Great Britain, he holds the qualification of Master of Wine, the British certificate which is globally recognized as the toughest set of written and tasting exams of all. Most years fewer than a dozen applicants pass, and fewer than 250 people have been awarded the qualification. He taught an elite group of extremely grateful students a splendid summer class on the history of European grapes in America. He had enthusiasm, knowledge, and incredible respect for the first wine pioneers of the new continent. Needless to say, his classes were always booked solid. Students from as far as Japan and South Africa came to attend his excellent courses.

Although I could have daydreamed for hours, I finally kicked the sheets aside and got up to face the busy workday ahead of me. I showered and made coffee. Carrying a steaming cup of espresso to my desk, I turned on my computer and got started. I worked on my piece about Chez le Chat, and it didn't take me too long to feel satisfied. Draining the remaining drops of coffee, I sent it off to Oscar and then faxed it, too, holding his assistant hostage on the phone until she confirmed receiving my pages.

I made flight arrangements with my trusted travel agency and also asked for a rental car. I told them not to worry about sleeping accommodations. For some reason, I wanted to wait until I got to Oregon and then decide where to sleep. Despite the short notice I felt excited at the thought of leaving in a couple of days. I got up to make something to eat and break the news to Peridot. He took it better than expected. The fact that I had filled his bowl with fresh tuna helped a great deal.

I made a quick salad and got back on the Internet to find out more about the Willamette Valley. I must admit, just because I write about wine doesn't make me an immediate expert on every wine producing region out there. I wasn't very familiar with this one and found myself fascinated as usual, engrossed in learning about one of the most promising new wine-growing areas in the country. The area came alive with winemakers, soil, and descriptions of ocean breezes breaching the Coast Range to the west, the Cascade Mountains to the east, and the Willamette Valley nestled in between. A valley that, thanks to Oregon's northern latitude, benefits from long hours of summer sunshine adequate to fully ripen its vineyards' grapes. The addition of the occasional marine breezes rifting through the Coast Range barrier helps to temper the climate, causing the ripening process for wine grapes to be gradual, encouraging complex fruit flavors, deep aromas, and just the right amount of acidity and subtle nuances. All of this combines to allow Oregon wineries to compete well on the world stage.

From the information I deduced the Willamette Valley wine region is considered a cool-climate viticultural appellation—grape-growing region—similar to Burgundy, France. So we were talking about cool-climate grape varieties such as Pinot Gris, Riesling, and Chardonnay, but most importantly, Pinot Noir.

I couldn't wait to get there.

I called Benedetta and told her the news about my trip to Oregon. She told me it wouldn't be a problem, as usual, to drive me to the airport and cat-sit for me while I was gone. I worried a bit about Eros and Peridot sharing living quarters, though. She must have sensed my concern for she soothed me by saying it would all be fine. For some odd reason the certainty coating her voice eased my worries.

I trusted her.

"Once I get back I might need you to take Peridot again."

"Where are you going next?"

"I'm shooting for Australia."

She whistled softly. "Finally, Porzia. I bet you can't wait."

"You have no idea," I said, venting my frustration.

We talked a bit longer; actually *I* talked a bit longer, she just listened to me as I rambled on.

"Porzia, I could listen to you for hours, but you're beginning to sound like a broken record." Benedetta's citric comment healed me quickly.

"I know. I'm sorry."

"It's OK. Just shoot me if I ever get so pathetic," she begged me, chuckling.

"I feel like shooting you right now," I told her, half seriously.

"I'm gonna have your cat. Be nice."

"Maybe I should ask Evalena."

"Can't do that."

"Why not?"

"A familiar can be devoted to only one witch at a time."

"Are you calling me a witch, Benedetta?" I didn't quite understand if she was being serious or not.

She just laughed and never answered. As soon as we hung up my phone rang again with Oscar on the line.

"Hello. What are you up to?"

"Work, work, work," I told him, walking back to my desk.

"Find time for fun, Porzia, dear. Life is short."

"You sound like the antithesis of il grillo parlante."

"Who?"

I shook my head, as if he could see me. "It's the cricket in the Italian *Pinocchio*," I said.

"I see." He still sounded a bit confused. "Well, the reason I'm calling is because I've read your piece and loved it."

"You did?" I asked, smiling.

"Absolutely."

"Thanks, Oscar," I said. "And how are you doing?"

"Doing well. Talked to Joel about Camille's proposal. We're fine-tuning the details, some of them major ones, like his worries about employment in Miami, and moving once again, and blah, blah, blah . . . I shouldn't bore you."

"You're not boring me, Oscar. Remember, we're in this together."

"How about you? Have you spoken with your heartthrob?"

"Not yet. We have a lot of things to discuss, but over the phone it's extremely difficult."

"I hear you, Porzia. And I wish you the best."

"Thanks, Oscar."

"Any other assignments or exciting happenings?"

"I shouldn't talk to you about it—trying to scoop out the competition?"

Oscar laughed heartily. "Oh, absolutely not!"

"*Right.*" I was grinning as well.

"Keep in touch between adventures, Porzia, and thanks again for a stunning piece."

"Thank you." I hung up feeling pretty good about myself.

CHAPTER 31

I flew into Portland on a very foggy morning, leaving behind sunny Florida, my cat in Benedetta's hands, and a spotless condo since I'd spent the day before my trip thoroughly cleaning. I'd hoped I would hear from Gabe before I left but didn't.

I had called the photo agency in Portland and spoken to Hannah, the assigned photographer. We arranged to meet and decided it would be fine not to make sleeping reservations. "It will be an adventure. Kind of exciting," she promised.

My kind of woman, I thought.

I packed a light suitcase with boots, jeans, layering shirts, and, on a whim, Joséphine's amber pendant.

After a bumpy flight from Pensacola to Denver and an even more turbulent one to Portland, the plane slit through a thick layer of rain-laden, gray clouds, which re-closed, unperturbed, above us, and landed on wet concrete. My stomach felt so queasy I imagined my intestines wrought like clothes after a final spin cycle.

On weak legs, I found the rental car. I fastened my house and car key chain with the dangling set of dice onto the rental SUV's thinking that Gabe would be proud of my outback choice of wheels. I studied the map briefly and drove straight into downtown rush hour hell. Every other radio station I fidgeted with blasted alternative rock. What a change from Country Georgia or Cajun New Orleans.

Twenty minutes later, a tall redhead shrouded in a hemp outfit greeted me at the photo agency. "You must be Porzia." Wisps of untamed ginger curls framed her smiling face. I sniffed patchouli.

I nodded and extended my right hand. "Hannah, I presume?"

"Nice to meet you," she replied, offering a firm handshake.

"You're driving," I told her as aftershocks of road rage spasmed through my body.

"Oh, you've enjoyed our traffic, yes?" Cocking her head she regarded me, amusement dancing in her deep emerald eyes.

"Oh yes," I groaned, handing over the car keys.

"Pleasure's all mine," she said, laughing and taking the keys from me.

She grabbed a faux suede bag and her photography equipment and loaded them into the back of the rented yellow SUV and we sped off down the highway heading south, toward where the Oregon countryside timelessly spread.

"Where should we start?" she opened with, her eyes shining with excitement.

"How about the Willamette Valley?"

She nodded, smiling at me. "One of my favorites."

"Great!"

Serenaded by the hypnotic woop-woop of the windshield wipers fighting a lost battle against the unrelenting drizzle, we left the city.

"I wonder if we'll get to see anything," I mused. "Half the day's gone already."

"It won't get dark until about nine this evening," Hannah said, reminding me of how the Northwest benefits from extended daylight during the summer.

"Wineries will be open so late?"

"To make the most of business some will, yes."

"Do you have any particular one in mind?"

She turned her head smiling at me. "A few, but nothing special. I figured you might have an ace or two up your sleeve."

I dug in my carry-on bag for my blue ball cap and tied my hair in a ponytail, anticipating rain for the rest of the day. "There is one in particular I'd love to find," I said, thinking of Camille's Pinot Gris.

"What's the name?"

"La Maison de Pascal."

"Pascal's house? Never heard of it."

"You speak French?"

"Not really. Just what I remember after spending a summer in Europe."

I searched my notes looking for La Maison de Pascal's address and found it. "They're on the 47, just outside Gaston. It says about thirty-five miles west of Portland."

"Not far at all. Let's go there first."

About an hour later, amidst gentle rolling hills covered by thick rows of luscious grapevines, we found a simple sign indicating our destination: La Maison de Pascal. We followed a bumpy, unpaved, winding road up through a ripening pear tree grove to a charming winery nestled by the bank of a gurgling river. We parked the car among a few other visitors' vehicles and walked up to the main entrance where an older gentleman with gold-rimmed spectacles and a trimmed beard welcomed us. We introduced ourselves, mentioning *Grape Expectations*—much to the delight of the older man. He told us to please call him John. I dropped Camille's name and their superb Pinot Gris. John, casting formalities aside, hugged us.

"Pascal!" he called to a petite, brunette, middle-aged woman. A tiny pink barrette kept a mischievous lock of her hair away from her bright golden-speckled chestnut eyes.

She excused herself from a group of visitors and approached us, smiling shyly but sincerely. John introduced us and told her how we came to be there. Genuinely pleased, Pascal offered to show us around. We got the grand tour of the facility, from the cellars to the ceilings, with Pascal answering my questions while Hannah shot photos left and right.

We ended up in the tasting room where John awaited with samples of their wine. After so much talk, Hannah couldn't wait to taste Camille's Pinot Gris. John explained to us how the Pinot grapes have a tendency to lose their delicate natural flavors and their natural acidity (which, in the case of such gentle grapes, ought to be called crispness) if they ripen too quickly or, even worse, over ripen. Thanks to longer summer days extending well into late fall and cool latitudes, the Willamette Valley climate is perfect for the best development of such grapes. The conversation got technical as we discussed levels of residual sugars, malolactic fermentation, and the singular phenomenon of the Pinot Gris grapes having a tendency to emulate their soil and regionality. The French call this notion "*terroir*." It loosely translates as "taste of the earth," a concept that tries to explain why the same varieties, grown the same way but in different places, end up tasting different.

John believed in leaving his Pinot Gris the hell alone, no malolactic fermentation and no oak. He fermented his wine cold in stainless steel, got it in the bottles, and voilà, all done. The result was bright, clear aromas with the spice reaching the nose, and at the end of the palate a lush but clean sense. After all, it's Pinot, not Chardonnay; no buttery, oaky flavors but fruity, crisp, refreshing. "Not a wine to be masticated," he commented confidently. Hannah abruptly stopped sloshing it around her chipmunk-inflated cheeks.

I had enjoyed it in Miami and with my girlfriends a few nights back, but now I truly appreciated it. Almost disappointed, Hannah thought it too zesty, almost tangy. We moved on to try the Pinot Blanc, which I found, in turn, a bit too fruity, though I did appreciate the creamy-textured structure, tasting traces of vanilla on the finish. Of course, Hannah loved it. We tried the winery's Pinot Gris Reserve—made from his oldest vines and best grapes—last, and John's eyes twinkled as he filled our glasses. I took a sip. This one embodied a totally different profile than the crisp freshness I had tasted in the first Pinot Gris. Extremely fruity but not cloying, with a rich texture that wasn't in the least overpowering, it held a lingering, warm, spicy finish topped off at the very end with a whiff of smoke. Intriguing varietal characteristics indeed!

I ended up buying two bottles of the Reserve and two bottles of the Pinot Gris. Pascal, readjusting her pink barrette, cast John a conspiring look and offered us hospitality for the night. After just a moment of hesitation, we accepted.

I spent the rest of the evening with Hannah walking outdoors among the grapevines. Occasionally, the sky took a break from the constant misty drizzle, allowing her to take additional photos in better light.

With Pascal and John we shared a simple but regal pear and cheese salad for dinner, accompanied by their delicious Pinot Gris. I helped Pascal clean up after dinner while Hannah excused herself to take advantage of the lingering daylight and a break in the clouds to snap some more photos.

Sensing my need for some rest after such a long day, Pascal led me upstairs to a guestroom and bathroom. She graciously made sure I didn't need anything else and wished me goodnight. Grateful for some privacy, I took a warm bath and washed the day off my tired body. A sunset streaked the valley, tingeing the river waters with deep purples and oranges.

I must have been really tired, for I fell asleep right away while daylight still lingered outside, with a brief kiss sent out to meet Gabe in his adventure.

*

With my body set on Florida time I woke up early. I bundled up in flannel pajamas and thick socks and went to work at my laptop, entering all the information I had gathered the previous day. When my stomach begged for coffee I took a quick shower and slipped into a clean pair of jeans, boots, and a heavy, fitted, black silk blouse I don't wear often in Florida because it's so warm. At the last minute I clasped the amber pendant around my neck.

I found John, Pascal, and Hannah in the kitchen engulfed in the juicy aroma of frying bacon. I sat at the table with them and poured myself a steaming cup of coffee, added cream and loads of sugar, and took a sip. They offered me a simple but delicious breakfast of eggs, hand-cured bacon, and toast. I asked John if he knew of anybody who made Pinot Noir in the area. I specified that I wanted a smaller, off-the-beaten-path winery where I could find a gem or two for my article.

"I don't know how he's gonna take the idea of his wine in a major publication—" John peered at me over his spectacles, "but just about an hour and a half south there's a place called ToeKnight Cellars. They might have what you're looking for."

I wrote down his directions while Hannah traced the route on our map. We thanked our hosts for the warm hospitality and set off in search of this promising destination.

John told us the scenery would indeed be incomparably nicer if, instead of the highway, we decided to follow his instructions for secondary roads.

Above us the sky still looked undecided whether to give us drizzle or a sun break. Hovering clouds lazily collided against one another reminding me of trapped cows on a moving cattle trailer. But all around us the landscape sparkled brilliant, verdant, and luscious. I guess it pays to get so much rain. I had never seen so much green all at once. Hill after hill, valley after valley of it unrolled, ever shifting. Emerald fields swayed gently under the encouraging breeze. Rows and rows of endless, bursting grapevines sloped vibrant hills; I bet they shone like real gems when the sun kissed those leaves. In the far distance the stark silhouette of forest-covered mountains sawed a jagged line across the blue horizon. I rolled down my window as we passed a grove of evergreens. It smelled like Christmas.

"Douglas fir," Hannah told me. She pointed at more trees coming up the road. "Those are hemlocks." She cast a sidelong glance at me. "Don't see many of those down in Florida, huh?"

"No, we don't," I said, inhaling deeply with my nose out the window.

In a small town named McMinnville we stopped to fill up the car, and I read a sign advertising for the Oregon Wine Tasting Room.

"What do you think, Hannah?" I asked her, pointing at the billboard.

"It won't be your secret ace, but it's worth a quick stop," she answered, smiling.

Chased by the sky's decision of more rain, we rushed back to the car and headed southwest on Highway 18. We found the tasting room in no time.

We parked the car beneath a welcome sign announcing not only a tasting room, but a farmers' market as well. What had begun as drizzle now mutated into persistent rain; we ran inside. I checked my boots to make sure my feet were still dry, and Hannah whistled, "These people mean serious business."

The place echoed the hollow enormity of certain primitive caves. Only this cave had mutated into an impeccable and well-stocked cellar featuring rows and rows of wines. I grabbed a visitor's pamphlet and read that the place featured over 150 wines from over seventy Oregon wineries.

Hannah fidgeted with her camera lenses and flagged down a young man to ask permission to take photos.

"By all means," he replied, smiling.

I walked up to one of the several displays and began to read labels. Mostly Pinot Noir from Willamette and Yamhill, Syrah, and a few bottles of—*surprise, surprise!*—Sangiovese from the Columbia Gorge. In the crowded space I felt like one of the trapped cows I'd thought of earlier. Colliding with rain gear-shrouded patrons, I worked hard to reach each station. I found Chardonnay and Pinot Gris; I looked for La Maison de Pascal and didn't see it. Then I stumbled upon the dessert wines and lingered over an interesting label of Pinot Gris Vin Glace. Used to not judging a book by its cover, I asked for a tasting. By its stem, I held the glass up to the light and admired the warm honey overtones. I dipped my nose in and finally took a sip: fruity, almost like a cobbler, filled with Cameo apples, peaches, and a hint of cinnamon aromas. *Hannah would really like this,* I thought, looking around for my companion. Only a few feet behind me, she was sipping from a glass of dessert wine as well. I asked for a second tasting and called up to her, "You would like this one, Hannah." I raised the glass.

"Here, let's trade," she said, handing me her glass.

I tried it and thought of poached pears stuffed with Gorgonzola cheese, and walnuts. Not that the wine tasted like poached pears, but it would marry well with such a dessert. It presented a little too honey-ish on the palate for me, but rich nonetheless. I walked back to the Pinot Noirs and browsed for ToeKnight Cellars. Quite pleased, I didn't find it.

Cradling a couple of bottles, Hannah reached me at the cash register. Her pleasant smile told me it had been fun. One more surprise met us outside: no more rain. The earthy scent of upturned soil enriched the air and held a lightness incomparable to Florida's humid breezes. I offered to drive, but Hannah declined, assuring me she was just fine to continue.

By early afternoon I began to think about food when a brightly painted sign on the edge of the road announced our destination. Inside a grape-filled vat, a smiling knight in full armor danced with bare, oversized feet, splattering purple *mosto* all over the sign. With the engine still humming, we stopped for a few seconds to enjoy the jovial, contagious energy of the barefooted knight. We grinned at each other and drove on. I knew Hannah shared the same intriguing feeling I had churning in my stomach. I don't know how to explain it, but I knew without a doubt that this place made excellent wine.

Deep green—one shade shy of black—fir trees secluded the lengthy uphill driveway, barely giving us a glimpse of thriving grapevines in the background. The car wheels met gravel and a wide front yard opened suddenly in front of us. Right in the middle of a perfect spread of emerald grass stood a large fountain featuring a marble knight—twice the size of a real man—proudly holding a spear, his eyes fixed on a past lost in the distance.

A massive husky ran up to the car barking loudly. He sprang up on his hind paws and landed his front on the car hood as Hannah slammed on the brakes.

"Holy shit!" she howled, instinctively throwing an arm out to keep me from hitting the dashboard.

I could only stare at the growling, angry dog, hypnotized by his sharp fangs. His mouth foamed. Mine suddenly dried up. The space between my heartbeats immediately filled up with fear. Then, as if responding to a silent command, his ears twitched. He jumped off and sat down, still tense and suspicious.

"What a welcome," Hannah whistled softly. Carefully, she circled the car around the majestic fountain under the dog's watchful guard and throaty snarl.

I watched the dog stare at me through the window and wondered whether it would be best to just bail on the visit. Then we heard a voice calling the dog back. We both turned toward the sound. At first glance I thought the man to be the fountain knight come to life, standing on a wide porch that wrapped around the main house. I then realized he held a walking stick, not a spear.

Hannah cut the engine, tossed me the keys, and bowed. "After you . . ."

"Not without you as back up." I shot her a serious glance and closed my hand around the dice key chain.

She nodded. "Deal."

CHAPTER 32

Something eerie lingered in the air, and the feeling deepened once I left the safety of the car, colliding with a solid barrier of tangible discomfort. As if walking through the silver shards of a splitting mirror, I heard Hannah's feet crunch gravel right behind me. Summoning a drop or two of undiluted courage, I balled my fists and reluctantly walked up to the man, now crouched to hold the dog by its collar with both hands. His walking stick leaned lifelessly against the porch railing. I looked into a rugged, unsmiling face and stumbled upon the lightest blue eyes I had ever seen. Husky eyes, just like the dog he was restraining.

A deep sense of vertigo spun me into a timeless void. When he finally broke the spell, Hannah's soft gasp gave voice to the pang I felt, and I realized that my heart had suddenly stopped beating.

"May I help you?" he asked in a throaty whisper, exuding everything but the willingness to actually help.

With pure survival instinct, I clung to his arrogance with emotional claws, wondering why the hell I felt so defensive. Maybe I was overreacting, but my senses—especially the ones my proper self never speaks of—stirred, awakened by what I could only describe as an ancient, familiar summons.

The dog sat up and sniffed the air, as if reacting to my frenzied pheromones.

I shoved my sweat-drenched keys inside my pocket and took a step forward, subconsciously hoping not to be shocked, the air seemed so charged, and hesitantly extended my hand. "Hi, I'm Porzia Amard. I'm writing an article for *Grape Expectations* magazine—" I paused to read his face and gratefully noticed a hint of recognition at the mention of the magazine.

He said nothing but let go of the dog, got up, wiping his hand on his faded jeans, and took my extended one. He looked straight into my eyes.

I felt extremely uncomfortable. *No way in hell this man was gonna let us taste his wine.* I struggled to continue: "This is Hannah, the photographer." Hannah stepped forward but merely waved, since his hand still held mine.

"Hi," she said softly, bravely attempting a smile.

Barely glancing over my shoulder at her, he acknowledged Hannah with a curt nod.

"I hope you don't mind us dropping in like this, but John and Pascal of La Maison de Pascal mentioned your winery this morning, and I thought it would be great if I could possibly include your wines in the article we're working on . . ."

He finally let go of my hand, but the warmth of his lingered. "La Maison de Pascal, you said?" His eyes dropped down to my neck and the amber flared alive, hot against my skin.

If a wolf could speak it would have such a voice, I thought. My fingers flew to my throat and I nodded. The stone felt scorching to my touch.

"They're friends of the owner." He seemed to warm up a bit. "I'm just a guest. Zach is the one running things around here. Would you like to meet him?" His features shifted seamlessly right before my eyes.

Oddio! E' bellissimo!

"That would be great." I exhaled and released the tension in my shoulders.

"This way." He picked up his walking stick and leaned on it as he began to walk away, limping slightly, the husky at his heels.

Hannah hurried next to me, whispering to make sure he wouldn't hear, "He belongs on the cover of *Playgirl*, not at some remote winery in the middle of frickin' nowhere," as she cast an arm out to our surroundings.

I felt a pang of discomfort at the thought that she found him attractive, but it disappeared before I could even begin to reason over it.

We reached a red barn with a heavy sliding door. Our mysterious host easily opened it and motioned for us to enter. It was darker inside, and it took a moment for my eyes to adjust to the light's sudden shift until the winery's fermenting area slowly took shape, shrouded in dimness. Bent over a thermometer, in overalls and a ball cap, an older man straightened up and looked at us curiously.

"Hey, Zach. These ladies are from a magazine and want to talk to you about the wine. John and Pascal sent them," he said to the older gentleman.

With a skeptical smirk Zach approached us. "John sent you?" he asked, accepting my extended hand.

"Yes. I'm Porzia and this is Hannah."

"Which magazine?"

"Grape Expectations."

"I'll be damned!" he exclaimed and smacked his leg.

More at ease, I finally managed a genuine smile. "John makes great Pinot Gris. I asked him about someone in the area who made great Pinot Noir, and he recommended you."

He raised an eyebrow. "You just drove down?"

I nodded. "We stopped at the Oregon Wine Tasting Room on the way."

"We're not featured," he grinned.

"So I noticed," I grinned back.

He scratched his ball cap, then, not satisfied, sneaked a finger under the cap and *really* scratched. The ball cap bobbed back and forth, precariously hanging up there. He resettled the cap down his forehead and grinned again. "I'm Zechariah ToeKnight, but you can call me Zach."

It was my eyebrows' turn to shoot straight up. "Your last name *is* ToeKnight?" I heard Hannah behind me stifle a chuckle.

"Yep. Waddayathink? That I dreamt the catchy name up one starry night?"

I laughed. The guy had great self-irony. "I guess you were blessed from birth."

"Or doomed." He laughed, spreading his arms. "What else could I have gotten into with a name like that if not wine?"

"Wine is a great business to get into," I stated.

"I agree," Hannah chimed in.

"Is wine a great business?" Zach turned to ask our mysterious guide.

Leaning against a thick wooden table, with arms crossed over his chest, he shrugged and looked straight at me. "It's not great unless you have a passion for it. Like everything else in life." He unfolded his arms and bent to scratch the dog's ears, breaking eye contact.

"That's right!" Zach approved. "How about a bite, young ladies?"

Hannah and I exchanged glances. We hadn't eaten since breakfast. "Sounds like a great idea," Hannah replied for us both.

"Ya coming?" Zach asked the mysterious guest.

"No, thanks. I ate already."

"Fair enough."

Via a well-manicured grass path, we reached the house's back door. Zach took a moment to wipe his muddy boots on a porcupine-shaped brush and then, with a wink, he opened the door, and we stepped into a cozy family room where a fireplace crackled happily beneath a mantel adorned with an abundant spread of family photos.

"My wife should be in the kitchen. Let's surprise her," he said. With the look of a mischievous child about to start trouble, he tiptoed up to a tall woman washing dishes by a deep sink. He grabbed her waist, swept her in his arms, and swirled her around. With soapy hands fluttering suds like snowflakes, she screamed, kicking her feet, and finally landed laughing. Thrilled with the result, Zach introduced us to his 'Missus' and told her we were from *Grape Expectations*. Her hands shot up to her plump cheeks.

"La Maison de Pascal sent them down," Zach added.

"And how are John and Pascal?" she asked, delighted.

"Doing great, from what we saw," I told her.

Pleased with my answer, she got busy with a tray of cheese and tomatoes, country ham, roast beef, dark bread, and a platter of—believe it or not —juicy Mission figs. The kind with thin purple skin and crimson pulp I could die over and just about did right on the spot.

Zach, ball cap doffed, hands washed, and hair sleeked back, sat with us and uncorked an unlabeled bottle of red wine.

"Is this your Pinot?" I handed him an empty tumbler.

He nodded and poured us the thickest wine I've seen this side of Chianti. I expected an overbearing power but was irrefutably wrong. The wine had finesse, opening with currants and dried cherries; a well-balanced acidity followed, thanks to dried strawberries and a hint of cassis. The finish was short and clean, yet luscious flavors lingered.

I looked at Zach. "You haven't won any awards for this yet?"

"Never bothered with it," he shrugged and topped our glasses.

"Why not?" Hannah asked. "This is excellent."

Zach looked at me.

"I agree," I told him. I rolled up my sleeves. We had found our secret ace. "How long have you been making wine, Zach?" I asked as I helped myself to some food.

"My whole life. My father made wine. I followed in his footsteps."

"Pinot Noir?"

"Is this going in the magazine?"

I nodded. "Probably, but not all of it and not as we're saying it. I'm just getting a feeling here."

"Fair deal," he said. "Father didn't care for Pinot. He had Cabernet grapes, but the final product was always average." He looked at me. "Stuff for just the family to drink. Wine was a hobby, a passion of his, but what brought bread to the table was cattle." He looked at both Hannah and me. Leaning on the table with an elbow, he pointed outside. "After we eat, I'll take you two outside and show you around."

"May I take photos?"

He pondered Hannah's request while chewing on a piece of bread. "Of everything but our guest."

"Agreed," she said without any further questions.

Zach resumed his story. "In 'Nam I met a French fellow married to one of the local gals there. He had joined the fight just to protect his own and in between dodging bullets told me about Pinot Noir. I spent long nights in filthy foxholes in the jungle surrounded by darkness. While rain pounded relentlessly on my helmet, I listened to this kid talk to me in broken English, describing summer and fall in his beloved France: hills covered in fragrant grapes, harvest time, and Pinot Noir." Here Zach paused to take a long sip of wine. Mrs. ToeKnight pushed the fig platter under my nose; I almost wept.

"I don't even remember how long we stuck together, but we both survived. After 'Nam he moved his family back to France, and I went to visit him. Turned out he wasn't really French but Dutch—born in Holland by French parents who went back and forth between the two countries. Nonetheless, he knew about grapes and hooked me up. My Missus here is his youngest sister."

"That's a great story, Zach. May I write about it?"

"Nope," he said, refilling my glass. "Write about the present if you like."

I looked at the plump woman sitting in front of me with curiosity.

Hannah got up to shoot photos.

I ate a fig, thinking about Zach's story, then ate a second fig and a third, until I was the only one left at the table with Mrs. ToeKnight cleaning things around me. Zach and Hannah had walked outside, and I was left contemplating the thought of eating the remaining figs and the promise I had made Zach not to disclose his Vietnam tale.

Hmm . . . tough choice.

"You like my figs?" Mrs. ToeKnight interrupted my train of thoughts.

I looked up at her and smiled. "I love figs and yours are delicious."

"Thank you," she said. The hint of French in her words felt so familiar to my ears.

"The young man you met is my nephew," she told me, as if explaining something I hadn't quite grasped.

"Is that why I can't write about him? And is that why Hannah can't take photos of him?" She nodded, pleased, perhaps thinking I had gotten the drift, and asked me if I would like some tea. *But why were they hiding him? And what kind of secret lay behind all this?* I declined the tea and a chance to ask more questions I knew wouldn't get answered anyway and resolved to look for Zach and Hannah instead. I found them in front of the knight statue, taking photos.

"An ancestor?" I asked Zach. Brushing mysteries aside, I had every intention to continue my interview and cast the mysterious "wolf" out of my mind.

"Naw! Just for fun," he chuckled, dismissing the knight. "Here—let me show you the important matter." With a brisk step, he motioned for us to follow him into the fermenting area where we found out that he did have labels for his bottles, all portraying the happy knight smashing grapes. He also had a reserve and vintage section and a lot more wine than I expected.

"People find us," he told me, answering my silent question. "Special folks like you and Hannah. And now with your article, even more people will find us."

"Does it please you or does it bother you, Zach?" I asked him. "You just have to say the word and I won't mention you at all."

"No. It's fine. I'm kinda pleased, actually. *Grape Expectations* has an excellent reputation. I'm still in control." He grinned at us. "If you'd like, we're harvesting in a couple of weeks. You're more than welcome to join us."

"I'd love to, but I have another commitment," I said, thinking, *I'll be in Australia in a couple of weeks.*

I bought a case of Pinot Noir and Zach told me he would ship it to my address, while Hannah took a final photo of Mrs. ToeKnight waving at us from the veranda. We shook hands with Zach and asked for the correct address so I could send him a few copies of *Grape Expectations* featuring the article with his winery.

"Don't bother. I have a subscription." Tilting his ball cap, he bade us farewell.

We drove away in silence, close to one another physically but light years apart emotionally; our private thoughts, unfolding in distinctive paths, finally converged and met.

"What are your thoughts?" Hannah asked softly.

I shrugged, not sure I wanted to share what I was thinking with her. "I'm not sure, Hannah. I'm a bit perplexed."

"About what?"

"How has he managed to remain anonymous for so long? His Pinot Noir is prize quality."

Hannah agreed with me. "I don't know much about wine, but I really liked his."

"He seems not to care at all about fame or wealth."

"Many people don't." She smiled. "I'm not one of them, but I also know I won't do what I repute as immoral to gain status like paparazzi do, following celebrities, invading their privacy."

"I see."

"Would you write a fake review if they paid you enough?"

I shook my head. "No." I looked at her, turning the question around. "Would you take child pornography photos for a million dollars?"

She cast me an obscure glance I had a hard time interpreting. "No. But I wonder *who* would pay *what* to know about that handsome fellow hiding up there."

I looked at her. "Do you think he's famous? Do you know who he is?"

"No, I don't." She brought the car to a stop to read a road sign indicating McMinnville to the north, Albany to the south and Salem to the east. "How about you? Did you recognize him?"

"No," I answered curtly. "Which way now?" I could feel her eyes studying me intently as I pretended to look left and right.

"How about Salem? I know a small country inn where we could spend the night. It's not too far from here. I don't know how tired you are, but if we see something else that interests us on the way we could stop if you'd like."

"Sounds good to me."

Salem. Benedetta would be proud. Fancy how no esoteric endeavor had tinged this trip yet. I touched my amber, thought of *his* eyes . . . and reconsidered.

CHAPTER 33

From a glass of wine in Miami to the hills of Oregon to the winemakers themselves, I journeyed in quest of the source of liquid passion. A successful winemaker holds the secret to the fascinating alchemy necessary to bottle passion. Once a bottle is opened, it's a magical experience to see this passion pour into the glass, to anticipate the aromas in the colors of a job well done. When they finally explode in the mouth, all the elements swirl into place in a complex dance. From the fiery heat of the sun . . . to soil, wind, and rain . . . earth, air, and water . . . all are spellbound into a perfect liquid potion.

As I wrote my article in the privacy of my room at the Salem Country Inn, I realized that my words were infused with magic. I lifted my fingertips to touch the amber still hanging around my neck.

Was magic still dwelling?

I saved my words, turned off my laptop, and went to bed wearing only the pendant.

I slept soundly and woke up with a vague memory of dreaming about wolves. I rubbed my eyes and stretched slowly. I looked out the window and couldn't believe my eyes. The sun! Shining! A few clouds lingered around, but I could tell it was going to be a gorgeous day.

After a light breakfast, we hit Interstate 5 north and branched right outside of Portland to go east. Thinking about the Oregon Wine Tasting Room and the Sangiovese from the Columbia River Gorge, I had told Hannah that we should head up there next.

We left the highway, followed the directions I had gotten off the billboard, and climbed up until we reached a plateau at an elevation of about 800 feet. The sun ruled strong up there and it felt great to step out of the car. The pure air welcomed us to River Gorge Vineyards. The difference between a winery and a vineyard is that the vineyard grows grapes to sell to the wineries where the wine is actually made. What intrigued me about this particular vineyard was the fact that it supplied local producers with the Sangiovese I had seen at the tasting room and, amazingly, Barbera grapes as well.

My article was going to be a lot more interesting than expected. I had so many questions. We ended up spending most of the day right there with Mike Olson, the owner of River Gorge, and some of his helpers. Hannah came and went, snapping photos left and right. We tasted a few finished wines that Mike had gotten back as presents from some of the wineries that had bought his grapes. One particular bottle from a small winery across the river caught my attention: Wind Bluff Sangiovese and I asked Mike if he would be willing to sell me a couple of bottles.

"I won't sell it," he said seriously, "but I'll give it to you."

After thanking him for everything, we finally headed on our way. I held on to the Wind Bluff bottles while Hannah tucked away half a dozen rolls of film. We'd skipped lunch, and the day was almost over. We decided to turn around and drive back to Portland, and Hannah graciously invited me to stay at her place for the night.

*

The following morning, with heavy clouds hanging daringly low, my plane took off in a turbulent effort and was soon soaring above the clouds. The sun shone bright all the way home as I fidgeted with my laptop. Hannah had wanted me to choose the photos I'd like to have printed along with my words and to assemble the piece. I thought the magazine editors would do that as usual. But Hannah firmly believed otherwise.

"I'm sure in the end they'll have the last word, Porzia, but we did this together. We shared the experience and the energy. I'd like my photos to echo your words and our feelings about the whole trip," she told me on the way to the airport.

We had agreed she would send me everything she thought might be worth considering and then we'd decide what we would send along with my article to the magazine.

I worked all the way back to Florida. I declined airplane food and drank only apple juice and water. By the time I landed in Pensacola I was famished.

Benedetta waved at me as I emerged from the jetway. "You look horrible," she commented, hugging me.

"Nice to see you, too!" I groused. My empty stomach was making me grumpy.

"Bumpy flight?"

"No, just starving," I grumbled.

"Well, we can fix that. I forgot your cat at home, so we can swing by Central Market and eat." Benedetta reached for the wine box.

"Oh, that sounds great! Thanks!" I said, feeling a little guilty about postponing seeing my kitty. Food over pet; my stomach made up my mind.

We drove downtown on a beautiful September afternoon, the summer mugginess just a memory swept away by the salty breezes.

Central Market used to be just that, the market where all the local restaurants bought their produce, seafood, and meats. Now the market is a thing of the past, but the name still stands on a small restaurant serving the best salads and sandwiches around.

We parked and climbed the few steps up to the dining area. I wasn't dressed for warm weather and kept peeling layers off as we seated ourselves on the front porch overlooking a small marina down below.

Benedetta ordered her usual seafood salad, and I asked for the crab cakes. We always order the same dishes and then share. They know us by now and bring extra plates automatically, along with a chilled carafe of the house white. I have no idea what it is. Joe, the owner, won't tell me, but both Benedetta and I love it.

"So, now that you're stuffing your face—," Benedetta asked me, while I tried folding half a crab cake into my mouth, "how was your trip?"

I chewed the heavenly, oversized morsel and took a sip of wine before replying. "It was a lot of fun; a lot of incredible scenery, a lot of wines, and a handful of great winemakers deserving a lot more recognition."

"That's what you were there for."

"Give them recognition, you mean?"

"*Grape Expectations* is the gospel of wine aficionados, Porzia. Of all people, you should know that."

"I do. And I'm actually happy about putting some of these folks in the spotlight, but I'm not sure about one of them." I told her of Zechariah ToeKnight.

"You mean there are people out there who would rather keep away from becoming famous?"

"I mean there are folks out there that had been faring quite well on their own. People who make wine because it's a passion." What had the mysterious "wolf" said? I tried to remember his exact words: "The wine business is not great unless you have a passion for it. Like everything else in life," I quoted.

"And whose words are those? Are you saying that there are still people out there not obsessed with making money? That they're happy to just live for their passions and leave aside profit?"

I nodded but didn't feel like sharing with her my mysterious encounter, so I steered the conversation toward safer shores. "Why are you so surprised?" I stuffed the other half of the crab cake into my mouth and waved my fork at her. "You're one of them."

Benedetta smiled. "Because I only teach music?"

"*Si*," I said. "You could be out there doing concerts and recording your own music. You're choosing to spread the word instead, as you say, touching one life at a time in your classroom. Making a lot less money than if you'd sell yourself."

She looked at me. "You're right. It's just hard to believe there are others out there like me."

"How's your salad?" I asked her, pointing at her untouched half.

"Not as good as your crab cakes, I guess, judging by the speed you're inhaling them at."

"I didn't eat anything all day."

"Then you should probably not drink so much wine." She moved the carafe away, out of my reach.

"It's OK. If I drink with food, I'm fine." I tilted my head and committed to finding the last drop at the bottom of my glass. "I wish Joe would tell me what this is."

Benedetta chuckled. "Maybe it's Italian-style house wine. That's why he doesn't tell."

I smiled as well, remembering how I once fibbed to Benedetta about some *trattorie* way of pouring leftover wine from the evening bottles into carafes and selling it as the house white or red the following night.

"Good call, but it's been way too consistent in taste," I said. I felt a little lightheaded. Actually, I had a pretty good buzz going. I tossed Benedetta one of the crab cakes, leaned back in my chair, and took in the view below me. A few people had docked their boats and were climbing the narrow staircase up to the restaurant. I squinted to read the name of a sleek yacht moored at the end of the main dock and couldn't focus.

Hic! I hiccuped, looked at Benedetta, and saw two of her. I heard thunder in the distance, but the sky looked pretty clear to me.

"I think I'm tipsy." I hiccuped again.

"You are?"

"I hear thunder."

She looked up. "It's the Blue Angels flying above us."

"Oh! I'm not *that* drunk then." I smiled at her and took a bite of seafood salad. It was delicious. I gave Bene the rest of the crab cakes and finished the salad. My head cleared up a bit, but I still felt tipsy.

We paid the bill and got back in the car. We drove to my place where she helped me unlock the door and take my shoes off as I climbed into bed. She pulled the sheets up to my chin and told me she would be back shortly with my cat.

I fell asleep right away.

I didn't hear her come back with Peridot, but I felt his purring against my neck as he settled on the bed and fell asleep with me.

*

Waking up with that incredibly satisfying feeling of knowing I didn't have anything to do, I stretched and looked out the window, wishing it was raining. That would have been a perfect morning: rain outside and nowhere to go. I reached over to grab Peridot, still asleep against my back, and flipped him over to scratch his chin.

"*Buongiorno, micio,*" I greeted him. He slit open a swampy-looking pupil and immediately re-closed it to better focus on the feeling of my nails on his cheeks.

I was feeling pretty content to just lie there, until something caught my eye on my nightstand. I shot out of the blankets and grabbed my key chain. A single die hung amongst my keys. I looked on the floor, idiotically believing the other one might have somehow rolled down there, somewhere. I jumped up and made for the front door, remembering that Bene had helped me unlock the previous night, and I felt a surge of inexplicable fear at the thought that I had lost one of the dice. It could be all the way back in Oregon for all I knew, perhaps in Zach ToeKnight's yard. In a vision I saw the piercing, crystal eyes of the mysterious guest. Spellbound, I watched him lean forward, sided by the husky, to pick up my die, almost buried in a spread of gravel.

I opened my fist and stared at the remaining die in my hand. It stared right back at me. *One.*

A subtle, fleeting longing began to dull my heart. I shook it off and wondered if Gabe had made it back yet. Clark had said about a week . . .

I ran to grab the phone only to notice that the answering machine was blinking at me. I hit play and heard his voice asking me about my trip and to call him back.

I dialed his number, frantically adding hours randomly in my head, concluding that it was probably late at night there. I hoped I wasn't calling too late but then heard his voice answer.

"Hi, it's me."

"Hey, luv! How you going?"

"Great! I'm home and glad I caught you."

I heard him laugh. "Me too."

"I didn't mean it like that," I grinned. "I meant *awake*, but how are you?"

"Knackered, about ready to fall asleep."

"Busy day?"

"Can say that again. Busy bloody week."

"I won't keep you then."

"No worries. I like talking to ya. How was your trip?"

"Went great. I'm almost finished with the article. I actually worked on it on the plane flying back yesterday. Now I just have to choose some photos and send it in."

"Did you have a good time?"

"Yes, it was intense. A lot of driving, but interesting. Found a couple of great undiscovered places I'm featuring. One for Pinot Gris and the other for Pinot Noir."

Peridot stretched to sniff the phone and purred loudly.

"What's that?"

"The cat. Purring."

"I just love how you say 'purring' with those *R*'s rolling." His voice stroked my skin like fingers.

"*Puuurrrring.*"

"Tease."

I heard him groan. "*Moi?*"

"Wait until you get here."

"Oh, you're gonna make me wait," I crooned innocently.

"Don't push it." His voice dropped to a hoarse whisper.

"That's right. You're . . . what's the word you used? Knackered—that's it. You wanna go to sleep," I chuckled, turning the knife in the wound. "Didn't mean to keep you . . . ahem . . . *up*."

I heard him laugh. "You're impossible."

"I can't wait to see you too," I said only half jokingly.

"So what dates will work for you?"

"As soon as possible would be wonderful, Gabe. Especially right now. I miss you. I missed you this morning when I woke up in my bed all alone."

"Get on a bloody plane tomorrow."

"I wish I could, but I have things to sort out, the article to send for *Grape Expectations*, other assignments to book and perhaps even postpone so I can do this and not worry about pending stuff. And you? Working everybody to death down at the shop?"

"Got that roight. They're mad at me. Can't wait until you get here so I'll be off their backs. Clark asked about you."

"Wants to know if I'm still around?"

Gabe laughed, "Roight."

I chuckled. "He can see for himself in a few days. Did you guys have fun?"

"Oh, heaps of fun!" he said. "The car we sponsored got a good placement. We didn't win, but just to be able to be there was bloody great!"

"How long did it last?" I asked him, infected by his enthusiasm.

"About a week of real racing, but a few days longer if you consider the getting-things-going time."

He described to me his feelings about sleeping under the vastness of the Australian outback sky. I listened, imagining him out there, knowing that my imagination wouldn't be enough to understand such a boundless expanse. He painted the memory of a sunrise with such poetic respect I could almost see him standing still as the sun peeked through the shadowed, distant hills, holding his breath so as not to disturb nature while his heart filled with the warmth of the golden sun slowly lighting up the miracle of another day.

"I thought about you and how when that warm sun filled me I could honestly say 'Thanks, but I don't need to have it all, for I already have the warm love of a splendid creature sustaining me.' So I bowed and put my cap back on, telling the sun to go find someone who really needed warmth."

"Gabe, that's absolutely beautiful."

"You should have been there. There is nothing like daybreak in the desert."

"I could almost see it as you described it to me."

"We should go when you come over. I'm working my schedule out so we can have time together, luv."

"That would be great, but I don't want to intrude on your schedule, Gabe."

"Wouldn't make much sense for you to get here while I'm stuck on some project and can't take time off. I'd end up chuck a sickie the entire time."

"Chuck a *what*?"

"Calling in sick at work without being sick."

I laughed. "That's funny. What are you guys working on now?"

"My pipedream, luv."

"Really?"

"Yes."

"Am I going to see it when I get there?"

"I hope it will be done by the time you get here so I can take you for a ride in the desert and show you how sunrises are truly meant to be."

"I can't wait, Gabe," I whispered.

"We're going toward the nice season, Porzia. It will be a perfect time for you to be here and see things around. Let me know the exact dates, and I'll have a plane ticket ready for you."

"You don't have to do that."

His voice deepened, became more intimate. "I just wish it was a one way ticket, luv."

What do you say to that?

"I don't know what to say, Gabe."

"No worries, we'll talk about it when you get here." He paused, then, with humor in his voice, continued, "I might be able to persuade you to stay."

"How?" I teased.

"Get you a job down at the shop," he replied, laughing.

"That's not what I was hoping for," I said, not falling for it.

"No? What were you hoping for?"

"A warm bed and the promise of an occasional lazy morning, rain falling outside, and more local Aboriginal tales from paintings hanging on your walls;

cooking side by side; forgetting about food and tearing clothes off each others' bodies; holding hands, drinking coffee, showering together, and other moments that make days, weeks, and a lifetime."

Silence filled the distance between us. "I love you, Porzia."

"I love you, Gabe." My heart about broke at the thought of being so far away from him.

"Goodnight, luv."

"Bye."

I hung up and languidly savored the feeling of his voice still rippling through me. He might have not been lying next to me, but this wasn't a bad way to begin the day. It could have been a lot worse. I could have been going through life without ever knowing him.

CHAPTER 34

The following days blurred with activities: typing, faxing, and talking on the phone with Hannah and Professor Wyvill at *Grape Expectations*.

Hannah had managed to shoot a picture of "The Wolf" as he walked ahead of us, the husky at his side, to the barn where we first met Zach ToeKnight. I stared at his straight broad shoulders. Despite the walking stick, he exuded strength and felt somewhat familiar. I tried to recall his eyes but to no avail, although his words about passion still vibrated through me. I ran a finger along his figure almost expecting him to turn and answer my silent question: *Ma chi sei?*

After sorting the rest of Hannah's photos and editing drafts until everybody agreed on a final layout, I turned my attention to Oscar and the *Scoop* deal still pending. Camille was being extremely patient, especially with Oscar sorting out his private life to make things happen, but with me as well. Without knowing what the future held, or how serious things were getting with Gabe, I felt reluctant to commit or make promises I wasn't sure I could keep.

I still managed to find time to jog every morning. I saw Evalena for tea and a nice relaxing chat to bring her up to speed on things happening. Her house was almost ready to move back into; the paving on the driveway the last missing piece of the puzzle. So by the time I'd be back from Australia, they'd be settling back into their own home.

I talked to Gabe every day. I guess the excitement of seeing one another again was contagious, and we found excuses to talk as much as possible—sometimes more than once a day. And if not by phone, we used e-mail just to say hi. I barely slept to accommodate the time difference, and I knew he did the same. Neither one of us minded. Sappy as it might sound, love sustained us.

In a whirlwind, a week went by, and I received my plane ticket in the mail, making my trip an unquestionable reality. A few more days and I would be in his arms.

This time I packed my luggage with plenty of sexy outfits and lingerie. I also added a few things in case we'd end up camping in the desert as Gabe had mentioned over the phone.

As usual, Benedetta drove me to the airport. With only a minute to spare for a hug, we hastily said good-bye. In a daze from that moment on, my trip became a physical act to be barely remembered, eclipsed by my emotions. Even my snacks didn't help this time.

About eighteen hours later, I found myself about 30,000 feet above Adelaide, splashing cold water on my face, wishing for a bed and at least two days of uninterrupted sleep. Once again I flew from Pensacola to Houston to LA to Melbourne, where I had finally caught my last plane, the last leg of my journey to Gabe.

Walking back from the lavatory to my seat, I glanced at my hands. The skin of my palms was transparent, showing a pretty, intricate pattern of greenish-blue veins. It reminded me of a geographical map leading nowhere. *Must have something to do with the pressurized cabin,* I thought absentmindedly. My thoughts drifted through the filamentous barrier of time, and I remembered my last conversation with Gabe before leaving. I smiled.

"I haven't been sleeping much lately, luv."

"Are you alright?"

"Yes, just missing you heaps."

"I'll be there soon."

"Then I really won't sleep," he had laughed.

Goose bumps crawled on my skin just remembering his laughter. As I rubbed my arms, the pilot announced our imminent descent into Adelaide, and my attention perked when he mentioned being just above Adelaide's hills. I glanced outside the window thinking I could spot Gabe's place, but Adelaide was a black velvet spread of winking gems. My watch read almost midnight local time.

Critically, I eyed my blue yoga pants and tank top. The fleece zip-up that completed the set had served its purpose to keep me comfortable but was nonetheless just that: comfortable. I tilted my head to see if my sneakers were still under the seat in front of me and wished I had brought a change of clothes, something a bit more feminine. *Even jeans would have worked better than this,* I thought, pinching the stretch jersey of my pants. I wore no makeup either; I never bother when flying, only this time the lack of mascara seemed to matter a huge deal. Why was I fretting about my usual choice of comfort over appeal when flying?

It was only Gabe for heaven's sake!

Panic began to drum against the walls of my heart. I sieved a hand through my hair, restoring a brick on the crumbling wall of my confidence. I had washed my hair and dried it straight just hours before leaving. I knew at least that looked great.

I thought of Benedetta. *Great! The ugly duckling wears a wig!*

We hit asphalt and the jet's tires hiccuped on the runway. I tied my shoes back on and waited for the seatbelt light to turn off.

It took an eternity. I contemplated the idea of beginning to count my heartbeats thumping loudly in my chest. I unwrapped a piece of gum instead and chewed. The sharp peppermint flavor somersaulted in my nervous stomach. Looking around for a garbage bag I found a small one and quickly got rid of the gum. I thought of Gabe waiting for me just on the other side; the closest we'd been in weeks. I got impatient and pulled a royal blue thread off the upholstery of the headrest I was leaning on with every intention of unraveling the entire seat if things didn't get going.

Finally, people began to move up front. I took a deep breath, gathered my jacket and bag, and followed, wondering why the hell I was so nervous.

I never got an answer. I saw Gabe as soon as I stepped out of the tunnel and ran into his arms, forgetting all about my bag and the rest of the world. His strong arms wrapped around my waist and lifted me off the floor. All that mattered was the ache lifting off my heart and his mouth on mine. His calm heartbeat echoed in my chest and mine finally slowed down.

"Welcome back to Oz, luv," he said. His hand caressed my hair, and I lifted my head to look at him. His blue eyes smiled and his grin spread, still warm from the contact with my lips.

"Thank you." I fluttered back to the floor and then reached on my tiptoes to kiss him again. I ran my hands up to his head and plunged my fingers into the thickness of his blond hair, deepening the intimacy of our mouths. I leaned against him and felt his hands caress my lower back. I pulled back and slowly tilted my head. His hair had gotten longer and the lines fanning at the corner of his eyes sexier than ever. He looked so much better than what I remembered. *So real, alive and vibrant; a painting come to life.*

"Ready?" he asked as he reached for my bag with one hand while the other grabbed mine.

I nodded and finally took in the rest of him: faded jeans, hiking boots, and a thick suede jacket over a black shirt.

"Is this all you've got?" he asked, pointing at my bag.

"Yes."

"You're staying for three weeks and all you're going to need is packed in this bag?" he asked, incredulous.

"I'm not planning on wearing a lot of clothes." I winked at him. "As a matter of fact, I can't wait to get out of these." I pinched the fleece and shook it a couple of times, making him crack a grin.

"No worries, I'm sure we can work something out." He tugged at my hood.

I blushed with pleasure.

He pushed open the exit door and I shivered against the dark night. As we hurried through the deserted parking lot I quickly slid into my jacket. I suddenly felt disoriented. The strangeness of my surroundings rolled over me and amassed onto my already confused state of jet lag and lack of sleep. I tightened my grip on Gabe's hand.

Shielding against the artificial light of the parking lot, I blinked several times; *Australia*, I thought, barely able to focus. I observed the unfamiliar cars, the fresh air crisp and clear around me, stirring my senses. Inhaling slowly and deeply, I registered the foreign scents and blinked again.

"Won't be long now, luv," Gabe comforted me, unlocking the Rover. I climbed in while he stored my bag in the trunk. I sat and leaned my achy back against the cool seat leather, deeply inhaling Gabe's familiar scent. The ethereal feather hanging from the rearview mirror trembled when he opened his door and climbed in.

"You must be exhausted," he said.

My head nodded.

He drove swiftly along deserted roads with only the occasional car passing by until we left Adelaide behind and began to climb, the only vehicle on the winding road. A plane flew over us, aiming at the airport down below, and I found it hard to believe a few minutes earlier it had been me up there.

Snared in a web of exhaustion, I barely had the energy to talk. I squeezed his hand and brought it to my lips to lay a light kiss on his palm. He glanced over to look at me. "How you going?"

"Tired. Exhausted. And immensely happy." I smiled.

"We're gonna be home in two minutes. I'll run you a bath and then you can sleep."

"Sounds great, as long as you hold me."

"Deal."

Two minutes later, the gate silently opened in front of us. The house's austere silhouette hid until the headlights swept it briefly. When Gabe cut the engine and the headlights with it, I saw a soft glow spilling from the high windows.

"We're home, luv."

I waited for him to get out and come around my side to open the door, and summoning my last crumbs of energy to get out of the car, I slid into his arms. He cupped my face and kissed me lightly; his long fingers pulsed warm on my cheeks.

"Let's go inside and get you comfortable. I'll come back for your bag."

I nodded dreamily and held his hand up the steps to the front door. A dog barked inside, and the tawny muzzle of a butterscotch-coated golden retriever peeked through when Gabe opened the door. The dog stepped back, gave us room, and then walked back to Gabe, swinging a long tail, its mouth open as if smiling.

"Porzia, this is Tess," he said, kneeling to scratch the dog's floppy ears. I extended a hand to Tess to sniff and she warmed up to me. I knelt next to Gabe so Tess could do her dog thing and smell my fingers. Once satisfied, she bent her head, encouraging petting.

"Hello, Tess. Nice to meet you, girl," I said, scratching her head. "She's incredibly sweet, Gabe." I looked into the dog's warm brown eyes. She looked back at me, then took a step back and pushed Gabe with her head until he ended up sitting on the floor. I sat next to him and forgot how tired I was. I wanted the moment to last forever, to linger, unfazed, forever.

"We need to get you settled so you can relax, luv," Gabe suggested, swiftly getting back on his feet. He leaned over to help me up and walked me back to the bedroom. While he went back to grab my bag, I sat on the bed and swept my eyes around the room. Everything looked as I remembered, only more tangible. The same mesmerizing Aboriginal painting hung on the wall; the same *garra* and *galpu* and the same trophies doubled as bookends. I inhaled deeply—the same smell of wood and Gabe's subtle energy infusing the air. Comfortable at last, I rested my head against the pillows. I relaxed and kicked off my sneakers. My feet felt like squished marshmallows. Hopefully they'll remember which shape to restore to.

I was almost asleep when Gabe walked back in with my bag. He quietly asked me if I still wanted a bath, and I nodded groggily. Exhaustion anchored my body, but I needed to wash the trip off my limbs. With enormous effort, I got up and walked the short distance to the bathroom, summoned by the gurgling welcome of the tub filling up fast. Gabe had switched the light off and had lit candles instead, but he was nowhere in sight. And then I realized he was giving me privacy and space to adjust. I felt touched by his attention. I got rid of my clothes and teased the water with my still-swollen foot, finding it the perfect temperature. I coiled my hair up my head and sank into the deliciously scented, bubbly waters.

Instantaneously, the trip tension began to melt.

In the flickering candlelight, I noticed a pile of fresh towels, toothbrush, toothpaste, soaps, a loofah, and other necessities I knew he went out of his way to gather for me. On the towel rack a clean white T-shirt hung neatly. I smiled, remembering how I had chosen the same one to sleep in last time. So much for the lingerie I had packed; I was going to spend my first night back in a T-shirt. I rinsed off beneath a jet of healing, warm water, visualizing the ache from the long trip, willing it to run down my body and disappear, along with the swirls of soap spiraling down the drain, to leave me cleansed.

I stepped out of the tub renewed and briskly dried my body. I brushed my teeth and looked at my reflection in the mist of the steamed-up mirror. Livid blue circles framed my eyes. I looked dead tired. A shadow of a suntan lingered on my nose and cheeks. A couple of extra lines at the corners of my eyes caught me by surprise. I knew they weren't there a week ago. Trying to smooth them off with my fingertips, I only managed to blotch my skin red. I gave up, put on the T-shirt, and walked out of the bathroom. My bare toes sank into the thick carpet of the bedroom where a blazing fire greeted me. I looked around for Gabe and called his name.

"Out here, luv," his voice answered from the veranda.

I walked though the sliding doors and a sharp slap of cold whipped my bare legs and feet. I hugged myself, hid my hands under my armpits, and bravely walked up to him. He turned around, taking his hands out of his jeans pockets. He looked tall and invincible, one with the surrounding night. A sliver of orange moon skimmed the black ocean. In a minute or so it would dip below the horizon, and I almost expected it to sizzle and dilute the water's darkness, but it didn't.

"It's cold out here, Porzia. Let's go back inside, luv. You're all warmed up from the bath." He wrapped his arms around me.

"What are you doing?"

"I'm waiting for Tess. She asked to go outside while you were taking your bath."

I looked around. "Where is she?"

"Around here somewhere." He whistled softly, and from beneath a shrub on our right, the dog magically appeared. She trotted happily behind us and disappeared in the direction of the kitchen.

Back in the bedroom, Gabe pulled the blinds, casting the room in intimacy, and asked me if I needed anything. I shook my head and climbed into bed. I laid my heavy head on the soft pillow and caught him looking at me. I blinked a silent question and was rewarded by that grin of his.

"It's great to have you here."

"It's great to be here, Gabe." I stifled a yawn that almost dislodged my jaw.

I fell asleep and barely felt the bed shift when Gabe climbed in minutes later. The warmth of his body wrapped a solid shield around me. I sighed, happy, knowing that nothing would trouble my sleep.

*

Heat, shadows dancing on the walls, and the song of the wind tangling branches outside woke me. It took me a moment to remember where I was. Miraculously, the fire still crackled in the fireplace. Golden light from the flames danced on Gabe's body next to me, sound asleep, free of covers all the way down to his waist. One arm was thrown above his head while the other rested carelessly on his stomach. His breath held a steady rhythm, controlled, but just as powerful as the wind blowing outside.

I rolled over to one side to get a better look at him. I tried to control my own breathing so as not to disturb his sleep and—honestly—to give myself a chance to observe him silently. I wondered where Tess might be . . . if she minded my intrusion on their harmony. The wind outside gained strength; its song swelled into a symphony and interrupted my thoughts. Branches bowed and some snapped like frenzied violin bows against the forceful power. Gabe slept, undisturbed.

I clenched my fists to keep my hands from touching his body. He looked absolutely stunning in the firelight. His hair shone like liquid gold and his chiseled profile incited an irresistible temptation. I bit my lower lip and my eyes wandered to his mouth, lightly parted, on down to his shoulders and the rippling of his muscles, defined even while he slept.

He's absolutely gorgeous, I thought. I took in his smooth chest with its golden skin and the thin trail of darker hair from his navel that disappeared under the crumpled sheets. I couldn't resist and pushed up on my elbows, careful not to trail my hair down to tickle him. I dropped my mouth on his upper stomach and lightly kissed him. He stirred and raised a hand to caress my hair. "You're awake, luv?" His husky voice reached my ears, and his fingers raked my hair.

I turned my head to rest my cheek on the tautness of his stomach and felt the rising and lowering of his breathing against my skin. "Yes, but don't worry. Go back to sleep." I pulled away and relaxed back on my pillow.

Outside, the wind slowed to a soothing lullaby, and I drifted back to sleep.

I woke up hours later to a crisp, sunny morning and Gabe next to me, wide-awake.

"Hey," I mumbled, rubbing my eyes.

"Hey, yourself."

Under the covers his warm hand inched up my bare leg. His eyes never left me as he drank the yearning my face revealed. I held my breath, for it distracted me from the sensation his hand slowly evoked. We locked eyes and I forgot to blink. My eyes burned. My stomach burned. My entire being was on fire. A mere caress of his fingers along my thigh had stroked me aflame.

"I want you," I mouthed softly.

I heard his sharp intake of breath and his hand inched higher. I rolled on one side to face him and slightly parted my legs. He took the invitation and pressed his fingers into my warm flesh, parting my legs wider. I lowered my eyes to his mouth and lifted an arm to wrap around his neck. I used the strength of his body as leverage and pulled myself closer to him. I rubbed my nose against his neck, deeply inhaling his strong masculine scent, intoxicating myself. His hand still lingered, dangerously close; his eyes, still locked on my face, reflected the fire flames.

"It's like I'm seeing you for the first time," he whispered hoarsely. "And yet, I have the feeling I've known you forever."

I looked at him and something tore within me.

As if by magic, pain lifted and fears dissolved.

I accepted the consequences to love this man unconditionally. No matter what, my heart agreed to take in not only the immense love, but the risk of pain as well. For the first time in my life, the taste of unconditional love rolled over my tongue. I took a moment to savor the feeling.

I felt liberated. I had defied fear and allowed this love to grow stronger than the dread of pain. The fear of being loved and giving love no longer gripped my heart. What I faced was this new me, this Porzia: determined to let go and obliterate herself with this love.

How the hell did it happen?

I felt torn between the blessing to feel such emotions and the surprise at finding such strength in me.

I looked at him and, in the clarity of his gold-speckled blue eyes, all doubts faded. "I know what you mean."

The daylight filtering through the blinds seemed to shift; the crackling of the fire ceased as if waiting for Gabe's hand to resume exploring.

Who is this man holding the power to still time? I wondered, fascinated. And then it dawned on me. Nature had been waiting for *my* breath to resume. I was the one who had held time!

Gabe's eyes narrowed and looked at me for a few moments longer, then he leaned over and hugged me. Hugging him back I rested my head in the curve of his shoulder.

"If I'm dreaming, please don't wake me," I said against his skin. He tasted warm.

"What if reality is better than the dream?"

I sighed. "What can be better than this?"

"This." He parted my legs with his knee. His body shifted and we sank into the mattress. His mouth found mine, and I lost touch with this world. I entered a dimension of swirling senses. I shut reason off and surrendered to the rising pleasure his tongue inflicted on me. His hand mercifully resumed its caress, and

I used mine to explore his sensuous body. My fingernails trailed along the curve of his spine until they met the elastic of his shorts. I slid my hands on his hips and pulled the shorts down. I rose off the pillows to get rid of the T-shirt and laid back.

"Hang on a sec, luv. I wanna look at you."

We shared the intimate look of two lovers as our heavy-lidded eyes met in the intoxicating anticipation of lovemaking. Desire rippled through me like a subtle shock. The clear blue of skies after a summer thunderstorm sparkled through the thickness of his eyelashes, eyes that drew me to his mouth with wanton need.

I parted my lips and kissed him deeply, finally closing my eyes to fully enjoy the pleasure building up within me. My whole being stirred and quivered in anticipation; at last! such long-awaited fulfillment.

My breasts ached and my nipples hardened with memories of our past lovemaking. I felt so ready I could taste sex in the air around us. I knew he fed off such pleasure and so did I. I lost cognition and the boundaries of where I ended and he began. Our skin touched, melting reality away. When I slid over to lie on top of him an intense, scorching heat took over, fusing us to make one. What had begun as a gentle nibble along his strong jaw became a game of biting and teasing. With agonizing slowness his hands slid from my shoulders, contoured my back, all the way down, and sank in the round swell of my bottom. I felt him ready, hard and strong. In a slow, circular movement the tip of his swollen head parted my waiting lips and I took him in, stealing his breath away.

I stilled to fully enjoy the pleasure of him filling me deeply. I savored the strength of his thick hardness. The length of him pulsed within me, ready to please me. *Oddio! One more push and I'll melt* . . .

I resisted his throbbing, quick shocks of pleasure stroking . . . *Not yet* . . .

I tightened my legs against his hips and moved slowly while his impatient hands kneaded my flesh, guiding me deeper, until I threw my head back on the edge of climax. Surging with the buildup, I steadied my hands on his broad shoulders and thrust down one last time. I crashed through a thick tide of rising pleasure and felt him shake, echoing my own ecstasy.

*

Minutes went by, silently rolling like notes of a fading piano.

"Now, for real, welcome back to Oz, luv," his hoarse voice whispered in my hair.

"Thanks," I said, lifting my head to look at him. "Feels good to be back."

That brought laughter up to his lips. He ran a hand through his thick hair and leaned over to kiss my nose.

"Hungry?" he asked.

"Yes, starving."

"I'm sorry, I should have asked last night if you wanted something to eat."

I shook my head. "I wasn't hungry last night. The bath was all I needed."

"How about a quick shower with me?" he asked.

"Ok, but let's make it quick 'cause I am *really* hungry," I said, throwing off the covers.

Tess walked into the bedroom wagging her long caramel-colored tail. She came up to Gabe and then looked at me, tilting her head.

"She's probably wondering what kind of weird creature I am."

"You can tell her all about how weird you are, just be gentle," Gabe teased.

I grabbed the first thing I saw and threw it at him as he ran for the bathroom. It happened to be the T-shirt. Tess, thinking we were playing a game, got excited and jumped to intercept the flying bundle. I walked up to her and asked nicely if I could have it back.

"I'm not weird, Tess. I'm just not from around here," I explained, scratching her ears.

She looked at me with her big brown eyes and released the shirt. I heard the shower and asked her if she wanted to play. She gave me a conspiratorial look and wiggled her tail. *Good girl,* I thought. Together we walked into the bathroom, and I let her in the shower with Gabe.

"Porzia! What the hell?" I heard his voice exclaim above the shower.

"That's how weird I am," I yelled over the pounding water.

Tess, all wet and grinning, was shoved out of the shower and shook herself right in the middle of the bathroom. Surrounded by a cloud of steam, Gabe's face appeared from the open shower door.

"Get in, luv."

"No more games?" I asked warily.

"Fair dinkum, no more games."

"Ok then—" I walked around Tess's water puddle when suddenly Gabe grabbed me and pulled me in under an icy jet of water.

I screamed.

He switched the water back to hot, and I hugged his icy-cold body.

Finally signing an armistice, we dried off and decided coffee sounded really good.

We made breakfast, although we didn't really have much to do. He had bought some delicious pumpkin crumpets which we smeared in rich butter and ate with soft-boiled eggs and a large pot of coffee.

I enjoyed breakfast so much I offered to do the dishes. The phone rang while I filled the sink, and I heard Gabe talking to somebody about an upcoming race; his help was needed down at the shop. He hung up the phone and walked up behind me at the sink. He slid his hands around my waist and rested his chin on my shoulder.

"That was Gomi. I have a couple of things to sort out down at the shop." He kissed my neck. "Wanna come along?"

"Sure." It felt like a déjà vu.

"Won't take long. We'll probably knock off in a couple of hours or so."

"How about Tess?" I asked.

"She can come along as well."

As if she understood his words, Tess walked to the front door and looked at us impatiently. I laughed and hurried to grab my shoes, jacket, and bag.

I thought to myself, *I could really get used to this drive,* as we headed down through the hills into town. The ocean sparkled in the far distance. The silhouette of cargo boats interrupted the straight line of the horizon. On the way to Tasmania? Perhaps New Zealand? No Mexico or Miami around here. I glanced at Gabe next to me, wearing jeans and a heavy heather-gray sweater. His leather jacket was on the back seat along with a gym bag and a few racing magazines. I was a guest in an utterly male domain.

"Once I get things going, my mates should be able to take care of business alone, and we'll take off and disappear somewhere, luv."

"Where were you thinking of going? The desert? Like you mentioned over the phone?"

"Yes, but not too far from here." He took his eyes off the road to glance at me. "What do you reckon?"

I smiled. "I came to see you. Where we go doesn't really change that."

"I know, luv, but I'd like you to see a little bit of Oz while we're at it."

"So—why the desert?" I asked, intrigued.

"Well, I thought we should give it a go from the beginning of things and go from there. Like every great story ever told." He smiled at me. "The origins of this land still vibrate in the outback. If you understand the desert, then you come to respect the land and every creature that has adapted to survive on it. Take a look at some of the animals still roaming out there. Some of them—actually, most of them—can only be found here, like kangaroos, dingoes, and Koala bears." He cast me a serious look. "And the people, from the Aborigines to every human being choosing to call this challenge home. Not to mention the unspoken traditions, legends, and beliefs that map this land making every rock, animal, and weather phenomenon a landmark in a web of surviving ideals."

"Is Ayers Rock one of these landmarks?"

"According to Aboriginal Dreamtime it's one of the most important. They call it *Uluru*."

"Where does the name Ayers come from then?"

"The premier of South Australia in the 1800's: Sir Henry Ayers."

"I see."

"The Aborigines believe in *Tjukurpa*, an energy source. It translates to Dreamtime, but it's also used to refer to the record of all activities of a particular ancestral being, from the very beginning of his or her travels to their end. These travels and events took place and are recorded at many separate sites. That's why I was saying earlier that the desert is a map. Although most of the legends and traditions aren't disclosed to the *Piranypa*—the non-Aborigines —it is common knowledge that *Uluru* and its surrounding area are inhabited by dozens of ancestral beings whose activities are recorded at innumerable places." Gabe looked at me as if debating about going on or not. "Am I boring you?"

I shook my head. "Absolutely not. Go on, please."

"At each site, the legendary events can be recounted by just recognizing a physical feature representing both the activities of the ancestral being at the time of its formation, and the living presence of *Tjukurpa* within that physical feature today. Now, this is where the concept gets slippery. You see, for the Aboriginal people, that physical feature, whatever its form or appearance, animate or inanimate, is the *Tjukurpa*. It might be a rock, a sand hill, a grove of trees, a cave. For all these, the creative essence remains forever within the physical form or appearance."

"That's why they don't need to write things down?" I asked. "Because they have it all mapped out in the landscape. And how do you know so much? Who told you all this?" *And all you're not sharing with me,* I wanted to add, but didn't.

He brought the car to a stop in front of the shop and looked at me, turning the key off in the ignition. "More of your questions, eh?"

"Those you're so afraid of?"

"I'm not afraid, Porzia, just sworn to secrecy."

"So I have to be satisfied with what you can share. Is that it?"

"I'd like to go out there with you. Show you the desert and give you a chance of knowing this ageless land from the beginning. Isn't that how things start anyway? From the beginning?"

"I'd love to."

"It's a mind-blowing experience, luv, to let your thoughts melt by the heat of an outback campfire." He shot me a long silent look, then leaned over and lightly kissed me. "And I wanna share it with ya."

*

Gomi's familiar face greeted us inside the shop. Garbed in an oversized midnight blue coverall, sporting a nametag with an embroidered white garbage bin instead of his name, he gave me one of his million-watt smiles and asked how I was going. Tess walked up to him and nudged his hand for petting.

"Pretty well, thanks. And you?"

"Going good. It's nice to see you again. The boss here has been pretty pissy these last few days." He winked at me, scratching Tess's head.

"Gabe? Pissy?" I raised a questioning eyebrow.

"Just trying to get things done before you showed up, Porzia. As you can see, it didn't really work out or we wouldn't need to be here now," he fired back at Gomi.

"No worries, mate. I've got it all under control," Gomi said, flashing a smile.

"And what are you doing to the bloody Holden with that rear anti-roll bar, Gomi?" Gabe asked, walking away from us.

"Just making sure you'd have something to deal with, boss." He winked at me again and followed Gabe. I wasn't sure I wanted to get into it and made up my mind not to interfere when I heard them start discussing technical stuff like long-range fuel tanks, inlet geometry, and re-mapped engine management systems. I noticed a trophy display on the far wall and saw that it not only featured cups in various sizes and shapes but photos and plaques from regional races dating over fifteen years earlier, as well. On the second shelf there were photos of Gabe and Gomi almost unrecognizable. *Oh dear god! Was that a mullet on Gomi's head?* I couldn't quite believe my eyes, but it must have been him. The smile was just as dazzling. I shifted my gaze onto Gabe and took a long look at him. My nose brushed the glass case, fogging it up.

Daring and fearless. Those two words came to mind first. He had an aura of invincibility that only youth, inexperience, and arrogance can give. He had changed a lot since. On the third shelf, at my eye level, I noticed the Paris–Dakar trophies and photos. In these Gabe looked more mature, but still younger. I frowned, observing him. He focused on something distant, as though he was in search of something. Answers? *Was this quest for trophies a way of quenching such thirst?* I shook my head. I was no Freud. Why was I even bothering with it? The Gabe I knew now had replaced the invincibility aura with experience and scars. Somehow, it made him the man I loved. I turned my head, searching for him and saw his head bent under the hood of the Holden, only steps away from me. I shifted my attention back to the trophy case. Photos of Gabe and a group of guys in front of a red race car caught my attention; *Miller's Team, Duneblast,* someone had scribbled in black marker at the bottom of the photo. It must have been after the accident as Gabe was crouched next to a man in full driving gear. The man held a cup and was giving the thumbs up signal. Gabe sported a jacket covered in sponsors' patches, jeans, and a crooked but yielding smile. Clark stood right behind him, a hand on his shoulder.

"Darwin Duneblast, seven years ago." Clark's reflection in the trophies' glass case spoke.

I spun around, startled.

CHAPTER 35

"Welcome back, Porzia," he said, leaning over to give me a quick hug.

"Thanks." My answer exhaled in veiled surprise. How long had he been standing behind me?

"It's been a while," he sighed, letting go of me.

Did he mean a while about the photos I was looking at? Or perhaps how long he'd been standing behind me? Or about last time we'd seen each other? And why did I feel like I had been caught snooping?

"I don't know how to answer you, Clark," I admitted candidly.

He raised an eyebrow and rocked on his heels, thumbs stuck in his jeans pockets. A slow grin spread across his face and I saw Gabe, years from now. His grin was so contagious, I found my own.

"When did you get in?"

"Yesterday."

His bushy eyebrows shot up in disbelief. "And he has you down here already?" he chided, turning his head in Gabe's direction.

"No big deal," I shrugged. "Gomi called the house asking for help."

"I thought everything was under control," Clark remarked.

"What's going on anyway?"

His eyes clouded just like Gabe's before a storm. "Oz Endurance, Porzia, that's what's going on. Or to be more precise, will be going on here—in a couple of months."

"Is it an important race?" I asked, having no idea what I was getting myself into.

"You could say that."

"Maybe this visit wasn't good timing," I murmured softly, almost to myself.

Clark's hand squeezed my shoulder. "My dear . . . you couldn't have picked a better time," he answered enigmatically.

Gabe chose that moment to walk up to us, dissolving my chance of asking Clark what he had meant.

"You don't have anything better to do than come to work today?" Clark rebuked his son.

"Got called in, Clark, but we're out of here." Gabe took my hand, whistled at Tess, and gave his dad a mock military salute. Without waiting for an answer, he turned on his heels and stormed out the door, dragging me with him. I barely had time to wave good-bye. Once we were inside the car I asked him if everything had been alright in there.

He handed me his cell phone. "Keep this off, somewhere I can't see it, luv. For the entire time you're here."

I took his cell phone. "Are you serious?"

"Yes. I promised myself I would stay away while you were here, and I will keep the promise."

"OK," I said and stuffed the phone in my bag. "But if you're doing it for me, don't worry. I don't mind if you have to work here and there. I can find things to do."

He turned on the engine and skillfully backed out of the parking spot. "I know. It's not a matter of entertaining you. It's a matter of them being able to keep up without me and me not thinking about work for a while. You're what matters now." He looked at me before merging into traffic. "*We're* what matters now."

I leaned over to squeeze his hand. "Thank you. Where are we off to?"

"Shopping," he told me. "There's a place I want to show you."

We quickly drove a few blocks downtown and parked. Gabe pointed at a store across the street. "That's it, luv."

"A bookstore?"

"And more." Gabe let Tess out and told me she was allowed in the store we were about to enter. We crossed the street, and Gabe gallantly opened the door for me. I walked in followed by Tess. A massive monolith-shaped marble fountain took center stage in the middle of a carpeted floor. It gurgled happily, echoing the soothing rhythm of the Indian melody uncoiling smoothly, like a spellbound fakir's snake, from hidden speakers. A metaphysical bookstore like I had never seen before spread out in front of my enchanted eyes. Rows and rows and more rows of books lined the walls. Jewelry sparkled in a glass counter case; candles, incense, essential oils, and dried herbs made the place smell the way I imagined magic would smell in the fairy tales of my childhood. A sprinkle of new age customers, the kind of folks blessed with auras confidently walking with magic as a familiar companion, so much like Evalena, read or chatted quietly in comfy chairs upholstered in bright orange and green chenille scattered here and there. A buffet offered a scrumptious selection of organic coffee and herbal teas, scones, and cookies. Tess walked up to the jewelry counter where an older lady with a shiny bob of silver hair recognized her and offered her a dog biscuit. She waved at Gabe and cast me a sincere, welcoming smile.

"Where are we?" I asked Gabe, sweeping a hand around to encompass the place.

"Paths," he answered, taking my hand. "Come and see, luv."

"The name of the store is 'Paths'?"

"Roight." He walked up to a beautiful display of local art. Bright paintings, rudimental musical instruments in wood, strings, and leather I wouldn't know where to begin to play, and tribal clothing came together in a unique collage of Aboriginal folklore.

"Incredible," I murmured softly.

Gabe had walked up to the book section. With tickling nostrils I began to explore the scented candles and incense display. I grabbed a shopping basket.

"May I be of assistance?" the silver-haired woman asked me with a smile, startling me.

"This is an incredible place."

"Thank you," she said with a pleased smile and a slight bow of her head. Her hair was genuinely the color of liquid silver. "I'm Maureen, the owner. Delighted to meet you."

I took her extended hand. "Porzia. My pleasure, Maureen. I'm afraid I don't know where to begin."

"You came in with a special intent?" she inquired in that typical Australian way of casting a question out of a statement.

I shook my head and pointed at Gabe. "No. He brought me. It was a surprise."

"I see."

"So I'm kind of lost."

"Oh no, honey. You're most definitely not lost."

"Excuse me?"

"You're not lost," she stated simply.

I had no idea what she meant, but I believed her. "I'm afraid I'm not really following," I frowned, perplexed.

"No worries. Just take a look around and rest assured whatever brought you here will find you. I promise." She smiled and looked me straight in the eyes. "It always works." She walked back to the counter where a few people were queuing, ready to make their purchases, and I almost gasped when I noticed that around her body a light energy field radiated subtly. I closed my eyes and shook my head. Incredulous, I opened one eye, then the other, and gave her another look. The aura had disappeared. Not trusting myself, I decided I had imagined it.

Yet the feeling lingered.

Thinking of how much Evalena and Benedetta would enjoy a place like this, I walked to Gabe who was still by the book section.

"What are you looking for?"

"A book." His eyes scanned the shelf until he found a thin hardcover featuring a colorful mosaic on the front.

"What is it about?" I asked, curious.

"It's a story."

I looked closer, trying to make sense of the mosaic design and pulled back to refocus. Like Icarus flying too close to the sun, I almost got burned. Defensive chills flared up my spine.

Gabe turned the book in his hands so I could have a better look. "What do you see, luv?"

Wings.

Tiny white dots in what at first appeared to be a random pattern became wings against the black background. I looked at him and saw his eyes shone deepest blue, waiting for my answer.

"Wings, Gabe. I see wings." I dropped my gaze to the book cover once again and read the title out loud, "*The Cloud Dweller.*"

"It's a legend I'm very fond of," he said quietly, handing me the book.

I took the book reverently and opened it, cautious. "How do you know it?"

"After the accident, I needed to make sense of what I had gone through, and one of the doctors told me about this place."

Time stilled as I took a long look at him. "Did you?"

"I did, somewhat. Believe it or not, the book I just gave you makes more sense than anything else I read." He returned my intense stare. "I'm not the man in your past life regression, Porzia. I'm a Cloud Dweller and being one eliminates the other. And roight now I'm wishing for supernatural powers so I could erase the sadness spilling off your eyes. But you've been gambling with two dice, and it's time you make a decision."

My head jerked upward. He had no idea I no longer held two. I had no idea what that meant.

Tears stung in my eyes, and I clenched the book tight. I lowered my head to hide my pain and stared at the swirling pattern on the book cover. I wished it would swallow me. Dot after dot, seed after seed, it manifested wings instead.

This was Gabe's way of explaining to me some of the unspoken questions I had about his accident, and despite the surging tide of my own curiosity, I was grateful but not ready to face my own part of the bargain yet. I had too many unanswered questions.

I lifted my grief-stricken face to him. "Maybe I can read it with you in front of that outback campfire we talked about."

"Deal." His eyes shifted to a lighter blue.

Mine remained turbulent as I took time to browse through the books and the other mystical tools the store offered. At the counter, a heavy-bellied snake statue caught my eye.

"I see you've found Eingana." Maureen interrupted my thoughts.

"Eingana?" I raised my eyes up to this woman's sincere gaze and asked on a whim, "Maureen—what can you tell me about Cloud Dwellers?"

"Nothing. But I can show you Eingana." She pulled out the powerful figurine and sat it on the counter. "The Cloud Dwellers call her Mother Eingana: the world creator, the birth mother, maker of land, animals, and kangaroos. This huge snake goddess still lives in the Dreamtime and occasionally stirs to create even more life. She's also the death mother. They say Eingana holds a mystical link to each of her creatures, sort of an umbilical cord that has never been severed. That's why she's represented swallowing her own tail. When she lets go, that life stops. If she herself should die, they say life itself would cease to exist.

"I'm familiar with such ties," Gabe whispered right behind me.

"I hope that answered your question, Porzia. Would you like to see more?" Maureen offered, after a silent moment.

I shook my head. I had suddenly remembered another snake swallowing its own tail in *Le Monde*, the tarot card Madame Framboise had pulled for me. Pieces were finally falling into place. Torn between relief and despair, I realized I had no right to question Gabe's choices. I was surrounded, naked, stripped like the woman in the card. We paid for my purchases and thanked Maureen for all her help. Gabe whistled to Tess, and we left the store.

Outside, it was still daylight, and I was surprised to find out that the day had gone on, while inside time had stilled among legends, mystical beliefs, and choices.

*

Back at the house, I quickly changed into a comfortable set of lounging pants and tank top, excited to prepare dinner while Gabe started a fire in the living room.

And then we forgot entirely about eating.

I walked back into the living room and one look was enough. I sank in the depth of his eyes reflecting the orange flames of the blazing fire and surrendered against a power I wasn't expecting to surge and challenge me so suddenly. I found myself in his arms, madly kissing him, oblivious to how I had crossed the distance. One second earlier I was standing on the threshold of the living room; the next, I was kneeling in front of a crackling fireplace, safe in his embrace, tasting liquid lust off his lips.

Clothes were impatiently cast aside while flames flickered in our direction, teasing our oversensitive skin.

I wrapped my legs around Gabe's waist, held him tight, and we became one. The fireplace heated my arms and hands as I straddled him and began to move, slowly. Ecstasy skimmed, teased, and finally flared with each agonized thrust of my hips. My mouth locked onto his. My eyes shut to fully absorb his strength but still echoed the blazing flames dancing madly behind my sealed eyelids. The fire within met the heat of the fire crackling behind Gabe's muscular back. I felt the building wave of climax lap at my shores. Pleasure rose, boundaries disappeared, lust thickened, and it all melted once his mouth reached the firm tips on my breasts. I dug my nails in his back, lost control, and surrendered to ecstasy.

One slow, overwhelming wave of pleasure at a time.

I couldn't control the mad pounding of my heart ricocheting against his chest but managed to untangle my eyelashes just enough to look at his face and not get blinded by the bright fire behind him.

"I think we're stuck," I croaked hoarsely, my tongue sheathed with thick pleasure not yet swallowed.

"Not a bad thing to be with ya," Gabe whispered, and magically he managed to lower our bodies onto the soft rug without sliding away. He swept my hair off my back and caressed my arched spine with his warm breath. His sensuous lips found an erogenous spot on my neck, and I choked on my own purring. I struggled to grip the short fibers under my nails, and gave up when I felt him penetrating me deeper.

"You're hot and sleek." He curled his arms around my shoulders and thrust in one last time. Deep inside me, his body shuddered with spilled pleasure and his teeth sank into my shoulder. His trapped voice escaped against my skin in a low, intense moan.

Ecstasy unleashed from earthly boundaries.

*

Spent, he rolled back on the soft rug, blinked, and cracked a grin. Words took flight once again.

"Look," he said, pointing out the window.

"I don't see anything . . ."

"The sky has darkened to a perfect level of intimacy, luv." He got up and offered a hand. "Come on—time to eat."

I opened a bottle of Umeracha Shiraz and set the table while Gabe tossed a salad of scrumptious veggies and cheeses. I warmed up a loaf of bread and dumped al dente fettuccine in a skillet with goat cheese, sautéed Portobello mushrooms, and a couple of secret ingredients.

We sat at the table while Tess slept in her bed by the fireplace. In the frenzied passion of our lovemaking, I hadn't noticed her till now. My glass toasted Gabe's above her loud snoring. Laughing, I wished him *buon appetito*.

"How come English doesn't have a word for it?"

"You mean the equivalent to *buon appetito*?" I asked him, rolling some fettuccine around my fork.

"Roight."

"Interesting. What do they say in the States? 'Enjoy' I guess is one of the words. 'Dig in' if you're with friends or family. But you're right; every language I know except English has a way of wishing happy eating."

"*Bon appétit* in French," Gabe said.

"*Buen provecho* in Spanish."

"Japanese?"

"*Itadakimasu*," I said and bowed.

Gabe broke into one of his deadly grins. "Have you got any more?

I nodded. "Dutch, Greek—I think that's it." I looked at him, smiling. "*Eet smakelijk!*"

"Is that Dutch or Greek?"

I chuckled. "Dutch. The Greek version is *kali orexi*."

He poured me some wine. "I bet after a few glasses of this stuff we can make up some words."

"Pretty powerful, eh?" I said, sipping the rich wine.

"Perfect with the pasta." He reached for some bread to wipe his plate clean and got every last bit.

"What would you like to do after dinner?" I asked.

He leaned back in his chair. "A second helping of the *appetizer* would be nice. But I need to have a walk with Tess before it gets too late. Would you like to come?" he offered.

"Go ahead," I told him. "I'll have the kitchen cleaned up by the time you get back."

"Don't worry about the kitchen. I'll take care of it in the morning."

I shrugged and finished the last bit of my fettuccine. "It's OK. I don't mind doing it now."

"I should be cleaning up, Porzia, you did all the cooking."

I winked. "Tomorrow you can do both for me."

"Breakfast?"

"Deal."

"Turn on the TV if you'd like. Get a taste of Oz entertainment."

"OK, I will."

He pushed off his chair and called Tess up. Startled from deep sleep, she waddled up to him and let him clip the leash onto her collar. Gabe handed me the remote control, kissed me, and walked away. I followed the sound of his fading footsteps and managed to struggle with the remote until it gave up and, blessed gadget, turned the TV on.Drowned by the sound of water quickly filling the sink, I hardly paid attention when a newscaster's grave tone forecasted extreme weather conditions and the possible connection between

Aboriginal end of millennium prophecies and the current meteorological phenomenon.

Barely listening, I rinsed the dishes and loaded up the dishwasher. I dried my hands and poured the remaining wine into my glass.

"... It's now official, the race will be going on despite a record heat index expected to hit the Alice Springs area. Organizers believe the extreme weather conditions won't be a deterring factor in the choice of itinerary for the Oz Endurance.

"As of now, Gabe Miller hasn't been available for comment on the rally of the millennium—"

In my ribcage, a rapacious claw squeezed my heart until blood and tissue sponged out through clenched talons.

I grabbed my wine, reached for the remote control, fiddled once again, and finally managed to turn the volume up. Hypnotized by the images rolling on the screen, I sat down on the edge of the sofa.

"The atmosphere is heating up in preparation for the Oz Endurance, the end of the millennium ultimate challenge.

"The event is staged to follow a ruthless itinerary of 3000 kilometres spanning Oz's most difficult terrain, part of which consists of off-limits, legendary Aboriginal sacred grounds.

"The weather conditions are expected to be extreme.

"Heat, heat, heat... lethal for human and machine.

"A centennial weather pattern last witnessed at the end of the 1800's is estimated to slowly surge in the next couple of months and build up to record-high temperatures.

"The Aboriginal tribe—guardian of the sacred-ground segment of the course—associates the weather pattern with ancient legends undisclosed to the non-initiated. After long negotiations they have finally agreed to a select group of individuals.

"Who is to face such a grueling test?

"Only those who live by the rules and obey the rules as nature dictates will be called to participate.

"The list of names is to remain secret until the tribe's wise man deems it to be *a propitious time. Invitations will follow suit, but speculations are already flying about Gabe Miller resuming his career for such a challenge."*

*

The images on the screen shifted to a short report on Gabe's suddenly interrupted career.

I shifted and sank deep into the sofa's welcoming pillows and gave the TV my undivided attention.

Pictures of a very young Gabe rolled on-screen while the voice droned on about his steady and consistent rise among the racing circuits. In less than five years he had climbed from victorious regionals to triumphant nationals. When Gomi joined the Miller team, their first victory in the Australian Safari catapulted them into the international scene. In their first attempt at the Paris–Dakar, they arrived second. The following year, they won. And then they successfully completed an encore and won again, two years in a row.

At the peak of such an accomplished career, Gabe spent one year meticulously working on a custom-built vehicle. Finally he drove it and crashed, putting an end to his brilliant future. A sequence of images of the almost-deadly accident reeled on my heart like an intolerably heavy rolling pin: the vehicle reduced to a heap of burnt, crunched metal; the racing number folded on itself, barely readable in a distorted crease; Gomi's devastated face as he briskly followed paramedics carrying a gurney with an unrecognizable Gabe strapped onto it; Clark's sleep-deprived frown impatiently waving journalists away in front of a hospital.

And now this last chance.

The news ended and a cheerful commercial jingle for pet food mocked my sense of despair.

"Oh, Joséphine, what have I gotten myself into?" I lamented and drained my glass.

Oz . . . Wizards . . .

All of a sudden I understood Evalena's warning and her question about fairy tales. *The Wizard of Oz* is one of my favorite stories.

CHAPTER 36

The front door opened and Tess ran up to me. The chilled shadow of late winter clung to her fur. She burrowed her nose in my hands, and I felt pure sour panic rise up my throat. Choking, I hid my face in her thick coat. *Oddio!* I inhaled brisk winter and damp upturned soil.

She felt soft and alive.

Gabe added wood to the fire and then sat down next to me to unleash Tess.

Enveloped in panic, I barely lifted my head; in a whisper I asked him about the Oz Endurance.

"Where did you hear about it?"

"On TV."

"What did they say?" he demanded as his head snapped to the screen.

"That it will be going on despite the expected extreme heat."

"So—it's official?"

I nodded, not trusting my voice.

"Bloody hell." He grabbed the remote control to search for more news.

"What exactly is it, Gabe?"

No answer.

"Gabe?"

He turned the TV on mute, tossed the remote back on the coffee table, and cast me an unfocused look.

"It's a race, Porzia." He ran a hand through his hair and air rippled like water. I felt adrift, impotent against the sweeping tides.

With effort he resumed, "A race that will go through Aboriginal sacred grounds near Alice Springs for the first time in history."

"How long has there been talk about it?"

He shook his head, "Oh, forever—years."

"Why now?"

"Because not only is it the end of the century, but the end of the millennium as well. And according to secret legends, a favorable time." He sighed before continuing on. "You know how weather comes in patterns like that *El Niño* phenomenon. When is it? Every seven years or so, roight?"

I nodded and tucked my feet under my hip.

"Last time we had heat like that was at the end of the last century. Only this time it will be even more powerful because the millennium is coming to an end as well. We're exuberant people, Porzia. Leave it to Aussies to come up with the idea of an end-of-the-century endurance challenge to go out with a bang!"

"Exuberant doesn't do you guys justice, Gabe. This race makes the Paris–Dakar look like a beach walk."

Gabe smiled and reached over to ruffle up my hair. "I love the way you see things sometimes."

"Are your guys involved?" I blurted out.

"Not yet."

"Would you like to be?" I asked in a breath, staring straight into his blue eyes. I tasted the fever that burned in his soul. Heat reached up from within and unleashed its power.

His eyes spiraled into pools of impenetrable darkness. "*Yes.*"

An immense power surged in the ensuing silence.

With a deep suspicion of inadequacy, I realized I faced an unequal enemy. This fever, consuming him from within, was his nature. This true essence that made him the man I loved might ultimately destroy his life.

Evalena's warning rang through my mind: *He leads by example, Porzia. Beware.* Now I understood. Gabe might not be Xavier, but he was showing me the way through the portal of my own fears. And how to walk beyond.

"But I don't think I will."

"Pardon?"

"They won't call me."

I blinked and absorbed his words. "Why not?"

"Luv, don't ask." He pulled me into his arms. I untangled my legs and stretched my body on top of his.

"I won't ask," I conceded, surfing the tide that had suddenly changed its course. "Thanks," he whispered, caressing my hair.

We held each other in silence while the fire warmed us up.

Mute images from the TV rolled on. Tess whined in her sleep, and Gabe's heartbeat drummed steady against my ear.

"Ready for bed?"

"In a minute," I answered. I wanted to bask in this eye in the middle of the storm for a while longer.

"We're getting up early tomorrow."

"Why?" I lifted my head. "We have nowhere to go."

"In that case, we're getting up even earlier so we don't have to hurry to get to *Nowhere*."

I shot him a confused look. "What?"

He smiled. "Nowhere, South Australia."

"Is that a real place?"

"You got that roight."

"You're making it up."

"Naw! Fair dinkum, we're going to Nowhere tomorrow."

"Where is it?" I realized the silliness of my question and broke into laughter.

"Out that way." Gabe pointed to the front door.

"Is Tess coming?"

"Where?"

Still laughing, I answered my own trap. "Nowhere."

"Yes, luv." Gabe swept me up defying physical laws. "She's been before."

In a fit of giggles I managed to ask, "Tess has been to Nowhere before?"

"Twice."

In the warm atmosphere of his bedroom, serenaded by the crackling fire, we crawled in bed and began to kiss.

Our lovemaking unfolded like a sinewy riverbed slowly filled by warmed, sun-melted snow.

*

In the middle of the night I rolled over and stretched a hand on Gabe's side of the bed.

Cold.

I blinked to adjust my eyes to the darkness. The dying fire cast a faint amber glow across the room, offering barely enough edging between shadows and darkness.

"Gabe?"

No answer.

I shifted back on the mattress and went back to sleep.

Minutes later, in that horizonless limbo between sleep and seraphic dreams, I sensed him. His cold body pressed against mine, and my dreams scattered like basement creatures exposed by a suddenly switched-on light.

"Were you outside?" My voice sounded pasty.

"Yes. Needed some fresh air."

"You're cold," I mumbled.

"You're not." He planted a kiss on my bare shoulder. "Go back to sleep, luv. We got a long day ahead of us tomorrow."

"*Buona notte, amore.*" I drifted back to sleep.

*

The following morning the smell of coffee startled me from my dream realm. I yawned and focused, manifesting Gabe by my side of the bed. Steam blurred my vision, my nostrils twitched, and I zoomed in on the cobalt blue coffee mug only inches away from my face.

"Time to get up." He waved the coffee under my upturned nose.

With slow-motion, wading hands I made a futile attempt to reach for it. "What time is it?"

"Seven."

"I still have jet lag."

"This will help." He set the steaming coffee mug on the nightstand. "Drink up and I'll be back shortly to see if you're awake. We need to pack a few things and be on our way. Tess is ready to go."

I lifted myself up and cupped the hot mug with both hands. The aroma of freshly brewed coffee laced with cream reached my nose. I sipped, careful not to burn my tongue with the scalding yet welcome concoction. I had reached the bottom of the mug when Gabe walked in carrying an empty travel bag and smiled. "You look much better."

"Like I'm awake now?" I set the coffee down, pushed the covers off, walked up to him, and gave him a quick hug. "What all do we need to pack?"

"Not much; clothes to layer, hiking boots or sneakers, comfortable socks, and a jacket."

I nodded, reached for my luggage, and helped him with the packing.

After a quick shower and a light breakfast, we loaded Tess in the back of the Rover and took off to . . . Nowhere.

In the brisk early spring morning only a few sheer clouds hung low in the crisp cerulean sky. A radio station broadcast a Midnight Oil special while the enchanting scenery quickly changed right under my spellbound eyes. Nature crept up to the edge of town and suddenly took over. Right outside Adelaide fragrant eucalyptus trees led the way toward a destination I knew nothing about.

Gabe was being mysterious.

I glanced at the back of the vehicle, stuffed with camping gear, and met Tess's ecstatic face.

We stopped for gas beneath a bright yellow sign warning of kangaroos crossing. In a small hut that doubled as convenience store, Gabe paid in cash for the gas and a dusty bottle of lukewarm water. The weather was warming up and our car was the only one in sight.

I was glad to be with him.

The radio buzzed and we lost Midnight Oil when we drove off the main road to edge the dry bed of what, eons ago, must have been a river. On our right, the desert stretched like a roll of endless burlap. What a postcard it would have made.

"I don't believe my eyes."

"Pretty impressive sight, eh?"

"Are we going out there?" I asked, pointing at the desolate expanse.

"Not all the way in. Nowhere is about another 25 kilometres east," Gabe reassured me. "Another half an hour and we should be there."

When we arrived at the park center, a smiling Aboriginal man, with skin the color of rich cocoa, welcomed us. He gave us directions, a receipt for the camping fee, and a colorful pamphlet featuring bright photos of several poisonous creatures and emergency contact numbers.

Oh, merda! I thought as I read about how to act in case of a kangaroo attack. How to dislodge limbs from the mouth of a voracious crocodile. How to apply pressure to the bitten area in case of a poisonous snake or spider bite until the nearest hospital is reached.

With my body postured as far as possible from the window, I glanced at the dormant scenery of beige dried brush, throat-gritting sand, and distant faded orange hills edging the horizon like an unaccountable mirage, and worried.

But then, slowly, I noticed a tiny bell-shaped purple flower here, a scurrying of tiny prints there. Wings flocked above us, and I realized that in its own unhurried way, in a monochromatic expanse, the desert lived and gave life. To better observe I scooted closer to the window and even rolled it down to inhale deeply the parched scent of dried brush. It reminded me a bit of the warmth of Italian Septembers when the farmers cut the dry golden wheat fields and trap summer in the packaged, dried hay for the ensuing cold season.

I discovered the old cliché that the company you keep means everything to be absolutely true. Gabe turned out to be a blast to camp with, and Tess was an incredible example of how to just relax and enjoy the moment.

We set up camp in a clearing away from main roads, civilization, and any possible trace of human progress. We explored, with Tess ecstatic to discover this plant or that bush. Gabe proved to have an immeasurable knowledge of the surrounding nature, from animal tracks and what they meant as far as hunting or migratory patterns to herbal folkloristic stories and remedies. I was intrigued and fascinated by the simplicity of life in the outback and stunned at the amount of life actually dwelling in such harsh territory.

No TV, no phones. The radio in the Rover was perfectly functional, but we chose not to use it; willingly we surrendered and forgot civilization. Our pace slowed, our words acquired stronger meaning, and Nature began to communicate with us.

Through the wind, the birds, the clouds, with infinitesimal messages, the Mother reached us. Shy and curious at first, a gentle breeze brought echoes of distant scents. A scurrying of fast paws told us we were being closely watched, perhaps accepted. The crumbs of bread we left out disappeared, and the warm wind coiled around our bundled bodies and kept the fire alive and crackling. Glad to have spectators, the sky stunned us with a breathtaking sunset and we watched in awe, silently taking long swigs of chilled beer. We roasted sausages on a warm fire and cozied up in heavy wool blankets in the company of an eagerly darkening sky. Tess barked at invisible shadows. Stars twinkled shyly at first against dusk and then brighter and more confident as night empowered them, opening up an unlimited display. Of course, it was all backwards from my familiar Floridian sky, but once I persuaded Gabe to humor me and take a look at it with his head between his parted legs, the firmament flipped back to almost normal.

Time slowed until it didn't matter anymore. Destiny took a break from unfolding and pleasure stirred, branding our hearts as our bodies merged and melted in the darkness. In the far distance, right above Earth's rim, an electric storm flared in a wild dance. It scared Tess so badly she burrowed her nose between us and then fell asleep at our feet, reassured, warm, and safe.

CHAPTER 37

I woke up to stark silence. I sat up, pulling the sleeping bag up my bare breasts trying to remember where I was.

"Gabe?"

Silence answered.

With irrational, unexplainable, rising panic drumming out of control, I realized I was alone in the middle of Nowhere, Oz. I tightened the grip on the silky fabric of the sleeping bag until my knuckles turned white with effort. Struggling not to give in to fear, I brushed aside the thought of wondering where such intense panic could be coming from and chose to be my practical self instead. A poor choice to make as the ensuing events would later reveal, but no matter how powerful the warnings, I still hadn't gotten used to trusting my intuition. Only when we truly stare at our enemies in the eyes do we learn what we're capable of, or not.

I scanned the tent in search of a note he might have left me. And found nothing. With practicality failing miserably against the overpowering surge of intuition, I succumbed to it. Despite my fears, I closed my eyes. I inhaled deeply against my clenched hands stretching the tight grip I had of the sleeping bag and then exhaled, relaxing my shoulders, opening my eyes. The tent looked somewhat brighter, but I knew this to be just an optical illusion. Something told me I was alone and he was nowhere nearby. Not spiritually, at least. Tess felt intangible as well. The call for magic was the only present vibe along with my frightened breathing. But one annihilated the other. In the darkness, at the bottom of my cozy sleeping bag, my bare toes curled. Yes, bare—just like Venere in the Uffizi. I was about to step off my shell to face the Wizard of Oz wearing no ruby slippers.

I slit my head through the thin fabric split of the tent and scanned my surroundings. Outside nothing had changed.

The fire had died to a meager scattering of ashes. The Rover stood dormant, parked about ten yards from me at the end of a double trail of tire marks. Now, that was a thought. I dropped my eyes and scrutinized the campground dirt for foot and dog prints, only to find neither. It was as if Gabe had taken flight.

The wind stirred and brought words. *He can't take flight. Not with his broken wings.*

Chilled to the bone, I realized that *It* had heard my thoughts.

I stood, stark naked, paralyzed with what I believed to be my fears. I swallowed and tasted focus instead.

It is when we are most afraid that we are most alive, with all our wits stretched to their limits and beyond, clawing for survival. With inadequate blindness fighting the dark unknown, we resort to the other senses—including the sixth—the portal to magic.

I was sure I had not imagined the vibe. It felt familiar and recurrent, like a persistent nightmare.

Or a watchful, silent guardian: A warrawarra who held the power of Gabe's breath.

I recalled it in the yellow-eyed snake biting his own tail surrounding the naked woman in the tarot card of *Le Monde* and in Eingana, the goddess. I recognized its powerful barrier, in a flutter of wings, when I tried to scrutinize Gabe's privacy. It had spilled from Gabe's mouth speaking of having defied death in a thick, almost unrecognizable, Aboriginal accent. It awoke us from a distant nightmare shared in the privacy of my own bedroom, and finally, had stared at us through the disturbing eyes of a cat, coiled in a flowerbed in New Orleans.

Yes, I faced an unequal opponent.

But why opponent?

I had only one way to find out.

This time I would not barricade my will behind fear. And so I rose to the challenge and met it. Consciously aware that a pinch of ignorance in the face of my inadequacies might turn out to be a crucial advantage, I summoned the power and rose from the quicksand. As Evalena had explained, in the gap between heartbeats I stepped out of the tent with only my hair as witness. My feet met the warm, packed desert dirt as I caught the tail end of my incoming breath and cast my question.

"Who are you?"

"*I'm the wind and the messenger.*"

I exhaledand stretched the space with silent words once again. "Where is Gabe?"

"*On the outer land's edge. In the timeless. You must let go of him.*"

"Why?"

"*Your journey.*"

I inhaled. With my left hand I caught hold of a web of fears, rolled it around my fist, and finally cast it aside. With my right hand stretched outward in front of my heart, I shielded and spoke. "No."

"*He is not the answer.*"

Something pulled and I took an involuntary step forward into the timeless. My face pushed through and caught the midst of a spinning tornado. I could see nothing, but I held my ground. Despite the spiraling force, I braced myself and focused. With all my strength, through my connection with Joséphine, I called upon my magic lineage. My chest swelled, filled, and when I felt about to burst, I pushed at the whirling wind, willing it to stop.

It barely slowed down.

I searched for a gap, a portal, for a moment when I could leap. The warrawarra's power seemed unfazed by my attempt and soon regained speed. It was going to pull me in and all of a sudden I wanted out.

"No!" I screamed.

I drew back as a dog barked.

I spun around and saw Tess at my side. Gabe followed at a distance of at least sixty feet away from me still. Tess's barking had covered my scream and dissolved the mystical sinew, but it was too late.

Gabe had crossed over. From the distance separating us I observed him as he approached me and Tess, already at my feet. His step held the determination and will of someone ready to leap once again. His energy hummed with years of suppressed drive now finally released.

And I as well had taken my own step.

I reached down to Tess and scratched her floppy ears. "I owe you one, Tess."

Life's warning of bends in the road can be as inexplicable and sudden as a wind in the desert.

And then time resumed its rhetorical course.

The day to return home approached.

The star-filled night glittered and dimmed against the city lights fanning off the horizon.

Gabe fell silent on the drive home, his eyes focused on the desert road ahead.

On the back seat, tucked snugly on my folded sleeping bag, Tess's ears twitched, and her tail flicked in her sleep, probably dreaming of chasing desert creatures.

I stared out the Rover's window at darkness moving like a black screen on fast-forward. My own image, reflected off the spinning blackness, stared back and didn't recognize me. I felt different from the Porzia of few days back. I tuned the outside off to focus within. The desert had changed me. I felt a deeper connection and respect for Mother Nature, Her eternal strength and survival powers. I discovered I didn't need comforts to appreciate what life offered. And most of all, I had faced a wizard with my own magic. I had embraced my powers, extinguished my fears, and as a prize, I survived. But at what price?

Prize and price: only one letter distinguishes the two.

I turned to study Gabe's sharp profile. Long strands of hair grazed his forehead, brushing against his darker brows. Like gems framed by thick eyelashes, his eyes glimmered dark blue, focused on his driving. His straight nose reminded me of the Greek gods of Benedetta's myths. His defined lips curled relaxed, and the dark stubble he had let grow in the desert left the dimple on his chin barely visible.

"You cold?" he asked, interrupting my observations.

"No. I'm fine."

He took his eyes off the road and looked at me. "Tired?"

"Not really. Hungry."

His sensuous lips broke into a grin, and his eyes shifted back to the road. "After a week of campfire food I reckon Miss Gourmet is ready for real food?"

"*Miss Gourmet*?" My right eyebrow arched in mock disdain.

"Just teasing, luv." He glanced at his watch. "I'm afraid you might have to wait until tomorrow for a real meal. We have another couple of hours before we get home, and by then the shops will be closed for the night."

"How about restaurants?" I teased.

"I need a shower and a slow ease back into civilization. Can't do mobs of people tonight. Please forgive me."

"Good point."

"We can see what we have at home and maybe throw something together."

I nodded. "As long as there is wine, I'm fine."

"Got heaps of that. If I remember roight, there might be a couple of Umeracha's bottles left."

"No, you don't," I said, incredulous.

The headlights of an oncoming car lit his crooked grin. "Oh yes, I do."

"Great!" I replied, getting excited. "Now we really don't need civilization."

"When you have me?" he teased.

"And the wine you provide," I shot back. Then I looked at him for a second and asked, "How long is it going to take us to adjust to people again?"

"It depends. After a week in the desert, I'd say a couple of days at home and you should be fine. Since this was your first time, the impact might be more intense and you might end up needing more than a couple." He looked at me. "Just take it easy and don't force anything, luv."

"How about you?"

"No worries. I'll be fine in two days tops." His face got serious. "I remember times when it would take me weeks."

"Weeks?"

"When I trained I would often be gone a month or longer at a time. Got really focused and absorbed with the outback. Runners talk about that plateau they reach where heartbeat, breath, and stride merge into one and endorphins kick in. The run becomes effortless and one could keep on going to the edge of the earth. The same happened when I drove out there, Porzia. It's a bitch to unwind from it. When we competed, Gomi used to go into retreat for weeks to snap back. I personally miss it. Even the pain of coming down from it. He doesn't," Gabe added. "Gomi's happiest under the hood of a rig down at the shop."

Adelaide's lights sparkled in the far distance as I listened to him speak of his driving days and tried to understand. Occasionally I would ask him a question and noticed that even if the answer would somewhat upset me, he never faltered. His honesty was brutal.

I wondered if I had the strength to truly defy the gods.

"Gabe, I know I don't have the ability to fully grasp the depth of your experience, all that you've done in your life before I became part of it." I took a deep breath. "I will not pretend to know something I have not experienced. Hell, before that night at Umeracha, I had no idea who you were and honestly had no knowledge whatsoever of the racing world. I still don't know much about it. But what I do know is that some people live a life fueled by passions. One of mine is for food and wine and the compelling urge to write about it, to share my knowledge and discoveries with people out there, to educate them to appreciate the pleasures and passion of gourmet food and wine.

"Yours is to race. Even after what happened to you, you've kept that passion alive." I struggled to find the rights words to continue on. "I guess what I'm trying to say is that our passions have found a way of merging and getting to know one another. I respect yours and love the man you are deeply. I'm also grateful you've made me part of your life and showed me how Earth and Nature are so incredibly beautiful and unselfishly giving. I had never been camping before. I've never seen a desert night sky. The moonlight is so much more intense away from artificial light. I've never felt the smoky scent of a campfire tickle my nostrils as food roasts and never felt my body glow in the heat of the bright flames. It was just as you said it would be. I glimpsed the origin of time, life, and the beginning of this ancient land, thanks to you." I sighed and found the courage to continue. "But it was a lot more than physical. Out there my fears were transformed into another passion that has been dormant within me. Now I can move on, into this new realm, confidently and somewhat eagerly. Only I don't know how to express my gratitude." Frustrated, I dropped my fluttering hands in my lap.

His hand caressed my cheek, and I gave in to his loving fingers. "You just did, luv."

CHAPTER 38

It didn't take long to unload the car, and the most pressing thing to deal with then was finding a hot shower. We washed the days of desert camping away but instead of lingering in the rejuvenating water, our stomachs reminded us it had been way too long since our last meal. I cut my shower short and got into some comfy clothes before heading into the kitchen to try to figure out something for dinner.

With my head stuck in the fridge, I eyed the miserable selection in front of me: a couple of shallots, parsley which needed to be used soon, tomatoes at their ripest. Gabe promised to set the table if I could come up with a miracle and left to unpack our bags.

I moved to the pantry and found penne pasta and vodka. An idea stirred in my head, and I smiled, thinking of my father's favorite recipe—*Penne alla Vodka*, a perfect ending to our adventure.

Soon the kitchen was filled with mouthwatering aromas.

"Smells great, luv." Gabe walked in and began to set the table, then opened a bottle of Umeracha Shiraz and poured us each a glass. We toasted to a great desert adventure and the warm feeling of being back home. I took a sip and allowed the thick wine to coat my palate. It brought back memories of my last visit to Australia. I looked at Gabe over the rim of my glass. "I will always associate this wine with meeting you."

"I think we should skip eating."

"Not tonight. I'm hungry."

He reached for my hand, slowly pried my fingers from my glass, and brought them up to his mouth. His sensuous lips opened and closed around my fingertips, and his teeth nibbled, shooting scalding flames of lust through my inner core. I took his face in my hands and brought his mouth a breath from my lips. I looked straight into his clouding eyes and lowered my mouth to brush his, barely giving him a taste.

"Gabe. *Amore mio*—you're gonna have to wait because I'm hungry, and I would like to eat." I rotated my hips against the hardness of his body that instantly responded to my teasing. I pulled away and sat in my chair. As if nothing had happened, I took a forkful of penne in my mouth and invited him to sit as well. He was staring back at me through thick eyelashes, his mouth parted, his eyes still clouded by desire.

"Eat up. It's delicious," I told him, chewing my first bite.

He sat, took a forkful of the penne, and brought it up to his lips. "Not as good as what I had in mind."

"Try it and then tell me." I knew he would love my sauce.

In no time, he had dusted his plate up and gotten up for seconds. I laughed and poured us more Shiraz. He returned to the table with a second plateful and asked me if I wanted more.

"No, thank you." I leaned back and sipped the wine. "Don't forget to mop up all that good sauce."

He did and then offered me the first bite. I brushed his fingertips as I bit into the soaked bread and looked at him, silently promising dessert.

The mantle clock struck midnight.

"Come." He offered me a hand.

Not worrying about cleaning up, we walked back into the bedroom where our hands spoke eagerly, silently.

*

We must not have moved at all during the night because the pale morning light found us deeply asleep in the same position. I stretched the full length of my body against his. Gabe's solid arm wrapped around my waist, holding me tight. His heartbeat drummed softly against my curved back while his breath teased loose strands of my hair.

It tickled me.

I giggled.

He stirred, tightening the grip of his arm around me.

"Gabe, you're tickling me."

"Can't be," he mumbled. "I'm not even hard yet."

I giggled again. "That's not what I meant." I smoothed my hips against him, checking . . . or perhaps I'm just a chronic tease.

"But it's not a bad idea," I offered when I felt him respond.

"I can't believe you called it tickling."

Fully awake and aroused, he pinned me, face down, with the weight of his body.

"It was your breath," I said with my voice muffled by the pillow. I turned and gasped for air as he parted my legs and wound my hair around his hand.

"My breath?" he whispered, gently biting into the curve of my shoulder.

"Never mind—just stop teasing." The feral urge to have him inside me was unbearable.

"What do you want, luv?" he asked, sinking his teeth into the softness of my earlobe. A pang of pain ricocheted through my spine, echoing in ripples of desire, and I grasped for the sheets as my back arched in silent begging.

"You." I ached.

"Say it." He lifted his fingers to brush my mouth. I took his thumb into my parted lips and ran the hot tip of my tongue along it. I felt him inch closer against the tender flesh between my legs.

Not close enough.

I moaned and bit his thumb. "I want you inside me." I flexed my left arm behind me to guide him.

He let go of my hair to take hold of my wrist and lifted it away, back above my head. His right thumb was still inside my mouth, but the hardness pressing between my buttocks remained a yearning.

"I can't wait. Please, Gabe," I moaned, stripped of inhibitions.

"But I like this." His rich voice dripped in my ear. He kept from penetrating but slid down deeper and found the swollen heart of my desire. I felt the pulsing of his hardness rub against it and met it with my hips thrusting backwards. My mouth found the rest of his fingers and sucked, one at a time. "That's what I was looking for." Its head stroked me intimately.

I smiled against the pillow and lifted my hips in one swift move. He slid smoothly deep inside me. And I contracted my inner muscles and trapped him.

He gasped as the tight grip sucked, pulsed, and brought him to finish suddenly.

"That's what *I* was looking for," I whispered when, seconds later, he crashed against my back.

"You're wicked."

"And more." I smiled.

Tess's head peeked through the door and looked at us.

"I think she's checking to see if we're done and if it's safe to join us."

Gabe lifted his head. "Looks like it." He patted the blankets to encourage her.

In two huge jumps she hopped up on the bed, wiggling her tail like a busy feather duster, and settled right between us. She took a look at me and smiled, turned her head to look at Gabe, and gave him a huge lick on the chin.

"G'day to you too, Tess," he said, pushing her face away.

"How about I leave you two to enjoy your morning effusions and I jump in the shower?" I moved out of their reach.

"How about we join you?"

"How about coffee?" I yelled, closing the bathroom door behind me.

I took a long, warm shower and spent extra time caring for myself. I used extra conditioner on my hair and combed it through, detangling it before rinsing in the relaxing warm water. Once out, I wrapped my head in a dry towel and took advantage of the lingering steam to carefully apply, with a soothing massage, amber infused lotion all over my body.

I opened the bathroom door in a cloud of amber scented steam and met the beckoning scent of coffee.

In the kitchen, Gabe was loading the dishwasher, wearing only a pair of flannel lounge pants and the phone trapped between chin and shoulder.

"I'll be there. Just don't bloody fuck with it, mate, 'til I get there." Anger burst in sparks flaring from the sharp metal blade of his voice.

I froze in the doorframe.

He spun around and saw me. Our eyes met for an instant, but he quickly shut me out and focused away.

Maledizione!

He backed against the kitchen counter and braced himself, turning his knuckles white with effort.

I pushed off the doorframe, steered away from him, and poured a cup of coffee. Gabe silently pointed to a steaming mug on the dining table all set for breakfast, and I attempted a contrite smile. "Do you need privacy?"

He shook his head and abruptly ended the phone conversation. "Gomi, just be on it, but don't bloody talk to them. Whatever you do, mate, don't let them in. I'm on my way." He set the phone down on the counter behind him, folded his arms across his bare chest, and dropped his chin. I took a sip of scorching coffee and waited.

For what seemed an eternal lapse of time.

Suddenly, Gabe turned the dishwasher on and walked out of the kitchen, mumbling something about a shower.

Ma che caz . . . ?

The soft whoosh-whoosh of the dishwasher filled the silence. The coffee mug radiated heat into my hand, but my bare feet were getting cold on the floor, so I brought them up on the chair and tried to stretch Gabe's robe, which I had borrowed, over my toes. The crimson toe polish had chipped and looked in dire need of being wiped off and reapplied. I lifted my head and caught Tess watching me from the pantry door. Her head tilted to one side, she walked up to me. I scratched her ears and asked her if she knew what was going on. Instead of answering, she walked away down the hall toward the bedroom and the muffled sound of running water.

*

Several minutes later, they both walked back in, Gabe wearing a pair of faded jeans and a burgundy polo shirt. He had showered and shaved his desert stubble but had left a sexy goatee to shadow his sensuous mouth. He took the coffee mug he had abandoned on the counter, nuked it for a few seconds, topped it with fresh coffee, and finally walked up to the table and sat next to me. Still wet from the shower, his hair hung in soft spikes down his forehead. He took a sip of coffee, pushed the chair back, rested his elbows on his knees, and leaned closer to me, holding the coffee mug with both hands. I followed his golden head as it bent and remembered the chipped polish. I made sure my toes were safely tucked away.

Gabe lifted his clear blue eyes at me. And the burdened sky, tired of holding its load, finally exhaled.

"Drivers are being summoned."

I frowned.

The dishwasher paused, switching cycles, and in the silence, in that momentary gap of noise, I understood.

With trembling hands I set the now-tepid coffee mug down. "And . . . ?"

He looked at me for an eternity before shaking his head. "Gomi said there's an envelope at the shop."

"You need to go down—"

"The place is surrounded by reporters."

"When did it happen?"

"While we were in the desert." His eyes never left mine. He blew at the rim of his cup to cool the steaming black coffee. "Gomi's been trying to reach us for the past few days, but you've got my mobile." He had the spirit to wink at me and took a sip of coffee.

I had completely forgotten about the damn phone. Heck, I didn't even take that bag to Nowhere.

"I see."

I did more than just see. I tasted metal at the back of my throat. His fever reached out to me, but it wasn't all darkness. A tiny seed of excitement stirred, eager to grow, fed on by the flame of challenge. Like our love did, from seed to flower . . . following its destiny.

"Who's at the shop?"

"Gomi, the crew, and Clark." The shadow of a smile appeared on his lips. "Barking at the mob of reporters, I reckon." He took a long look at me. "If we give it a burl and head down there now, it won't be a piece of piss to give them the flick, luv. It's London to a brick they'll be all over us."

I nodded. Not only would we face the media frenzy about the breaking news, but we'd expose our relationship to their devouring jaws as well. I couldn't begin to imagine the sensation the news would raise, especially now with the Oz Endurance casting Gabe back in the midst of headline news.

Were we ready for all the attention?

I shook my head and he nodded once. We agreed.

He leaned back in his chair and stretched his legs. "Gomi's so excited he's splitting out of his skin. Even offered to head up this way and bring the envelope to us, but I don't want him to lead them back to the house. Sometimes I think the kid's got kangaroos loose in the top paddock." Gabe tapped a finger to his right temple.

"You mean he acts like a nut?"

He nodded.

"I thought the race isn't supposed to take place for another couple of months."

"That's right, Porzia, but it takes time to get things ready, and two months to prepare for something this big is nothing. Especially with all the secrecy around it. I still don't know how many, who they are and—"

"And you've been preparing," I finished for him, thinking of his almost-completely outfitted pipe dream. "You're one of them."

*

I left Gabe to call Gomi back. In the bedroom I dressed my body as one would dress an inanimate puppet, my amber-scented skin the only familiar comfort.

Sharing silence, we drove into town together, but he dropped me off about four blocks away from the shop and gave me Tess on a leash. The plan was for me to walk to the shop and check out the crowd of vans and cameras parked outside the main entrance. Nonchalantly walking amongst them, I would shoot for the back door, heading straight into the garage. Gabe, meanwhile, would drive straight into the midst of the madness and leave it to the reporters to get the hell out of his way, as he mildly put it.

Nice plan.

The morning sung crisp and bright in downtown Adelaide. Despite the fabulous weather, I walked in a daze, holding my breath still in the eye of blurred, out-of-control events. I dreaded the moment my so far belated, yet unavoidable, reaction would come crashing down on me. Tess pulled on the leash, forcing me to quicken my step. I tried to detangle the knot of feelings churning in my stomach, but to no avail. I barely dared inhale and exhale. In order not to stir dormant demons, I wasn't breathing properly.

The sun peeked from behind high clouds. A hint of warmth hung in the flower-scented air, and passersby sharing the sidewalk with me seemed to feel it too. Scarves hung loosely from unbuttoned coats, smiles were exchanged, and "G'days" wished. A few people stopped to pet an ecstatic Tess basking in the extra attention. We passed a bakery, a small bank, a travel agency advertising specials to Thailand, and the lavender restaurant where I'd had lunch with Gabe on my last visit. I glanced inside to read the special of the day—meatloaf. Despite all, I smiled. I was about a block away from the shop when a rush of TV vans buzzed up the road, madly driving away from Gabe's business. I quickened my pace and arrived at the now deserted main entrance. Gabe's Rover pulled in right behind me.

Clark swung the front door open and cast me a forlorn look. "G'day, Porzia. Nice to see you're still here."

Uncertain what he meant by this remark, I arched an eyebrow and was about to reply when I felt Gabe's hand at the small of my back. "Let's get inside before anybody spots us, Porzia."

"So it worked?" Gomi asked, flashing one of his stunning smiles.

"So I reckon." Clark took a seat on a wheeled chair by an old metal desk.

"What did you guys do?" I asked, intrigued.

"They anonymously tipped one of the local TV crews about having spotted me somewhere else, far away from here," Gabe explained.

"That's about right," Gomi beamed. "Only you don't know where we sent them."

"But you're about to tell me," Gabe replied, taking off his leather jacket.

"You're down at the Thai parlor getting a massage." Gomi grinned from ear to ear.

Gabe chuckled, "Did I have a gift certificate?"

Clark shook his head and unleashed Tess.

"Porzia, you haven't met the rest of the team." With a reassuring, if not somewhat possessive, hand at my back, Gabe encouraged me closer to the three intrigued fellows. "Matt, here, is our brakes and suspension expert. Matt, this is Porzia."

I shook Matt's strong hand and smiled at his freckle-covered face. "Nice to meet you." His smile broke wide and his nose crinkled.

Dan, a balding fellow in his mid-thirties, with piercing dark eyes, was next. "Porzia? That's a Latin name. It almost sounds like 'portal.'"

"That's right," I said, returning his firm handshake.

"I took Latin in school for a while," he offered.

"Yeah, leave it to Dan to waste time with dead things like Latin and ancient carburetors," the last fellow I shook hands with said in a friendly, mocking tone. Almost as tall as Gabe, but not as broad, his honest eyes twinkled with barely disguised sarcasm. "Rohan. At your service." He bowed.

"We keep him around for moral entertainment mostly." Gabe's own tone was coated with similar friendly sarcasm. "The fact that he's the best hot-wire in the country is irrelevant."

"Hot-wire?" I asked.

Rohan nodded. "That's only one of my many talents."

I was afraid to ask what else he was good at.

"What's going on then, mates?" Gabe asked. He rolled Clark's chair aside, with Clark sitting in it, to lean against the desk, and folded his arms across his chest. It was becoming a habit.

"The Aborigines released a number of international invitations—I reckon it's invitations by mail—'bout two days ago, and the international media's been all over them," Rohan explained. "We're getting our fair Oz share."

"Who's going?" Gabe asked.

"Everybody we thought of," Gomi answered.

"So that narrows it down to—what? Twenty at the most?" Rohan snickered.

"Just about," Gomi continued. "Funny thing is—they're all keeping quiet. Nobody's talking." He shot Gabe a searching look. "They're all waiting to see what you're going to do before accepting—"

"Then how does the media know who's going to participate?" I asked.

"They don't have a bloody clue, Porzia." Clark answered my question. "They're just targeting whoever got an envelope."

"Boy, we were crowded this morning. This place hasn't seen so much action since we came back from Dakar—," Gomi blurted.

As if cued by a maestro's invisible stroke, the mood changed instantaneously. They all exchanged uncomfortable glances and suddenly found things to do: Matt mumbled something about coffee; Dan silently bent to pet Tess; and Rohan patted a pack of cigarettes in his shirt pocket and walked out. Dan took Tess and followed Rohan out the back door.

That left Clark, Gomi, and me.

"Would you like me to leave, Gabe?" I asked him. I thought he might need some privacy to discuss things with his father and best friend. I honestly didn't know if I wanted to be there.

"No, Porzia. Not unless you'd like to."

I locked eyes with Clark and answered his silent plea. He didn't want Gabe to accept.

Did I?

"I'm fine for now," I conceded, not breaking eye contact with a desolate Clark. "But I'm going to walk out if I need to."

"Fair enough," Clark accepted, gaining a questioning look from his son. He held the gaze and leaned forward in his chair, reaching for the front pocket of his denim shirt. With his middle and index fingers he peeled out a thin white envelope. "Here it is, son."

I blinked and he suddenly looked as though he had aged ten years. With a spasm of pain and fear gripping my own heart, I realized Clark was scared to death.

No. Not to death. Of death.

Fear streaked his features like etching on leather. I felt it slither up my skin. He faced the chance of losing his only son.

I selfishly shut him out. Shut out the depth of his pain. I didn't want to go there. I had my own pain to deal with, my own challenge to face.

Gomi leaned against the hood of a white Subaru covered in sponsors' decals. The short walk in the crisp air that I had enjoyed minutes earlier seemed a dream; my labored breathing remained the only tangible effect.

It was suddenly hot in the garage. I brought a hand to my throat and felt my frenzied pulse against my sweaty fingertips. No gap between heartbeats. No room for magic.

Gabe reached for the envelope and, without a word, shoved it into his jeans pocket. Unopened.

He took my damp hand and spoke to Clark. "I'll ring you later. Keep Tess tonight?"

Clark, massaging his eyes vigorously, barely nodded his agreement with shut eyelids.

Gabe steered his gaze toward Gomi, and Gomi nodded as well.

We walked out, climbed into the Rover, and drove away.

"Where are we going?" I asked, buckling up.

"Grocery shopping and then home," he said, merging into the slow traffic of the Parade.

"Clark is keeping Tess tonight for a reason."

"Roight."

I understood. "I don't know if you need me to be around at the moment." I looked at him. "I know what the envelope means."

His eyes never left the road. "You want to talk about it *now*?"

"Yes, why not?" I insisted. "I'm not a patient person, Gabe. We're not going to have a better time. It's the feelings involved that rule—not the time." I was having a hard time controlling such feelings, pushing, spilling out like a launched locomotive. I physically fought my emotions in an unmatched effort to restrain the surging pain. Sparks flared as I braked in the darkness of my chest.

"Don't keep from accepting because of me."

"I won't."

"I couldn't bear the guilt. It would kill our love."

"I know."

"I think you need to be alone," I blurted out loud, the last thought of the crashing train running through my heart, leaving a gaping, blackened tunnel in its wake.

"Not yet." He took my hand in his, and I wondered how much time we had left. How many more times would he touch my hand?

"Your father's scared."

"He's not the only one, Porzia. We're all bloody scared."

"No, you're not, Gabe." I felt rage spill out of my whole being along with tears. "You're not scared. You've been *Dreaming* your own Aboriginal beginning for this time to manifest. But it's absurd!

"You can't believe that now, all of a sudden, you might be invincible. I remember you telling me you defied death once and you could do it again. Are you out of your goddamned mind? How can you think that with only a touch of a superior being inside you you're no longer facing mortality? Who the hell do you think you are? And who the hell does he think he is? You don't fuck with the gods! And don't tell me that it's not true. He's kept you alive this long. Why would you think that now you can make up your own rules?"

Enraged, I attacked him, my fears pressing the verbal abuse until the eagle feather hanging off the ignition caught my eye, and I stopped abruptly. All of a sudden, I connected the dots of the bloody wings. The Dhamala Gabe killed in mercy must have been the first, initial contact. Trapped by a broken wing, the warrawarra spirit could not return to its human form. Gabe and his kind sense of justice. *Oddio!* The price he paid! Feeling the pain of killing an innocent creature actually released the powers and, ultimately, a responsibility. The warrawarra was freed but bound by debt—a debt of life proportions. He had eventually returned the favor when Gabe found himself trapped in the gap, in the metal of his wreck. For the eagle, the wizard had to sacrifice wings, but managed to keep Gabe alive through the umbilical power of the Aboriginal goddess Eingana, whom he must worship. What had Maureen said when she met me in her metaphysical store? *"Whatever we seek, we shall find"*? Or did she say *"It shall find us"*? Suddenly her words became a crucial piece in the puzzle of my understanding. And now Gabe would face the ultimate transformation: to challenge the strength of his medicine protection, to rise above his limits and leap. That's why his ankle's tattoo wasn't complete: the ending had yet to be written. Like a true empowered god, Gabe would write it himself. If he survived.

"You can't help it." I understood what this meant for him. It was the ultimate race. A once-in-a-lifetime chance to satisfy an ageless hunger. Before he became the man I was in love with, Gabe was a Cloud Dweller.

I wiped my eyes with the tip of my fingers, smearing tears left and right. "I want to go *home*, Gabe."

"Me too, Porzia."

*

We drove back up Adelaide's hills and made it home right before the sun lost its battle with gathering clouds, and rain began to pound against the double-paned windows. As soon as we stepped inside, I asked Gabe to please light a fire. I left him in the living room with wood and matches and walked to the kitchen where I opened a bottle of Umeracha Shiraz and grabbed two glasses. Outside in the darkness, thunder echoed lightning while inside, flames finally flickered in the fireplace. Gabe sat in front of it and accepted the glass of wine.

"We're gonna get drunk."

"*Salute*," I said, sitting on the sofa. I kicked my boots off and tucked my legs under my hips.

"We haven't eaten anything all day." He touched his glass to mine.

"I can't think of food."

He smiled sadly. "That's a first."

I tilted my glass and took a long sip. The rich wine splashed in my stomach, a foaming wave against a strong cliff, and warmed me from the inside out. I leaned against the soft cushions and looked at Gabe's face reflecting the blazing flames. He sipped the wine, inches away from me. My knees almost touched his shoulder. Every contact with his body now took on a stronger, infinite meaning, enhanced by limited time, impossible to enjoy fully.

I finished my wine, poured myself another, and topped Gabe's. My head was getting lighter and my fears crawled drunkenly toward the recesses of my mind. I locked them back there and drank more wine. At the end of the second glass, sad to say, I felt pretty wasted, all my belligerent arguments, as the gods would have them, forgotten.

I fell asleep on the sofa and barely felt Gabe's powerful arms lift me up to carry me to the bedroom where he undressed me. A vague idea of blankets covering my body skimmed my consciousness before sleep mercifully took over.

*

I woke up to darkness and silence.

Alone.

Heaven up above had tilted the bucket in one last surge of rain, like a child crying empty tears at the end of a tantrum. The sky was drained, and we both knew it.

I shoved the blankets off and got up, realizing Gabe must have slipped his white T-shirt on me before tucking me in bed. Silence engulfed the house; only dim light guided my steps.

Gabe was on the couch, awake, wearing black boxers and the exhausted look of a warrior who has defeated demons, at a price.

I walked up to him silently but knew he'd heard me.

On the mantel, the clock chimed two A.M., the darkest hour before morning.

The envelope lay open on the coffee table. Unsurprisingly, a pattern of wings was barely visible in the folded invitation.

I sat next to him, and he took my right hand in his. His lips brushed my open palm, and I exhaled.

"I'm going, Porzia."

His golden hair shone thick and within reach, a mere brush away from my fingertips. Once again—just like that day, months ago on the plane, before I knew him—fear of reaching and pull paralyzed me.

Instead of fighting such fear, I nodded slowly as if the air had suddenly thickened into an amniotic liquid I had forgotten how to breathe in. I was going to drown instead.

I got up and walked back to the bedroom. I lay in bed and closed my eyes, thinking, *If I fall back to sleep it will all go away.*

But I knew better.

When I heard his soft footsteps, I spoke quietly to the shadow in the doorframe. "I'm going home."

Silence.

"Not because—"

"I know why, Porzia. No need to explain." He stopped me in mid-sentence.

"OK then," I said to the darkness.

I felt him in bed next to me a second before his heat hugged my chilled body.

"You know I love you."

I started sobbing uncontrollably. "That's why it hurts so much."

CHAPTER 39

Clark would never forgive me.

He had counted on me to hold Gabe back. But how do you stop the wind from blowing? The rain from falling? A Dreamtime seed from blooming?

Blinded by love, he had underestimated his son and the need consuming Gabe from within.

Gomi knew better and probably suspected some of the mystical. So he'd quietly done his best to prepare, not only securing state of the art equipment, but ultimately focusing on what mattered most: endurance.

The day I left Oz, he hugged me, flashing his dazzling smile. I guess he respected the fact I was stepping back, allowing Gabe to live his life no matter what the price.

"This is ultimate love, Porzia," he whispered in my hair. "The unconditional, selfless kind. The one that means you love somebody to the point of allowing them a chance to their fate—if that's what they need to do."

*

I will not talk about saying good-bye to Gabe at the airport.

Nor will I mention our last night together. It's impossible to even summon the memory of it. That's for me to cherish alone.

How do you love that which you don't know? I had wondered long ago. Now I *knew* him and love. And what if he was the *one* I shared more than a lifetime with?

Now I faced the excruciating chance he would be taking in two months.

No, I will speak no more about it. But I will talk about the endless flight from hell I endured with distance spreading against my will.

I left him.

For fuck's sake, I did.

I loved him so much I left.

And we're not talking about trying to be brave or fishing for a standing ovation. What he loved the most was going to take him away from me.

In the last hours, his heavenly eyes burned with damning fever, the racing in his blood come to life once more.

I didn't tell anybody about the change of plans.

I wanted to crawl back home unnoticed.

I should have known better.

In a comatose state, I walked out of the connecting tunnel into the airport's unforgiving, artificial neon light and saw a human-size owl. I squinted and the owl shifted into Evalena. Still dealing with the vision, almost expecting to embrace feathers, I felt her arms close around my trembling shoulders, and, hating myself for thinking it, I wished she was Gabe.

"I know, Porzia."

"How can you?" I burst into loud sobs.

"I just do, honey." She let me hide my tears against her shoulder.

We drove away in silence. Still crying, I stared out the window through diluted images. Pensacola looked strange. Adelaide was home.

What the hell?

My future with Gabe hung from a thin line. I knew nothing. How could I even think of Oz as home?

I guess when distressed, the mind plays awful tricks.

"Peridot is at home, Evalena?"

"Yes, dear. I stopped by Benedetta's this afternoon and brought him home," she said. "I thought you'd like to have him waiting for you."

"Did you see her?"

"Of course. She opened the door to let me in." She smiled. "I haven't mastered walking through walls quite yet."

Too bad.

"You told her I was coming home?"

Evalena nodded in the beams of an oncoming car. "Yes. She didn't ask questions. She's a smart girl. Whenever you're ready to talk, she'll listen."

"OK. And how about you?" I asked suspiciously. "One thing is to *feel* I was having trouble, but to be waiting for me at the airport, and for the exact flight, is pushing it."

"Gabe called."

My heart shot up my throat. "When?"

"I guess right after you left."

"How does he have your number?"

"We're listed, dear."

"But you're not even living at your house."

"Moved back two days ago."

"*Caspita!* Perfect timing, eh?"

"Why are you surprised?"

A pang of irrational anger tinged my words the color of bile. "Well, since you know everything—tell me why the hell is this happening?"

Evalena pulled into my parking lot and rolled the car to a halt before answering me. She cut the engine and faced me, leaning one elbow on the back of her car seat. "You don't want to talk about this *now*. You ought to climb upstairs, say hello to your kitty, and take a bath, if you have the energy, then go to sleep. Answers can wait 'til the morrow."

"I don't want to wait," I complained in a petulant tone I didn't know I was capable of. I hated it.

Evalena smiled. "You have the answers already. That's why you're back here."

I burst into tears and hid my face in my cupped hands. They smelled stale and dirty. The forward motion of flying still rattled my bones. "I want to know if he's Xavier. I want to know why? And I want to know if he's going to die. And why didn't I recognize him?"

There, I said it all out loud. My fears concretized into real enemies in front of me and I wasn't even armed for bloody battle!

"Porzia, you're in no condition to discuss these matters right now. Please let me help you get settled upstairs, and we can talk about it calmly tomorrow sometime."

I finally agreed but only because I was exhausted.

We got out of the car, unloaded my bag, and walked by the oleander. The tree was thriving. In little over a week it had bloomed beautifully.

In a little over a week?

I cast a silent prayer.

Evalena waited for me and then helped carry my bag up to the front door. Right behind it we found Peridot standing at full attention. He welcomed us with loud purring and serious leg rubbing. I scooped him up in my arms and gave him a proper thank you. His fur felt soft and warm to the touch, unconditional comfort and love. *Just what I needed.*

Evalena brought my bag to the bedroom, gave me one last hug, and left me alone.

Way past midnight and no moon in sight.

She had switched the bedroom lamp on, and I followed the light with Peridot still curled in my arms. I switched the lamp off, sat on the bed, and kicked off my shoes, then relaxed, stretching my achy back on the familiar softness of my pillows, and closed my eyes to face the demons.

In the dark.

Two months.

The Oz Endurance was set for the end of December, right before the end of the millennium. There was plenty of time to drive myself crazy.

I opened my eyes and released Peridot from the constricting hold I had on him. Purring happily, he snuggled in at the foot of my bed.

The answering machine was blinking furiously, and, impulsively, I reached to hit the play button.

Gabe's voice came on as if he were standing there in the darkness, one of the demons. I closed my eyes, carefully focusing on his words. "Porzia, I hope you've made it. Give a ring when you get in will ya, please?"

A second message followed. "I forgot to say thank you."

The third message was from my father; to call home and where the hell was I?

I deleted my father's message, making a mental note to call them tomorrow. I hit play one more time and fell asleep listening to Gabe's voice thanking me.

*

I slept soundly, like a rock at the bottom of a deep ocean, oblivious to the turbulent surf above.

Trapped under my chest, my right arm was dead asleep. Slowly, painstakingly, I pulled it free and felt it tingle as blood rushed through it, and with blood came the memories.

The fear of the looming day and lacking the strength to deal with it all made me want to crawl back under the covers and sleep through it.

Slowly, groggily, I got up instead.

I walked to the bathroom and jumped at the grotesque face staring back from the mirror. I looked like a frozen pizza. A still-wrapped frozen pizza. How ugly. Red sleep folds streaked my right cheek like stiff mozzarella. My eyes resembled swollen olives and my nose had mutated into a cluster of iced tomato sauce. Let's not mention the bitter line thinning my lips and the blotched blemishes on my chin. *Mamma mia!*

I washed my face and rinsed with plenty of cold water. I looked a bit better but still felt like somebody had rollerbladed all over me. I walked back to the bedroom where I noticed a small aromatherapy burner on my dresser. My nose twitched, catching a subtle scent. No wonder I had fallen asleep so easily.

Evalena, I thought. The smile cracking my lips felt foreign.

CHAPTER 40

The following days became a blur of dull pain, fogged up emotions, and the piercing sound of the phone constantly ringing.

I called my family and spoke briefly with my father. I told him I had just gotten home from a long flight and would call back later on when I felt better. I hung up thinking that I had no intention of ever calling home again. I had no intention of ever speaking again. I felt so depressed and tired I didn't even return Gabe's phone call. I barely ate or fed Peridot. I didn't go out, not even to check the mail. I drew the curtains and slept. I drank water, munched on stale cookies, and never changed out of my pajamas. I hardly washed my face or brushed my teeth. I switched the answering machine off and, after a few hours of unceasing ringing, I yanked the phone cord from the wall, hid my head under the pillow, and fell back asleep. The few times I climbed out of bed, Peridot followed me silently and came back to the bedroom to curl at my feet as I gratefully found relief in Morpheus's arms.

*

I honestly don't remember how much time I spent in such a state, but I most definitely remember thinking that people should mind their own damn business—friends especially—when the loud banging at my front door startled me from a dream I could not recall to save my life, but had a sense it might have been important. I smashed the pillow on my head to muffle the incessant noise, but I knew whoever was causing such havoc wasn't going to stop any time soon.

"Porzia! Open the door before I call the cops, for heaven's sake!" a strong voice commanded.

Interestingly enough, I had no idea to whom the voice belonged. I unburied my head and waited a few seconds for the voice to resume talking. It didn't, but the loud knocking carried on.

I scrambled out of bed and grabbed my robe. "OK, OK . . . I'm coming!" I yelled above the thundering. I peeked through the eyehole and caught the rim of a wide straw hat tilted over a sharp profile. The acrid smell of cigarillo reached my keen nostrils as I cracked the door open, and Camille Weir stormed in like a stale-scented genie unleashed from a tobacco-plantation magic lamp, if one can imagine such a novelty.

"What the hell is wrong with you?"

Perhaps instead of genie, I ought to have used the word demon. I opened my mouth to speak but tightened my robe against my chest instead. She closed the door and took two steps back to get a better look at me. "Dear heavens, Porzia, you look awful."

"Thanks."

"And what is this smell?" she asked, crinkling her posh nose. Wasting no time, she extinguished her cigarillo, walked up to the windows, and spread the curtains open; all of them, including the bedroom ones. She walked all over my place with her designer shoes clicking disapproving noises on the hardwood floors while I stood like an idiot, frozen by the front door. I held on to my robe, a lifesaver, and wondered what smell was she talking about that could be worse than what she smoked.

"What are you doing standing there like a freeze-frame? Have you got any coffee?"

I took a few steps, not trusting my legs, and pointed at the kitchen. She walked in and began to open and slam shut cabinet doors until she finally found a canister of Illy and began making us espresso. I followed and leaned against the doorframe. Forgive my cowardice, but I was scared to death. Then, realizing it wasn't all fear I felt, I mumbled an apology and rushed to the bathroom, locking the door behind me. I ended up washing my face, brushing my teeth, and even made a futile attempt to comb my hair, finally throwing the brush back in the basket. The smell of fresh espresso beckoned me back into the kitchen, the need for it stronger than my unjustified fear of Camille. I set my shoulders straighter and crossed the line.

"How much sugar do you take?" she asked.

"Three," I responded sheepishly, dropping my shoulders involuntarily.

She didn't flinch but handed me a cup. She took a sip of hers and nodded approvingly. "I guess there's a man behind this?" she asked, widely gesturing a perfectly manicured hand.

"Camille—" I cupped my coffee with both hands, summoning courage. "What are you doing here?"

"Protecting my interests, of course." She used a tone that openly diagnosed me with acute idiot syndrome.

"Your interests?" I dared.

"Helen got no answer for the last week. No machine, no way to contact you. You don't even have a cell phone, and according to her you haven't checked your e-mail in ages."

"The thought that I might have been out of the country didn't cross your mind?" I asked sarcastically.

She swatted at my sarcasm with her imperious hand. It dropped like a stiff fly. "You've gained my trust with your professional demeanor. You *always* leave your answering machine on or a phone number where we can reach you. I even have your parents' number in Italy, Porzia. Not this time. This time you disappeared. Until I spoke to an extremely distressed Oscar and he finally broke down and told me you're dating Gabe Miller."

"Not anymore," I hissed.

"That's none of my business." She tilted her head back to catch the last drops of her espresso. "Until now."

"What do you mean?"

"We're going forward with *Scoop*, Porzia. Oscar has accepted. He's been trying to reach you for the past week or so. Then he heard the news about Miller going to race again and called me. I put two and two together and flew up."

"I see," I said, finally taking a sip of espresso. Colder, but it still tasted great. "You make good coffee, Camille."

"Nonsense. Anybody can make good coffee with a Moka and the brand you use." With totally unexpected tenderness Camille leaned forward and tucked a rebel strand of hair behind my ear. "Go jump in the shower, Porzia. We've got business to discuss."

*

As if I give a shit, I thought as I walked back to the bathroom. My suitcase stood in a corner of the bedroom still unpacked. I kicked it.

I walked into the bathroom, making a point of avoiding the mirror. I quickly peeled off my—by now contaminated—pajamas and turned the shower on.

My skin tingled under the welcomed pelting. I turned the shower jet to full blast and felt my body drink in the moisture like a parched plant soaking in the year's first rainfall. I lathered my hair with invigorating rosemary shampoo and rinsed it thoroughly before applying a generous amount of conditioner. Ten minutes later, I had almost entirely restored my human status. I changed into some clean clothes, combed my hair thoroughly, and walked back into the kitchen. Fearless, this time.

Camille was speaking to someone on her cell phone, nervously swinging a high-heeled foot back and forth.

"Yes, Helen, go ahead. I'll catch you later." She hung up without saying goodbye, folded her phone shut, and smiled at me. "Don't you feel better?"

I nodded and sat down and took a look around my kitchen. "I would offer you something to eat, but I'm afraid I've got nothing," I apologized, passing a hand through my wet hair.

"Don't worry. I ate on my way from the airport, and I won't stay long." She got up, walked to the front door, and disappeared outside for a few minutes. Peridot followed her to the door and peeked out the curtain to see. Just as curious, I wondered if she had left when I heard her heels clicking back up the stairs.

"I had to tell Ambrose to just park it for a bit, but not to get too comfortable. We're going as soon as you and I are finished," she said, breathless. A thin attaché case snapped open under the light touch of her sharp vermilion fingertips. She handed me an official-looking folder and sat down.

"It's a contract, Porzia."

"I don't—"

She raised a hand silencing me. "No need to decide this minute. I just thought you might like some news other than what you've been dealing with."

"Oh—"

"I'm on my way to New Orleans for a week or so. I would like an answer by the end of the week." She paused, and I worried she would ask me to come along.

"Who's Ambrose?" I asked her instead.

"My driver; you met him in Miami." She smiled. "I flew up and had him meet me here. I absolutely detest flying into New Orleans."

I raised an eyebrow. "He drove up from Miami? So you wouldn't have to fly into New Orleans?"

Camille tilted her head and cast me a piercing look confirming my acute idiot condition. "He ought to be grateful to you for being such a pressing matter and on my way. So he was spared my tedious company almost all the way up."

Leave it to her to make you feel like anything she did, you owed her.

*

Once she left, I wondered if I really wanted to be subjected to her as a boss. I closed the door behind her, catching a glimpse of Ambrose and a shiny black Cadillac. I walked back to the kitchen and opened the folder. I sat down while Peridot rubbed against my legs and finally jumped on the table to lie on the spread-out contract. I scooped him in my arms—a dead weight like only cats can manage—settled him on my lap, and read on.

Everything she had promised during the meeting was listed, from my collaboration with Oscar to the monthly column and the quarterly featured article. She hadn't left anything out. Salary, special bonuses, deadlines, and penalties were all listed, including a special clause saying I was free to live anywhere I wanted and to continue with my freelance career.

I wondered if I needed a lawyer as I flipped pages looking for fine print.

There wasn't any. The contract was everything I had been working toward these past years as a freelancer: the security of a steady income doing what I loved, not to mention the freedom I would still be able to enjoy. Camille must have considered this thoroughly.

How ironic, I thought, *now that I can't really appreciate it.*

I got up, gently dropped Peridot back on the chair, and walked to the bedroom where I plugged in the phone and dialed Oscar's number at *Gusto* in New York. His secretary paged me through instantly, making me realize he must have been worried sick.

"Porzia! At last, honey!"

"Hi, Oscar." I rubbed my third eye. The opening act of a splitting headache arrogantly throbbed inside my forehead. Rubbing wasn't really going to help. Neither was talking to Oscar.

"Are you alright?" he asked, deeply concerned.

"No, but I don't wanna talk about it," I sighed. "Camille stopped by."

"I told her not to."

"Never mind, Oscar," I sighed. "She left me a contract and wants an answer within a week."

"It's not the best of times, honey, I know."

"Oscar, what do you know of what I'm going through?" *Let's see the extent of the damage.*

"About the Oz Endurance you mean?"

"Yes."

"Where have you been, Porzia, for the last week?" Oscar asked, incredulous. "The press has been covering the news nonstop."

"What's the bloody big deal?"

"Oh, nothing—just the biggest event of the end of the millennium. Besides this computer bug everybody's yapping about," he replied sarcastically. "The fact that your *beau* has decided to resume his brilliant career for such an event is raising the stakes—"

"He's not my beau, Oscar," I interrupted him through clenched teeth.

"My apologies," he said sincerely. "I didn't mean to sound demeaning, honey, but you've got to admit he *is* a beau."

I heard him giggle. Oscar will always be Oscar, even at the worst of times.

"Listen—," I began as my headache shot like a ricocheting bullet behind my eyes. "I just called to say I am this close to accepting Camille's offer and please don't worry, I will be fine."

"I don't mean to pressure you as I say this, Porzia, but you are aware that without you there is no deal, right?"

"Right."

"I'm fine with you declining," he said. "I'm honestly OK with what I am doing and with where my life is going, although the challenge of having my own magazine is appealing. So promise me you won't make any rash decision only for the sake of who's involved."

My head was pounding so loudly I saw flashes when I closed my eyes. "You have my word," I promised him.

We left off agreeing to get back in touch with each other by the end of the week, and I told him I would call him before I spoke to Camille, no matter what I decided.

I hung up the phone and thought about calling my family. My head was begging for me to grab an ax and split it open, it hurt so much. I took some aspirin with a tall glass of water and went back to the bedroom where I shut the drapes Camille had determinedly spread open. I yanked the phone plug out of the wall and lay back down on the unmade bed.

CHAPTER 41

I ended up taking it.

The job, that is.

After a week, I finally came out of the coma I had slumped into and replugged the phone in.

Sad to say, it wasn't that I had reached enlightenment, although after a week of fasting, I should have.

Nope, nothing so drastic or life changing.

Simply put, I got hungry.

I called my favorite deli in town and asked for a delivery of fresh bread, crab salad, a wedge of Brie, and a basket of fruit. I took a shower, opened a bottle of chilled Galestro, and, as I waited for the food to arrive, picked up the phone. I called my family first and talked to my father for the longest time. He just listened, as he usually does. I could almost picture him leaning against the heavy dresser in the hall, where the only phone in the house is kept, nodding or frowning as the conversation unfolded. He whistled softly at the mention of Gabe's name. I finally sighed and waited for him to speak.

"Take the job. Don't be an idiot."

I shook my head. Straight to the point, my father will never waste words.

My mother resonated a totally different vibe.

It took a while to share it all with her, and as usual, she listened patiently. "Why is it that Prince Charming always shows up at the end of the tale, Porzia?"

"I have no idea, Mamma."

"It's only when the heroine is ready that love finds her. Maybe he is not your soul mate," she sighed, but her voice held a hint of pride for my choice to embrace magic. "I remember Joséphine's words, *cara bambina mia*. Do you know yourself? Or how much of your essence have you stifled in the pursuit of this love?"

I was going to have to give her questions some thought.

"Porzia, I know what your next question is going to be. I can only answer that I know for a fact that pain spilling from delusion is every bit as hard and real as pain from a true love. But your illusion of happiness has been obliterated by knowledge you've summoned and now need to face, conquer, and use to your own benefit."

*

I hung up the phone somewhat revitalized, ready to face the rest of the music. I dialed Oscar on his direct line.

"Oscar—this is Porzia. I'm in."

He whistled softly and then giggled. "Great!"

"I don't have much time. I'll call you back in a couple of days. I need to reach Camille before she heads back to Miami and decides to stop back here."

"She's not that terrible now, Porzia."

"Worse, but I can handle it," I smirked.

"I need to talk to you about something I'd like you to write about for my last issue of *Gusto*."

"Ok," I told him. "I'll call you back."

The food arrived as I reached Helen at *A' la Carte*. *Thank God for cordless*, I thought, carrying the bags back to the kitchen.

"Helen, this is Porzia Amard. How are you?"

"I'm doing great, Porzia. Nice to hear from you."

"Is Camille available?" I scooped a bit of crabmeat into Peridot's bowl. After a week of stale dry food, he deserved a treat.

"Actually, she's still away from the office, I'm afraid. Would you like her cell phone number?"

Now that was a first. Moving up on the food chain, I thought.

"It's not necessary, Helen; just tell her I'm accepting her offer. I'm making you a copy of the signed contract and will send it in tomorrow. I'll keep the original as she requested."

"That's wonderful. I'll set things in motion, then and pass on the news to her." She paused before graciously adding that she would discreetly suggest to Camille not to worry about stopping on her way back from New Orleans to check on me because I 'mentioned' to her that I might be out of town.

"Thanks a lot, Helen. You're precious."

"You're most welcome."

I hung up the phone and took a sip of wine, debating whether to eat first or continue on with the phone calls. Food first, I decided, envious of Peridot wolfing down his share of crab. I set the table, turned on the radio, tuned it to a classical station I love, and sat down to eat my first real meal after over a week of dry cereals and frozen orange juice out of the can.

How sad.

I took my time and enjoyed every bite of zesty crab salad, crusty bread, and creamy cheese. I drank two glasses of Galestro and ended the scrumptious feast with a juicy pear and some more Brie cheese.

Who would have guessed that such a treat would end up being my last one for the longest time?

The phone rang as I wiped my fingers from sweet pear juices.

Funny how my heart knew even before answering.

"Porzia, it's me. How you going?" Gabe's voice kissed my ears from across the planet.

"Hi. OK, I guess."

"I've been bloody worried sick." He sounded tired.

"Yeah? Guess how I will feel for the next couple of months." As soon as I said it I regretted it. "Look—I didn't mean it."

"Yes, you did. No worries," he chuckled. "I was expecting worse."

"Worse?" *Should I throw a tantrum or something?*

"Yeah, like I'd never hear your voice again."

"I would have called, Gabe," I said, tired. "I just needed some time."

"You alroight?"

"You already asked that. No, I'm not OK." I winced. I could have held him on the phone for the next two months, keeping him away from danger.

How absurd.

I squeezed my eyes shut and exhaled, trying not to cry. If I had let myself, I would have told him I loved him, I missed him, I only wanted his arms to hold me and promise me it would all work out.

As if I had spoken out loud, he answered me. "Porzia, I know I can't ask you—but if you could find the strength through this to keep in touch—it would be . . . it would mean a lot."

I bent my head between my knees and realized I had collapsed on the floor.

"Also—please don't keep alone."

"What do you mean?" I asked him.

"I mean—please keep Evalena by you."

"Why?"

"In case I don't make it."

"Don't talk like that!" I screamed, angrily wiping tears off my stricken face.

"I have to, Porzia, please understand—"

I heard him exhale, getting impatient. "Listen, this was probably a mistake. I shouldn't have called. I just needed to know you made it home safe."

A surging red tide of anger flared inside me. I gave up controlling my tears, my vision blurred, and I exploded, "*YOU COULD HAVE BLOODY CALLED EVALENA!*"

I slammed the phone down and yanked the cord so forcefully that the plug came off with part of the drywall.

DAMN MY ITALIAN TEMPER!

I changed into my running gear, threw a bottle of water, Walkman, and a small towel into my gym bag, and stormed out of the house, barely remembering the car keys and to lock the door behind me. I actually slammed it shut, almost breaking a window. I glared at the oleander and almost kicked it before jumping in the car and heading to the beach to run away from everything for as long as I could.

And I ran for an entire week.

I got up every day, shot down an espresso and a protein shake, and rushed out to run. For two and a half hours daily. I bought AA batteries, more protein shakes, water, and cat food. I never turned the TV on, never bothered with the newspapers or calling friends. Eventually, I fixed the phone plug, turned on the answering machine, and even repatched the wall . . . with toothpaste. Who needed a man?

Gabe never called back.

But a week later I received a letter.

*

Dear Porzia,

I never wanted for things to end like this.

With your sweetness and warmth, you've captured my heart and made it glow again. These past months with you have been as intense as the rest of my life altogether. I opened myself to you in a way I didn't think could be possible. I can't imagine how I lived for so long without your laughter or soft curves pressed against my body as night fell. How many early mornings have I held my breath watching you peacefully sleeping and thanked the gods.

I know why you left and, if possible, now I love you even more for it.

But I need to do this, and although I know you understand, I need to write, to tell you about this ache that consumes me. I didn't think I'd ever be driving again after the accident.

This is for me a dream come true. A desire so much bigger than my fears; I have no choice and can't settle for anything else. I gave it so much thought I believed I was going crazy for a while, but once I recognized this need, I knew. I could never have been content or have looked at myself with respect if I'd chosen to stay behind. Even if it means to hurt and disappoint you and my father, I need to be true to myself. I am the man that I am, Porzia, and therefore, human and not perfect. I am aware of the challenge I'm facing, especially being 'wingless' this time. Although a speck of hope remains since I will be driving through Cloud Dwellers' Sacred Grounds. I know I will be breaking a vow, nonetheless, and the price to pay for such a transgression is my life. I wished to be your soul mate when you told me about him, just as much as I wish to drive again next month, but I'm not him, and I am certain I want to drive.

I need to thank you for the unconditional love with which you have graced my life and the sacrifice your heart is bearing. I won't ask you to wait. As you gave me the freedom to choose, I free you as well. I believe the chocolate quotes were correct; I'm about to leap, hoping for the net to open. And you are free from servile bonds of hope to rise or fear to fall; Lady of yourself, though no lands, And having nothing, yet hath all.

When life offers a last chance far beyond your hopes and dreams, it's unacceptable not to rise to the occasion, but most important is that it's not rational to grieve when it ends.

With love, always,
Gabe

*

He had included his Baci chocolate quote. I held the thin piece of paper reverently in my fingers.

He didn't want me to hold on.

My tears stained the crumpled sheet of paper I had been holding against my heart, ruining it. He was letting me go so I would not be sharing the responsibility of his death.

He spoke of my unconditional love. What about his? He was just as capable of offering such a precious gift. The letter I had just read the undeniable proof.

His words streaked as my tears melted the ink and I did my best to smooth the paper, careful not to smudge it any further. I opened my journal where I kept the lavender he had given me and carefully pressed the letter between the white pages. I went to bed that night wishing I still believed in prayers.

CHAPTER 42

October came and went in a blur of wind and clouds. Humidity hung on, unseasonably so, through Halloween and the first week of November, when it finally gave in to rain.

Gabe never called.

I, on the other hand, often picked up the receiver ready to dial his number, ready to apologize for anything and everything just to hear his voice one more time, but I never went through with it. Despite his request to keep in touch, I sensed the fragile balance of the elements. One phone call from me and he might change his mind. Regret his decision forever, and die by my side, day by day.

I kept my work connections to the minimum but still remained indispensable enough so as not to be considered entirely off the market. The news of Camille's project spread through the grapevine—no pun intended—actually giving me an excuse to keep a low profile with everybody else. *Scoop* slowly jelled under Oscar's direct supervision and feeble assistance on my part. Camille, as promised, kept out of it.

I finally spoke with Benedetta but asked her not to mention the situation, for I wasn't ready to deal with it. Honestly, I didn't know what to do. I raged from extremes of anger toward him and his selfish behavior to tear deluges, feeling so sorry and sad I wished the earth would open up and swallow me.

Benedetta respected my wish for peace and quiet but checked in on me often. Evalena, on the other hand, must have sensed my initial, unjustified resentment and left me alone. She knew exactly what I was going through, for I could sense her love around me. Without interfering, she left me to solve things at my own pace.

It was around Thanksgiving when she finally called, asking me to join them for dinner to celebrate the holiday. I politely declined but told her I would like to talk to her in person. As usual, she embraced me.

And I cried. For an eternity. Back in her restored home on Navarre Beach, I sat on a brand-new sofa much different from the past life regression one and told her everything I had understood of my quest. Finally, I blew my nose and accepted a fragrant mug of tea.

Evalena sat next to me and blew over the rim of her own mug.

"One thing is for sure, Evalena: I didn't stifle myself in this relationship. On the contrary. Whatever will happen, I feel that I have truly discovered some of my strengths and qualities and not for one single instant did I make myself uncomfortable. Not for anyone."

"You know, to quote one of those Greek myths Benedetta loves so much, Demeter could be compared to Eingana. She thought she could overcome the limits of human flesh by imposing immortality on a baby prince."

"Did she succeed?"

"No, the queen mother put a stop to it." She took a sip of tea. "I don't believe *The Wizard of Oz* is your favorite fairy tale either, Porzia. It's not really a fairy tale, anyway."

"Well, it *is* one of my favorite stories. But I discovered it later in life. I should ask my mother which ones I loved when I was younger."

"Not a bad idea, sweetie. She's right on track."

"With what?" I asked, suspicious.

"You. Now."

"Her theory of me facing my fears and surviving?"

Oh, I understood! Finally! I had confronted my own spirit. I killed the old Porzia in the desert; the events had brought me to the point of asking to know. And my wish had been granted: the wizard had recognized my power and opened the portal. Through the fire of the phoenix, I transformed and stood my ground. Ultimately, I survived the knowledge.

Evalena cast me a meaningful look. "You had a deadly combination of fear and pleasure, Porzia. Both are powerful stimulants to attain full consciousness. You've grown strong enough to demand sacred knowledge, faced it, and survived."

"What's next?" I sensed this to be only a partial transformation.

"It will come to you. Give it time."

"And him?"

"He's flying, Porzia. But if Gabe is fulfilling his own fate—" she held my gaze, "where is the *One*? Where is Xavier?"

"Still out there?" I sounded skeptical.

*

I left her house praying for time.

Time for what?

For hope to finally crush me?

I knew deep inside me that I hadn't given up. I was doing exactly what Gabe had set me free *not* to do. I was secretly waiting. Superstitiously, I thought that if I kept away from the escalating interest in the race, if I kept from listening to the news and reading the papers, I would keep from jinxing it, giving him a little more room to . . . what? Negotiate with his death?

My own accomplishment had rendered me utterly arrogant.

*

A week before Christmas the race began.

On Christmas Eve, Gabe died.

*

Right before midnight, an eagle perched herself on the oleander and began to screech, careless of the rain pelting her feathers. I had been folding laundry by the fireplace when I heard the wretched shriek and froze. My skin crawled and Peridot ran to the window, meowing loudly. I followed my cat in a daze and pulled the curtain to see the eagle illuminated by the artificial glare of the parking lot lamppost. It was so windy, rain fell sideways. Yet the oleander stood immobile, as if surrounded by an invisible protection. Still screeching, the eagle looked straight at me, then spread her wings and took flight, her piercing screams blending with the sudden noise of the phone ringing.

"Porzia?"

"Yes?" I whispered with a knife carving my heart.

"Clark here, Porzia," his voice cracked.

"I'm on my way," I sobbed.

*

Clark met me at the airport and drove me straight to the funeral.

I have a poor memory of the following events.

I remember the Jourdains, including Madame Framboise, who rose, trembling, from her wheelchair, to give me a surprisingly firm hug. Nicolas held my hand, and I hid my face against his shoulder, falling apart.

Gomi wasn't there. He had been in the car with Gabe at the time of the accident and was now in intensive care, having not yet awakened from a coma. No visitors allowed.

The rest of the Miller team spoke to me briefly afterwards, but I honestly don't remember much. The crowd was unbearable and the media worse, suffocating.

Clark took me aside and finally found a moment to give me a wrapped gift. Gabe had told him I had forgotten it. He had aged so much I was having a hard time remembering the Clark I had met only months earlier.

I had declined Madame Jourdain's offer to spend a few days with them and asked Clark to please take me back to the airport.

"I thought at first you'd be able to stop him," he confessed, and his already red-rimmed eyes welled up with tears again.

I leaned over to squeeze his arm. "I'm so sorry."

"No. I owe *you* an apology." He rubbed his eyes. "I'll take care of Tess, and you need to be strong," he said quietly. "Time will help us all." I hugged him outside the airport and told him to please not wait with me. He cast me a curious look, and I lifted the wrapped package he had given me.

He nodded and left.

*

I leafed through the book as the plane took off, and Australia became a distant map down below.

*

—*The Cloud Dweller*—

*

And I found out why Gabe lost his wings, to finally find them again.

Evalena had said it would come to me. Just give it time.

I had learned how to harness my powers. Now I needed to discover how to love what I feared.

*

Fine.

ABOUT THE AUTHOR

Giuliana Sica

Giuliana was born in Siena, Italy. At the age of 4 her father gave her a box of markers. She immediately began to doodle stories on the house walls, and after a few weeks of repainting, she finally received paper as well. She has not stopped writing since. She calls Whidbey Island, Washington, home where she settled in 2001 after globe-trotting the world teaching Italian in exotic places as far off as Japan.

She holds a Classic Italian Literature and Philosophy degree with a minor in English still laced with a Chianti-infused accent. She speaks fluent Spanish, has forgotten most of her French, and holds tightly to her Japanese, mostly by eating sushi every chance she gets. She currently teaches Italian for Skagit Valley College and Rosetta Stone. She shares a yellow cottage on the island with her husband, 4 cats, a vegetable garden, and a fig tree named Federico.

Every residual free minute of her life is spent working on Book Two.

CPSIA information can be obtained at www.ICGtesting.com
Printed in the USA
BVOW010459040912

299391BV00002B/1/P